HAMILTON'S BATTALION

A Trio of Romances

ROSE LERNER   COURTNEY MILAN

ALYSSA COLE

PROMISED LAND

BY ROSE LERNER

Donning men's clothing, Rachel left her life behind to fight the British as Corporal Ezra Jacobs—but life catches up with a vengeance when she arrests an old love as a Loyalist spy.

At first she thinks Nathan Mendelson hasn't changed one bit: he's annoying, he talks too much, he sticks his handsome nose where it doesn't belong, and he's self-righteously indignant just because Rachel might have faked her own death a little. She'll be lucky if he doesn't spill her secret to the entire Continental Army.

Then Nathan shares a secret of his own, one that changes everything...

For my uncle David. Thanks for everything you've taught me about military history. I finally wrote you a battle!

Introduction

MRS. HAMILTON,

As requested, I have read and sorted this week's correspondence and collected those letters pertaining to your husband's ever-growing biography. This account was received from Mrs. Rachel Mendelson in response to your query sent to those who served in your husband's light infantry battalion. She describes the experience of one Ezra Jacobs, who served under Colonel Hamilton. Corporal Jacobs's story is quite unconventional, but is that of an ardent patriot. It appears that Mr. Mendelson was also acquainted with your husband, and he has added some observations of his own. I have attached my notes listing specific interactions with your husband, as that is what most interests you. I hope that you will find this useful to your endeavor.

Your obedient servant,
M. Alston

Prologue

New York City, 1820

"Look at this letter I got." Rachel slid the unfolded sheet across the breakfast table.

Nathan skimmed it as he drank his coffee: ... *Writing to those who knew my husband in his military career...his command at Yorktown...a memorandum of all your recollections of him...most particularly anecdotes, even of the most trifling description...his style of speech...everything which will illustrate the elasticity of his mind, shrewdness of his judgment, excellence of his heart, forbearance, courage, authority, virtues, &c....Yours, &c., Elizabeth Hamilton.*

"Oy. She doesn't want much, does she?"

Rachel took the letter back, smoothing out the creases. "I'm honestly surprised she wants *my* reminiscences for Colonel Hamilton's biography. I left him mostly out of my memoirs on purpose, out of gratitude."

"She'll probably take your anecdotes and leave out your name," Nathan said caustically, spearing another herring. "She didn't address one to me, I see. I have recollections of Hamilton too."

"Then we can write a memorandum together." She smiled at him. "I have fond memories from the siege of Yorktown."

"I have *scars* from the siege of Yorktown," Nathan said, but he smiled back.

"'I beg you will sit down day after day for a short time and endeavor to tax your memory,'" Rachel read. "What time are you needed at the counting house?"

"Not for another hour."

"Then we can start now."

Chapter One

October 3, 1781
Outside Yorktown, Virginia

RACHEL'S MESSMATE Scipio was writing a letter by the faint light from the open tent flap. The light was growing stronger; the drummer would beat the reveille soon. Scipio frowned over his paper. "Last night I dreamed about Anna Maria, but I can't decide if I should mention it to her or not."

Rachel laughed as she combed the snags out of her thick brown hair. Even with pomade, it wasn't easy to keep Jewish hair smooth and neat enough to suit their captain's ideas of the example a noncommissioned officer should set for his men. "Why? Did you dream you were quarreling?"

"She was setting a hot johnnycake on the table, and I could smell the maple sugar," Scipio said ruefully. "It's not very romantic, is it?"

"A hot johnnycake sounds damned romantic to me." Rations hadn't exactly been plentiful the last month. To speak truth, rations hadn't exactly been plentiful the last four years.

Bugger this knot. Rachel dug her fingers through her hair, finding the stubborn tangle and carefully dismantling it. A clump of strands had to be sacrificed, crusted with old pomade. She shook them off outside the tent with a grimace. "I think

Anna Maria would want to know the truth," she said decisively. "That you were thinking about her."

In case she never sees you again, she didn't say, but they both heard it in the distant boom of the enemy's cannon, firing on the Allied camp. The British wouldn't give up Yorktown without a fight.

Rachel felt a little hollow, and not just from hunger. Of the other three junior NCOs of the First New York Light Company, Corporal Scipio Coffin had Anna Maria waiting to marry him when he returned to Albany with his freedom; Corporal Tench Goodenough and his wife had already left the tent to sneak a few minutes alone; and while Sergeant Zvi Hirsch Philips had no mistress, he wrote his bosom friend Daniel twice a week and talked of him unceasingly the other five days.

If Rachel died in the assault on Yorktown's defenses, who outside her regiment would mourn her?

Uniforms were scarce in the Continental Army, so soldiers were stripped before burial. Would everyone be angry when they realized she was a woman? Would they remember her fondly as a fallen comrade, as they would have remembered Ezra Jacobs, or would they only remember *that strange creature who tricked us and was most likely a whore besides*?

She thought often of the glorious future when there would be ballads written in her honor. The moment of discovery itself she shied away from.

Despite some teasing about her beardless face, no one had guessed the truth yet. Either she would be found out by accident or she would know when the moment was right to reveal herself. Neither could be prepared for, so why think of it?

"Will you plait my queue?" she asked.

Scipio obliged. He himself had given up trying to make his tight black curls meet regulations; his wig rested atop his knapsack in the corner.

Her queue neatly tied off, Rachel put on her hat and poked her head out of the tent. The reveille was beat when a sentry could clearly see a thousand yards distant, which was bound to be any minute now. She'd better make sure their drummer was awake.

Checking that the ribbon she wore around her neck was securely beneath her collar, Rachel shouldered her musket and stepped into the frigid morning air, wishing her uniform were less threadbare. She eyed with envy the warm, thick coat of a civilian making his way through the sleeping camp.

He wasn't the only one stirring: picket guards patrolled the avenues between tents, a few soldiers shaved and cursed their gooseflesh, and a woman carried a kettle towards the smoke rising from the kitchens. But her eyes lingered on him. Was it only because of his coat? Or did she know him?

He glanced about him, head turning towards her. She saw half his face beneath his broad-brimmed hat.

Recognition shook Rachel to the soles of her boots. Her heart pounded.

Nathan.

He disappeared behind the next row of tents, evidently not having spotted her. What was he doing here?

But even as she thought it, she knew there was only one answer. Glad her musket was unloaded—for God's sake, she couldn't shoot *Nathan*—she ducked between two tents and ran after him.

And here it is, she thought. *The moment of discovery.* There was no hope Nathan wouldn't reveal her sex. Maybe she should shoot him after all.

Quashing the thought, Rachel put on a fresh burst of speed. "Loyalist spy! Stop that man!"

Heads poked out of tents, and a few men stumbled forth in their stocking feet, blinking gamely about. She was already past them, gaining on him. "British spy!"

He glanced back, looking mildly curious. She was almost on him. Wasn't he going to run? If he did, a picket guard might shoot him. Her breath came short and blood roared in her ears.

Nathan stepped politely aside to let her pass.

Abruptly furious, she changed course and barreled into him, bearing him to the ground. He landed flat on his back with Rachel sprawled on top of him.

This was the strangest moment of her life, yet it felt familiar —Nathan's neat shoulders and narrow chest, their legs tangled together. His hat had landed a few feet off, and unruly curls fell across his face and straggled on the ground. *He* hadn't bothered to pomade his hair.

He stared up at her, and for a second she thought, *I've changed. He doesn't recognize me.*

He went white as one of the commander in chief's fine bedsheets. His lips parted, his dark eyes widened, and his body trembled beneath her. The drummers began to beat the reveille; at first she thought it was her heart.

"Rachel?" he whispered. His mouth opened and closed, as if he was trying to think of something to say. "R—Rachel?"

She felt awful for a moment that she'd made him unhappy, and that was how she knew she hadn't changed after all. Still the same weak Rachel. She should have shot him.

She wanted to scramble away. Instead, she checked that the sentries had arrived and were pointing their muskets at Nathan. Then she stood, brushing mud off her elbow as best she could. *Just focus on the next thing, and the next, and wait for him to let the cat out of the bag.*

She was so rattled that the adjutant's name flew right out of her head. But she took a sharp breath, and it came back to her. "Privates, help me escort this man to Major Fish for questioning."

They fixed their bayonets and stepped forward, a small glorious miracle that banished her nerves. Her deception hadn't suddenly become obvious only because Nathan was here. She was yet a soldier, and she would act like one.

Squaring her shoulders, she met Nathan's eyes. "Get up," she said curtly, for he had stayed on the ground, gaping at her with stunned, accusing eyes.

He'd put his hat back on, though. A good Jew should never go bareheaded. Rachel fought the urge to dive for her own hat and clap it on her head like a scolded child.

Damn Nathan anyway. She kicked him, not as hard as she wanted to. "Stand up." Backing away, she motioned her men back too.

Still staring, Nathan stumbled to his feet. There was a small pleasure in remembering she topped him by an inch or two.

"Keep your arms out of his reach. You, kindly search him for weapons. Be careful." Despite the warning, she didn't expect Nathan to have anything bigger than a pocketknife, and she was right.

It wasn't the walnut penny knife she remembered; somehow that rankled. Rachel freed the blade from its cheap bone handle and tested the edge. Dull. What business did he have in an army camp?

Shutting the knife and dropping it in her pocket, she retrieved her hat with deliberate carelessness. "Follow me, Mr. Mendelson." To the escort, she added, "If he runs, shoot him."

She wheeled on her heel with precision, as she'd trained for hours to do, and marched off towards the regimental colors marking the adjutant's tent.

☙❧

As SOON AS Rachel's name left his mouth, Nathan had felt like an idiot. Of course it wasn't her. It was some Jewish boy from New York who happened to share her accent and the shape of her chin. He braced himself for a puzzled sneer.

But when the soldier sneered at him, there was nothing puzzled about it. She wasn't surprised to be called "Rachel," because it was her name. That was Rachel. Rachel's angrily furrowed brow, the proud tilt of Rachel's head and the curl of her mouth. The familiar curve of Rachel's shoulders forced into a new military posture. It had been so long that he couldn't even be sure her beautiful voice was pitched lower than it used to be.

Nathan followed her. Well, he had no choice, did he, if he didn't want to be bayoneted. Honestly, at the moment, maybe he did want to be bayoneted, because at least then he wouldn't be miserably realizing that...

No. No, he refused to be sad about this. She was alive, and not dead of yellow fever and buried in Philadelphia. That was a *good* thing.

He couldn't make up a story for how she'd got from there to here. Had she...done it on purpose? How could she have managed that? Had she ever really been sick?

Was it a miracle direct from HaShem?

She knew perfectly well who Nathan was, though. She wasn't born again. She hadn't suffered a loss of memory and forgotten her old life. She'd chosen to let everyone go on thinking she was dead.

Actually, he didn't care about "everyone." She'd chosen to let *him* think it. That wasn't such a good thing. It felt—he didn't know what it felt like, other than Not Sadness. Like a sizzling ball of *something* eating away his guts.

It was almost nice to feel something this powerfully that wasn't fear. He'd spent a lot of time being afraid since last he saw Rachel.

He was seeing Rachel.

In a three-cornered hat instead of a cap, with a severe wool-wrapped queue marching down the back of her neck—but it was the same sweet nape of her neck. Tanned and thinner, maybe, but he'd know it anywhere.

Given the choice, he'd follow it anywhere. And since she'd ordered him to do so, for once they were in agreement.

He'd always known in his heart that given the choice, *she* would pick the Revolution over him, this new country of goyim over her own people. But even in his moments of bitterest resentment, he'd never imagined this. How could he—Rachel, a soldier?

Rachel, a soldier. Ah yes, there was the fear after all, fresh and bright and new again. The British were desperate. They wouldn't yield the town without a fight. How many of the men in this camp would be alive at the end of the week? He'd just found her! He couldn't lose her again. He *couldn't*. His body wasn't strong enough to bear such a terrible strain twice over.

She was taking him to her superior officer right now. If he told the truth, that she was a woman, she'd be safe. Safe, and angry at him—angrier, anyway—and humiliated, and he couldn't do it. He'd learned the value these last years of keeping dangerous secrets, and the peculiar depth of affection it took to watch someone you liked run a terrible risk and not stop them.

Drums started beating at one end of the camp and spread. Men poured out of their tents, making escape easier and harder at the same time. He tried to think, tried to do his job again. Better to brazen it out, he decided, than attempt to outrun an army of men in better condition than he was. Which meant he could keep following Rachel.

They reached a marquee tent with flags stuck in the ground before it. A slight, boyish figure in buff and blue, with a colonel's sash across his breast, was just going in. Nathan winced as the young man took in the situation and came towards them.

"Who is this, Corporal Jacobs?"

Nathan winced again, this time at Rachel's alias.

Stepping smartly forward, she stood at attention. "Colonel Hamilton, sir, I have reason to think this man a spy employed by the British."

Nathan's expression could probably have been described as a grimace by now. No—what was worse than a grimace? He cringed as Colonel Hamilton gave him a sharp glance.

"What reason is that, Corporal?"

Abruptly, Nathan straightened, eager to hear what she'd say.

She didn't hesitate. "This man is Nathan Mendelson, known to me from before the war. We shared a faith and a synagogue, and many times I have heard him speak ill of the rebels. When the British occupied New York City and the Patriots among our congregation fled, he remained. As late as a year ago I had news of him working for a supplier to the British troops of that city."

She'd been listening for news of him? Another fiery rush of unidentifiable feeling.

Hamilton nodded. "Bravely done, Corporal. Has he been searched for weapons?"

"Yes, sir. He carried a pocketknife only."

"May I have it?"

To Nathan's surprise, she paused before reaching in her pocket. But she laid the small knife in Hamilton's palm.

The colonel examined it and then eyed Nathan. "I'd better check him again. If he knows anything, the general will want to hear it immediately."

Nathan submitted to being searched a second time, wishing Rachel were doing it.

"I commend you for your swift action, Corporal. You may

return to your company for parade. On your way, kindly alert the commander of the guard that I have borrowed his sentries."

"Yes, sir. Thank you, sir." Again, Rachel paused. "Will you let me know if—I should want to—" She fumbled for words. "If he is to be executed, sir, I should wish to be present, and convey the news to his family."

Hamilton's face softened. "If it comes to that, Corporal, I will notify you. You're dismissed."

She saluted and marched off without a backward glance. Nathan watched her go, feeling a little panicked. How would he manage to see her again?

"Mr. Mendelson," Colonel Hamilton said sharply. "If you would be so good."

Flanked by sentries, Nathan followed the officer, only glancing back nine or ten times at Rachel's retreating back.

⁂

RACHEL'S BATTALION had been ordered to an early mess; they would spend the evening and most of the night providing cover for troops working on the fortifications. Rachel gulped down her food and took hasty leave. She couldn't possibly leave camp for the night without knowing if Nathan would keep quiet. About her secret, anyway—really *quiet* would be like wishing for the moon.

She presented her permission to the guards. With a roll of his eyes, one of them unlocked the door to the tiny room serving as Nathan's cell. "A friend of yours, eh? He hasn't stopped making noise all day. Will he listen to you if you tell him to shut his mouth?"

Nathan looked up from the pencil drawing he was making on the wall, vibrating with nervous energy. He had a split lip and a reddish, swollen place on his left cheekbone.

"It looks like you boys shut it for him," Rachel said grimly. "The fair treatment of our prisoners ought to be a shame and an example to our foes." She plucked the pencil out of Nathan's hand, trying not to let the heavy shackles on his ankles disturb her. "He's a spy and you didn't take his means of writing away? What's your name, Private?"

The soldier stiffened in surprise.

"Coburn," Nathan supplied helpfully.

Rachel didn't look at him. "Is that correct?"

"Yes, Corporal," Coburn said through gritted teeth.

"Would you like to tell me who struck the prisoner, Mr. Coburn, so I can include it in my report to Colonel Hamilton?"

In the very short time since his appointment to a field command in the Light Division, everyone had been made extremely aware of how the colonel felt about the just treatment of prisoners. Even ones who would probably be hanged. Even though the division was on edge and furious because Colonel Scammell—darling of the light infantry and the only man who could make George Washington laugh until he cried—lay dying at Williamsburg, shot in the back by the British *after* he surrendered to one of their patrols last week.

"It was him," Nathan said with edgy cheerfulness.

Rachel couldn't think about him being executed. He'd probably try to tell the hangman a joke. "I'm ready to hear your side of the story," she told the sentry.

"He wouldn't shut up, and he insulted Irish cooking."

Rachel bit her lip hard to keep from smiling. "He goaded you past the limits of your endurance, I see. Don't let it happen again. That will be all, Private."

Coburn went out and shut the door.

"Can I have my pencil back?" Nathan said in Yiddish.

"Of course not," she snapped in the same language. "What is wrong with you? You spent all day antagonizing armed men while entirely unable to defend yourself because…?"

"Because I had nothing else to do. I can't even pace in these things." One of his legs began to vibrate; the shackles made an awful clanking noise. "I tried to buy a book, but the only one any of them knew of the existence of was *Pilgrim's Progress*, and I haven't yet grown that desperate."

He'd picked the buttons off his cuff. Rachel's hand went to the needle and thread she carried in her pocket—but she quashed the impulse. "Have you eaten?" Not much better.

He stared at her in disbelief, leg still bouncing. "Have I *eaten*? Rachel, who cares?" He'd lowered his voice to protect her secret. Did that mean he wasn't planning to tell? Why not? "You're *alive*?"

She shifted uncomfortably. "Obviously."

"I sat shiva for you," he said intently. "I said Kaddish for you. I've remembered your yahrzeit three times. How can you be alive?"

That startled her. She'd never thought about Nathan mourning her, past the first few weeks. He'd observed the anniversary of her death?

She remembered lighting a candle on her mother's yahrzeit, tears blurring the flame. Every year at synagogue she'd sobbed brokenly in the women's gallery, listening to the mourners' Kaddish being recited below. Had Nathan cried for her?

Well, of course he had, he cried over everything. "I'm sorry, but—"

"Rachel," he burst out, lurching to his feet, "what if I had *remarried*?"

Chapter Two

RACHEL HADN'T CONSIDERED that either. Why not? She thought about it now, and didn't like how much it unsettled her. "Nothing would have happened," she said anyway. "It's not as if I was planning to come back."

Nathan's eyes nearly popped out of his head. Wrapping his fingers around their opposing thumbs, he muttered a charm against the evil eye. Not the short Yiddish one she'd learned from her mother, but a long one with Hebrew parts. "Don't *say* that! Why would you say that?"

Rachel sighed, annoyed both at his superstition and that she'd caught herself staring at his hands in the candlelight. "I didn't mean it like that. I meant I'd live somewhere else afterwards, with a different name."

He was uncharacteristically silent. "Oh," he said at last. "I…" He swallowed. The bruise looked very dark against his cheek. "I would have given you a get."

She wasn't sure she believed him. "That would have made your mother too damn happy." Mrs. Mendelson had been after Nathan to divorce Rachel since a year into their marriage, on grounds of barrenness.

Nathan winced at the profanity. His disapproval felt like a porcupine rolling over her skin. But Rachel was done trying to be a good wife. He wasn't the center of her world and his simple assumption that he was—she wanted to *shatter* it.

"I wasn't just running away from *you*. You were already a hundred miles away. I wanted to join the army. I needed to disappear and take a new name. If you'd given me a get, people would have expected to know where I went afterwards."

"You didn't take a new name," he pointed out. "You took your maiden name back."

"I see your hurt feelings come before everything, as always."

"You should go," he said abruptly. "If you don't, I'll start shouting and then all your hard work—how did you even *do* it? My mother said she washed your body—" He stopped short.

She wanted to throw the truth in his face. But somehow she did still shrink from hurting his feelings.

"My mother was in on it."

She bit her lip.

He put his head in his hands. "Of course my mother was in on it." His voice was muffled. "You should go."

She wanted to stay and finish the argument. *You're not his wife anymore,* she reminded herself. *The siege is what matters. Your comrades need you. You can't risk it.* She rapped on the door.

A different member of the guard answered her summons. Hopefully Coburn was abashed and wouldn't beat Nathan any more than he already had. She had one foot out the door when Nathan said, "Wait. You said something about eating? I'd love some food. I gave one of them money to buy me dinner and he never came back."

Rachel's fist clenched. She could have smashed it into Nathan or the sentry's face with equal pleasure. "When I come back tomorrow," she said, loudly enough that everyone in the guardhouse could hear her, "if I hear of one more instance of mistreatment or stealing, I will recommend an immediate court martial. Either give him back his money or give him what you bought with it."

"The last thing we need is for him to be drunk too," someone said behind her.

"I know he's a pain in the ass," she told them. "Believe me, I've known him for years. I *know*. I know he's a spy, and a Loyalist, and that he never shuts up. But you are Continental soldiers. Have some goddamned discipline."

Out of the corner of her eye she saw Nathan wince again at her taking the Lord's name in vain. Damn him too. He'd been dining with Hessian officers in New York while she was starving in the army. Why should she feed him?

Angrily, she pulled the hunk of bread from her pocket. It gave beneath the pressure of her fingers, not even stale. The light infantrymen had been paid in cash on the march south, their first real wages in months. Her mess had had beef for dinner. Not enough beef—she still wanted the bread. But she marched over and slapped it down on Nathan's pallet. "Let him eat it, Private. That's an order."

Nathan's hands came away from his face. He looked up at her and opened his mouth. She fled before he could say anything someone might hear.

"Is *Pilgrim's Progress* still available?" she heard him ask as the door shut behind her.

৩৩

October 4

PILGRIM'S PROGRESS WAS DRIVEL. It was trash. It was an atrocity. Christians were awfully smug about how not only heathens and Jews and so forth but also most of their own friends were bound for hell, weren't they?

That wasn't the worst part, though. The worst part was how often the word "wise" appeared in the book. With the long printer's s, it looked like: *wiſe*.

Every time Nathan saw it—every time—he thought it said *wife*. He still had a wife.

His candle was burning low. He would need to light a new one from it soon, before it burned out. A new flame couldn't be lit on a holiday, and it was the first day of Sukkos.

The guards, shamed by his wife's reproof yesterday, had actually brought him a little cheese and bread this morning. Fresh from the oven, so he shouldn't have eaten it on a holiday, but it was probably baked by a Gentile—he abandoned the line of reasoning. A prisoner was permitted some lenience. Besides, it felt like every month this war dragged on made following the mitzvos harder and harder, and less vital too. A pleasant luxury for when you were safe at home surrounded by your friends. Why would HaShem want him to go hungry?

To prove to these goyim that being a Jew meant something, maybe. That it gave Nathan more strength in adversity than mere cheese and bread.

Showing off, then. HaShem did seem to like His followers showing off.

How many mitzvahs was Rachel breaking? She was wearing men's clothes, to start, and maybe a forbidden mixture of wool and linen at that; she was working on Shabbos; she was lying; HaShem only knew what she was eating; she was taking His name in vain; she was probably taking her hat off indoors and showing her hair—

The candle guttered. He scrambled for the next one, but the windowless room was plunged into darkness before he could light it. Argh, he'd gotten distracted thinking about Rachel and the deep rich brown of her hair. He'd felt so special, back when they were married, when she'd started wearing caps and he'd been the only man she permitted to see her hair.

What did he mean, "back when they were married"? They were still married!

It's not as if I was planning to come back, Rachel had said yesterday with perfect indifference.

He'd known she didn't love him when he married her. Her mother was sick and someone had to pay for the doctor. But he hadn't really *loved* her either; he'd just liked her enormously. Husbands and wives grew to love each other after the wedding. Not always, of course. But often enough. He'd assumed…he'd hoped…

He'd been desperately in love with her two years later, when the British occupied New York in '76. It had been a wrench to send her and his mother to safety in Philadelphia while he stayed to protect his job and their little house.

Rachel had asked him to come with them! She'd *asked* him,

and he'd been so flattered he almost went. He'd thought she felt *something* for him, beneath…everything. Apparently not. And he'd lost the house anyway in the Great Fire just a month later.

Many Loyalists were convinced that fleeing rebels had set the town on fire as the British marched in. Nathan thought it more likely that fires started easily in empty cities.

What hadn't he lost since this war started? What was left?

Rachel, he reminded himself. *That is,* you *definitely lost her. But she isn't gone.*

So many times he'd imagined her sick and scared and confused with fever, with no one to take care of her who loved her. No one to kiss her forehead or hold her hand or tell her she would make it through this, she just had to *fight.* He'd thought, *Maybe if I'd been there…*

But of course Rachel never needed anyone to tell her to fight. She was born fighting.

He'd wasted so much time longing to atone for the pain he'd imagined he caused her, and she'd never spared a single thought for his, if the look on her face when he mentioned her yahrzeit was any indication. All through last night, when he tried to sleep, he kept seeing that blank, surprised look.

Strange that she and his mother had finally found something to agree on: that their marriage didn't matter at all.

He got to his feet, shuffled awkwardly and loudly across the room in his shackles, and pounded on the door. "Hey! I need a light for my candle. Has your fire been put out since yesterday evening?"

ॐ

"…AND he interrogated us for a quarter of an hour about when we lit our fire," the sentry finished complaining. "How should I know? It was here this morning from the last watch."

Rachel sighed. There was no point explaining to them about whatever holiday it must be; probably Nathan already had, in detail. "A quarter of an hour might be an exaggeration, don't you think?"

"Not by enough," another soldier muttered.

Nathan's head jerked up when she came in. He was sitting with his knees pulled up to his chest, perching a book on his shackles. "Have you read *Pilgrim's Progress*?" were the first words out of his mouth.

Since her battalion had been up most of the night, they had few urgent duties today, but she'd still put off visiting him until late afternoon, dreading what he would say. Planning her answers.

Instead, he said *this*. "Of course not. Why on earth would I read *Pilgrim's Progress*?"

"Boredom, obviously. Desperation." A British cannon boomed. His mouth spasmed. "This am haaretz Christian abandons his family—because that's what good goyim do, evidently—so he can go to Heaven without them."

You abandoned your family, she wanted to say. She crossed her arms silently.

"So he's walking along on his way to Heaven," Nathan continued, "and he meets this fellow, Mr. Worldly Wifeman—I mean Wiseman—who tells him that instead of...sorry, I'm not going to go back and explain the whole thing because it's very boring, but I *am* going to tell you that Mr. Wiseman is from the town of Carnal Policy."

The laugh burst from her tightly compressed lips.

He looked pleased with himself even as he wiped a drop of her spit off his cheek and twitched at another cannon blast. *Don't say anything,* she told herself. *Just don't say anything.*

"*What?*"

"Carnal Policy," he repeated.

"That can't be right."

He knocked his candle into the straw pallet when he stood, clanking, to show her the book. Rachel righted the candle with a sigh, grinding out the sparks with her boot.

But there it was in black and white: Carnal Policy. "Oy, der goyim," she muttered.

He laughed, the dark stubble on his jaw catching the light. He hadn't shaved in a few days, even before his capture. She wondered if it bothered him; Nathan had been particular about a smooth face, even though he blushed and hung his head whenever the rabbi harangued his congregation about their shameful beardlessness.

But that was five years ago now. It didn't feel like five years since she'd seen him. It felt like yesterday. It felt like he was her husband standing next to her and later they were going to share a bed.

She stepped away.

His smile faded. "Right. So Mr. Wiseman tells Christian that—"

"Wait. Christian is his *name*?"

He nodded. "He tells Christian that he doesn't have to go through this tiny gate he's been looking for, he can just go visit Mr. Legality and Mr. Civility, who live in Morality. And of course you know Mr. Wiseman must be a lying schemer trying to keep Christian out of Heaven, but I understand why Christian falls for it because legality, civility, and morality sound like a big improvement over my wife and children burning in a lake of fire to me."

He paused for her to laugh. How dare he come back after five years and still expect her to laugh?

She wanted to, and that made it worse.

"So there's an ugly high hill hanging over the path to Morality that our hero is worried will fall on his head. He's going along in terror and *flashes of fire* start coming out of this dreadful menacing hill, and guess what this hill turns out to be?"

She shrugged.

"*Mount Sinai.*"

Her jaw dropped. "No."

He dropped the book on the ground emphatically, and stepped on it.

"Mount Sinai isn't a *hill*. It's, it's—" The truth was, she pictured Mount Sinai looking like the Palisades along the Hudson River, which presumably wasn't close to the truth either. But—she knew it was beautiful.

"How can you live with them? They hate us," Nathan said, an edge in his voice, and the moment of charity evaporated as if it had never been.

"Your mother hates me too, and you didn't object to my living with *her*."

"She doesn't hate you. She's just difficult. You of all people can't condemn someone for that."

"I of all—of all people—" Rachel sputtered.

"She wanted my marriage to bring her naches at Shearith Israel," he said reasonably for the millionth time, "so she started out a little standoffish, and you never made a single attempt to win her over."

Because it was simply a fact that marrying Rachel was a step down, so why should Mrs. Mendelson's scorn offend her? "I don't care who she wanted to impress at synagogue. I was your wife, and she was rude to me from the moment I met her. And *you* never did anything about it but tell me to ignore her."

"If you had just had a little patience with her—"

"At our wedding she offered to take me to a dressmaker if I'd let her give my gown to the maid."

She could *see* him wanting to say that his mother had meant it kindly. How could he not understand how much that had stung? Rachel had tried to look pretty. She'd been nineteen and grateful for his proposal and she'd done her best to be a credit to him. She *had* tried in the beginning—to be a good wife and a good daughter-in-law, to hold up her end of their bargain—and been rebuffed every time. Mrs. Mendelson hadn't meant it kindly.

"So she made some petty remarks," he said. "For that you turned our home into a battlefield? But I suppose that's where you always wanted to be anyway."

Rachel gritted her teeth. "She told you I was barren and you should divorce me. Plenty of women take a few years to conceive their first child!" She stopped herself before she started listing examples from Shearith Israel; she hated that the names still sprang to mind, after all this time.

Nathan threw up his hands. "Why are you even here." His voice was flat. "Why visit me? Why have this conversation? *I* never even considered taking my mother's ridiculous advice, but you...well. We both know what you did."

As if him laughing and saying *Ma, don't be ridiculous* meant the subject was closed and there was no reason to think about it further. "You sent me to Philadelphia with her. Alone. Are you really surprised I ran away after *two years* of her carping at me and moaning that my childbearing years were slipping away? 'If you can even *have* children, dear.'"

"A year and a half," he corrected her.

"I beg your pardon?"

"It was a year and a half," he repeated, as if she actually hadn't heard him instead of merely expressing incredulity at his ability to miss the point. "You left New York on the fifth of Elul in 1776 and you died"— another pause for the Hebrew incantation against the evil eye—"you ran away on the seventh of Shevat in 1778, so that's a year and a half."

Rachel had left their little insular world behind without looking back; she didn't like the pang of loss she felt hearing Nathan mark time by Jewish dates. Sometimes she and Zvi managed to sort out when they were in the neighborhood of a holiday and maybe say a prayer or reminisce about home, and sometimes they didn't. She'd tried to say Kaddish for her mother each year, hating that she wasn't sure of the date.

"It's a holiday today, isn't it?" She hazarded a guess. "Sukkos?" That was the Festival of Booths, to remember the wandering in the wilderness after Egypt.

He grimaced. "The first day. I should be eating in the sukkah." He rubbed at his eyes with the heels of his hands. "Rachel, what do you want me to say? That I should have gone to Philadelphia with you when you asked? Are you telling me you'd have stayed if I did? You know, I thought…I thought maybe it was my fault you died. That if I'd been there, things might have gone differently. I kept asking my mother what the doctor said, and what you said, and were you afraid, and did you ask…"

He trailed off, but Rachel knew what he had been about to say. *Did you ask for me?*

"And when she didn't answer, I wondered if the answers were too awful to burden me with. I've spent the last three and a half *years* wondering if I could have changed it! I refuse to do it all over again, not over this. We both know you didn't really want me with you. I thought…I thought you might like some breathing room."

"So you did know." There was a roaring in her ears. Why, when everything else was gone, did this rage remain? She had wanted to be done with it, to leave it behind as surely as she'd left the lunar calendar and a life where eating outdoors seemed noteworthy.

"Why couldn't you just admit it instead of pretending not to notice?" The words spilled up her throat from some ever-springing well inside her. "Instead of acting like it was a joke every time I said something unkind in the vain hope you would *leave me alone* for half a second. You kept practically begging me to like you, giving me presents and telling funny stories and fussing over my dinner plate. Why couldn't you give me breathing room *then*, when we were living together, if you knew I wanted it?" She hadn't wanted him to send her away to Philadelphia. She'd only wanted space to stop resenting him.

Too late now.

"I'm not good at that," he said ruefully. So sure of his own charm. So sure she couldn't stay angry. He'd always underestimated her.

"'Did I ask for you,'" she mimicked. "Because that mattered more than anything, didn't it? Oh, yes, I died a terrible death of yellow fever, but let's ask the important question: was I thinking about *you* while I did it?"

"That's not what I meant."

He looked so innocent and wounded when that was *exactly* what he'd meant, and Rachel's anger burned so hot she spit out the one truth she had always swallowed. "I never wanted to marry you. *Never.* I did it to pay for Mamma's doctors, and then…" Then Mamma died anyway, only a few months later.

"I know that," he said, as if that somehow made it all right. "I didn't mind, I thought—"

"I know what you thought. You thought you'd grow on me. You behaved as if we were really married, as if I were really your wife and you could comfort me." She'd wanted it to be true too. She'd wanted so desperately to feel better and he'd tried and tried, but it was no use.

"The doctors said she'd recover." Her eyes filled with tears, still longing for her mother after all these years. She remembered trying not to impose on the Mendelsons with her bottomless grief, to cry discreetly and not to mope around the house, because they were all she had now and she'd still felt like a guest in their home. "It was all for *nothing*," she said viciously. "I made that great sacrifice for nothing."

He looked stung at the word *sacrifice*. "I wanted to help you," he said self-righteously. "Your mother was sick and I wanted to help you. We *were* really married. You said yes."

Her gorge rose. "You wanted to help me? You wanted to fuck me!"

She'd never said that word to him before. They'd been shy and respectful to each other about everything to do with the marriage bed. It had been months before she could even bring herself to explain where he needed to touch her down there. He'd apologized, and they both cried. They'd been ludicrously young.

She was a soldier now and said "fuck" all the time, but she still felt shocking and ashamed.

He swallowed, tried to take a step back, and almost tripped over his shackles. "Well. That too."

୬୬

NATHAN STOOD THERE, ankles smarting and bruised, pickled in the same sick shame he'd felt on their wedding night. He'd known she wasn't really enjoying herself, not the way she should have been, but he didn't know how to ask her about it, he'd never done this before either and he barely knew her, so he just kept trying and everything he tried, everywhere he put his mouth and his hands, made him harder and her shyer. Yes, he'd wanted to fuck her.

They'd figured that part out eventually. The rest of it, they'd never figured out.

He'd never meant to take advantage of her. He was a little older, but not by much: twenty-three to her nineteen. And he'd been a good match. Not a brilliant one, whatever his mother thought, but he'd had a steady job and a house and a kind face and her mother had liked him. Rachel had said yes, and he'd thought...

He hadn't thought that meant *Yes, I'll make an enormous sacrifice.* He'd thought it meant *Yes, I'll be your wife.*

"Were you only pretending to like me? At the beginning. I thought you liked me."

She crossed her arms. "I liked you well enough," she said reluctantly, and then threw up her hands. "And there you go again! Think about *my* feelings for once. Think about something other than whether people *like* you. It made it worse that I liked you, that you were nice to me, that I wanted you in my bed. I couldn't even be properly angry. I couldn't feel justified in resenting you. All I could feel was more and more awful, like my life was an apple slowly going rotten and I couldn't stop it."

She smoothed her regimental coat over her hips and straightened her spine soldier-fashion, as if reminding herself she had a new life now, a better one. As if it comforted her to remember she'd tossed their life together onto the slop heap like a rotten apple, and walked away from it.

He'd tried so hard to be a good husband. He'd never reproached her for being cold or snappish or disagreeing with him about politics in public. Now she told him that was an unforgivable crime too: *Why couldn't you just admit it instead of pretending not to notice?*

"I don't know why I'm even talking to you," she said. The words slipped between his ribs like a bayonet, cold and sharp. "What can you understand about wanting independence? All you ever wanted was for the British to make everyone behave themselves, like children. You can't even stand up to your *mother.*"

"That's not fair. Wanting legality and civility isn't childish," he said hotly, even though he liked the British much less now. He and Rachel had done this a thousand times and he still knew all the words. "Peace isn't childish. How many people have already died for independence?"

He ran over what she'd said again. "Wait! Am I the British in this analogy? As in, you heroically claimed your freedom from my tyrannical rule?" No, because he was a nebekh who couldn't stand up to his mother. "No, wait, my mother is the British, and I'm…Canada?"

"I want freedom for us more than I want to live." She was talking about literal American independence now. She'd breezed past the trifle of his existence, and moved on to the important things. "Aren't you tired of us always being simply Jews, no matter where we live? We're never English or Spanish or Polish. I wouldn't call myself a Pole if you paid me, but my family lived there for generations."

What's wrong with being a Jew? he wanted to ask, but for once he kept his mouth shut. He didn't want to hear her answer. Not today.

"I want to be American," she said. "Goyim think *they're* governed without representation! There isn't a single Jew allowed into Parliament, or even to vote for Parliament. Jews aren't even British citizens. Their army hasn't got one Jewish officer who didn't convert to take his commission. *Ours* does," she said proudly.

He snorted. "And you think *I* pretend not to notice things! How many of your Jewish officers have been court-martialed for suspect loyalties?"

That brought her up short, but only for a moment. "If you mean Colonel Franks, anyone who was Benedict Arnold's closest aide-de-camp would have come under suspicion, and he was completely exonerated. Anyway, I didn't say it would be easy, or quick. Things don't have to be easy if they're worth a hard fight. But you wouldn't understand that. You're a coward and you—"

She brought *herself* up short, suddenly. "I'm sorry," she said stiffly. "That wasn't fair. I shouldn't dredge up all this old history when you're— You've held up really well in here."

"Coward" stung: there it was, what she'd always believed. She had chutzpah, to say that to him. He wasn't the one who'd run off like a thief in the night so he wouldn't have to talk to her! But "old history"—that was far, far worse.

Had she thought of him once in the last three and a half years?

"I'm going to petition your court-martial for clemency," she promised, her voice tight. "I'll—I'll talk to Colonel Hamilton. He has Washington's ear, everyone says. We don't always hang spies. If you give your parole—"

"I'm not a coward," he said tightly. "Well, all right, I am a coward, but I work around that. I'm not a spy. Or—I *am* a spy, but not for the British. I've been supplying the British army and then passing information about their numbers and whereabouts to Washington. That's why I was here yesterday morning, to meet with the general about the state of things in Yorktown."

Chapter Three

THERE WAS total silence in the room. Nathan hated total silence.

"It's true," he insisted. "Cornwallis thinks I'm off scouring the countryside for beef for his men. Ask anyone. I mean, anyone who'd know. Washington, Hamilton, um…" He tried to remember who else had been at his briefing. At a day's distance they were a blur of powdered hair and Gentile faces and names. "John something? Sorry, that's half the men in your precious army."

She blinked at him. "That doesn't make any sense," she said finally. "Why would you do that?"

"It's been five years since you saw me," he pointed out. Old history. He wished it felt that way. "Maybe you don't know me as well as you think you do."

Her face hardened. "And that's supposed to make me trust you?"

"You weren't in New York for the occupation—"

"Neither should you have been!" she flared.

He threw up his hands. "You didn't want me in Philadelphia."

Someone pounded on the door. "Is everything all right in there, Corporal?"

She drew herself up again, that unfamiliar military posture.

"Yes, thank you, Private. Open the door, if you would be so good."

"Wait," he said, panicking. "I can explain. I'll explain. I'm happy to explain, I just got distracted, don't go—"

She went, and didn't look back.

Rachel couldn't quite bring herself to go to Major Fish, the adjutant, who would know where Colonel Hamilton was but would expect an explanation for why she wanted to see him. She felt raw and unsoldierly. Surely Major Fish would see right through her and say, *That man's your husband, isn't he?*

Did she have time to go hunting for Hamilton on her own, though? She ducked her head into her own tent to see if they'd picked up any assignments. No sign of the first sergeant or the Goodenoughs, but Scipio was playing patience while Zvi sharpened their bayonets.

"Oh, give me yours," he said.

As soon as Rachel handed it over, she missed its holstered weight at her side. *You don't need trappings to feel like a soldier, damn it. You are one.*

"Thank you," she said, feeling guilty that she'd been dealing with her private affairs while he worked. Like a woman.

"He's showing us up, isn't he?" Scipio said. "I shouldn't even have these cards; they're useless weight in my pack."

Zvi shrugged. "I needed something to do with my hands." He tested the edge with his thumb and grinned. "There she is. Maybe soon I can leave bayonets behind and go back to my cleavers." Zvi had been a kosher butcher in New York before the war—thankfully, not the one Rachel had patronized.

"Will you go back to keeping kosher after the war?" she asked with sudden urgency.

"Of course. Who'd buy meat from a butcher who cheats in his own kitchen? Besides, Daniel's stricter than the Shearith Israel mashgiach. Let's ask Sarah to get some crab this week; if we win the war with this siege, it may be my last chance." Zvi heaved a tragic sigh. "Never tell any of my customers. Or Daniel."

If we win the war with this siege...

Rachel had never been afraid of the end of the war. She'd planned her lecture tour and her fame and looked forward to a warm fireplace and enough to eat. But now she felt terrified.

Would she keep kosher after the war? She'd always disliked those countless rules, and she'd discovered she liked bacon very much. But when she was giving lectures on her service to admiring crowds, would it make her seem less a Jew if she ate it? Would it hurt her cause?

Nathan hadn't even wanted a candle if it wasn't lit properly. His disapproval still itched at her. Rachel was a bad wife. A bad Jew. A bad woman. What else would be left, when she wasn't a good Patriot and a good soldier?

Nathan was lying about becoming a Patriot. He must be. Trying to save his neck with a wild story seemed like something he would do. Colonel Hamilton would laugh at her and tell her not to be gullible, and Nathan would...

Go to prison, at best. The American prisons were nicer than the British ones, but not by much.

"Have you seen the colonel?"

Scipio checked his watch. "I walked past him half an hour ago, reading the sutler a lecture about properly rationing alcohol. As if the officers don't down a cask of brandy with every meal."

Zvi shook his head. "I will never understand how much goyim drink."

That was Rachel's cue to agree with him, but she couldn't muster up the good cheer to do it. These were her friends—Ezra Jacobs's friends, anyway—and she wanted to tell them about Nathan's claim and ask their opinion. But she couldn't explain who he was to her and why it mattered, and in the absence of that they'd gleefully pick the whole thing over like prime gossip. She was alone in this, as she'd been in everything since her mother died.

"I'm going to look for him," she said. "Thanks, Zvi, I'll clean your musket tonight if you like."

He grinned at her—well, at his whetstone. "I like."

"Is everything all right?" Scipio asked. "You look shaken. What do you need to talk to the colonel about?"

"I'm fine. I—" She hesitated. "I'm fine."

The sutler was able to tell her that Colonel Hamilton had gone to the artillery park with General Knox, and there she found him.

She had spoken to the colonel many times on the march south and in camp, and had never found him particularly difficult to talk to. But she'd never had to approach him on personal business before. She'd never had to approach *any* field officer on personal business before. She had no family to beg favors for or to visit on furlough.

At least, she had pretended to have none. What would the colonel say if he knew the truth? *Go home, you unnatural woman,* presumably.

But she had no home.

"Yes, Corporal?" Hamilton prompted.

Rachel stood stiffly to attention. Could he read anything in her face? "Sir," she said quietly, hoping General Knox, who had moved tactfully a few paces off, couldn't hear, "I was visiting with the prisoner Mendelson, as you had given me leave to do, and he told me he has been spying for His Excellency, and not the British."

She hadn't realized until this moment how much she hoped it was true: Nathan had changed his mind, he had come round to her way of seeing things, he was safe… *Please, let it be true.*

Hamilton's mouth made a thin, tight line. "The things a man will say to save his skin. The improbability of that must be as obvious to you as it is to me."

"Yes, sir. I—" Her throat closed. She was a fool, and Nathan must be desperately frightened, to tell such a stupid, pointless lie.

Unless he was just trying to impress her.

Hamilton's face softened. "As you were, Jacobs. Listen to me. Your friend is a Loyalist, not a deserter. I've no desire to see him hanged, and neither does General Washington. Indeed, the commander and Colonel Laurens were discussing just this morning if there was any prisoner of the British in Charleston we might exchange him for. Enjoin Mendelson to stop telling tall tales and provoking the guardhouse sentries, and he'll come through this with a whole skin."

His pity was worse than if he'd laughed at her. Her colonel saw her for the soft fool she was, who'd wanted to trust Nathan against all her common sense.

As if she would enjoin Mendelson to do anything after this. If she visited him, she'd be tempted to shut his mouth with her fist like Coburn. He wouldn't hang; she owed him nothing further. Let him lie and cajole his way to dinner if he could, and if not, let him starve.

❧

IT WAS GROWING late and Nathan was trying to decide whose arrival he would welcome more, his dinner or an apologetic Rachel, when the door opened to admit Colonel Hamilton.

It *was* Colonel Hamilton, wasn't it, and not another uncommonly handsome young commander of middling height? Nathan had never met him before yesterday, and it didn't help that the whole officers' corps wore their hair so thickly powdered its color was indistinguishable.

Nathan held up his candle. Red eyebrows, that was promising but still inconclusive. Should Nathan just wait for him to speak and hope he introduced himself?

"Mr. Mendelson," maybe-Hamilton said, very straight and slender and stern.

"...Yes, sir?"

"Did you confide the secret of your employment to Corporal Jacobs?"

His heart leapt. "...Yes?"

The officer sighed. "I suppose that's better than someone else spreading it." He gestured at Nathan's shackles. "We did not provide you with those out of spite, Mr. Mendelson. We have gone to great lengths to preserve your secret, and consequently your life. Show some sense and don't loosen your tongue to every distant childhood acquaintance."

Nathan tried to start upright and banged his shin on his shackles again. "Ow! So what did you tell him?"

"I told him no, and when you consider the matter rationally, you will thank me."

Nathan took a deep breath, trying not to panic or shout. "I really won't." Rachel thought he'd lied. That he'd dreamed up a wild story to make himself look heroic, probably. Or worse, that he was a coward grasping at straws to save his neck. He got carefully to his feet. "Go back and tell him yes."

The colonel stiffened.

"I mean, please. Sir."

"I beg your pardon?"

"Corporal Jacobs isn't a distant childhood acquaintance," he said with far too much conviction ringing in his voice. He clenched his fists so he wouldn't take very-likely-Hamilton by the sleeve for emphasis. Rich goyim started fights over things like that. "I know him well and I rely absolutely on his discretion. Inquire yourself, you'll see—" He almost said *she.*

Drek. If he spilled her secret, Rachel *would* be right about everything: that he was useless and weak-willed and incapable of keeping his mouth shut. "He won't have told a soul about any of this."

Probably-Hamilton's eyebrows winged upwards. "A close friend who arrested you."

I like her better than she likes me. But despite the bitter taste in his mouth, he knew she would have arrested a Loyalist spy she loved just the same. "Because he's…"

Nathan searched for a word to explain Rachel's infuriatingly uncompromising, burning sureness. This goy wouldn't understand "tzadeikes," and its English equivalent "righteous" was too silly to say out loud.

"Principled," he said inadequately. "Because he's believed in this cause since he was eleven and the first Liberty Pole went up on the Commons."

Eyes shining, she'd told him her memories of every pole that got chopped down by the British and every new one that went up in its place, as lovingly as Nathan might talk about a favorite book.

All this time, he'd wanted her to know he'd gone over to her side. Nathan bit his cheek until he tasted blood, thinking of the times he'd cried himself to sleep with a hand on the pillow where her head should have been, longing to talk it all over with her. To tell her that he was terrified but he was doing it, he was doing it for her, for the America she'd cared so much about and he'd never been able to imagine. It had broken his heart that she would never know, when—he'd thought, maybe, she would have been proud.

Now he just needed her to know how wrong she was about him. "You have to talk to him again."

"I'm afraid that's out of the question."

Nathan gave up and took almost-definitely-Hamilton by the white leather swordbelt crossing his chest. Gingerly. His shackles hit the colonel in the ankles. "Sorry, I—"

The young officer jerked away. "You forget yourself, Mr. Mendelson," he said furiously.

"I'm not forgetting." Nathan's voice came out low and thick. He wondered who was more shocked by his vehemence, himself or let's-just-call-him-Hamilton. "*You're* forgetting. I've risked everything for your army. You're planning to send me back into a town you're building artillery platforms to bombard. So I want to risk this one more thing—what's it to you?"

"The dangers you choose to run may be your affair, but the success of this siege is mine," Hamilton bit out, "and who knows but that secrecy about your role may materially affect it. Men desert every day. If any of them were to go over to the enemy with knowledge of your true loyalties—if we send you into Yorktown with false intelligence and they don't believe it— men will die. My men. Maybe Corporal Jacobs. I'm sure you see my difficulty," he finished in a tone that said he was sure Nathan *didn't* see, because he was a self-serving Jew and not an American.

Hamilton could be wrong about him all he liked. But Rachel...if Nathan died in Yorktown and she went the rest of her life smugly ignorant of all the dangers he'd chosen to run...

He crossed his arms. "You don't command me," he said stubbornly. "I'm not a soldier, I'm a contractor. Tell him, or I don't go into Yorktown at all. He'll keep it secret if you ask him."

"Since you insist." Hamilton looked utterly disgusted, but Nathan's heart thrilled feverishly with victory. "I hope we don't live to regret it."

Nathan hastily spat three times over his left shoulder. "Bite your tongue!"

Hamilton sighed, rubbing Nathan's fingerprints off his swordbelt with his sleeve. "Yes, I should have said, I hope we *do* live to regret it; hoping not to regret it at all seems a lost cause. But I'll engage to sound out the corporal's friends in a day or two. If he has remained discreet that long, I shall do as you ask, and on your head be it."

🐚

October 7

RACHEL'S FEET, knees, and back ached from standing in the cold trench, and her eyes ached from staring into the darkness for any sign of a British attack. She checked again with the men in her squad: *Are you awake? Are you pointing your bayonet anywhere stupid? Is your powder dry? Do you remember the orders?*

She was proud to find that, while a few of them were indeed pointing their bayonets somewhere stupid, they were all awake and they all remembered the orders: fire one round at an approaching sortie, rush over the parapet, and meet them with the bayonet.

Rachel thought they might relish the opportunity to bayonet a few redcoats. News was spreading through the division that in spite of prayers and hopeful prognoses, Colonel Scammell had died yesterday of his wounds; the men stamped their feet and blew on their hands and muttered angrily to each other.

Private Carvalho, only sixteen, had forgotten to bring anything to eat with him and had also failed to mend the hole in his jacket's elbow against the night breezes, even though Rachel had reminded him of both this morning. With a sigh,

Rachel handed him her packet of sugared almonds and her sewing supplies.

"You owe me sixpence for thread, Private, and don't drop the needle." Sometimes it amazed her how much an NCO had in common with a nursemaid.

Tench wordlessly held out his own almonds as she passed him. His wife, Sarah, who cooked for their mess, had brought the almonds with their dinner—a rare delicacy to relieve her feelings about Tench marching into the trenches. Rachel didn't want to deprive him of that little reminder of love, but they were delicious and it had pained her to sacrifice her own. She picked out two nuts, enjoying the buttery crunch and the lingering flavor of nutmeg.

Suddenly she wanted to ask Tench, who she knew had read *Pilgrim's Progress*, if he really thought Mount Sinai was an ugly black cliff belching smoke. If he thought she was going to burn in a lake of fire. But she didn't want to hear the answer.

Instead she asked Zvi, as she passed him to return to her place in the line. "Have you read *Pilgrim's Progress*?" In the darkness and secrecy of their position, she felt as if she ought to whisper, but the roar of the British guns made it both impossible and unnecessary.

"Obviously not. Have *you*?"

"No. Nathan Mendelson was reading it when I went to visit him. He said it describes Mount Sinai as a terrifying hill about to fall on Christians' heads."

She caught the edge of Zvi's smile in the darkness. "I wouldn't mind dropping a mountain on their heads some days." His face turned towards her. "You and Mendelson were talking about books? He must be a cool hand."

She laughed. "Nathan, a cool hand? Not likely." Abruptly she remembered him politely stepping aside to let her pass as she chased after him shouting *Loyalist spy!* A chill ran up her spine, a sudden queasy suspicion that she didn't know Nathan anymore.

Which made her all the more foolish for half believing his lie about working for the Patriots. For treating him as if he were the same old eager puppy nipping at her heels, when he'd grown teeth. Well, she'd learned her lesson.

"You wouldn't catch me talking about books if they were holding me for my hanging," Zvi said cheerfully. "I'd divide my time evenly between weeping, begging, and bribery, I expect."

"And what would you be bribing them with? If you've got more than a few dollars in cash left, you've been holding out on us."

Zvi spread his hands. "Anything I've got they might want. I'm not too proud to yield up my virtue to save my life."

Rachel laughed. "Well, the sages say that to save a life is the greatest mitzvah."

"Corporal Jacobs?" a third voice intruded.

She started guiltily, saluting. "No sign of movement, sir." Heavy clouds blocked the waning full moon. She could make out the buff facings of the field officer's uniform, but not the face or voice.

"Thank you, Corporal. Might I speak to you apart a moment?" As he turned away, her eyes caught the glint of a gold lace epaulet and a dim flash of aquiline profile—Colonel Hamilton.

There was really no "apart" to be found, not and keep behind the cover of the earthworks protecting them from British cannon fire. But he led her away from her own squad, and leaned in. "Your captive friend has importuned me most urgently to inform you that he is indeed employed by us. I hope you'll understand that my earlier liberties with the truth were a general caution, and no mistrust of you. Not only his safety but our own may depend on your keeping strictest secrecy."

She couldn't see Hamilton's face, but she felt his eyes boring into her. "Yes, sir," she said reflexively. "I shall be worthy of your confidence, sir."

In the last few days she had spoken more with officers of high rank than in the last two years. A few days ago, it would have seemed significant: an opportunity for advancement to be exploited, a risk of discovery to be carefully managed. Now… "For how long?" she demanded. "How long has he been working for our side? Sir."

A pause. "Two or three years?" Another pause. "Since the summer of '78, I believe. But we must both get back to work. Ask him the rest yourself tomorrow." He put a hand on her shoulder. "Remember, Corporal, French and American lives depend on your discretion."

"Yes, sir." He turned. She shouldn't badger him; he had more important business to be about. "And you're sure of his loyalty?" she asked his queue anyway.

He turned back, straight shoulders slumping a fraction. "There are very few people of whose loyalty I am *sure*, Corporal. I was sure of General Arnold once. But for whatever it's worth, I think Mendelson sincere. Now put it from your mind and return to your squad."

She returned to her squad, but she couldn't put it from her mind. She watched for British attack as the hours dragged by. Dawn broke. Noon neared. They had been awake nearly twenty-four hours, and her eyes drifted shut despite the booms and cracks of British fire aimed at the men building batteries. But still she couldn't put Nathan from her mind.

Is this a dream? she wondered suddenly. She did dream of Nathan now and then. Not in any particularly interesting way; his presence rarely surprised her in the dream. She was reading her own name on the casualty lists in the newspaper while they sat at breakfast, or some terrifying creature was pursuing her company and he was there in uniform, or she was quarreling with his mother and he didn't take her part. Had she fallen asleep on watch?

She strained to open her eyes—but no, they were open already. She felt for the ribbon around her neck—it was still there, the same fuzzy velvet it had been since the old satin one, worn to shreds, caught on the strap of her cartridge box during drill and ripped in half.

Nathan was a Patriot. He had been for two or three years. What did it mean? How did she feel about it, other than relief he hadn't lied to her face? Tired, mostly, and on edge, her nerves jangling even though they hadn't lost a man all night. One farther down the line had been hit in the arm, and another in the leg, but that was all.

At noon Baron Steuben's men relieved them, drums beating and colors flying. Rachel prodded her squad into its place in the column.

Back in camp, they were obliged to strike their tents and change ground a little to the right, to leave a wider path for the artillery to be brought up from its park to the trenches. Rachel was glad of it, after an initial moment of bright fury at being denied her bed. Send the men into their tents with their nerves still buzzing from a dangerous night, and half of them would have gone in search of liquor instead. Half an hour's steady work would calm them enough to sleep.

Tench gave her a gentle kick. "Wake up, Ezra!"

Rachel realized she was kneeling by a pounded-in tent peg, staring in the direction of the guardhouse. Should she go see Nathan? Had he eaten?

Should she eat something? Her stomach felt hollowed out...

Sarah Goodenough seized her arm and dragged her upright. "Come along, Ezra."

Rachel allowed herself to be shepherded into their tent. Exhausted and jittery and lingeringly afraid though they were safe in camp now, she knew a moment of envy when Tench slung an arm around Sarah and pulled her close.

She rolled over. *Don't think about it. Sleep.*

She slept.

October 8

RACHEL WOKE UP STILL TIRED, but her stomach churned too much to fall back asleep. She checked her watch: four o'clock in the afternoon. Sarah had brought them porridge salted with a few scraps of bacon at seven this morning. Rachel had thought nothing of it at the time, but now a voice in her piped up: *a Jew shouldn't eat bacon.*

It sounded like Mrs. Mendelson. In a flash, old grievances rose fresh and sharp—the time Shearith Israel's mashgiach inspected their kitchen and found the cheese grater in with the meat dishes, and Mrs. Mendelson loudly blamed it on Rachel, for example. Nathan had rolled his eyes and paid the fine out of his own pocket, and hadn't understood why that didn't settle the matter.

She rolled over. Sarah was asleep, Tench's face pressed into her arm. Rachel would have to find her own dinner today. Buy it, probably.

Had they fed Nathan anything since she'd seen him?

She sat up, felt that her queue was still mostly intact, and, covering her disheveled hair with her hat, went in the direction of the sutler.

But when she came to the guardhouse, haversack heavy with more or less kosher food, the door to Nathan's cell stood open and the room was empty.

Chapter Four

RACHEL'S HEART GAVE A GREAT, frightened bound. "The prisoner—" Had they hanged him in spite of his innocence? Had he demanded his dinner one too many times, and been beaten to death? Had he been taken sick and sent to the hospital? Had—?

"Oh, the little Jew?" a soldier said. "He made such a pest of himself they finally put him on fatigue duty. I think he's with the Virginia militia."

"Th-thank you, Private," Rachel stuttered. Outside, she leaned against the wall, heart pounding. What was wrong with her? She had been content—even relieved—never to know what befell Nathan again as long as she lived. She had been *annoyed* at chance mentions of him in letters to Zvi, amidst synagogue gossip from occupied New York. Now here she was, scared half to death at the mere idea that something might have happened to him.

She was light-headed from hunger and lack of sleep. That was all.

The adjutant of the Virginia militia informed her that Nathan was assisting one of their messes in making cartridges, and directed her to their tent.

Before she even put her hand on the flap, she heard Nathan muttering to himself. "Five and a half across, all right, now five and three-quarters up, two and three-quarters here, connect them, voilà..." The familiarity shocked her for a moment; he always talked to himself when he totted up figures.

Inside, the mess clustered around a table brought in for this delicate work. Nathan sat at one end measuring cartridge papers —the easiest part of the job—and passed the marked-up paper to a black militiaman on his right, who cut it to size. She was glad to see they hadn't trusted a prisoner with a knife.

Nathan's head was bent over his paper, dark curls falling into his eyes. For careful work with powder, the tent was illuminated by a covered lamp. Its light cut his face below his hat sharply in half: deep shadow and strong light. Unexpectedly, Rachel felt her face crumple.

She took a deep breath. Yes, he had beautiful curls, yes, his hands were beautiful—fingers curved around his pencil and bent to hold the ruler precisely in place. Yes, his nose was...

Surely there were other words in the English language besides "beautiful." She was only too tired and hungry to think of them. "Beautiful" swallowed up all her thoughts and she stood turned to stone, listening to the murmur of Nathan's voice until one of the militiamen looked up and saw her.

"What's to do, Corporal?"

Distracted, it took her a moment to parse his thick Dutch accent. A moment in which Nathan ripped a fresh page from his book with vindictive glee—oh. He was making cartridge papers out of *Pilgrim's Progress*.

"I'm an acquaintance of Mr. Mendelson's."

Nathan raised his head, his face somehow both tightening and relaxing when he saw her. She bit her lip hard.

"Ezra," he said, coolly but without a trace of hesitation or self-consciousness at the false name. She dug her teeth in.

"Oh, it's your friend!" His neighbor looked up, smiling. "Glad you came out of it safe. He fretted about you all morning. Paid out a dozen pennies to our drummer, sending him to the hospital for news."

Nathan flushed.

"I brought his dinner." Rachel was glad her voice at least

47

sounded steady. "I wonder if you might spare him a few minutes."

The militiaman looked reluctant. "Well...if you insist, Corporal."

Nathan's mouth twisted wryly. "Quacoe is the first person to be glad of my company in I don't know how long."

Rachel's hand clenched around the strap of her haversack. She'd chosen their dairy meal carefully, turning the sack inside out and digging her fingers into the corners to rid it of any crumbs of meat. "I can go," she said flatly. "If you aren't hungry."

He sighed. "Of course I'm hungry. Wait, let me finish this paper." He drew a last line and passed it to Quacoe. "I'll be back soon," he promised, slipping a strip of discarded paper into the book. "You can use the pages up to here. I haven't read the rest yet."

He jostled the whole table when he stood, making a sound of pain as his shackles caught on a table leg. "Sorry," he said, turning away from her again. "I keep forgetting about these. Did I make you spill your powder? Should I—"

"I'm hungry, and my shoulder is sore," Rachel bit out.

Nathan frowned. "What happened to your shoulder?" Shuffling his way to her, he reached out as if to touch it.

"I'm carrying our dinner across it," she snapped.

"Oh," he said in relief. "Give it to me, then."

She clutched the strap tighter, ducking out of the tent. "You'll just drop it next time you trip over those things." She wasn't his wife anymore, for him to carry her groceries.

He followed her without argument.

She headed for the first tree she saw with spreading branches, to come as near as possible to the commandment to eat under a shelter open to the sky during Sukkos. "I didn't think we'd be able to eat outside, but I—I bought a lemon. It's the closest I could get to an esrog."

He looked surprised and puzzled. "Thank you."

It's not a special favor to you, she wanted to say. *Maybe I wanted to celebrate. Just because I eat pork now doesn't mean I'm not a Jew.* But admitting she'd had a wistful impulse to celebrate a holiday with him would actually be worse.

Strange how much more charitable she felt now she knew he was a Patriot. As if she'd finally won an argument and could be gracious in victory.

She spread the meal on the dry grass: a quarter loaf of bread, a small hunk of cheese, two dry salted fish, and a bottle of wine half full. Not enough for two people, but all the money she could bring herself to spend at the sutler's, on top of what she'd already given Sarah for the week's meals.

Nathan didn't take one look and point out that he could have given her money for more, which she appreciated.

Instead, he picked up the lemon. His face contorted as he obviously tried to figure out how to tell her something she wouldn't like.

"What?"

"I can't use a lemon," he said apologetically. "It isn't an esrog."

She gritted her teeth. So much for charity. "We don't *have* an esrog."

"Right. Or a lulav. It's better not to fulfill a commandment than to fulfill it incorrectly."

Six hundred and thirteen pointless rules, and every one of them precious to him.

He was fidgeting with the lemon now. His thumb circled the stem end; abruptly, against her will, she thought of him touching her nipple.

"It was kind of you to think of it," he said, desperate as ever for her not to be angry with him. "A gut mo'ed." Happy holiday.

"A gut mo'ed," she answered with an ill grace. She hadn't done it to be kind. She'd done it because—she didn't know why. She'd wanted to feel comforted, or uplifted somehow, but she didn't. When he blessed the wine and passed her the bottle, all she could think about was that his mouth had been on it first, and the water for the ritual handwashing was freezing.

At home, she'd candied their esrog to serve on the fifteenth of Shevat. Mrs. Mendelson had come into the kitchen and told her to bite the end so she'd finally conceive. And Rachel had done it, consumed with longing for a child she could love the way her mother had loved her.

Her stomach rolled.

She was sick with hunger, that was all. Nathan began the blessing for bread, but Rachel couldn't sit still a moment longer. She tore the hunk of bread, set his half back on the ground, and began shoving hers in her mouth. Her queasiness retreated. Oh, thank God.

Finishing his blessing, he made an exasperated sound. "That prayer is two lines long! You never could wait for anything."

That's what he'd told her about a baby, too: *You're too impatient. There's plenty of time.* He'd been wrong. There hadn't been much time at all.

She'd never be a mother now. Rachel Mendelson was dead. A dead woman couldn't be given a divorce, so she could never remarry.

Unless Nathan died, she realized with a painful thump in her chest.

No. *No.* That couldn't happen. She'd made her bed, and she'd lie in it alone gladly. She should just be grateful that esrog hadn't worked, or she'd still be in Philadelphia, living under Mrs. Mendelson's thumb. She crammed more bread in her mouth.

In a few minutes every crumb was gone: bread, cheese, and fish. They passed the bottle back and forth until it was empty.

They sat there, looking at each other, still hungry enough that Rachel could feel the wine already. Nathan's eyes flickered down once, twice, his thoughts obviously going in the same direction as hers, and then he snatched up the lemon, digging his thumb into the peel. "Ow, ow, cut on my hand, ow."

He handed her half the sections. Rachel hesitated: it would taste better if she skinned each section, but it would fill her belly less. Nothing for it. She jammed half in her mouth and bit down, sourness exploding across her tongue.

It wasn't so bad after that first chomp, but she had to chew the skin for an eternity before she could gulp it down without choking. Steeling herself, she popped the other half in her mouth, laughing in spite of herself at the absurdity of it and the look on Nathan's face as he chewed his own.

Finally the lemon was gone, leaving behind an aftertaste that was merely unpleasant and lingering. Her eyes met Nathan's, and all at once she wanted to kiss him more than she'd ever wanted anything in her life. Her body knew in its bones that his mouth would wash this bitter taste away.

How could a body be so unreasoning, over and over and over again?

He was thinking the same thing—she read it in his eyes. She could do it. She could lead him a little ways off and kiss him. She could ask him to put his mouth between her legs, and when she was slick and sated she could ask him to fuck her. He wouldn't refuse.

Her body was different now, stronger and weaker than it had been the last time he touched it. Her limbs had new muscle and new power, and her ribs showed where they hadn't before. Her body had ached and blistered and bled, felt the frost at Valley Forge and the stifling heat at Monmouth. She had grown intimate with its mortality, with how easily it could be shot or sliced into.

She loved her new body, but the one thing it hadn't felt was pleasure. For years now she'd only come in her sleep, starting awake in a panic that she might have made an unmasculine noise. She wanted Nathan to put his hands on her.

❧

NATHAN WANTED TO KISS HER. But then, he always wanted to kiss her, and even as a new-married man of twenty-three he'd managed to restrain himself at inopportune times. Most of them—he remembered one Purim dinner at a friend's house, where they'd both fulfilled the commandment to get quite drunk. She'd been uncharacteristically cheerful and affectionate on the walk home, throwing her arms around him and telling him he was handsome, and he'd…

He'd been afraid it would wear off before they got home, so he'd pulled her behind a stack of barrels and kissed her, nuzzled her neck, and when she giggled and tilted up her head to let him, her hands trustingly on his waist, happiness had swelled in his chest so buoyantly and swiftly that for a moment he'd worried it would crush his lungs.

The memory didn't make him happy now. *You kept practically begging me to like you,* she'd said. *Why couldn't you just give me some breathing room* then, *when we were living together, if you knew I wanted it?*

He'd never been one to give anyone much breathing room. His mother was fond of saying she'd never had a moment's peace until he learned to read. He could still remember her telling him, *Nossie, let me hear my own thoughts now,* when she'd been trying to count stitches or flip a cake out of its pan and he was talking to her.

Rachel *wasn't* wrong about him, not really. He was a coward and he preferred things to be easy and he yammered on and on about nothing and he wanted people to like him far too much. He just wished…he wished she didn't think those things were so terrible. He wished she'd look at him and feel fond about them.

He looked at her, reluctantly fond of her stubborn, scowling silence, and in the silence and sunlight he really saw her for the first time since their reunion.

She was too thin, he realized with a shock, and so was the fabric of her clothes. It was nearly winter! Everyone knew Washington's army was freezing and half starved, but he'd never thought it was *Rachel* going hungry.

The miracle of it struck him afresh, that she was alive, that she'd been living all this time.

He could see the marks of it in her face: she was firmed and hardened, sure of herself in a way nobody managed at twenty-one. In the fading daylight he could see the dark, downy hairs on her upper lip. She used to carefully pluck them, not wanting to meet his eyes while she did it. He supposed they helped her disguise now.

He wanted to kiss her, and he wanted to ask her a thousand questions, he wanted to get to know this new Rachel. Now, while he had the chance. Before she left him again.

But he'd been living all this time too. He wanted to prove to her that he'd grown up as well, and could be quiet if he wanted to.

More than that—he wanted to give her the breathing room she'd longed for five years ago, when she was young and round-cheeked and didn't know how to ask for it. Quickly, he said the blessing to conclude the meal. Then he leaned against the cold tree, looked at the sun hanging low in the sky, and pressed his lips together.

Silence made him itch, even if it wasn't really *silent,* broken by unceasing cannon fire.

But to his surprise, when he left the silence there, she broke it. "When did you stop being a Loyalist?"

Don't talk too much. "The British weren't kind to New York City," he said finally. That about summed it up. "They didn't bring peace; they didn't even bring order as they promised. They kept the city under martial law, so there was no civil justice, but the police court can't try capital crimes and the courts-martial wouldn't punish soldiers for anything. The things I witnessed, perpetrated by drunk soldiers who knew they could quite literally get away with murder—" He shuddered. "People who lost their homes in the Fire were living in Canvas-town—it's just like the name suggests—while Patriots' empty houses were handed out rent-free to British officers and their personal friends, who hosted Queen's Birthday galas in them with money meant for prisoner rations."

That was definitely talking too much, but—she almost smiled at him. "You sound like a Patriot," she said, as if it was a happy surprise.

He looked away, afraid if he gazed too long at the sudden light in her face, he'd be right back at begging her to like him. "They...this is going to sound petty after all that, but they took the bronze plaques from the Shearith Israel cemetery and melted our names and memories down for bullets."

He heard her sharp intake of breath. "Whose?"

"I don't know. I didn't want to go look. No kin of yours or mine could afford bronze plaques anyway...but I was angry."

"How did you find someone to offer your services to?"

"I didn't," he admitted. "Do you remember Haym

Salomon?"

She screwed up her face. "The merchant? I thought the British arrested him in '76 on suspicion of starting the Great Fire."

"They did, but he contrived to get released again. I'd been seeing a lot of him at Shearith Israel after…that winter."

Loyalist Jews had eventually persuaded the British not to turn their synagogue into a barracks, but when it reopened, the changes unsettled him—congregants leading prayers with untrained voices from Hazzan Seixas's bimah, Hessian soldiers helping make up a minyan in a nearly empty building. Without his mother there to nag him, Nathan had begun to avoid services. But after Rachel's death, he'd needed both the prayers and the fellowship.

"Mr. Salomon was friendly, and I was pleased by it because he was older and richer than me, and I was lonely and missed my father. But he was sounding me out to replace him, because I handled my firm's contracts with the British army. He'd made New York too hot to hold him—" He laughed. "Probably not literally?" To his delight, after a pause, Rachel chuckled too. "He asked if I would keep my eye on his wife and baby and pass information to one of his contacts."

"And you agreed?"

"I thought—" He stopped himself from saying, *I thought you'd want me to.* That wasn't breathing room. "—it might help. I thought it sounded exciting."

"Was it?"

He grinned at the dubious slant of her eyebrows. "Yes. I'm good at it, believe it or not. Turns out I'm nervous enough already that I can ignore a little more and do quite daring things."

"Such as?"

"Walking into General Clinton's empty office and searching his desk, and saying when he caught me that I was looking for a pen to annotate my invoice. That sort of thing."

"And he believed you?" She looked impressed.

He shrugged, trying not to preen. "He didn't have me arrested or sack me, and sometimes that's all you can ask."

She shifted into a more relaxed position, her elbows resting on spread, raised knees, unselfconsciously comfortable in her breeches. Comfortable with him, even. Nathan tried not to look at her legs or where they joined.

"How did you get the information out of the city?" she asked.

He'd resolved not to talk too much, but maybe giving her space didn't have to mean not talking, if she was asking him questions. He told her about his codebook, and invisible ink (which they were always out of, but it sounded thrilling), and leaving messages in secret hiding places for men he'd never met. He didn't mention any names.

"We have to win this war," she said intently, chin propped on clasped fists, and for the first time she didn't say it to argue with him. *We* included him now.

He'd known, in the long years of imagining telling her, that it would feel wonderful to finally not be shut out by her fervent *we*. He didn't like that it was full of unexpected small resentments too.

"And we have to be part of it. Jews, I mean."

"Wait, what?"

"You know that quarrel…I was just a baby, but you might actually remember it." She lay on her back in the dry grass. "There was an argument about taking the window sash in the ladies' gallery out of its frame for the Days of Repentance, sometime in the fifties."

What did that have to do with the war? "Who could forget? Gitlah Hays and her Christian friend got rained on during Kol Nidre and she had her husband sneak into the synagogue next morning and rehang the sash." He stretched out gingerly beside her, carefully propping his hat over his forehead, and she didn't inch away.

It was growing dark and the ground was ice-cold, but high above them stars were coming out, brighter for the chill. In the near distance, British mortar shells tumbled sparkling through the twilight.

Nathan tried not to think about how they were hollow spheres packed with powder, sealed with a protruding wooden fuse that gave them their distinctively uneven arc, but it was hard to forget when he could hear them exploding.

"Everyone was still angry about it twenty years later," she said. "My mother's friends would talk over each other to tell you how hot it was that year—a good ten degrees hotter in the gallery than on the floor where the men sat—and if the parnas's son *did* lay hands on Solomon Hays, it was no more than he deserved. And then Mr. Hays prosecuted the parnassim in goyish court. What a disgrace!"

Nathan sighed. "My mother sided with the Hayses."

Rachel howled with laughter. They lay so close Nathan fancied he could feel the ground quivering. "I *know*! If you think my mother didn't bring it up when you asked to marry me…but that's my point. In twenty years, in thirty years, in forty years, everyone will still be talking about what everyone did in this war. They'll hold grudges and remember who was on their side and who wasn't. Only it will be worse, because it's a war and not the damn gallery window. I want Patriots to remember that the Jews were on their side."

He felt a little sad. This was hardly the burning idealism, the passionate belief in liberty that he remembered from her. A shell burst in midair in a shower of burning shrapnel. He shivered violently and refrained with an effort from offering Rachel his coat.

She didn't pay the explosion any mind. "That's why I have to be as famous as possible."

Nathan blinked. "What?"

Abruptly Rachel's existence was new again. She spoke, thought, moved, and all of it startled him—he couldn't understand or predict it. She was flesh and blood, not the pale ghost in his mind that answered him according to his own fancy.

She curled onto her side with sudden ardent energy, propping herself up on her elbow. *There* was the passion after all; war and the wide world of Christians hadn't dulled it. "I'm going to help win this war, and then I'm going to tell everyone I'm a woman. Have you heard of Hannah Snell?"

"The British soldier? Everyone's heard of her. Her memoirs are in every bookshop in New York." He remembered conversations like this in the nighttime dark: her talking animatedly, mashing her pillow with her hands, while he lay and listened happily. A breath away when their twin bed frames were pushed together, or her voice bridging the gap when her courses came and they were forbidden to touch. Sometimes he'd grown animated too, and they sat and talked half the night. Later, as war neared, they'd argued.

Later still, he had wanted peace and quiet in his bed and turned his back to her, feigning exhaustion.

She sat with a triumphant nod, wrapping her arms around her knees. He almost reached up to push her hair behind her ears, before he remembered it was in that tight queue.

"I'm going to do that," she said, trembling with enthusiasm. "I'll give lectures, I'll petition the government for my pension. I'll write my memoirs, even. No one will be able to forget me, and they'll know I'm Jewish."

She saved her passion for helping her people; that startled him most of all. He'd been so angry yesterday when she said, *I want to be American.* He'd thought she meant, *I don't want to be a Jew anymore.* It had never occurred to him a person could be both.

That was exactly what she'd been trying to say, wasn't it? And he hadn't been able to stretch his mind to hear her. He tried to now. A Jew *and* an American...

Would Americans ever accept as one of them a Jew who didn't leave his Jewishness behind and adopt their ways? Would they accept him even if he did? Did their acceptance interest Nathan one way or the other?

He might not be sure, but Rachel was.

When she used to talk eagerly of a new republic, he'd thought she pictured somewhere she could be a modern woman and forget the past—their shared Jewish past stretching back thousands of years, the accumulated stories and wisdom and tradition he loved so dearly and she found stifling. He'd suspected that by "freedom" she meant freedom from *him,* and everyone like him. Had he been wrong?

Maybe she *had* meant it that way, and living among goyim all these years had changed her mind. Or maybe it had never been Jewishness she wanted to leave behind at all—maybe it had just been Nathan.

But he remembered turning away from her in their bed, and wondered queasily if she was right, and he'd left her behind first.

"But…how are you going to be a famous lecturer, when you're pretending to be dead?" He tried to say it as if it didn't mean anything to him. A simple, curious question.

She made a face. "I was hoping I'd grown enough that no one would recognize me if I just changed my name."

I would recognize you anywhere. "Well, not many people know you as well as I do," he said, intending to be encouraging and probably just sounding proprietary.

She clearly decided to take it in the spirit it was offered. "You're right, it will be tricky." She hesitated. "I promised your mother I wouldn't bring shame to your family. More than I had already by marrying you, anyway."

He rolled into a sitting position, suddenly feeling foolish and exposed lying down. He'd been trying not to think about his mother. At least Rachel had had a goal lofty enough to half justify ruthlessness. Mrs. Mendelson had only wanted to get rid of Rachel, and she hadn't minded hurting Nathan badly to do it.

"I'm sorry," she said unexpectedly. "I…if I had it to do over I'd do it again, but I *am* sorry."

His breath caught. He blinked back grateful tears, a welcome relief from resentment and humiliation.

That surprised him, too: how deeply the words touched him. He would have said the two sentiments negated each other —*I'd do it again,* and *I'm sorry.* They didn't. He knew she meant both of them. His mother wouldn't mean the "I'm sorry" part, if she could even bring herself to apologize instead of just insisting she'd been in the right until he grew tired of arguing about it.

He thought of Mrs. Jacobs, suddenly. She'd seemed a reasonable sort of person. Even dying, she'd made an effort to think of Rachel's feelings and spare them. He supposed Rachel had had expectations for a mother and a home that he hadn't really understood.

An apology meant something to her, more than *this conver-*

sation is over now.

He couldn't quite tell her yet, "I forgive you," or "it's all right." His instinct was to rush on, to make a joke, to pretend she hadn't said it. But he'd learned to work around being a coward, hadn't he? He dug his nail into his thumb and counted cannon fire. One, two, three, four...

"I know." It wasn't much, but he meant it.

Her arms loosened their tight grip on her knees. Her face turned towards his, briefly, and she almost smiled before she looked away.

"Do you have another name picked out?" He made a genuine effort this time, and the words came out with cheerful unconcern, as if her leaving "Mendelson" behind didn't drive hot spikes into his flesh. Good to know captivity hadn't dulled his skill at subterfuge.

"I like Esther. It sounds like Ezra, and she was a Jewish heroine who fought for her people in disguise. Besides, things rhyme with it." She gave him a sly, self-deprecating look. A flirtatious look, even. "You know, for the ballads. 'Test her,' 'None could best her'..."

"Fester," he suggested blandly.

She giggled. "Nothing rhymes with Rachel," she said mournfully.

"Maybe if you mumbled a little you could get away with 'catch hell.'"

"Or 'satchel,' yes, very heroic." She sighed. "I should go back."

She sounded reluctant, as if she would have liked to stay. That was...*not progress,* he chided himself. *You aren't launching a campaign to win her back.*

The words struck his heart like lightning. A campaign to win her back sounded like the best idea he'd ever had.

"So should I," he said, with more of that cheerful unconcern. *Be here, and give her room to breathe. Start there.* "Quacoe will be waiting for me." He got to his feet with an effort.

Her eyes went to his shackles. "Let me see your ankles."

He shuffled a step back. "Oh, they're fine."

She raised her eyebrows. "Are they?"

"As fine as they can be after wearing irons for four days," he said impatiently. "Don't—" *Don't fuss.* That was something a man said to his wife, so he didn't say it. *Room to breathe.*

But this was something a woman did for her husband, crouching down, pushing up the knee of his breeches and pulling down his stocking, even if she did it with a stoic soldier's face. Even if she carefully didn't touch his skin.

He wanted her to touch his skin. He would die if she touched his skin.

She peeled the stocking gently away from his ankle, taking a few hairs and a scab with the linen. "Ow," he protested. Her mouth set in a grim line.

He couldn't see in this position, but he'd looked earlier and he knew he'd told her the truth: it wasn't bad. A lot of bruises, some shallow scrapes, and a general puffy redness. Who cared?

He should be relishing her attention, but he wanted too much for it to be real, for it to be out of love and not duty. The only reason he didn't yank up his stocking was because their hands might brush. "It's nothing," he repeated. "It won't be for much longer. I'm sure your feet have been worse after a day's march."

He didn't like that idea either. He'd heard too many tales of blood in the snow; his heart felt swollen and black-and-blue as a plum to think it had been her blood. And he hadn't been there to frown at the damage, the way she was doing now over a few scratches.

"I marched in order to get somewhere," she said. "These are for nothing."

"What do you mean, 'nothing'? These are keeping my secret. They're keeping me useful and they're keeping me safe. Is that nothing? Let them be."

Her frown deepened.

What do you care? he wanted to say. It was on the tip of his tongue, jumping up and down and pushing at his lips, demanding to be let out. Not saying it was probably the hardest thing he'd ever done; he felt a fierce, hot pride when he managed it. She rocked back on her heels, and he retied his garter, and that was that.

Chapter Five

❧

October 9

THE NEXT DAY was fatigue duty again for Rachel's brigade, a long day of fetching wood and water, digging new sinks, and other hard, dull labor. The only break was the cheer that went up through the camp when the first Franco-American batteries opened, accompanied by a ceremonial firing of every gun in the trenches.

And then, when they had nearly finished their work, a last-minute order came for sixty saucissons, eighty fascines, two hundred palisades, and eight hundred pickets by five o'clock. In other words, hours of bundling brush and branches securely together, stripping and sharpening small tree trunks, and picking splinters out of men's hands.

We're digging a second parallel soon, whispers went through the camp. *But what about those British redoubts?*

The squat dirt towers filled with guns sat out ahead of the British defenses and fired on anything that came near. Even though the American troops had all seen the earthworks give cover to the trenches, even though the redoubts themselves were made more or less of the same stuff, it was hard to believe that some dirt thrown over these bundles of sticks they were making could really ward off cannonballs.

Rachel breathed a sigh of relief when it was finally time for mess. The day's rations were meager, and the beef would have to be boiled for hours to be edible, but Sarah grinned with suppressed excitement. "We'll eat this tomorrow," she said. "There's plenty of food tonight. Do you want to invite your spy friend? We'll be very careful not to let drop any state secrets."

Rachel wished she could honestly answer that question in the negative. She hated the eagerness that flared up in her at Sarah's words, like breathing on a banked coal. What was wrong with her? If she did invite Nathan, in five minutes he'd embarrass her in front of her friends, and she'd remember she was glad to be rid of him.

"Thanks, Sarah. I'll go and fetch him." She couldn't *wait* to be rid of him again, and feel glad of it.

Sarah's surprise was crab, big blue ones already turned a gorgeous vivid red in the mess's tin kettle. The steam smelled of shellfish and wine.

Rachel's heart sank even as her stomach rumbled and her mouth watered. "Is there bread or something for Nathan?"

Sarah's face fell. "Oh, I didn't even think. Zvi asked for crab this week, and these were so fine! I…" She cast about, hands fluttering.

Nathan looked at the crab with trepidation. He looked at Rachel's messmates, impatient for their dinner. He took a deep breath.

"I'll eat it," he declared. "Once in my life, why not?"

Rachel's jaw dropped. "Are you sure?"

To her surprise and dismay, the idea discomfited her. As if it had only been all right to break every rule because Nathan had been at home keeping them for her.

Zvi sighed heavily. "Once won't be enough when you've tasted it. Even without vinegar or pepper or mustard—"

"You don't have pepper?" Nathan asked.

They shook their heads mournfully.

Smiling, he reached in his pocket and held out his closed fist palm up, as if to surprise a child with the gift of a penny. "Allow me to solve this problem for you." He opened his fingers to reveal a flat brass spice box, double-curved like the body of a guitar. "They took my nutmeg grater, but the salt and pepper, being in an inner pocket, escaped their notice."

So much for her friends disliking Nathan. Judging by their expressions, any of them would henceforward gladly step into the path of a bullet for him. They gathered around the fire, and Sarah dished up dinner.

Nathan poked dubiously at his crab, shuddering when its legs wobbled. "How hungry do you think the first person to eat one of these must have been?"

"It's not too late to change your mind," Rachel said.

But her friends vied with each other to show him how to break it apart and pull out the meat, and Nathan, visibly flattered by the attention, succumbed. Rachel held her breath as he screwed up his face and put the first piece in his mouth.

"It's...sweet," he said in surprise.

Zvi sighed again. "I know…"

Sergeant Flanagan rolled his eyes. "You sound like boys stealing communion wine. It's just crab."

"Tell that to my mother." Nathan seasoned another bite and popped it in his mouth. Grains of pepper stuck to his wet fingers.

Rachel couldn't bring herself to dip her fingers into his spice box, but she ate a piece of crab. It felt intimate even to taste what he was tasting, to let the sweet briny crab melt over her tongue and know that the same forbidden flavor was in his mouth.

This was ludicrous. There was nothing intimate about sharing food. She broke bread with her messmates every day and it had never once seemed a prelude to carnal conversation.

"Hey!" Scipio said. "Maybe Mr. Mendelson knows about the ring."

No. *No.* Damn it all to hell. Rachel's face flushed and her heart pounded. "Shut up," she said sharply.

Unfortunately, that rarely had the desired effect among a group of soldiers not under one's direct command. Flanagan smirked. "Oho, yes, let's ask him."

Zvi hesitated. "Maybe we shouldn't spoil the mystery."

"Pfft," Scipio said. "Do you know whose ring Ezra is wearing, Mr. Mendelson?"

There was no profanity terrible enough to relieve Rachel's inner agitation, but Nathan still looked merely confused. His eyes went to her hands, sticky with crab. "He isn't wearing any rings."

"Around his neck," Sarah clarified. "Come on, Ezra. Show him."

"Ah, leave the kid alone," Zvi said.

Tench reached for Rachel's collar. If she made a fuss now it would only be worse. There might be a scuffle; those were dangerous when you were hiding breasts.

Why had this eventuality not occurred to her when she invited Nathan to dinner? Why had she kept the ring in the first place? Oh, she'd come up with a hundred excuses she could have fed to Nathan in an argument, even though she'd never expected to see him again. For instance: *They won't expect me to romance anyone if they think I have a sweetheart at home.*

But in truth, when it came to it, she didn't know why. She just hadn't been able to leave every scrap of herself behind.

She stuck her thumb inside her collar and pulled the ribbon out, not meeting Nathan's eyes. Her wedding ring dangled, a plain gold circle that could have meant anything. He was the only person on earth who would recognize it.

There was silence.

"Well?" Tench said. "Do you know whose it is? He won't say, which is how we know it must belong to a girl."

"It did belong to a girl," Nathan said slowly.

Rachel shoved the ring back inside her collar, feeling guilty for smearing crab on it. Treyf. Her fingers shook. There were so many damn rules, how was she supposed to know which ones mattered? Which shame was nonsense and which was the voice of her soul?

Tench leaned forward. "What was her name?"

"Rachel." Her head jerked up before she realized Nathan wasn't talking to her. "I, um, I loved her too, actually. But she chose Ezra." He tugged at a stray piece of thread on his waistcoat pocket. "It broke my heart at the time, but I think I understand why now."

Every cannonade from the trenches echoed in her chest. *Boom. Boom. Boom.*

"Why?" Tench pressed.

Nathan grinned. "Because he's taller than I am."

Rachel let out her pent-up breath in a startled laugh. "That wasn't why."

"Well, go on," Scipio prompted. "Tell us about her. Is she beautiful?"

She actually wanted him to do it. To talk about the girl she'd been. But he didn't. "Pass my pepper," he said innocently, and ignored all further attempts to pry information out of him.

⚜

AFTER DINNER, she escorted him silently back to the guardhouse, bayonet fixed for show. She couldn't look at him. She wanted to blurt out, *Do you still think I'm beautiful?* She traced her faint mustache self-consciously, and hoped he didn't notice.

"Rachel," he said quietly. "Stop for a moment."

She started, glancing around for anyone who might have heard him use her name. "*Nathan.*"

"There's no one in earshot. I checked."

To her surprise, she believed him. She made herself meet his gaze. "What is it?"

"I…if *I* had it to do over again, I wouldn't do the same thing. I'd give money anonymously to the rabbi to pay for your mother's doctors, instead of asking you to marry me."

He shoved his curls out of his eyes, restlessly, but he looked her in the eye. "It didn't occur to me then, and if it had I don't know that at that age I'd have had the courage to hide money from my mother, but…it's what I should have done. I'm sorry. You were right. I thought only of myself. I generally do. My nerves make so much noise I can't always hear other people. I should try harder. I should have tried harder with you. Sorry, I'll stop talking."

He'd been thinking about what she said? Really thinking about it? She looked at her boots. "Thanks."

She was even more shocked when he waited silently to see if she had anything else to say.

She tried to imagine her life if he had done that. Who would she be? Where would she be? Would she be someone else's wife? A spinster seamstress in Philadelphia?

Or would she be right here, but free? Free to marry one day and have children, free not to care about Nathan's worried dark eyes, or his hands visibly fidgeting in his pockets. Maybe she wouldn't even remember his name. *Nathan Mendelson? It sounds familiar. I'm sure if I saw him I'd know who he was.*

She couldn't decide what to say next: there were too many things on the tip of her tongue, and too many things she suddenly wanted to believe he'd do differently now. *If you had it to do over again, what would you say to your mother when she suggested you divorce me?*

Rachel counted ten rounds from their new batteries before he nodded and set off towards the guardhouse.

A stray thought from earlier came back to her. "Wait," she got out, before she could think better of it. "I need to get something from my tent first." He accepted the detour without question.

She ducked under the tent flap and stood there, irresolute. She should duck back out and pretend she'd done something. This was too great a sacrifice, and why should she?

Nathan poked his head into the tent, holding his hat in place with one hand. "So this is where you and your friends sleep." He eyed the ground. "Five men fit in here? *And* Mrs. Goodenough? How do you avoid kicking each other in the night? How do they not—" He gestured at her breasts.

Rachel flushed hot. *Not everyone sleeps as restlessly as you do.* She couldn't say that. Just thinking it, just knowing what it was like to sleep next to him, was an unbearable intimacy.

She turned away to root through her pack. "I worried about that too. But my—they're small. Nothing's happened." The memory of his hands on her breasts felt tangible, so vivid he must see it too.

"Enough is as good as a feast." He snickered. "Sorry."

Her face flamed. The memory changed—he was suckling at her bosom, and then it wasn't a memory anymore, but desire. She wanted to tear off her linen wrapping and press his unshaven face into her sensitized flesh.

She elbowed him aside to get out without brushing up against him, gulping in night air. "Here. Tear this in half and wrap it around your ankles to pad them."

He looked at the bundle she'd shoved into his hands. "I can't take this. How many extra shirts do you even have?"

Just the one, and it was a precious commodity. Not having it meant that when Sarah was doing their mess's washing, she'd have to wear her uniform against her naked skin, and it *itched*.

"The war will be over in a few weeks. It's fine." She winced at the ripping sound as he tore it—easily; it had been worn to shreds anyway.

It took him a few false starts to tie the linen snugly around his ankle. If she saw one of her men struggling like that with a bandage, she'd take it out of his hands and do it for him.

She stuck her hands in her pockets and looked away. If she touched him, she'd have him back inside the tent in a flash, never mind that one of her messmates might stick his head in at any moment. Bruises or no, Nathan had a well-turned calf. She used to love how in the right light, if she was sitting close enough and he'd crossed one ankle over his knee, she could see the hairs peeking through his stockings. It was too dark for that now, thank God.

He tied off the second ankle and stood, taking a careful step. An expression of surprised pleasure spread across his face. "Thank you," he said earnestly. "*Thank* you."

She shrugged and shouldered her musket.

⚜

October 10

THE NEXT DAY AT NOON, their battalion marched to their posts in the trenches in a silence broken only by their drums and marching footsteps. The lack of cannon fire felt eerie, unnatural. The guns were the promise of their deliverance, beating Cornwallis into submission.

New batteries had opened just this morning; the American artillery park stood half empty. Already the little town was visibly damaged by the Allied guns, the handsome manor house where Cornwallis had made his headquarters nothing but a windowless pile of bricks.

The silence was on account of that house. It belonged to a rich old man named Nelson, and as a favor to his three sons, all American officers, Washington had asked for a ceasefire to get their father out of Yorktown.

"If I were a Virginia man, I'd riot," one of the men said in German. "For officers, we stop the whole war to rescue their father. 'Oh, *your* father, Private? Don't be so sentimental!'"

"The cannon don't cover your gossiping now," Rachel said sharply in Yiddish, with a meaningful glance at their own officers, some of whom spoke German. The soldiers rolled their eyes at her accent when they thought she wasn't looking, but they shut up.

After half an hour or so, an old white man made his careful, limping way out of the Yorktown gates to the American lines, aided by a black servant with a heavy bundle under one arm.

A black soldier spat on the ground. "A good day to be Mr. Nelson's favorite slave. The others will be fine, I'm sure."

"If he stayed, he might be free," a friend pointed out. As the Allied cannon resumed firing, a tall chimney fell with a crash. "Ah…on second thought, I'll take my chances here."

That was the prevailing sentiment in the trenches as the day wore on: *it's bad here, but God have pity on the English bastards.* Less than a day after the opening of the Allied batteries, the British embrasures and platforms were so damaged they couldn't protect their crews or support the weight of their guns, which one by one ceased firing. The Allied cannon poured shells and roundshot into the little town unopposed.

The artillerymen in the American Grand Battery had heavy work, but the light infantry covering them had little to do but take it in turns to assist the pioneers in digging the second parallel—a shorter trench than the one behind it, carefully stopped short just out of range of the British redoubts' mortar shells, if not quite their grapeshot or cannon—and watch for a sortie that never came.

Sarah brought their supper at twilight: stringy boiled beef today and some bread that had not *quite* risen. Rachel knew bitter disappointment that Nathan did not come with her. For him to struggle all the way to the trench with shackled ankles would have been both painful and stupid, and she knew it. Yet the faint, unacknowledged hope that he *might* come—and he might speak, and he might look at her, and he might, even, laugh—had sustained her all day, more than the sure expectation of supper.

She couldn't stop thinking about what he had said: *It broke my heart at the time, but I think I understand why now.* Did he truly understand? She wanted to push him against a wall and make him repeat back to her what she had said to him, to explain it to her, to—

To prove that he was different now.

As darkness gathered and the British began another go at bombardment, Rachel made herself face it: *to prove that it would be safe to go back to him.*

The thought was nonsensical. She couldn't go back to him, unless she meant to give up all her plans. A respectable Jewish clerk's wife couldn't leave her children—she refused to believe there might not be children—with her husband while she wore men's clothing and traveled on Saturday and ate treyf food at taverns.

Besides, Mrs. Mendelson had told the rabbi she'd washed Rachel's body and buried her. There was no explanation for what had happened but the truth, and the truth would bring shame to the Mendelsons. Rachel refused to see her great accomplishments become Mrs. Mendelson's dirty linen.

She was so tired of shame.

But in the gathering dark, Rachel remembered how Nathan had been the only person besides herself who didn't lower his voice respectfully in her mother's sickroom. Mrs. Jacobs had hated those hushed, gentle voices.

Nathan had acted just as he always did, and Rachel had been so grateful every evening when he came home from the counting house and talked her mother's ear off for a while, because acting just as she always did with leaden weights on her heart and her hands and the corners of her mouth made Rachel so tired she could barely keep her eyes open.

And then, after Mrs. Jacobs died, he'd walked home for dinner every single day for weeks and told funny stories about his fellow clerks, talking right over his mother when she interrupted him pointedly, *Doesn't your boss mind you leaving in the middle of the day?*

At the time, Rachel had felt oppressed by his eager pauses after every joke, but…it had been better than being alone. It had been *much* better than being alone with Mrs. Mendelson.

He'd gone to say Kaddish for her mother three times a day for eleven months, as if he were her own son, even though Mrs. Mendelson said, *Oh, hire a student!*

He hadn't known what to do, but he'd tried.

It had been five years since they'd lived together. She'd changed. God knew she'd changed. Why not him?

She had chafed at all the rules of Jewish life, but the army was full of rules too, some of them equally arcane and purposeless, and they didn't bother her too much, because she'd chosen them. If she *chose* to be Nathan's wife…

Was that a fresh noise in the continual roar?

Rachel stood, listening intently. Did the sky seem less dark than it had a moment ago? The crackling sound increased—

Fire!

Men were climbing up on the banquettes, gaping at the town. She would have to restore order among her squad in a moment—beside her Scipio shouted, "Keep the line, knuckleheads!"—but first she followed them onto the ledge along the back wall of the trench and stood on her tiptoes to see.

Her breath caught. Three of the British ships anchored in the river were ablaze, struck by French hotshot. One flamed from its waterline to the top of its mast, a great burning torch lighting up the night.

Rachel glanced around for the officers; they were dazzled

too. A tall lieutenant colonel from another light battalion climbed out of the trench to shout, "We've had word her crew is safe. Enjoy the view!"

A cheer went up, and Rachel huzzahed with them, tears pricking her eyes that kindness was possible in the midst of destruction. Whispers ran up and down the line: *That's John Laurens. Henry Laurens's son.*

Behind the whoops and whispers, though, she heard another sound: a bloodthirsty murmur of disappointment.

Destruction always had an element of beauty, didn't it? Even this brutal war. She'd felt it from the moment the first shot was fired in New York City. They were burning the old world down.

But lately she'd been wondering more and more what would be left when everything was in ashes. What would be built on the rubble, and who would do the building?

She remembered what Nathan used to say, when she spoke of the people ruling: *Mobs never bode well for Jews. How long before those Liberty Boys who dragged their fellow New Yorkers through the streets and tarred and feathered them for supporting the King remember they don't like us very much either? What's going to stop them when they do?*

Everyone here knew Henry Laurens's name. The former president of the Continental Congress had backed General Washington during that dreadful winter at Valley Forge and fought to get them food and clothes, and every soldier would remember him kindly to the day they died.

No doubt Washington himself felt the same. When the commander in chief was leading their new nation, his friends would be listened to and his enemies shut out.

Would she and Nathan be remembered kindly? Would they be remembered at all?

Any day now, the Allied commanders would judge York-town sufficiently starved and battered, and the army would storm the town. Rachel's eyes turned to the British redoubts, along the line of the truncated second parallel. They'd have to take those first, wouldn't they, to finish the trench?

Determination and fear were a bitter taste at the back of her tongue. Not fear of death. It was easy to say, like Queen Esther,

And if I perish, I perish. No, her terror was of failure. Of doing nothing of note, of fumbling ingloriously, of being finally found out for a woman before she even got to the battle. Of being forgotten after the war, or worse, remembered with disgust.

She had staked everything on this new country, on its being better than the old one. She'd never rated the sacrifice very high, but today being Nathan's wife felt like a large thing to leave behind. A heavy thing, a sacred offering.

She had to make it worth it.

She watched the ship burn until there was nothing left. In less than an hour, that tall craft that took skill and love and years to build went down without a trace, and the water closed over it. They all watched. They all cheered. It was beautiful. Better than fireworks.

Chapter Six

❦

October 11

IT WAS NOON. Nathan could hear the drums beating. That meant Rachel's division would be leaving the trenches.

Could he go and inquire after her health? Was that giving her room to breathe?

The British guns had barely fired yesterday—and then in the evening they'd resumed with a vengeance. Nathan had grown up in New York City and was accustomed to sleeping through noise, but Yorktown was putting him to the test.

But of course, it wasn't the noise itself that bothered him. With every boom, he wondered, *Did it hit her?*

He didn't understand how she did it, how you got used to walking into bullets and just hoping they'd hit someone else. At least when he went back into Yorktown, he wouldn't be expected to march in columns. He could duck and dodge and hide behind things.

The messengers he'd sent to the hospital this morning all said casualties were low, and they hadn't seen her.

He was assisting the quartermaster sergeant of Rachel's division, a friendly Dutchman named Rinckhart, in dividing up peas and rice for rations.

"Either sit down or go," Rinckhart said, not unsympathetically.

Nathan realized he'd been standing up and sitting back down continuously for... "What time is it?"

"Four past."

...For four minutes. He sat down and tried to calculate how many pounds of flour they could spare each mess in the 2nd New Jersey today. Rinckhart had two barrels to last the siege, at one hundred ninety-six pounds of flour each, and one hundred twenty-one men in that regiment out of a total of five hundred forty-two in the division, with six men to a mess.

He gave up and put his head on the desk. *At one o'clock,* he told himself. At one o'clock he could go and she would probably be done with all her urgent corporal business and probably she would be asleep in her tent, but at least he'd know she was safe and then he could divide numbers correctly.

"What time is it?"

"Nine past."

He banged his head on the desk.

"I'm sure he's fine." The sergeant sounded bemused that you could worry so much about one single person in an army. How many friends did Rinckhart have to worry about? How many of them were already dead?

All through the camp, they were saying this siege could end the war. Nathan hoped with corrosive desperation that they were right, because he couldn't stand another year of it. No one could. The country couldn't.

You could only tear something apart so far before it couldn't be put back together. New York City was already not much better than a country market town. How many people would come back?

How many Loyalists still in the city would flee to England if the rebels won?

"Is he sleeping?" Rachel's voice said.

He bolted upright. "No!" *Just waiting for you,* he managed not to say.

He couldn't see any signs of injury, but she looked asleep on her feet. She came and stood by his chair for only a moment before slumping to the ground and leaning her temple against it. "Good morning."

It was afternoon, but who cared? "How are you?"

She gave him the casualty figures for her regiment as if that was an answer. "Could you see the ship burning?"

"No, I was in the guardhouse. But I heard all about it."

She sighed. "It was pretty."

"New York was pretty when it burned too." He could hear the bitterness in his voice. Not for her. For HaShem, maybe, for forming humans to feel awe at the fires and floods He rained down on them.

She yawned. "I'm sorry about—your house." She had almost said "our." She was far too tired. He should get her out of here before she said something stupid.

"I could get another one," he said instead, because just for this moment "I" meant "we" and they were the only people who knew that. "When this is over. If I wanted to."

That wasn't room to breathe and it was also probably just another chance for her to break his heart, but he let it hang there anyway, long enough for her sleepy eyes to widen. When she started to look nervous, he asked her a question about the distribution of rations.

After explaining, she asked, "Have you heard anything about old Mr. Nelson? Was he useful, or did he just have sentimental value?"

"Word in camp has it that he told them Cornwallis has been hiding in a hole in his garden. I also heard he told them about General Clinton's confidential communications from New York, but as I heard six different accounts of what the communications were, I don't know if I credit it."

"Mm." Her eyes drifted shut, hat sliding off her head into her lap. She didn't pick it up.

Nathan fought his instinctive impulse to cover her hair. Her observance of the Law was between her and HaShem.

"It's Shemini Atzeres," he said. He shouldn't be working on a holiday. But the soldiers needed to eat; that was a matter of life and death, surely. Everything felt like a matter of life and death now. "Simchas Torah begins tonight."

The name meant "Rejoicing with the Torah," the day when the year's reading through of the Torah was completed and begun again. In the ordinary course of events, it was celebrated with dancing in the streets, and much noise and sugarplums and wine. Very little of that was possible at the moment.

"Mm," she mumbled again. "We'll…we'll…"

"Do you want to celebrate?"

She made another exhausted sound of acquiescence. "Tonight. With Zvi."

He was quiet after that, to let her sleep. It wasn't easy, but—

She stirred uneasily. "Keep talking. Sssss…'s'peaceful."

He caught his breath. His heart—it *blossomed*, in a shower of petals and warmth and a peculiar, aching pain.

"In this week's Torah portion, HaShem shows Moses the Promised Land," he said. "But Moses never reaches it. We will. You and I are going to come out of the wilderness and drink our milk and eat our honey."

It was bad luck to say out loud, it was asking for trouble. But he needed to say it. He needed to believe they were going to survive this. Both of them.

He'd thought for so long that even if he waded through this war to the other side, he'd have to stand on the far bank without her.

He bent to his figures, calculating in as soothing a murmur as he could manage. The numbers arranged themselves perfectly this time, and Rachel began to snore.

He hadn't been able to say *I forgive you* yesterday, or *it's all right*. But nothing was all right, anywhere in the colonies. What had he ever done or felt, himself, that was so deserving of praise? There were dark circles under her beautiful black eyes and dirt under her fingernails, and he didn't feel angry anymore when he looked at her, only glad she was still alive and where he could see her.

He should take her to her tent. She'd get a crick in her neck sleeping against his chair like that. He'd do it when he'd finished the week's rations.

"I forgive you," he told her sleeping form, adding "for capturing me," for the sergeant's benefit. "It's all right."

He understood now why she'd left. At first that understanding had seemed like a tragedy, almost a crime. An unbearable thing to carry in his heart. But maybe…maybe it was his
chance to make her want to come back. Now he knew what he'd
done wrong before, he could try not to do it again.

She didn't hate the sound of his voice, as he'd thought she
might. That was something.

৩৯৩

WHEN TATTOO HAD at last been beat and the NCOs had made
their nightly visits to the tents to see that the men were at least
making a pretense of resting, Rachel and Zvi made their way to
the guardhouse and were let into Nathan's little room. The
windowless cell was pitch-black. With the siege intensifying, the
guards had been forbidden lights to avoid making their window
a target and to keep their sight keen, and Nathan suffered
with them.

"We should have candles," Nathan grumbled as Rachel and
Zvi sat on the floor in a rough circle, hats respectfully kept on
their heads. "It's a mitzvah."

Rachel, too annoyed to answer, was glad when Zvi spoke
up. "It's a joyful holiday. Let's say a shehecheyonu and try to be
joyful, and not worry so much about details."

"Boruch atoh Adonoy," Rachel started, and the others
joined in. *Blessed are You, Lord our God, King of the Universe,
who gave us life, sustained us, and enabled us to reach this moment.*

Let us live to celebrate again next year, she added silently.
Maybe no one was listening, but it couldn't hurt. *Spread the
wings of Your protection over Scipio and Tench and Flanagan too,
and over my squad. Please.*

"We can't do any of the usual things," Nathan said. "We
don't have a minyan, or a Torah, or enough wine to bring joy.
I asked and the guards told me singing made too much noise.
So let's go around and each talk about the Torah for a
minute."

Panic thumped in Rachel's chest. What did she have to say
about the Torah? She'd never even learned to understand

77

Hebrew beyond a few common prayers. Only boys needed to know that.

"I'll start," Nathan continued, because of course he did. "I've been thinking about legality, and morality, and civility, because I was reading *Pilgrim's Progress* and I suppose to some people, those things are the enemies of faith. But when HaShem gave us the Torah, He told us He didn't simply expect us to love Him more than we loved anything or anybody else. He told us that following His law and being fair to one another were the most sacred things we could do. And I want to thank Him for that."

His shackles clanked in the darkness as he tried to shift position. "In the first half of this week's Torah portion, Moses dies before reaching the Promised Land. But in the second half we start again. We don't even wait for next week to say, 'In the beginning.' In the beginning there was darkness, and the earth was formless and empty. I want to ask HaShem's blessing for this new country we're trying to create out of nothing. I want us…"

He paused. It was dark in the little room, but Rachel could feel him look at her. "And by 'us,' I mean not only Jews but all of us, all Americans."

Rachel's heart stuttered. He'd been listening when she said she wanted to be American. He'd remembered, and he'd made her hope a tenet of his faith.

"I want us to fight to make this a place where justice and integrity and kindness are first in our hearts. I want us to create light after the darkness."

"Amen," Zvi said, and Rachel hurried to echo him. Her voice came out a little hoarse, as if she'd scraped the last word from her empty throat. She felt—she felt as if she loved Nathan more than she loved anybody or anything else.

It's just a moment, she told herself. *It's just because he's good at talking. Gam zeh ya'avor. Everything passes, and so will this.*

She waited for the moment to pass, and it didn't.

She'd forgotten what it felt like to love Nathan, the strength and joy of it. Affection overflowed her chest until it was impossible to believe she had ever felt anything like it before, until she couldn't believe her body could hold one drop more. She felt a kind of wonder and awe at the mere fact that she hadn't burst apart, or spat affection onto the dirt floor.

Maybe she never had felt anything like it; maybe she'd needed to grow until she could hold it inside her. She was glad Zvi was here, because if he weren't, she'd kiss Nathan and that would be a catastrophe.

But why? she asked herself, forgetting that too. Forgetting everything but this feeling and how good it felt to be stretched and strained by it. *Why would it be a catastrophe?*

Maybe love was beautiful, like Mount Sinai, and she'd been twisting it into an ugly black cliff belching flame.

So you want to live with Mrs. Mendelson again? she asked herself, to calm the racing of her heart. *You want to get kicked out of the army?*

"I'll go next," Zvi said after waiting politely and Rachel saying nothing. "I, um, I keep thinking about one of the very first laws You gave us. 'Don't kill.' You told us not to kill and here we are, killing. But there are wars in the Bible, so maybe You just meant, you know, 'Don't murder.' This isn't murder, right? What they did to Colonel Scammell last week, killing him after he surrendered, that was murder, but in battle, it's not?"

He drew his bayonet from its sheath and laid it on the ground. "I'm a butcher, and I'm used to killing and blood. I remember the first time I slit a chicken's throat, it horrified me, and now it's nothing. I hate that killing men might feel like nothing after a while, too. So I want to pray that the war is over before the next new year." He laughed. "Next year in Jerusalem, right?"

"Amen," Nathan said with conviction. Rachel's was a thread.

There was a long silence.

"Ezra?" Zvi prompted.

"I never…" It came out too quiet, and she had to begin again. "I never liked all the rules," she said slowly. Talking to Nathan, really. "When I was a kid, I hated that I worked all week, helping my mother, and then on the only day we didn't work, we couldn't do anything because it was a day of rest. I hated all the things I had to memorize, and all the things I couldn't eat and the places I couldn't eat in and the people I couldn't eat with. When I learned what the prayer we sing every Friday night meant, I laughed...that we knew God loved us with an eternal love because He gave us 'Torah umitzvos, chukim umishpotim.' The Torah and the Commandments, the laws and the precepts. I thought we were the fussiest religion in the world."

Nathan had been the one to translate the Shabbos prayers for her, horrified she'd been saying them every week her whole life without understanding above a tenth of the words. He'd leapt out of bed and fetched a prayer book and gone through them with his finger under the words. Most of them had disappointed her. They sounded so fine in Hebrew.

"But I've realized since I enlisted that the rules we choose to follow make us who we are. If we want to stop being British, we have to follow the rules they won't: don't loot, don't hurt civilians, don't take unfair revenge on Loyalists, don't starve prisoners, don't beat a man after he's surrendered. Even the little stupid everyday rules that don't make any sense but some general thought they were a wonderful idea—well, I still hate them and sometimes I brush them aside, but even they bind us together, make us a community."

She laced her fingers tightly together. "I don't follow every rule God gave us, and I probably won't ever. But I'm glad He gave us the rules and made us who we are because I love us. I love being Jewish, and what...you said."

She couldn't say Nathan's name. It would make the moment too much, too intimate. "I like that Jewishness is about what you *do*, and not how much you say you believe in God in your heart."

"Amen," Zvi said. Nathan followed suit a moment later. Rachel couldn't tell how he felt about what she said. But it was the truth. That had to be good enough.

October 12

THE ALLIES HAD OPENED a second parallel overnight under the noses of the British. They were razing Yorktown to the ground with their guns, pounding its few thousand square yards with dozens, maybe hundreds of rounds an hour.

For Rachel and the rest of Colonel Hamilton's battalion, it was a long day full of dull chores in camp and a constant earnest but triumphant gratitude that one wasn't inside Yorktown. The neat little town was a slaughterhouse, spattered and dripping with blood.

Since the enemy could more or less drop shells directly into the new parallel, only two hundred yards from the British lines, it was also a good day not to be inside the trenches. But Rachel tried not to feel triumphant or even too grateful for that. That kind of luck was always fleeting and could never be deserved.

Her mess bought their dinner; Sarah Goodenough had been summoned to the hospital early in the morning to help with the heavy casualties, and kept there.

Rachel was kept too busy to visit Nathan—at least, that's what she told herself, and was glad of it. Even walking past the guardhouse sent a shock through her. Sitting beside him in the dark last night and listening to his voice had changed things, had pushed her past some boundary in her mind.

It wasn't lust and awkwardness she felt now—it was more like a fundamental recognition. The irksome fever of the last few days had become a steady, clear-burning flame.

She didn't like it. She didn't like that her body had made some kind of decision without consulting her. She was a corporal, not a wife. She had chosen that.

Everything turned on the success of this siege. She had drilled her squad, trained them, scolded them into cleanliness, tried to keep them healthy. Now she had to see them through this. She owed it to her comrades, her commanders, and her people. She owed it to Nathan. So they could all go home.

Home.

She was so tired. When had she last gotten a full night's sleep? Now and then her mind dwelt peacefully on being a wife: on living quietly at home, on her greatest responsibility being a dinner served hot and on time. Lectures and ballads sounded like an awful lot of work.

She liked that even less than she liked this love that sat like a smoothly polished stone behind her breastplate.

☙❧

October 13

RACHEL'S BRIGADE relieved the trenches at noon, and around two o'clock marched into the second parallel to defend against any British assault.

For the moment, the enemy were firing mainly on the French troops to their left. For days there had been rumors Cornwallis was running out of ammunition, and it was true that the British rarely seemed to concentrate their firing on more than one place at a time. But the siege stretched on.

A battle was one sort of ordeal, and tedium another, but this buzzing, fearful waiting was almost worse than either. It gnawed at the army's fraying nerves and wore away at their hope. Beside her, Scipio restlessly turned a piece of shrapnel over and over in his fingers.

Surely the British could not withstand this pounding forever. Surely soon they would pour out of the ravaged town and make a desperate attempt on the American guns.

"I reckon Secretary Nelson is glad to be out of it," one of the men said. "Did you hear one of his slaves was hit by a cannon-ball in his living room, just a few feet away from him?"

"Yes," Scipio muttered. "I've been hearing that all day, as if it's a story about Mr. Nelson's narrow escape and not about a human being who died because Mr. Nelson forced him to stay in a besieged city."

Mouth tight, he drew a square in the trench wall with his shrapnel. "Did you hear the one slave he brought out with him was carrying the family silver? Good to know he had some use that justified saving his life." Slash, slash, slash, cutting the lines deeper in the dirt. "Nelson kept them there for his own convenience, and now he's left them there defenseless for the same reason. Cornwallis won't let them share his hole, I'm sure."

Only a week ago, Cornwallis had already turned out hundreds of escaped slaves who had fled to him for protection, because they were sick or he couldn't feed them. They were dying in the forest around camp and all over the countryside.

"Do you think anything will really be different after the war?" Rachel asked. She felt afraid even to voice the idea. Did one wilderness only give way to another, on and on into eternity? Did somebody always get left behind in the desert? She had felt so hopeful on Simchas Torah, hearing Nathan's voice in the darkness. "Keynehore," she muttered, warding off the evil eye, and wished Nathan were there to chime in with his learned Hebrew.

Scipio hurled the shrapnel back at the British lines, a fierce, abortive motion. "It had better be."

As the sun sank low in the sky, camp followers began to bring men's dinners into the trench. Rachel's stomach grumbled as her squad cheerfully ate bread and nuts, but eventually Sarah came into view far down the trench, kettle held in apron-wrapped hands.

Behind her trudged Nathan.

Rachel had avoided him for the better part of two days, and all she had accomplished was to make herself happier to see him.

He carried a bundle in his arms, visibly apologizing to everyone he jabbed in the shins with his shackles. Since the trench was crowded, that was a lot of people. A wave of grumbles, insults, and rude gestures followed them as they got closer. Rachel remembered when that would have flustered Sarah; after a few years with the army, she rolled her eyes and marched determinedly onward. Rachel felt a surge of pride in all of them, how they had grown up and grown strong.

If Mrs. Mendelson asked to give her dress to the maid now, Rachel would have choice words for the woman.

Dinner was an approximation of beef stew: a few pieces of potato, onion, and the tough remains of yesterday's beef floating in greasy water. Rachel would be hungry again in an hour, but for now the food was hot and Nathan let her use some of his salt.

There was also water for their canteens, a few slices of fresh bread, and new packets of candied nuts, carried by Nathan. The sun hadn't set, yet he had helped carry fresh-cooked food. It was stupid, and maybe unkind, to feel such hope over that. "It's Saturday," she said, and then wished she'd let it pass without comment.

He shrugged, looking a little sad. "I don't know what higher purpose would be served by not seeing you."

"Keeping civilians out of the trenches." She felt sad herself. In not rushing him back to camp, she was breaking a rule whose rationale was far more self-evident. But she realized with a shock that their motives were the same: they wanted to see each other. "You should go back. It isn't safe."

"They're barely firing on this position," he pointed out, although he flinched and sucked in a breath at every crack of the guns.

Sarah lingered too, sitting in Tench's lap. It was hard for Rachel, so hard, not to at least press her shoulder against Nathan's, or knock his knee with hers as they sat side by side. Her desire for closeness felt more dangerous than the British cannon. She should make him go.

But he stayed, fidgeting and flinching and talking the ears off a couple of her privates as it grew dark. Every half hour or so, she told him to go, and didn't argue when he shrugged and said, "A little longer."

Around ten o'clock the engineers began building a battery just ahead of their position, aimed at the British redoubts. The infantrymen were instructed to make noise all along the line, to hide the construction from the British. Flanagan and Scipio were in the work party with some of their men, but she could hear Zvi singing and Tench leading a group in prayer.

Since enlisting, Rachel had tried never to talk too much or too loudly, afraid that in an unguarded moment her voice would give her away. She walked grimly up and down the line, inquiring after each man's health and listening to the answer— or shaking him awake if there wasn't one—and sharing her candied nuts with anyone who seemed colder or more scared than his fellows. She barely felt a pang of regret as she parted with them; just now she wanted to feel like a good NCO more than she wanted the nuts.

No deaths yet, thank God. Rachel sat with the few men who were shot, or struck with shell fragments, until someone came to take them to the hospital. For all the new skills she'd learned in the army, she'd enlisted already knowing how to sit cheerfully by a sickbed.

She still hated it. Nathan's voice helped, even telling an unpleasant ghost story. Soon half the men had joined in with ghost stories of their own. Elijah Sutton—ordinarily a cheerfully levelheaded fellow—spun the most hair-raising tale Rachel had ever heard, beginning, "My true love, Kate, had this from a woman who witnessed it, and Kate says her hair was white as snow, though she was a young thing...." The men hung on his every word, eyes wide.

"That'll keep them awake," Nathan whispered to her as she passed.

He'd been trying to help? That fountain of affection over-flowed again inside her. In truth, having the men jumping at shadows was less than ideal—but it was better than asleep, and they were all so tired. She wanted to curl up on the ground and put her head in Nathan's lap, herself.

"You should go," she told him firmly. His leg had not stopped vibrating for the last hour.

"I'm not frightened," he said, not particularly trying to make it convincing. "I'm clanking to aid the Patriot cause."

She hid a smile. "You're not a soldier. You don't have to be here." She knew he'd go if she insisted. If something happened to him, it was on her head.

"It's less frightening here than back there." He laughed nervously. "I mean. Sorry. I'm trying to give you room to breathe. Do you want me to go?"

He had asked her, point blank. "Yes" would be a lie. What would he think it meant if she said no? What *would* it mean? He had just told her he would be more afraid in safety than in the trenches, because there he wouldn't know how she fared.

We could build a new house after the war, he'd said. *If we wanted.* What did she want? She hesitated, frozen.

"A shell!" the sentry called. "A shell!"

She whipped around, searching the sky for the idly skipping arc of light that meant a shell—just slow enough they were worth trying to dodge, unlike cannonballs.

It landed at her feet, throwing off sparks.

"On the banquette," she shouted. "Everyone on the banquette!" Men scrambled onto the raised walkway along the back of the trench, hurling themselves flat atop the muskets they'd been storing there.

Nathan.

He was curled into a ball on the ground, arms protecting his head. "I'll be fine," he lied repeatedly to no one in particular.

"I'm going to die, and it will be your fault," she shouted. "Get the hell up!" She dragged him to his feet and realized the problem: he couldn't climb in the shackles. But he got his arms on the banquette and heaved, and she was able to tip his legs gracelessly up.

He was a civilian. She should have made him go. She climbed on top of him and pressed them both into the banquette. He shifted as if to push her off, which would land her right back down in the trench with the shell if he managed it. "Stay still, you piece of shit!" she yelled in his ear. He wriggled an arm free anyway, and used his hat to shield the back of her neck.

The shell didn't explode. They lay crushed together, her legs tangled with his, her chest against his chest, her hands splayed over the sides of his face. He was trembling, whispering—she strained and made out the words. The Shema, greatest prayer of all, small and frequent and supposed to be said one last time at the hour of death. *Hear O Israel, Adonoy is our God, Adonoy is one.*

She fought the overwhelming urge to kiss his temple. "We'll be fine," she whispered. He nodded, his nose brushing her cheek.

The shell exploded.

Chapter Seven

RACHEL WASN'T MOVING.

Rachel *wasn't moving.* In a panic, Nathan put his hands on her shoulders and pushed her up so he could see her face, but it was too dark to make out anything. Her eyes were open, but people died with open eyes, they—

She blinked. "Are you hit?"

Air rushed into his lungs, freezing and welcome. "I don't know," he said honestly. "Are you?"

She shrugged, sitting up and patting her head and legs. "I don't think so."

He should sit up and check himself for shell fragments. He was probably unhurt, even if he'd heard that wounded men often couldn't feel it. The body spared them that, somehow. *Boruch atoh Adonoy, Eloheinu melech ho'olam, asher yotzar es ho'odom b'chochmo...Blessed are You who in wisdom fashioned the human body...*

Making a frustrated sound, Rachel ran her hands over his body, quickly and carefully. Nathan let her. He deserved something nice after all that terror. "You're whole," she said brusquely. "Go back to camp. Now."

Only now she'd moved away did he realize how close they'd been. He could feel the imprint of her body on his, the stiffness of her pomaded hair against his cheek.

He wished there was something he could leave behind with her, some charm against misfortune. His amulet had shared a pocket with his nutmeg grater, and been stolen in its company. He wished now he'd made more of a fuss.

Nathan had always wanted so badly to protect her, to take care of her. He'd never managed it.

"When my mother was dying," she said. "You helped. I should have said so before. Thanks."

He...had? He breathed in, full of emotion—

"Brearley's company, form here!" someone called out.

"That's me." She turned away. "Prescott, he's talking to you too! Carvalho, are you hurt? Then why are you holding your arm like that?" She strode off.

In the sudden merging of past and present—the new bride caring for her sick mother and the corporal commanding her men—Nathan saw how impossible it had been for her to handle Mrs. Mendelson the way he'd asked her to. Rachel was built to face fear and injustice head-on. To deal as directly as she could, and to stand and fight.

He'd never fully understood that until now, any more than she'd understood that Nathan's nodding agreeably when his mother talked didn't mean he was under her thumb. It was just easier to pretend to go along, and then do as he liked.

To name an obvious example, he'd married Rachel.

He glanced at the battery under construction. The Allied guns were smashing Yorktown to splinters, but Cornwallis refused to surrender, hoping for help from Clinton in New York. The Allied armies wouldn't wait forever. If Cornwallis dawdled long enough, Rachel and her comrades would charge his earthwork walls and bristling wooden spikes.

She had her way of fighting. He had his.

Rachel skidded to a stop in front of him and crossed her arms. "Why are you still here?"

"Just thinking."

"Carvalho, kindly take your musket and escort Mr. Mendelson to the guardhouse before going to the hospital to have that splinter pulled. Report back here when you're patched up."

"Yes, Corporal." A scrawny Jewish adolescent tried to salute with his injured arm and stopped with a frightened whimper.

Her voice softened. "Do you remember the password?"

The boy nodded.

She put her hand on his shoulder. "It's just a scratch, Isaac. Keep it clean and you have nothing to worry about."

As they walked off, Nathan wished the awkwardness of shackles didn't prevent him from slinging a friendly arm around the boy's shoulders. "Do you know where Colonel Hamilton is, Mr. Carvalho?"

Carvalho frowned suspiciously. "Um. Why?"

"I want to talk to him."

"Look, sir, I may be young, and"—the poor kid gulped —"maybe I seemed a little scared just now because I'm bleeding, but you won't make me compromise the safety of my commanding officer by sharing information with a known spy."

Nathan pressed his lips together very tightly and shoved his hands in his pockets to keep them from vibrating with frustration. "I gave my parole," he tried. "I swore on the Bible. The front half, anyway. The part that's ours."

Silence.

"If you don't want to tell me where he is, can you take me to him?"

"What if you assassinate him?"

Nathan rubbed at his eyes. "Search me for weapons, then! Tie my hands together. Whatever you need to do. Believe me, it's of the utmost importance I speak with him. I know something about Cornwallis's troops." Did the lie sound plausible? Did it matter?

The boy pressed the tip of his finger to the shell splinter in his arm. People did the strangest things when they were nervous. "Ow. And why do you want to tell him now if you didn't before?"

"Because Corporal Jacobs is my friend and I want him to be safe."

That sounded plausible, apparently. Carvalho took a deep breath and capitulated. "I like Corporal Jacobs too," he confided as he led them through the trench.

"That's because you have good taste," Nathan said. "Who do you dislike?"

"I'm not sure I should tell you."

"Fair enough. Just chitchatting."

※

AFTER HIS MEETING WITH HAMILTON, Nathan said his evening prayers and made himself sleep. He needed to have his wits about him tomorrow—or maybe the day after. Who knew? But best be prepared. He lay down on his pile of straw, shut his eyes, breathed in and out, and repeated part of the prayer to himself over and over, the part that began, *Hashkiveinu.*

He didn't think about anything but the Hebrew words. He didn't even think about who he wasn't thinking about. *Spread over us the shelter of Your peace…*

He slept.

※

"BUT YOU HAVE to say what happened at *the meeting," Rachel interrupted. "Mrs. Hamilton will want to know."*

"It was more or less what you'd expect," Nathan said. "At least, I'm sure it was."

She raised her eyebrows.

"I don't really remember anything Hamilton did or said," he admitted. "I was extremely *nervous. Just mention his coolness under fire. I remember that it annoyed me at the time."*

※

October 14

NATHAN SPENT the morning staring at his watch, waiting either to be summoned to Washington's presence, or for it to be noon and for Rachel to return from the trenches. To pass the time, he also kept track of how many times he was threatened with violence for absentmindedly kicking the wall between his room and the guards'.

He tried to finish *Pilgrim's Progress*, but could only absorb the meaning of a sentence or two at a time, so he flipped to the end to see how it turned out. He discovered a second part, written later, in which Christian's wife followed him to Heaven. Nathan could only assume the author had been deluged by angry letters on the poor woman's behalf. That gave him hope; even Gentiles were not entirely heartless.

Please, HaShem, let all this be worth it, he prayed. *Let America lie down in peace and awaken to life. Let Rachel awaken to life. I don't suppose I have anything You need, but if I do, it's Yours—well, everything I have is Yours anyway, but…*

Noon came and went. Nathan tried to count how much time for the soldiers to form up, how much to fuss about with drums and flags and saluting the new troops, how much to march from the trenches, how much for Rachel to escort her men back to their tents… Maybe she would be too tired to visit and he should try to bribe one of the sentries into sending a messenger.

The door opened.

It was only one of the sentries, who tossed a scrap of paper at him and shut the door again.

Nathan dove for the paper, tripped, and fell on his face. He felt about on the floor in darkness, seized the paper, and, still kneeling, stretched it towards the light. *I'm well. I'll be there soon. Ezra.*

That had been kind of her, to remember that he worried.

He had ascribed to her any number of wonderful qualities, but he had never particularly thought of her as kind. He'd even had a sneaking admiration for her hard-heartedness, had fancied himself the rose twining round her briar, like in the song. But now he thought it over, the song was nonsense: roses had thorns and briars flowered. He had deluded himself that kindness came in one guise, and that was a sweet voice and never saying anything that might wound his own delicate feelings.

She had hurt him, it was true. But she hadn't done it out of cruelty or lack of feeling. She'd pricked his fingers because he'd been poking at her.

The door opened again. This time it *was* Rachel. The door shut behind her, and the sentries locked her in with him. He didn't know when he'd started smiling. It hurt where he'd scraped his chin on the floor. "I was just thinking about you."

There was a pause. "I don't—" she started. "I'm not—I should sleep—" She took two abrupt strides forward, fell to her knees, and kissed him, their hats knocking together and tumbling to the floor.

Five years went up in smoke. His whole life went up in smoke, and it was pretty while it burned. His hands flew to her waist and were confused by her uniform, layers of threadbare wool so different from anything they'd felt on her body before. He felt underneath her coat, underneath her waistcoat, there was her shirt and it might almost have been her nightdress but her body—was her body different or did he just not remember?

It must be different; she had marched a thousand miles since he touched her last. Her lips were chapped and her hair smelled like lemon, cloves, and slightly rancid fat. Lard, he thought. That was disgusting, pig fat in her beautiful hair, he couldn't think about it.

But it was easy not to think about it, it didn't matter, nothing mattered because she was climbing into his lap and her lips were on his, her breath warm in the autumn chill. She kissed him with silent desperation. Was he allowed to pull her shirt out of her breeches and put his hands on her skin? Better to wait, better not to do anything that might make her stop.

She pressed her forehead into his shoulder. "Oh damn, this is ill-advised, I'm so tired I can't think straight." She turned her face into his neck and kissed it. The shock of it went all through him. "Shut up," she murmured. "Don't make a sound. I'm begging you."

He dug his teeth into his lower lip and kept them there, a bright sharp reminder as she clumsily unbuttoned first his breeches, then hers, and pushed him eagerly inside her.

"Not a *so-o-ound,*" she whispered. He shook his head. She was rubbing at herself, she moved against him with tiny silent jerks of her hips. She kissed him as if she was driven to it, and he had to stop biting his lip to kiss her back.

Not a sound, he chanted silently to himself. *Not a sound.* Oh, but it was hard, he had missed her, she was hot and wet and wanted him. She was a magnet and every atom in his body was an iron filing turning towards her, straining painfully to get closer, screaming in pleasure and relief at finally having somewhere to point.

But he couldn't come inside her. He was proud of himself for remembering that. "I, um, pregnant," he got out under his breath.

Rachel froze. Once, they had made sure he always, always came inside her, because they'd wanted a baby and it was a mitzvah not to waste seed. *Never mind,* he almost said.

But she nodded. "Can you wait just another half a minute? I'm almost—"

"Yes, yes." He squeezed his eyes shut and dug his teeth into his lip again. He tried not to think about her arm rubbing against his waistcoat as she frigged herself, or the flatness of her chest beneath her shirt where her nipples pressed into tight linen, or her gasps, or the blunt pressure of her teeth through the wool of his coat where she'd set them on his shoulder.

She convulsed around him, her body shuddering, her teeth spasming on his shoulder. He waited and waited until he had to push her away. Sensation dimmed all at once but orgasm came anyway, pulsing weakly but intently. Seed dribbled down his cock. He wanted to take himself in hand but he wanted this to be all hers, too.

Oh, he couldn't help it, he wrapped his fingers around himself and felt her slickness, it was sordid to say HaShem's name at this moment but he knew the impulse anyway. When he opened his eyes she lay watching him, her fingers still working, slowly now.

Boruch atoh Adonoy, m'chaiyay hameisim, he thought out of nowhere, the daily prayer taking on sudden urgent meaning. *Blessed are You, Lord, who gives life to the dead.*

She was still for a moment, then wiped her hand on the inside of her breeches before buttoning them hastily. She smelled her fingers with a grimace and, reluctantly, put them in her mouth to clean them. Nathan's pulse raced despite his satiety.

"Do you think it smells in here?" she asked.

"Probably." Nathan replaced his hat. He felt disoriented by how she was a separate person again when she had been part of him—but she hadn't been, had she? He had had no idea at all what she was thinking or why. She had wanted him, and he had given himself to her. He'd done it unquestioningly, and loved doing it.

Now, questions crowded in. But did he really want the answers?

Nathan fastened his own breeches. "Um. Stay a few minutes. I need to talk to you."

She rubbed at her eyes. "I need to get back to my men. And sleep. I need...sleep." Her voice almost trailed off. She must have been awake since yesterday morning. "They said we might be going out again soon. For some action."

"That's what I want to talk to you about. I'm going back into Yorktown."

RACHEL SAT BOLT UPRIGHT, exhaustion receding to a sort of dull jitteriness. "*What?*"

Nathan looked pleased by her reaction. "They're sending me into Yorktown. Before your action. Probably to give false information, or...to help you. To help the army, I mean. Originally, I was hoping maybe you wouldn't see any action at all, but it's too late for that, evidently. Cornwallis would do everyone a favor if he—"

"That's absurd," she said firmly. "Going *into* Yorktown? They can't send you. Not now. Have you seen Yorktown lately?"

Nathan took a deep breath. "Yes."

"Tell them you won't go. They can't force you. You're not a soldier."

"I asked to go."

That stopped her in her tracks. For several breaths, she

simply had nothing to say. "You asked to go," she repeated carefully.

He nodded.

"What if I ask you not to?"

She hadn't meant to say it. She didn't know where the words came from. She waited, heart pounding and head aching, for his answer.

He watched her solemnly. "What if I asked you to leave the army?" he said finally. "They'd let you go if you told them the truth."

Her eyes stung. "I wouldn't do it," she admitted quietly. "Not if you begged me."

There it was, then. They had no hold on each other anymore. For one glorious moment she'd had him, his hands had been at her waist, he'd been hers but...it didn't mean they owed each other anything. She felt like crying.

He shrugged and nodded. "I...I want you to know I'm not doing it for you," he said. "To protect you. I do want to protect you, obviously. But I would have done it anyway. Well, not this exactly, I'd be in Yorktown right now if you hadn't arrested me. But you know what I mean—I thought you were dead and I was doing it anyway."

He fingered a scrape on his chin. "You know, when I'd get really scared, I'd think, *Rachel could do it,* and that helped. It inspired me. I didn't do it for you, but you made me want to do it, and I think it was a good thing to do. So thank you. Thank you for giving my life meaning."

Rachel felt ashamed. He'd inspired her too. Sometimes when she'd been afraid, early on, she'd thought, *Nathan couldn't do this, but you can.* That had given her so much stubborn courage. A welcome conviction that being a soldier was about more than being a man.

She'd underestimated him. Maybe he couldn't fight in a battle, or march ten hours without complaint, but he'd go into Yorktown and lie to Cornwallis's face and risk cannonballs and hanging, flinching at every loud noise. She didn't have the nerve for that.

He was waiting for her to answer him, but her heart was a

stone weighing down her throat and mouth, holding them closed. She didn't even know what to call this emotion. Fear? Anger? If she spoke…that would be something like a blessing, or permission, or acceptance.

All she wanted to say was *Don't go,* and he was going.

"When…" She could see Nathan considering his words. Trying to decide what would tempt the evil eye least, probably. "When all this is over," he settled on, "I'll give you a get if you want one."

She couldn't speak.

"If you want one," he repeated. "You said that last time I didn't ask you what you wanted. So I'll ask this time. I, um, you probably know I'd take you back if you wanted that instead. That is—sorry, that sounded wrong, 'take you back.' I don't mean to say I'd be doing you such a great favor. I mean to say I love you. But can I ask *you* for a favor? Please don't tell me the answer now. I want you to think it over. I want you to be sure. And if you *are* sure and it's 'no,' I'd rather…is this a terrible thing to ask?" He fisted a hand in the beautiful, filthy hair at the nape of his neck. "You can say no, if you need to. I just would like hope. In case. If you don't mind."

Her heart swelled, closing off words even further.

She had to say something. He didn't want to die knowing for sure she didn't love him. If he did die, and she hadn't said anything…

She'd told herself so often, *Nathan couldn't do this, but I can.* But Nathan was able to say he loved her, and she was terrified to say it back. She had plenty of reasons, but in the end it was just cowardice, wasn't it?

"And I won't let my mother be rude to you. I lived with her all my life, you know. But I've been on my own now, and to be honest it was a bit of a relief. I know you wanted me to come with you to Philadelphia, so I hope that doesn't pain you to hear. What I mean to say is, I understand now why she was a shock to your system, not being accustomed to it. If she can't control herself, she'll have to live somewhere else. If you say yes."

Shame at her weakness pushed the words out of her throat. "I love you too."

Her voice sounded grudging, but she felt calmer for having said it. What was the worst that could happen? Later maybe she'd add, *But I won't live with you*, and maybe he'd believe she'd promised him something and not delivered it. She could live through that. It was better than letting Nathan go to his death, fidgeting bravely and without a single word of comfort.

"I do love you," she said again, stronger. "And I'll answer you when all this is over."

She wanted to say something more, but there wasn't anything. Not meeting his eyes, she took his hand in both of hers and crushed his palm against her lips. So hard it stopped being a kiss and became a demand. A direct order to be careful, because there was no point saying it out loud.

He smiled, a wide, incredulous smile. His teeth caught the light of the candle.

It used to make her angry, how much he loved her. How much he wanted her to love him too. It still did, because he was going into Yorktown and he shouldn't be happy. He should be solemn and afraid.

The latch rattled. She dropped his hand, and the door opened. Two soldiers stood in the opening. "We're here for the prisoner."

He was led away, still smiling.

Rachel sat on the floor, very still, until her face stopped trying to cry. She went back to her tent and went to sleep.

***

NATHAN'S MEETING with Washington was brief, to the point, and left out any information about what Rachel's battalion would *really* be doing.

"...After staging your escape in the sentry's uniform, you will tell Cornwallis that while assisting in fatigue duty you overheard orders given and discussed in regards to an attack on the Fusiliers Redoubt on the British right flank this evening, to be supplemented by a simultaneous attack on the British position in Gloucester across the river."

"What's a fusilier?" Nathan's ability to keep his mouth shut was severely compromised by nerves.

"They are an elite Welsh infantry regiment who wear a distinctive hat," Washington said without a hint of a smile. "However, I don't suppose Lord Cornwallis will expect you to discuss the military aspect of affairs. In fact, the less you know, the better. Tell him we were lulled into a false sense of security by your unprepossessing manner and that you used your previous friendship with a noncommissioned officer and coreligionist in the Light Division to—"

"Corporal Jacobs didn't tell me anything, sir."

"I hope not."

"Is my manner really that unprepossessing?" Now he was just trying to see if he could get the general to crack a smile, even a scornful one. "I like to think I'm very impressive on first acquaintance. Dignified. Statesmanlike, even."

Nothing.

"I see why everyone thought it was so remarkable that—" He bit the words off before he could bring up Washington's dead friend Scammell, who had made the general laugh. "Never mind. I'm sorry, I'm a little on edge. Are you expecting heavy casualties in the Light Division tonight? No, don't answer that, it's bad luck. Is there anything else you want me to tell His Lordship?"

"I believe that will suffice." Washington regarded him gravely. "Lives depend on your steadiness, Mr. Mendelson."

"Not my *steadiness*, I hope." He tried to pull himself together. "Don't worry, Your Excellency. My unprepossessing manner is part of my stock in trade, as you so tactfully pointed out. I won't fail you."

In very little time, Nathan found himself skirting the edge of the trees behind the first Allied parallel, in company with a very large, very Irish sentry. "Well, uh." He made a fist.

"Lord love you, you'll break your thumb," the fellow said, and showed him how to do it properly. "A good solid blow, mind. I want a black eye to show the boys, and you want scraped knuckles to show the lobsterbacks."

Nathan winced in anticipation. "Sorry," he said, and swung.

છ્જી

RACHEL and her messmates were woken after only a few hours' sleep by Major Fish, who informed them that the whole division was returning to the trenches at five o'clock.

"We'll all need to be at our sharpest," he told them. "If we keep a cool nerve, we can deal Yorktown a killing blow tonight. Most of all, we cannot allow a single man to desert, or a single deserter to make it into Yorktown with advance information of our attack. We *must* surprise the British."

Flanagan rushed off at once to consult with the captain. Major Fish looked at Rachel. "Your spy friend escaped. I hope to God you didn't tell him anything. You spent a lot of time in his company."

"Nothing, sir," she said firmly, and the adjutant left with a shrug.

She felt sick. *We must surprise the British.* Was that Nathan's task? To ensure they were surprised?

Her thoughts full, Rachel began packing her knapsack. Did her queue need retying—

Scipio cleared his throat. Rachel glanced up to see her messmates regarding her gravely.

"What?" she asked, unnerved. "I didn't tell Nathan anything."

"We know the truth," Scipio said.

Time slowed. Her stomach hurt. What would she do if there was nothing to know?

She blinked. "What truth?" Maybe she should offer up Nathan's secret as a distraction. No, of course she couldn't—it was too late, anyway.

Zvi shifted uneasily. "You're going to be embarrassed if we're wrong," he told Scipio.

"We're not wrong," Tench said. "You're a woman."

Chapter Eight

RACHEL TRIED to laugh and keep her voice low at the same time. "What? A *woman*?"

"You don't grow a beard, none of us have ever seen you bathe or take a piss, and you're in love with Nathan Mendelson."

"I am not in *love* with Nathan Mendelson," she scoffed. Oh God, was that bad luck to say? "And you don't grow a beard either, Tench."

"A lot of us might not make it through this attack," Scipio said quietly. "We're not going to let a woman walk onto a bayonet."

Tench, just turned twenty-two, fingered his chin self-consciously. "If it were Sarah, I'd want someone to stop her."

Rachel's heart pounded angrily. *Then Nathan's a better husband than you are.* "How dare you?" she demanded. "I've fought beside you for three years. I'm not a woman."

"If you're not," Zvi interjected, "it's easy enough to prove it and we can all forget this ever happened."

"I'm not going to forget it," she snapped. "I don't owe you anything. Definitely not a peek at my cock. I thought we were friends."

They almost backed down. But they didn't. "Prove you're a man, or we're going to the captain," Tench said.

Rachel cast about desperately. Glancing out the tent flap, she saw Colonel Hamilton hurrying by, his face a thundercloud.

He was slim and small and pretty. Had anyone ever accused him of being a woman? When he wasn't giving orders or scolding, he was easy enough to talk to. If she had to tell someone her secret, she'd tell him.

"I'll prove it to him," she said, and leapt out of the tent. "Colonel Hamilton!"

Hamilton wheeled impatiently. "Yes, Corporal?"

Her courage almost failed her. But Tench, Zvi, and Scipio looked abashed that such a high officer had now become involved in their pettiness. She stepped forward smartly, saluting.

"Sir, my messmates have convinced themselves I'm a woman, and nothing will satisfy them but that I prove myself otherwise. I refuse to submit to the indignity of such a personal examination by my peers, but if we might have a few moments' private conference…"

Words ran out. If he didn't back her, that was that, and Nathan was already in Yorktown.

Hamilton looked reluctantly amused. "You're too proud to show your friends your cock, but you'll show me?"

She stood ramrod straight. "Yes, sir."

He sighed. "My lucky day. But I suppose we slight fellows must stick together." He looked at her friends. "I presume you'll accept *my* word, gentlemen?"

A chorus of "yes, sir"s.

He led her behind a few trees by the creek. "Well, out with it. Lafayette aims to deprive me of command of this assault, and I must hurry if I'm to thwart him."

She took a deep breath. "Sir, promise me you'll hear me out. I'll be quick, I swear."

His face changed. "Jacobs?"

She squeezed her eyes shut for a moment. "I *am* a woman, sir. But I'm also a corporal in the First New York Light Company. I was at Monmouth with you. I'm good at my job, and I lead my squad. You need me tonight."

Hamilton passed a hand over his eyes. "Damn it, Jacobs."

He grimaced, abruptly unsure if he could curse in front of her. Rachel knew a moment of despair. "You know I can't just pretend I didn't hear this."

"You can," she said urgently. "Please, sir. This attack could end the war, or it could prolong it another year. I can't allow my comrades to go without me. And—I want to be useful to my people after the war. I need this. When they sit down to write our new country's laws, I want them to remember that Jews were among the first into Yorktown's defenses. That a Jew was as brave and loyal and true as they were. *Please*."

She didn't mention the lectures. That wouldn't convince him this was safe for him.

Hamilton chewed his lip. "You don't seem to think of what it will do to *my* reputation after the war if I knowingly allow a woman to participate in a bayonet charge."

Her burst of rage felt like a shell exploding behind her eyes. "You sent my husband into Yorktown," she said between her teeth. "And—"

His eyes widened. "Your *husband*? Who, Mendelson? But he's—"

She didn't want to know how that sentence ended. *Shorter than you—nervous—so* Jewish—*an annoying chatterbox.* "Yes," she said tightly, to all of them. "And I am *damned* if I will sit in camp in a cursed petticoat instead of trying to get in there and fetch him back out. That's womanly, isn't it? People will understand that? There have been women in every battle in this war. Don't you remember Mrs. Hays, who manned her husband's gun at Monmouth when he fell?"

And before that, Mrs. Hays had been carrying water to the men on the battlefield. Sarah went into the trenches with their dinner, like camp followers everywhere. No one fretted for their *safety*. Only that they followed the rules.

A gleam of humor lit his eye. "An Amazon, I see."

Oy gevalt. When the war was over, she'd be a woman again. She'd nearly forgotten what it was like, to have men think she was funny.

She drew herself up, face blank, trying to remind him with her posture and her uniform and the green epaulet on her shoulder of the hours of training, the fighting experience, the thousands of miles of marching she represented. Trying to remind him that she was a soldier and had earned her rank, and he couldn't spare her. That she was as tall and as strong as he was.

He sighed. "I may live to regret this, but then again, I may not. We may all be dead tomorrow. You understand that?"

"Yes." She bit her tongue to keep from adding "keynehore" to ward off the evil eye.

He nodded. "God willing, we will both live to see our new country's laws written, and scrawl in our corrections and additions. Your people's fate holds a peculiar interest for me." The corner of his mouth curled up. "Did you know I was taught by a Jewess when I was very small? I could say the Decalogue in Hebrew, once."

৩৯

"WHAT'S THE DECALOGUE?" Nathan interrupted, looking up from the notes he was taking for Mrs. Hamilton.

"That's what I said."

Dubiously, he eyed what he'd just written. "And how do you spell it?"

Rachel shrugged.

"What did he mean by 'a peculiar interest'?"

"I don't know," she said slowly. "It might just mean he was one of those goyim who natter on about the glory of the Chosen People or believe Christ will come again if they convert us. But I thought —I imagined, maybe—that he looked at me with special meaning when he said it. For a moment I wondered—well, he said he learned Hebrew as a boy, didn't he?"

"You wondered if he might be Jewish."

She nodded. "Why not? The Caribbean is full of secret Jews. But I certainly don't intend to suggest any such thing to his wife."

৩৯

RACHEL'S HEART jittered in her throat. Was this really the time for reminiscences? "The what?"

Hamilton laughed. "The Ten Commandments." His brow furrowed. "Anochi Adonai Elohecha…"

With a pang of remorse, she remembered Zvi's words on Simchas Torah. *Don't kill.* Here she was, fighting tooth and nail to do just that.

"It's no use. It's gone now." Genuine sadness passed across his face. "I was so small she stood me on a table to teach me."

"Gam zeh ya'avor, my mother always said. Everything passes, and so will this." What would Mrs. Jacobs say now? *Go home to Nathan,* probably.

I'm trying, Mamma, she thought, and then caught herself. She hadn't made up her mind yet. Had she?

Hamilton seemed to think that over for an eternity. His eyes, she noticed, were nearly purple, their lashes long and thick. "Maybe," he said. "Sometimes I think so. But we had better act as if what we do here will last."

Rachel's heart thumped and steadied. Yes. That was right.

"Very well," he said. "If your husband permits it, I suppose I have no prerogative to overrule him. You win, Corporal. Let's talk to your messmates."

Her friends were waiting by their tent in an anxious clump. Rachel refused to feel sorry for them.

Colonel Hamilton gave her a brisk shove towards them. "You can rest easy, soldiers. Your friend appears normal in every respect." He grinned. "Well, perhaps an inch or two past normal. Now let's consider the matter settled."

Zvi looked relieved, Tench mortified, and Scipio suspicious. No one spoke.

Hamilton raised his eyebrows. "Is the matter settled, gentlemen?" His tone indicated that "No" was not an acceptable answer.

Rachel felt a sharp burst of gratitude. Every soldier had learned there was nothing officers hated more than being called liars. If they did it to each other, it meant a duel. The colonel had thrown his full weight behind her, simply out of a sense of fair play, and maybe kindness.

A chorus of "yes, sir"s.

"Good, because I have more important business to attend to —and if I hear you've been wasting time and embarrassing us all by spreading this sordid anecdote, you will regret it bitterly. I'll see you and your men at five o'clock."

And he strode off. Rachel tried to decide if it was possible to be in love with two men at once.

She looked her friends coldly in the face. They didn't meet her eyes. "Let's get back to work," she said shortly. "I never want to hear about this again."

And *that*, somehow, broke the tension. "Oh, please," Scipio said. "I'll be telling this story to my grandchildren. It's side-splitting."

Tench laughed. "Had he ever seen a circumcised one before?"

Zvi rolled his eyes, visibly begging her not to be angry, to "oy der goyim" with him like always. "Sorry. I didn't want to say anything in the first place."

She couldn't forget what they'd done, but there was no point in holding a grudge—not when they might all be dead tomorrow. And it would be an exciting episode in her memoirs someday.

Suddenly, she had to stifle an exhilarated laugh—she'd gotten out of it! "You're all awful and I hate you," she said. "Just because I'm short! And no, he'd never seen a circumcised one before. He asked me *questions*."

Her comrades had only wanted to protect her. She believed that. But Nathan wanted to protect her, too, and he hadn't tried to stop her.

She had actually been hurt by that. *Doesn't he believe we owe each other anything? Doesn't he think of himself as my husband anymore?* Colonel Hamilton had said it without thinking—*if your husband permits it.* Everyone—even Rachel, deep down, a little—believed it was Nathan's place to make this decision for her. Everyone but Nathan.

Who had offered her a get, too, if she wanted one.

The nervous laughter bubbling in her throat changed, nearly became a sob. She didn't want a get. She wanted Nathan. She wanted to share a home with him again. She wanted to be the mother of his children.

Men would think she was even funnier when she was a mother. *Oh, see how she worries and nags. See how she thinks her children are clever and handsome. What a fool.* Never mind that she'd stormed Yorktown.

She couldn't dither about this now. She was a soldier, and she had work to do.

৶৻৶

THE BLOOD SEEPED through Nathan's fingers and dripped onto the floor. "Do you think I could get a bandage or something first?"

"Steady on, Mr. Mendelson. We'll tend to your arm very soon. Can you show me on this map what you mean?"

"Do I look like I have a sense of direction to you? Harlem is north and the Battery is south. They said across the river." He pointed with his elbow to where he thought the river was, spattering more blood on the floor. "So…that way? And the fusilier something. Redoubt. What *is* a fusilier?"

৶৻৶

RACHEL LAY on the cold ground just before the first parallel. Around her lay her battalion; only Gimat's battalion and the pioneers with their axes were before them. The rest of the Light Division made up the supporting column behind.

All week, the trenches had meant danger and exposure. Until the time came to climb out and lie in the open ground between them and the British redoubts, she hadn't realized how much protection they actually gave. Now there was nothing at all shielding her from the British guns, except British ignorance of their position.

All the cannon in the trenches were silent, so the signal would be clear: three mortar shells from the French grand battery coming quick, one after the other. She glanced west and nearly leapt up, ready for the march—

But the two brilliants spots in the air weren't tumbling like shells. They hung, too bright and big to be stars. The planets Jupiter and Venus meeting, Scipio had told her. Rachel blinked, half expecting them to fade when she opened her eyes.

George Washington himself had spoken to them before they marched out of the trenches. Rachel couldn't remember what he'd said. Her mind was a jumble. What was the watchword? For a moment, panicked, she couldn't call it to mind.

No, no, it was "Rochambeau"; she remembered because everyone had agreed it was good for a charge, because it sounded like *Rush on, boys!* if you said it fast enough.

Distantly, guns began to blaze: the diversions at the other end of the town and across the river.

She went over her battalion's orders: at the signal, creep a quarter mile forward to the right-hand redoubt, while the French crept to the left-hand one. Fixed bayonets only, to avoid a misfire alerting the enemy. Break off when the head of the column reached the abatis—the wooden spikes and mass of sharpened branches circling the earthworks—and come up quick on Gimat's left to extend the front line.

Unloaded muskets were a clever strategy that had been used before with success. Rachel still felt strange and naked going into battle with her weapon unloaded. She put out a hand and laid it on her musket—a curiously intimate gesture. Just so, home in bed, she might have reached out for Nathan's hand.

She had learned to use this musket at Valley Forge, Baron Steuben teaching them to load and fire as one without breaking formation. She'd practiced until she couldn't lift her sore arms, until she could do it perfectly. So they would have no reason to doubt her, to send her away. After her promotion, she had taught her men to do it.

She had earned her place. She had labored and fought to be here. She had drilled her squad in bayonet charges, and she could get them through this.

She would get them through this, and they would take the redoubt. Men from the Pennsylvania Line would march in with shovels to link the British earthworks to the Allied second parallel, bringing the whole besieged town into the line of fire.

Horses would drag the last waiting, eager cannon from the artillery park, and Yorktown would be razed from the face of the earth like Jericho.

Nathan was in Yorktown.

Her hand crept instinctively to her chest. Nathan's ring under her clothes was so small her fingers could barely make it out, but it dug into her breastbone when she pressed.

She still didn't know what she'd tell him if she survived the night. But if she died…

If she died, she wanted Nathan to believe she would have said yes. She wanted him to have that much comfort, at least.

Rachel tugged the strip of velvet out of her collar, looping the tip of her index finger through the ring. When the old ribbon ripped, she'd been so afraid to dig through her clothes in the presence of her comrades that she'd almost let it be lost. She was glad now she hadn't.

After half a year's use, the knot was too tight to untie and the fabric too new to tear. Feeling for her knife, she sliced the ribbon clean through and dropped the ring into her hand. A warm circle in her cold palm.

She closed her fist tightly, squeezing her eyes shut. When she opened them, there shone Jupiter and Venus, that had stood sentry in the sky for thousands of years before men learned to make mortar shells, and would guard the Earth still when all the swords had been beaten into plowshares.

She remembered Nathan translating the evening prayer service for her in their warm bed: *You assign the stars to their watches…*

Kaddish, that in Hebrew sounded so solemn and spoke so eloquently of longing and adoration and grief, was just *may His name be glorified and embellished and covered in gold leaf with little flourishes drawn round it, &c., &c.* But she'd liked the one about the stars.

The ring stuck at the second knuckle when she tried to slip it on her finger.

Panic seized her. Her hands had changed. It didn't fit anymore. She had changed and she couldn't go back. She'd thought back then that standing watch sounded fine and noble, and now she'd done it herself in the snow, thoughts full of nothing but hot johnnycakes and hoping they wouldn't find her frozen corpse in the morning—

But she twisted and pushed, and the ring scraped over her knuckle and settled comfortably at the base of her finger.

She let out a breath. *Mrs. Nathan Mendelson.*

She smothered a laugh. No. She was *Corporal* Mrs. Mendelson now.

No one would ever call her that, but she liked how it sounded.

❦

THE SIGNAL CAME AT LAST: a boom and an arcing shell from the French grand battery, then a second and a third.

Halfway to the redoubt, they were halted.

"They'll need a volunteer from each company for the forlorn hope," the lieutenant whispered to their platoon. He stepped out of the column to confer with the officers.

The forlorn hope! Rachel had been so distracted she'd forgotten. Composed of volunteers from the column, they would lead the assault and be first into the redoubt, earning the largest share of casualties and glory. Should she volunteer?

Isaac Carvalho was before her, elbowing past and pushing his way to the cluster of officers. She couldn't hear their low-voiced conversation or make out their faces, but she saw Carvalho march away, to the front of the column. Was this her last sight of him alive?

She thought of the knapsacks they had piled neatly in the trench. How many would go uncollected on their return?

The moon was a sliver. The column crept forward in the dark. Rachel couldn't tell how far they had gone, or where the front line was. She saw the burst of light before she heard the long cracks of cannons and the short pops of musketry: the enemy in the redoubt firing with everything they had.

Up ahead, the American column broke out in cheers. "Now," the order came. "Now!" Their battalion split off—she was watching her squad to make sure they stayed in formation

—and then the column broke apart and they were all racing toward the light and sound of the British guns, determined to get there before the fight was over. The air was filled with screams and huzzahs.

"The fort's our own!" men shouted. "Rush on, boys!"

A whoop broke from Rachel's throat. Her heart was a drum —finally!—finally after all this waiting it was time.

Chapter Nine

THE GAP their pioneers had cut in the abatis around the fort was blocked up with men. Soldiers simply swarmed over and through the bristling wooden teeth. Rachel wormed her way between two sharp stakes and scrambled up onto the earthwork. She tried to turn to see if any of her squad needed a hand over —but already someone shoved at her, trying to get past.

The light of the British guns was fainter now; the men were fighting hand to hand inside the redoubt. The Americans must be winning—how could the enemy withstand this flood of men? It would all be over before she could get inside.

Rushing forward through the trench littered with little crackling hand grenades, Rachel passed two soldiers trading musket blows. Was that a British officer? Why had he left the safety of the redoubt?

"Have you read anything lately?" the redcoat shouted. No, she must have misheard. She would never know what he had really said; they were behind her and gone. Scrambling over another row of sharpened tree trunks, she stepped on something that moaned—a man, she realized—and kept going, up the breastwork and into the fort at last.

It was dark inside, lit only by gunpowder and a couple of dark lanterns. That was enough to make out the British soldiers' neat red coats, all identical, all in good repair. Rachel jabbed her bayonet into one with a rending of good wool cloth and a sharp spurt of satisfaction.

As she forced her way through the crowd toward the single British cannon still firing, she caught a glimpse of Captain Olney of the Rhode Island Regiment through the tight protective knot of his men, holding his bowels in with both hands as he shouted an order.

A British soldier blocked her path. Rachel parried his jab with her musket, pushing the point of her bayonet into his flesh. He wrenched the weapon out of her hands and tossed it to the side.

Possessive fury leapt in her chest. She wrestled him for his firearm, digging her fingers into the wound she'd made. Blood ran down his arm. He cried out and she didn't care at all, she was glad, she hated him. Was that wrong?

"British soldiers, surrender your arms!" a crisp British voice shouted. The cry was taken up by other voices: "Major Campbell's men, lay down your arms!"

The soldier she was fighting bared his teeth at her and let go of his musket. Stumbling backwards, Rachel slipped in something wet, landing hard with her hand in a pool of blood. She glanced reflexively at the body beside it and recoiled when she knew its face.

Isaac Carvalho.

Oh. Oh, that instinctive drawing back was wrong, was dreadful, she had to help him. She hauled him into her lap to feel for his pulse with cold, bloody fingers. He was warm, but so were new corpses, she couldn't find his heartbeat, she couldn't find it—

Through the press of still and silent men, she saw Colonel Hamilton ceremoniously receive the British officer's sword. Fury rushed back, hot and dancing. The prisoner would give his parole now and be sent home to his wife, and Carvalho's pack would lie in the trench for eternity.

A captain in buff and blue stepped toward Campbell, bayonet lowered. "Remember Colonel Scammell?" he demanded.

I *remember Scammell,* Rachel thought. *Kill him.* But her

fingers trembled on the boy's neck. What would happen when that bayonet sliced forward? Would the whole fort rise and slaughter the British?

Voices clamored in her head. Nathan's: *Mobs never bode well for Jews.* Hamilton's: *We had better act as if what we do here will last.* Her mother's, repeating the old piece of Jewish wisdom: *To save one life is to save the world.*

Her own: *The rules we choose to follow make us who we are.*

She stood in a rush, letting Carvalho's corpse thud to the ground. But Colonel Hamilton had already stepped between Major Campbell and that lowered bayonet.

"Remember yourself, sir," he said coldly. "This man has surrendered. Are we to imitate the enemy's barbarity?"

Rachel pushed forward, ready to defend him if necessary. On the far side of the redoubt, she caught sight of Elijah Sutton doing the same, but the press of men was too great for even a giant like him to move quickly—

The captain shouldered his gun with a scowl.

Her knees gave out. She sat in a heap by Carvalho's body. "We'll do it," she promised him. "I swear to you. We'll make light in the darkness."

The boy stirred, his eyelids fluttering. His lips moved, mumbling something that might have been "Corporal?"

Rachel staggered, light-headed, to her feet once more, blinking away tears, a hand on the earthen wall to keep from tumbling back down. "Doctor!" she cried out, hoarsely. "*Doctor.*"

And like a miracle, a doctor came, there was already a doctor in the fort. Rachel gripped his hand—oh no, she'd gotten blood on him. But his hands were already bloody. It was all right.

"Take care of him," she said. "I've got to find my other men."

Her other men were hale and jubilant. Their battalion had had no casualties at all, and only four wounded. The wounded were carried out, and the others were told they might rest while the Pennsylvania Line dug fresh trenches. They lay down where they were, amid blood and cartridge papers. *Yorktown won't be able to stand against us now,* everyone agreed.

Rachel touched her wedding ring with her thumb. *We did it,* she told Nathan.

۞

October 15

THE SECOND PARALLEL was complete by the time they were relieved at noon the next day. The British guns in the redoubt, set on new platforms, had been turned on their former masters. "We're giving them ten thousand rounds a day," she heard one artillery officer tell another, incredulous and triumphant.

Was Nathan still alive in there, cowering behind something? *Please,* she prayed. *Adonoy. Please.* If he was already dead, if her battalion had suffered a casualty after all—

She *missed* him. Had she missed him when she left him in New York and went to Philadelphia? It was so long ago she couldn't remember.

Well, she missed him now. She wanted to talk to him. She wanted him to talk to her. She wanted to lean her head against his chair while he muttered arithmetic under his breath.

If he came back, she was telling him *yes.* She didn't know how they could go back to New York together when he'd sat shiva for her. She didn't know what his boss would think of a clerk with a soldier wife. She didn't care. If she could storm a redoubt, she could face some cold shoulders.

Nathan couldn't do this, but I can. The familiar words floated into her head unbidden. But they weren't true anymore.

Nathan and I can do this together. There, that was right.

If he'd only come back.

۞

"WELL, I DID COME BACK," Nathan said. But nearly forty years later, he still looked smug about how frightened she'd been.

Rachel crossed her arms. "Took you long enough."

"Pass over it, then. Nothing much happened."

"Nothing happened? Only the end of the war. Besides, I talked to Colonel Hamilton twice. Mrs. Hamilton will want to hear about it."

"Twice?"

Rachel sighed. *"You never remember anything. The next day we built another big battery and the weather was dreadful. We were all huddled in our tents listening to the guns, with water streaming through the canvas, and I...I tracked down Colonel Hamilton and demanded a cease-fire for you like Secretary Nelson got."*

"Then I could never have been useful again, and anyway they wouldn't have given me back once they realized I was a spy. Spies aren't entitled to the courtesies of war."

"That's what Colonel Hamilton said." But Rachel looked unconvinced. *"Then after Cornwallis surrendered, there was a ceasefire for a couple of hours before the cannonade started again and I thought maybe it was over."*

"I was safely across the river in Gloucester the whole time. You didn't need to fret."

"You were safely across the river the whole time in the hospital because you were shot the first day, so I think I did need to fret!"

"My arm is fine."

"It wasn't fine then. You had a fever."

"That's true, I did. It was dreadful. I needed tender nursing. A cool, gentle hand on my brow."

"Shut up."

"'O, Woman! in our hours of ease—'"

"Anyway, *after the guns started again I went back to Hamilton. He told me Colonel Laurens was negotiating the surrender and he'd already talked to him about you, and not to bother him anymore."*

"Firing stopped again a few hours later anyway. I remember the quiet."

"And of course I was glad, but it was too *quiet. I could hear myself think."*

Nathan rested his chin on her shoulder. *"You know, Corporal Mrs. Mendelson, I was worried about you too. I didn't even have a colonel to pester about it."*

"I was fine."

"The British said they killed dozens of you in the assault."

"The British flattered themselves."

"I didn't know that!"

"And then you didn't come to the surrender ceremony. I watched for you."

"Only soldiers went to the surrender ceremony."

"Well, I thought you were dead."

"I almost went on that ship of Loyalists Cornwallis sent to New York, you know. He offered. It would have preserved my cover so beautifully."

She poked him. "And why didn't you?"

"Because I couldn't wait another month for news of you."

❦

October 21

RACHEL WAS on her way back from visiting Carvalho in the regimental hospital when Scipio walked straight into her.

"Sorry," he said, beaming. "I was reading my letter from Anna Maria. She says she'll make me a hot johnnycake with maple sugar every day for breakfast when we're married, and that I'd better end the war so you New Yorkers can go home and stop ruining Albany. Do you believe peace is really here, like everyone says? I have to serve until the war ends, and I'm tired of letters. I want to see her."

"I don't know."

"Oh! I almost forgot. A messenger came for you from the commissioner of prisoners. Mendelson's turned up. The commissioner says he needs you to loan him some money, but since Mendelson's richer than all of us, I assume that was a pretext to see you."

She should feel relief. Instead she only felt a more concentrated dread, as if this might all be a trick. "Where is he?"

"With other nonmilitary prisoners of war in one of those big brick houses on Main Street. I'm told you'll recognize it by how it's still mostly standing."

She went over her duties for the rest of the day in her head. Could she shirk them? Could she bear to wait until after tattoo?

Scipio's nose was buried in his letter again. He wouldn't see Anna Maria for who knew how long. She could bear another few hours.

"Go," Scipio said without looking up. "I'll shift for you."

Impulsively, Rachel threw her arms around him, careful not to crumple his letter. The other corporals hugged all the time, but she'd always been afraid to, in case they felt her breasts.

Scipio raised an eyebrow, but he looked pleased. They'd all been trying to worm their way back into her good graces since their accusation before the assault.

She kissed him on the temple for good measure and ran off.

۞

IT TOOK Rachel half an hour to find the house. After another ten minutes of inquiring after Nathan through the tightly packed crowd of prisoners, her heart was in her throat. It wasn't real, he wasn't here—and then she heard his voice.

"...I'm sure he's all right. He's just busy. Indispensable. He's a corporal, after all. I know his officers rely on him, so probably he can't come until after—what do they call that drumming at night?... Tattoo? I thought that was any drumbeat generally, are you sure?"

The lump in her throat so high she felt she might scream, Rachel squeezed through a clump of men sharing a brandy bottle and saw him. He sat cross-legged in the corner, drawing patterns on the floor with a finger. The man next to him listened with thinly veiled irritation.

"Nathan," Rachel said. "Why is there blood on your coat?"

He stopped talking midword. Up close, the pattern was a map of Manhattan; his finger stopped halfway through drawing Cortlandt Street in the dust.

He looked up, and at last she saw his eyes, dark and beautiful and gleaming. For a second he tried to contain his smile, and then it burst across his face.

That used to make her angry, how happy he was to see her.

It made her angry now, after everything. Her heart felt as if it was in ribbons and Nathan was just…happy to see her.

He pushed himself to his feet. He'd lost weight since last week; his drawn face was pale and dirty, his eyes red-rimmed. His dark curls were matted to his skin. She'd never seen his beard so long.

"Oh, this?" He picked at the long bullet hole in his sleeve. "I haven't had a chance to wash it out yet. Don't worry, the coat's not ruined. I'll patch it and it will be good as new."

"And your *arm*?"

His smile widened. "Oh, that's already patched. A graze. It will be as good as new too. The fever only lasted a day or two."

"The fever?"

"I worried about you too."

She could feel it, the pressure on her chest. "Why are you always so happy to see me?" she burst out.

Nathan glanced around. There wasn't anywhere in this crush to be private. He switched into Yiddish, which wasn't guaranteed to be private either, but it was something. "Because I love you. You know that."

She sat in his map of New York, defeated. "I love you too. I just—" She could feel tears pricking at her eyes. She sniffled.

He sat next to her. "You're happy to see me too," he said softly. "You just had a hard week."

She wanted to curl up in his lap and press her face against his shoulder and cry. She wanted to kiss him. She wanted to go home to their own two narrow beds, and instead here they were in the middle of this horrible crowd…

She supposed that *was* being happy to see him, in its own way. Nathan's way looked more pleasant for both of them. He seemed content with her accusatory interrogation, but didn't he deserve more? A smile?

That felt impossible, unimaginable. A kind word, then.

She had been so angry that he always pretended, that he never came out and said anything. But she'd been just as bad. She'd never come right out and told him what she felt, what she wanted.

What was the truth? What did she feel?

"I'm glad you're safe," she said slowly. "I missed you. I missed you kibbitzing in my ear. I think I...I don't have any feelings left after worrying all week. I feel like a pumpkin with the seeds scooped out. I think I might cry. I—"

She didn't have any more words. She pulled the ring out from her collar, where it hung on a fresh piece of butcher's twine.

"I wore this into the redoubt," she said, not meeting his eyes. "If I didn't make it, I wanted you to know..." But the words that flooded her mouth were all qualifications and conditions.

She choked them down. That wasn't what she'd wanted him to know. "I can't...I can't stop hedging. I'm afraid to. It feels..." It came to her, what it felt like. "Like bad luck. Like if I say it out loud, the evil eye will snatch it away. We'll be miserable and I'll break your heart again..."

"Say it," he said. "Say it and say 'keynehore' afterwards."

She straightened her shoulders and prayed no one was listening who could understand. "I destroyed our marriage. I burned it to the ground, and I can't be sorry I did it. But I'm going to build us a better one, if you want to build it with me. I love you and I want you for the rest of my life and we'll have to sort the rest out. Keynehore."

She'd thought he couldn't smile wider than he had a moment ago. He managed it somehow, eyes shining as he clasped his thumbs and chimed in with his Hebrew.

But she couldn't leave it there. "I can't give up my plans. Not even to raise your children. Our children." She pressed a fist to her stomach with how badly she wanted to have a child that was half him and half her. "And I don't want your mother raising them if I'm traveling."

He nodded. "I don't want her raising them either. She raised me, after all, and look how I turned out." He made a *tsk*ing noise and shook his head.

She laughed, astonished that she was actually beginning to feel happy. She would feel happy, if she didn't crush the feeling in her chest out of fear.

"We'll sort the rest out," he said. "We're imagining a new

way to be a country, where our leader isn't a king. A new way to be a Jew, where God isn't a king. Let's imagine a new way to be married, where I'm not a king either. I don't want that anyway. I don't want you to be my subject, or even my queen."

"What do you want?"

"I want us to go hand in hand." He blushed. "Sorry, I never said I wasn't sentimental."

She slipped her hand in his.

"If you're giving a lecture, I want to be there to bring you tea and lozenges." He leaned against the wall. Getting comfortable in his visions of the future. "Lecturing is hard on the throat."

"I don't understand how you do it. How you shake off everything. I left you, and you're just going to take me back? Why aren't you afraid?"

She remembered a hundred conversations with him, where she'd been the one consumed with visions of a bright future. She remembered how she'd fought to keep her mother alive, how she'd refused to believe it wouldn't turn out all right.

But what she really remembered was the lump of fear in her throat, because she'd needed that future too desperately to admit it might not come.

She'd thought Nathan such a coward. But she'd never been able to hope like he was doing right now, had she? If she had— before her mother got sick, maybe—she couldn't remember it. Not a drop of it.

"Rachel, I'm afraid of everything. What's a little more?" He gripped her hand tightly. "If I might remind you, you didn't *leave* me. You died. I lived through that. I didn't enjoy it, obviously, but I lived. What could happen now that would be worse?"

She loved him so much it felt like a catastrophe. But he was right. What was a little more fear?

She'd survived Yorktown. She'd buried her mother, and survived that too. She'd been trapped in the Mendelson home, and she'd left. She'd made a life for herself that she loved, and now she'd make another one.

We had better act as if what we do here will last.

She took a deep breath and leaned her head on his shoulder. "Your mother could kill me. If we go back together, the rabbi's going to know she lied to him." She took another deep breath and let her heart expand, let happiness fill her chest.

"Oy, the disgrace!" He shrugged. "We'll make up a lie. Or not. I'm sorry, I know you had your heart set on people calling you Esther."

"Nothing rhymes with Mendelson either."

He was quiet for a moment. "What do you want to do next?"

She thought about it. She'd reenlisted in January for the length of the war. She shrank from going back on her word, abandoning her friends. On the other hand, she could have left in January and no one would have blamed her. She'd done her part. The war would be over soon.

She'd always meant to reveal her sex sooner or later. She could do it now. When her friends thought she was a woman, they'd wanted her to leave; maybe they wouldn't even realize it wasn't fair that she could and they couldn't. Maybe they wouldn't hate her.

They hadn't been angry or disgusted. They'd just wanted to protect her. That was something.

"I could keep my cover and go back to New York," Nathan said. "I'll have to wait in a prison camp to be exchanged—two escapes in quick succession would strain even British credulity —but they'll send me back eventually. If you want to stay in the army. Or...we could both quit and go to Philadelphia together."

She'd hated Philadelphia. But suddenly she missed its careful grid of brick buildings with white trim, the prim Quaker way they'd named all their streets after trees instead of people. With Nathan, it could feel like home for a little while. Just until the British left New York.

"That," she said decisively. "Let's go to Philadelphia."

NATHAN LEANED in to take the pen from her hand and kiss her.

Rachel held on to the pen. "Wait, but I talked to Hamilton one more time."

He retreated with a peck on her cheek. "She can't chronicle every moment of the man's life. Imagine the printing costs. Are you planning to send her a list of our grandchildren's names and Mrs. Freedom's johnnycake recipe too?"

Rachel shrugged. "It is a very good recipe."

"True. You should make it when Zvi and Danny come for dinner next week."

"You really want a dairy meal when Zvi and Danny come?"

"No," Nathan said hastily. "Can they bring steaks again?"

Rachel's lips twitched. Zvi still ran his kosher butcher shop in Manhattan; he lived above it with his friend Daniel, who taught Hebrew. "Maybe I should do dairy. Zvi always complains about how I cook the meat."

"Let him grill the steaks, then. Uch, this time can you two not spend half of dinner recounting disgusting meals you shared in the army? I have a sensitive stomach."

Rachel ignored him, digging in her desk for her memorandum book. "I'll include everyone's addresses, in case they aren't as easy to locate as I am. She might not know Scipio's changed his name to Freedom. Let me see…"

Scipio had gone to work as a waterman after the war, and was now a skipper, with a thriving family and his own towboat company in Albany. Tench and Sarah were farming in Orange County with their seven children; Rachel could never remember how many grandchildren there were. Sgt. Flanagan was a tobacconist in Poughkeepsie.

"Maybe we ought to take another trip upstate," she said.

"You just want another chance to eat crab without any of our friends being the wiser."

"Maybe. I wouldn't tell them if you wanted to have some too…"

Nathan laughed. "Once was enough for me, thank you." He heaved a sigh. "I'm old," he said plaintively. "Too old to jounce upstate in the stagecoach and sleep in lumpy inn beds." But he pulled out his almanac and began looking at dates.

"You are old," she agreed. "You'll be seventy next year. Maybe I'll go without you."

Nathan shook his head. "This is the trouble with these May to December romances. You're only sixty-five and you'll make a fool of me."

"You don't need any help from me there."

"I suppose I asked for that—"

Rachel put a hand over his almanac. When he looked up, she kissed him.

Author's Note

Thank you for reading "Promised Land"! I hope you enjoyed Rachel and Nathan's story.

Would you like to know when my next book is available? Sign up for my newsletter at roselerner.com, follow me on twitter at @RoseLerner, or find me on Facebook at facebook.com/roselernerromance.

Visit my website for free short stories, plus *Hamilton's Battalion* DVD extras like deleted scenes, Pinterest boards, juicy tidbits about Hamilton, Burr, and the Founding Fathers (John Adams once claimed people only liked Washington because he was good-looking, and I'm pretty sure Thomas Jefferson had a journalist murdered at one point), a full bibliography and guide to further reading, and much, much more.

For a historical note on this novella, acknowledgments, and a list of other titles, please skip to the end.

To read *The Pursuit Of...* by Courtney Milan, just go to the next page.

THE PURSUIT OF...

BY COURTNEY MILAN

What do a Black American soldier, invalided out at Yorktown, and a British officer who deserted his post have in common? Quite a bit, actually.

- *They attempted to kill each other the first time they met.*
- *They're liable to try again at some point in the five-hundred-mile journey that they're inexplicably sharing.*
- *They are not falling in love with each other.*
- *They are not falling in love with each other.*
- *They are... Oh no.*

For everyone who waited to be included in the sequel—and particularly for those who are still waiting.

Introduction

❧

MRS. HAMILTON,

Enclosed you will find the summary of John Hunter's interview, during which he recounted his time in Hamilton's battalion; the Battle of Yorktown and its conclusion (with which you must be exhaustively familiar); his personal interaction with your Hamilton; his journey to Rhode Island with a Mr. Henry Latham, with references to your husband that may be of interest; and, oddly, his taste in cheese. I hope that you find the notes to your liking and that they are of as much assistance to you as the countless other interviews I have transcribed.

Your obedient servant,

M. Alston

Chapter One

Yorktown, 1781

IN THE HEAT OF BATTLE, Corporal John Hunter could never differentiate between silence and absolute noise. Years had passed since his first engagement, but every time, the sheer discord of sound blended together. The cry of bugles sounding orders, the clash of bayonets, the rat-tat-tat of firearms somewhere in the distance, the hollow concussion of the cannons—each one of those things heralded someone's doom. To take heed to any of it was to fall into fear. To fear was to make mistakes; to err was to die. No matter the odds, the sounds of battle were so overwhelming that they were no different than silence.

Yorktown was just like any other engagement.

Oh, the strategists might have begged to differ. There were more clouds, more night. Less frost than some of the battles he'd taken part in. Someone had talked prettily at them about how the freedom of this nascent nation was at stake and some other things John had listened to with his hands curling into fists. The colonies didn't care about John's freedom, so he returned the favor by not caring about theirs.

In the end, all battles were smoke and shit and death, and John's only goal was to see the other side of this war without being forcibly acquainted with the Grim Reaper. Fight. Survive. Go home to his family. The most basic of needs.

The night was dark around him and his fellow infantrymen. The spiked branches of the abatis had left scratches on his arm; the charge up the scarp had John's heart pounding.

They'd crept through the ditch and were approaching the final defenses of Redoubt Ten—a wall of sharp stakes, somewhat battered. A group of fools ahead of him was negotiating how best to storm the parapet. John held back. Apparently, the idiot in command of this maneuver wanted to lead the charge. Sutton, one of the other black men assigned to storm the redoubt, was hoisting him up.

Nothing to do but join them and hope for the best. Nothing to do but survive, fight, and return to his family before anything ill happened to them. Fight, survive—

John stilled, the chant in his head dying down.

There was a reason he let the background noise of battle fade to nothingness in his mind. It left room for wariness and suspicion. There. Behind them, back toward the abatis—there was a shadow.

It moved, man-shaped.

The person behind them was large and almost invisible, and he lay in wait. John's comrades hadn't noticed him. In their haste to get in, they'd all left themselves vulnerable.

All of them but him.

Damn it all to hell.

Silence and noise mingled in John's head. Perhaps the gunfire from the feint on Fusiliers Redoubt a ways off was loud; perhaps it was nothing. Perhaps the man he saw screamed in defiance as John turned toward him; perhaps he was silent.

Fight. Survive... *Damn* it.

There was no hope for it. John couldn't wait to see what would happen. He lowered his weapon, said a prayer for his sister, should his soul become irreparably detached from his body, and sprinted back toward the shadowed branches of the abatis.

The man's head tilted. John braced himself, waiting for the

man to fire a weapon or raise a blade, but instead the fellow just waited in silence. One second. Two.

John crashed into him at full speed, driving his shoulder into the man's chest. God, the other man was huge. The impact traveled bruisingly through his body. Still, John wasn't exactly tiny himself. They fell together, hitting the ground. It took one moment to get his bayonet into position, another to drive it forward, blade seeking the other man's belly.

It didn't make contact. Instead, the fellow hit John on the head with the butt of his musket. John's head rang; he shook it, pushed the echoing pain aside, and rolled out of the way of the next bayonet strike.

There was no time to think, no time to come up with any plan except to survive the next instant, then the next. No room for fine blade work, either; John swung his musket like a staff.

The other man blocked the strike, and the force of gun barrel meeting gun barrel traveled up John's arm. The battle had all but disappeared into a pinprick, into this moment between two men.

"God," the other fellow said. "You're strong."

John refused to hear his words.

John had neither energy nor emotion to waste on conversation. Fight. Survive the war. Go back to Lizzie and Noah and his mother. He'd *promised* them he would—stupid promise, that —but he'd break the entire British Army before he broke that promise. Men who let their attention slip perished, and he had no intention of perishing. He gritted his teeth and tried to smash the other man's head.

The other man ducked out of the way. "Nice weather for a siege, isn't it?"

John's almost perfect concentration slipped. What the devil was that supposed to mean? Nice weather for a *siege?* Did that mean the weather was good—it wasn't—or that bad weather was preferable during a siege? And what did *preferable* even mean between the two of them? Siegers and the besieged had different preferences.

Ah, damn it.

This was why John couldn't let himself listen to battle.

Anything—everything—could be a distraction. He shook his head instead and threw his entire weight behind his next strike.

It wasn't enough; the other man was taller and heavier, and their bayonets crossed once more. He was close enough to see features—stubble on cheeks, sharp nose, the glint of some distant bombardment reflected in the man's eyes. They held their places for a moment, shoulders braced together, their heaving breaths temporarily synchronized.

"It's your turn," the man said with an unholy degree of cheer. "I remarked on the weather. Etiquette demands that you say something in return."

For a moment, John stared at the fellow in utter confusion. "I'm bloody trying to kill you. This is a battle, not a ball."

He pivoted on one foot, putting his entire back into whirling his weapon. This time he managed to whack the other man's stomach. A blow—not a hard one, he hadn't the space to gather momentum—but enough that the fellow grunted and staggered back a pace.

"Yes," the man said, recovering his balance all too quickly, "true, completely true, we *are* trying to commit murder upon each other. That doesn't mean that we need to be impolite about it."

Fucking British. Would he call a halt to take tea, too?

"If you prefer," the man continued, sidestepping another blow, "you could try, 'Die, imperialist scum.' The moniker is somewhat lacking in friendly appeal, but it has the benefit of being true. I own it; we are imperialist scum."

What the *hell?*

"But aren't we both?" The conversation, like the battle, seemed interminable. "You colonials are displacing natives as well. I will give you this point. You'd be quite right not to use that particular insult. It would be rather hypocritical."

Not for John, it wouldn't. His presence in this land could not be put down to any volition on the part of his black mother, who was the only ancestor the colonials counted. But now was not a time for the fine nuances of that particular discussion. It was not, in fact, the time for any discussion at all.

He swung his musket again, heard the crack of the weapon against the barrel of the other man's musket.

"It just goes to show. Politics is obviously not a good choice of conversation among strangers, I suppose. My father always did say that, and damn his soul, he is occasionally right. What of books? Have you read anything recently?"

There were still a few soldiers making their way through the abatis, streaming past them. One went by now, glancing in their direction.

"Can't we try to kill each other in silence?" John snuck out a foot, attempting to trip the other man. His enemy danced away.

"Ah, is that it?" The man brightened. "I see. You can't fight and talk at the same time? My friend, Lieutenant Radley, was exactly the same way. I drove him mad, he used to say."

Used to? Ha. As if anyone could ever become accustomed to this jibber-jabber.

"He died in battle," the other man continued, "so possibly he was right. You probably shouldn't listen to my advice on this score. I don't have the best record."

Their weapons crossed again.

"Except"—unbelievably, he was still talking—"I obviously should not have told you that. I've given away an important advantage. Damn it. My father was right again. 'Think before you speak,' he always used to say. I *hate* when my father is right."

John didn't want to think of this man as someone with family, with friends. War was hell enough when you were just killing nameless, faceless individuals.

There was nothing to do but get it over with as quickly as possible, before he started thinking of his enemy as a person.

He threw himself forward, caught the other man's shoulder with his, and managed to send him off balance. A moment, just a moment; enough for John to clip his hand smartly with the butt of his musket. The weapon the man had been holding went flying. John hooked one foot around the man's ankle; his opponent landed flat on his back. John pushed the tip of his blade into the man's throat.

The man's hands immediately shot above his head. "I surrender the redoubt!"

John froze in place. "Have you the authority to do that?"

"No," the other man answered, "but let's be honest, it's only a matter of time, don't you think? Excellent tactics on your part. I almost didn't see you coming. Somebody ought to surrender it eventually. Why not me?"

"Sorry," John said, and it was quite possibly the first time he'd ever apologized to an enemy on the battlefield. "I'm going to have to kill you."

"Ah, well," the other man said. "You know your duty. Be quick about it, if you must. Better me than you, don't you think?"

Literally no other person had ever said that to John on the battlefield. John frowned down at the man in front of him, and…

And, oh Christ. He suddenly realized that he'd heard of this man. His friend Marcelo had mentioned something about encountering him before. British officer. Tall. Meaty. Blond. He'd chalked the tale up to campfire boasting. When he'd heard there was a madman who couldn't stop talking, John had imagined something along the lines of a berserker, frothing at the mouth. He hadn't expected a mere prattle-basket.

"*I* think it's better me than you," John said, frowning down at the man. "You can't possibly agree."

A flare from the battle reflected in the other man's eyes, temporarily illuminating him. John didn't want to see his face. He didn't want to see the haunted expression in his eyes. He didn't want to remember him as a person. He should never have let the clamor of battle give way to the sound of conversation, because he suspected that the tone of this man's voice—all gravel and regret—would stay with him all the rest of his days.

"Don't make me go back," the man said, so at odds with his cheery conversation on politics. "I can't go back to England. Dying is not my preferred form of non-return, but for the past months it's the only one I've been able to think of."

John tightened his grip on the musket. He couldn't listen. He couldn't think. In battle, he could only allow himself to be a husk, an automaton. Fight. Survive. Killing was a necessary part of war. He'd learned not to look too hard at his enemies, not to ask too many questions. He'd learned not to let himself dwell too much on the men who perished at the other end of his musket.

It was always a mistake to listen during battle. Here he was, hesitating, when it was either John or the man who'd asked him about books and the weather. He could make it painless—as painless as death by bayonet ever was.

The man gave him a sad smile. "It's nice weather for dying, isn't it?"

He was lying. He had to be lying. This was the sort of thing for a lying officer to do—to converse politely, as if manners meant a damned thing on the battlefield. John pushed his bayonet down a quarter inch.

"Go on," the man said.

His permission made it even harder. John didn't want to do it, but it was John or the prattle-basket, John or the prattle-basket, and John had come too far to perish now.

A bugle sounded.

John looked up into chaos. He could hear cheers, could see the lieutenant colonel in charge of this attack—Hamilton, was it not?—clapping one of the soldiers on the back. Ah, the idiot in command had survived storming the parapet after all. While John had been fighting, his fellow soldiers had stormed the redoubt and taken it.

It was done. They'd won.

He eased up on the bayonet. "It's your lucky day. You're a prisoner now, instead of a dead man."

"No." The man's hand clasped around the musket barrel, holding the bayonet in place. "No. You have to do it."

"What?" John stared at him.

"You have to do it," the man instructed. "Do you under-stand? If you Americans take the redoubt, Yorktown falls. If Yorktown falls, the war is over. If you don't kill me now, they'll make me go back to Britain, and I *can't* go back."

"Can't?" John swallowed and looked down.

"Can't." The man shut his eyes.

They'd called him a madman, and John had imagined a demon on the battlefield, not a man who talked of politics.

Perhaps it was mad to prefer death to a return to a place that could never be called home, but if that was madness, it was a madness John knew. He'd once been enslaved. He knew what it was like to yearn for freedom, to prefer death to a return to a state that robbed him of choice, of freedom, of humanity. The fellow was obviously given to dramatics. John doubted anything so horrid waited for him back in England. Still... He understood.

He didn't want to have anything in common with a blond British officer...but he did.

He should take the man prisoner. Should call for reinforcements. Who knew what this man would do if John gave him the opportunity?

"I can't go back," the man said again.

John should never have listened. Damn it, damn it, damn it. He swore and threw down his weapon.

The man struggled, propping himself up on his elbows.

"Then don't." John took off his coat. "Here." He held the garment out.

It wasn't much—a bit tattered, and God knew what it smelled like; John couldn't detect the stench any longer.

The man stared at it.

"It's not red." John shook the coat. "It's a mess out there as it is. Get muddy enough and nobody will know who you are. If you don't want to go back to Britain, turn into an American. You talk enough; I'm sure you can come up with a believable lie. Get out of here. Don't go back."

The man stared at him. "Why would you let me go? I'm the enemy."

"Enemy?" John rolled his eyes. "Take a good look at me. I have little love for...what did you call them? The colonial brand of imperialist scum. I have no enemies, just people I fight on a battlefield."

The officer sat up. Looked at John. John knew what he was seeing—not the broad shoulders, not the determination John knew flashed in his own eyes, nor the set of his square jaw. No, this blond prattler who talked of manners and politics would see only the brown of his skin.

John was an idiot to offer anything. But he knew too well what it was like to have no hope of help and to find it anyway.

Here, he thought to the woman at the well who had shaken her head, denying his existence to the man who sought John. John had crouched hidden behind the bushes until the threat had passed. She'd looked at him then. She hadn't spoken; she'd only nodded and left, as if she hadn't changed his life with that simple denial. *Here. I'm paying you back for that after all.*

"I don't want to talk to you," John said. "I don't want to be your friend. I'll kill you on the battlefield if I have to. But if you're desperate enough to die, you're desperate enough to abscond. If you don't want to go back, get rid of your damned officer's coat and take mine."

The man stared up at him. He looked at the coat, at the musket that John had tossed aside.

Slowly, he took John's coat. "I won't forget this," he said. "I'll pay you back someday."

John had heard that particular promise before. He'd heard it when he saved his father from being crushed by a falling mast. He'd heard it when he'd rescued another man in the Rhode Island First on the battlefield. Half the time, white men didn't even bother with empty words to assuage their consciences—at least not to the likes of him. The other half? They never remembered their promises. They didn't have to.

John shook his head. "Don't bother."

"John?" Elijah's call came from further in. "John, is that you down there? Are you wounded?"

He turned, leaving the British officer alone with his coat. He was already faintly regretting his choice—the late-autumn night was cold enough that he'd want that coat before morning struck.

He would never see the man again.

In the dark of the night, the man had no idea what John even looked like. Even if it were day, he'd never be able to distinguish John from any other black man. White men rarely could.

"I'm Henry," the officer called after him. "Henry Latham, at your service."

Henry Latham no doubt thought he was an honorable fellow. He'd tell himself that one day he'd return the favor, just as he assiduously avoided contact with anyone who looked like John. There was little use puncturing his illusions.

John knew that the roll of his eyes was hidden by the night, so he took care to imbue an extra dose of sarcasm in his tone. "I'll be sure to remember that."

"John?" Elijah was coming closer. "John, are you well?"

"I'm alive," John called in return. "Alive and unharmed." His body was already protesting the *unharmed* designation, his shoulder twingeing, his head still hurting.

Ha. He had already forgotten the name. He'd never hear from the man again.

֍

Some days later…

HENRY LATHAM KNEW that time was running out.

Well. Not in the literal sense. Time never ran out. It only ran on, continuing at its own inevitable pace. But in a little while the Continental Army would be on the move again, following the inevitable peace accords. The time it would take him to find John would be massively increased once that happened.

In addition, there was the problem of Henry himself. Some men prided themselves on remembering and repaying every obligation. Henry…well. He always *intended* to pay his debts, but then…he forgot. He could never keep any one thing at the forefront of his mind long enough to concentrate on it. This time, though, it would be different. This was New Henry, and New Henry was…

New Henry was confused, baffled, and on the run from the British Army. That made him exactly like Old Henry, except he'd overtly committed treason and absconded in the heat of battle.

Technically, it had been after the redoubt was surrendered,

but not by much. If that wasn't the heat of battle, it was perhaps the warmth of it.

The good thing about war was that it had proven all too easy to sell a few items of personal jewelry for funds—so many others were fleeing—without drawing much attention. New Henry had money. New Henry had clothing. New Henry just needed a plan. His started like this:

1. Find John. By his uniform, he was a corporal, most likely in the Rhode Island Regiment, although Henry had not been able to verify that for certain. Family name? Hometown? All unknown, but that was no reason to discard a perfectly good first step, especially when the remainder of his plan looked like this.

2. ...?

3. ...!?

4. ...

5. Cheese? Maybe cheese. Cheese was good.

Taking John's jacket and running off had been undoubtedly the most impulsive decision he had ever made in a life predicated upon what his father called rash whim and unpremeditated fancy.

As it was, he had a name—John—and a face and a rank. He'd made inquiries—not careful ones; nothing Henry did could ever truly be called careful—and found that there *had* been black soldiers under the First Rhode Island Regiment, and as the Rhode Island forces had been decimated, the resulting Rhode Island Regiment been pulled piecemeal into the assault on Yorktown. It was a start.

John, maybe from Rhode Island. He *could* wait years and lose all hope of the trail, or he could do what he was doing now: He could walk up to the enemy encampment with nothing more than a smile and a pack containing his secret weapon.

He sauntered up to the soldiers standing guard at the entrance to the camp and smiled as if he belonged.

"A good day to you, gentlemen."

They exchanged suspicious glances.

Ah, damn. The accent. Henry's accent marked him as a creature of exclusive British public schools and that terrible year at

Oxford before everyone—from his father to the dean to the unfortunate brace of goats that he really hadn't meant to send down the Cherwell on a barge—agreed that further schooling was probably not in anybody's best interests.

But Americans came from Britain, too.

The two soldiers frowned at him.

Henry just smiled at them. "If I could impose on you for some assistance, I would be deeply in your debt."

The men continued to stare at him without blinking. How they managed to do that, Henry would never know. It was a useful skill, not blinking. Did their eyes not dry? How did they accomplish that?

Oh. No. The one on the right blinked. Ah, well. So much for that theory.

"I am a cheesemonger," Henry said. It was a complete lie, but the story almost didn't matter. "Cheese is my livelihood. I am here for the purpose of purveying cheese."

The men exchanged confused glances and Henry made a mental note: Next time, less emphasis on cheese.

"We don't want any cheese," one finally said. "Move along."

"Oh, ha! I'm not here to mong my cheese at you."

Blank stares met this.

Was *mong* even a verb? It had to be; what else did a monger do, if not mong?

"I encountered a soldier of your company in town," Henry said. "He coveted my cheese—my delicious, crumbly, fragrant cheese." Emphasis on *fragrant*. Henry had smelled infantrymen five months from a bath who reeked less than the cheese wrapped in his pack. "He wanted a bit for his journey home and asked me to bring a goodly amount by."

The two men softened incrementally.

"I'd hoped you might be able to direct me in his...ah, direction."

"Who is it?"

"John," Henry said brightly. "He's a corporal!"

"John. *Which* John? What regiment?"

"Ah... I've forgotten his family name."

Oh, *that* made the story *so* believable. Who introduced themselves as only John? What a mess.

Henry went on brightly. "He's an inch or so taller than I am. Muscular." Henry still had bruises. "Deep voice. In the Rhode Island Regiment, I believe. He's one of the Negro soldiers."

Their faces changed on that last word, closing even more than they'd already closed before.

"One of the Black Regiment, then." The one on the right gestured. "They're over there. *We* wouldn't know any of them by name."

Henry thanked them and left.

He wondered, briefly, how they managed the headaches that must plague them with that attitude. He'd struggled with his own confusion for long enough before coming to his not-so-ideal strategy, but then, he was no great intellect.

He'd thought maybe in the infantry, it would be different. After all, these men were fighting for their ideals. It wouldn't, he'd told himself, be like the British Army, with its rules and regulations and safeguards.

It seemed exactly like the British Army, down to the sneers. Maybe sewing stars and stripes atop a flawed fabric didn't change the cloth. But there he went again. He was going to give himself a headache trying to puzzle it out. Henry shook his head and made his way in the direction the two men had indicated.

"I'm looking for John," he said, when he'd found the encampment of black soldiers. "This tall"—he gestured —"strong, taciturn, participated in the assault on Redoubt Ten, from...the Rhode Island Regiment?"

A fellow stood. "What do you want with John?"

"I'm a cheesemonger." Henry considered the rest of his speech. "He asked to buy some of my cheese."

The man looked at one of his fellows. "Huh," said the one who was sitting, examining boots that were as much hole as leather. "Cheese. I hadn't thought..."

"It's very excellent cheese," Henry assured him. "And I promised him a discount."

"What can it hurt?" one of them said. "Hunter is heading out. It's not impossible. I'll take you to him."

Hunter. Hunter. He was John Hunter. Excellent.

"Cheese," one of them muttered.

They conducted Henry through the darkening camp to a fire at the edge where a few men sat.

"John, this man—"

John looked up. In the days since the assault, Henry had tried to remember what his… benefactor? enemy? looked like. Tall, he remembered. He could have drawn the line of the other man's profile, the prominent, chiseled ridges of the eyebrows, the shape of his nose.

This was the first time Henry had seen him in daylight, fading though it was. John, last name previously unknown, learned and…drat it, immediately forgotten again. Their eyes met, and Henry felt a current sweep through him. *Him*, Henry thought, one hand going to his heart. *Him.*

This man. There was a scar down his cheek—not prominent, just a line of darker brown slashed across his face. His eyes narrowed.

They'd talked that night—well, to be fair, *Henry* had talked. Still, fucking was the only thing more intimate than fighting. He'd seen *something* even in the darkness. In daylight it was more obvious.

John was utterly, bewitchingly lovely, and Henry had been already predisposed to bewitchment. His cheekbones were high. He wasn't as tall as Henry remembered—something about a man trying to kill you made him loom in the imagination—but he was well muscled. John's arm was bound with some kind of cloth in a sling, holding it against his chest. His lips pressed into a thin line as he looked at Henry.

Something deep in Henry's gut awoke in that moment. It felt like a fundamental shift in his makeup. It was like the circular all over again. He changed again now, his breath cycling through him. He would never be the same.

Henry forgot everything he was going to say.

"John," the man beside him said. "This fellow says you're buying his cheese."

"Cheese?" John frowned. "I didn't want any cheese."

"Cheese?" Henry said, momentarily forgetting his own story. "What cheese?"

The man who had brought him looked at him. "What do you mean, 'what cheese'?"

"Oh. *Cheese*. Right. Never mind the cheese. John, it's Henry Latham." There were various other titles and whatnot that people often insisted on adding to his name, but they were all embarrassing and irrelevant in the moment.

John wrinkled his nose in confusion. "Who? I don't know a Henry Latham. What do you have to do with cheese?"

"The cheese is a lie," Henry explained brightly.

"What the hell?" the man muttered behind him. "I *knew* something was amiss. Wait. I recognize him. John, this man is a British officer. I've fought him before. I told you about him."

John looked up. His eyes narrowed, and he looked at Henry in something like astonishment.

"Nonsense," Henry said brightly. "If I were a British officer, I certainly wouldn't be waltzing around over here out of uniform, would I?"

John stared at him.

"You remember me, don't you? We met outside Yorktown. We talked about imperialism?"

"My God," John said slowly.

"You actually know him?" That was from the man in the back. "Are you sure he's not a British officer?"

"I do." John swallowed. "I suppose that if he says he's not a British officer, he's not a British officer. How curious, though. He's shorter than I remember."

Henry couldn't help but smile. "I knew you'd not have forgotten! And how could you doubt me? I told you I would find you, didn't I? And here I am."

John just looked at him. He did not look delighted. He looked surprised and suspicious. "Here you are," he repeated. "What the devil are you doing here?"

Chapter Two

JOHN HAD NOT THOUGHT of that bizarre conflict since the battle. There had been no point. The entire encounter felt like a dream, possibly a nightmare. The scene from his memory was tinged with the dark blue of midnight, with a sense of confused detachment from reality.

Did that really happen? He wasn't even sure, now, with the man standing directly in front of him.

But the man was here and he had a name. In daylight, he made less sense than he had at night. He was tall—but not, as John seemed to remember, *taller*. His hair was not blond; it stood up in little tufts that were not quite orange, not quite yellow. His eyes darted about with a sense of curiosity reflected in the nervous energy he radiated.

"Why the devil are you here?" It made no sense, and John didn't trust things that made no sense.

"I told you I'd search you out."

"Neither of us believed that."

"Speak for yourself." Latham gave him a brilliant smile. "I owe you my life. *You* may think that's a debt of little value; *I* have another view on it."

"He's not selling cheese?" Elijah, standing behind Latham, frowned. "John, do you want us to…?"

"He's harmless." At least, he was unlikely to do harm at this point. John would shake his hand, or whatever the man expected, and see the last of him. In fact, there was one sure way to drive the man off—invite him to sit with the black soldiers. "Here," John said with a casual solicitousness. "Sit down. Share a campfire. Stay for supper. What was your name again?"

"Latham." The man set his pack down and sat cross-legged on the ground. "Henry Latham. Can I offer anything for the common pot?"

Behind him, Elijah shrugged in confusion. And no surprise —even the most committed abolitionists often balked at sharing food with black soldiers. Then again, Latham had already proven himself to be more than a bit unusual.

He was rummaging in his pack. "I've a bit of bread and butter, if that wouldn't go amiss, and rather a lot of cheese. I don't recommend the cheese. It's a decoy."

"What is decoy cheese?" Marcelo had enlisted alongside John—not for the exact same reason, but for a very similar one.

Latham reached into his pack and brought out a heavy block wrapped in waxed paper. "I'm warning you." He had an easy smile—too easy to trust. His fingers were long and lithe, and they undid the paper with ease.

The first whiff of the cheese was the worst. It brought to mind old socks, or perhaps corpses rotting in airless caves. John choked.

Marcelo pinched his nose shut. "Damn, man. That is *rank.*"

John managed a second whiff, and discovered that the cheese was indeed a lie. His second sniff of the cheese was even worse than the first, and how that was possible, he didn't know.

"Isn't it terrible?" Latham grinned, and picked up a knife. "It's the most useful disgusting cheese I've encountered. Tell people you're selling cheese, produce this, and suddenly everyone's eager to have you on your way. They don't even pay attention to your questions."

"Are you a liar, then?"

Latham shrugged. "Maybe. Probably? Not so much. I suppose it depends on your particular point of view." He cut a thin sliver of cheese and held it out. "Here. Want some?"

"Tastes better than it smells, does it?"

"The man I bought it from told me it was an acquired taste," Latham said. "I've yet to acquire it. I have been trying, though." He paused. "Anyone else?"

Heads shook around the fire. John made the sign to ward off the evil eye, but Latham just chuckled and carefully wrapped the cheese back up, tucking the ends of the paper into the folds.

"Here's the question," Latham said. "When I tell myself this is the most delicious cheese in the world, that I'm going to absolutely *love* it—am I *lying*? Or am I *hoping*?"

"Fantasizing," John muttered.

Latham slid the cheese in his mouth. His nose scrunched. "Still terrible. I've not acquired the taste for it yet, I see. No worries; I've six pounds of the stuff to go."

All British were odd, John reminded himself. They might seem rational, but why else would they fight so many wars, just for the dubious pleasure of ruling the ungrateful?

John shook his head and divided the soup into bowls. The bread Latham produced was good, at least—soft on the inside with a crisp, flaky crust.

For a while, they didn't speak—*a while* being approximately ninety seconds, during which their mouths were occupied with spoons and soup.

Then Latham snapped his fingers. "Bugger it," he said. "I've spent *days* thinking of this moment, and the instant it arrives, all I can talk about is cheese, cheese, cheese. Good heavens; what is wrong with me?"

It was a very good question. John had no idea.

Latham turned to him. "You saved my life. I am in your debt. How can I ever repay you?"

John was not going to roll his eyes at this particular specimen of drama. Who *said* that sort of thing to another human?

Latham apparently thought the same thing, because he frowned, tapping one forefinger against his thin, pale lips. "You know," he mused, "in all the stories, they never mention how utterly *awkward* it is to say such a thing. It sounds terribly pretentious, actually. I assure you, I have very few pretensions. Maybe one of them. Two of them. I am a regular bundle of anti-pretension, in fact."

John raised a single eyebrow. With *that* accent? Unlikely. Pretty British officers like him undoubtedly had more than a few pretensions.

"I'm making things worse, aren't I?"

John nodded.

"Well, then. Is there anything I can do for you?"

It was, perhaps, irrational to feel angry under the circumstances. Here was this man, with his cheese and his smile, sitting before him, offering his help.

It wasn't as if John didn't *need* help; he did, in fact, a thousand times over. His last letter from his sister, Lizzie, six months past, had spoken of trouble at home. *Now that Noah's freed, people don't want us here.* Every week in which no further correspondence arrived diminished his ability to make excuses. Something was wrong, and the only reason John wasn't in a tearing panic was that tearing panics had never accomplished a damned thing. Here he was, in Virginia, with his sister and mother five hundred miles away.

He'd fought. He'd survived. Damn it, he ought to be able to go home.

Home might no longer exist.

He needed help. He needed a goddamned legion of soldiers to put down whatever unrest his family faced. He needed constables who cared about the peace of black freedmen, and not just the whispers of their white comrades. He needed laws that would protect the ones he loved.

All he had were his own two hands, and one of them was presently in a sling.

A true offer of help would have been welcome. But this one? This offer wasn't honestly meant. Any of the things John desperately needed were off the table.

This man didn't want to help; he wanted a handshake. Even that was off the table; after they'd parted ways, John had stupidly injured his right shoulder tripping over a rock on the way up the redoubt. Latham wanted a modicum of reassurance that he was a decent fellow.

John's shoulder hurt. He was too tired to reassure anyone, let alone pretty British officers with undisclosed pretensions.

John exhaled slowly. "I know how this dance is supposed to work. I say there's nothing I can think of. You press me to think of something; I demur, because we both know you don't really mean it. We shake hands, or I try to"—he gestured with his head to the sling—"and you leave, convinced you've done everything possible."

"Is *that* how it's supposed to go?" Henry looked at him with wide eyes. "That's a good bit more fleshed out than my list."

John ignored him. "It turns out that I'm tired. Nobody ever taught me which fork to use, and I ran out of etiquette somewhere around the time I was trying not to lose my toes at Valley Forge. I *do* need something, and I don't care about pinning a polite little medal saying, 'Well, at least you tried' on your shoulder."

"You Americans *have* medals saying that?"

John stopped, shaking his head. "No. Of course we don't. It's figurative."

"Of course it is. Pardon the interruption. You were going to tell me what you needed."

"I—" Latham really *was* rather odd. John paused, regrouping. He almost felt like a bit of a heel doing this, but—

"I'm taking my leave of the army tomorrow," he said. It had taken a bit of negotiation, that, but the doctor hadn't known if he would recover the use of his arm. John had been desperate to go home, to find his family; the Continental Army was counting the cost of soldiers lying about doing nothing while the peace accords started.

"They've no need for an injured soldier, and I may never be able to use my arm." John, in fact, believed no such thing. He had exaggerated the pain with the express purpose of convincing the doctor to declare him officially an invalid. He had to get home.

"I have a long journey ahead of me. Anyone who might otherwise accompany me on the road is either white or dead. And—" No. He wasn't about to disclose his worries about his family to this man.

"Right. Is that it?"

"Is that *it?*" John echoed. "I'm going on foot. There are

bandits on the road. We'll be living off the land as we move, so I hope you know how to set traps." He glanced at the man. "I hope you have a taste for squirrel meat, too. It's rather late in the year."

"Where is your home, then?"

"Rhode Island," John said pointedly.

"Ha, I guessed right!"

"It's some five hundred, maybe six hundred miles distant," John said repressively.

Latham folded his arms. Right. Here it came. The polite refusal.

"Sounds better than selling cheese," the other man said. "When do we leave?"

John blinked and looked over at the man. He was sitting contentedly in place, breaking the crust of his bread into pieces. The firelight made his hair seem even more orange than it had before. He didn't look as if he was lying.

He had to be lying. He didn't mean it.

"Tomorrow morning," John said in slow disbelief. "You understand that people like me aren't...loved in these parts? We'll move fast. We'll have no luxuries. I have no money to speak of."

A tiny frown touched Latham's face. *Finally*. It had taken long enough to put him off. But instead of protesting and suddenly discovering he had other things to do, Latham just bowed his head and considered his soup bowl.

"Well. That makes my head hurt all over again. Does that not make your head hurt?"

John looked over at Marcelo, who shook his head in equal confusion.

"You can't *say* the cheese is delicious and not eat the cheese," Latham muttered. "It's just not done."

Maybe he caught their disbelieving stares, because he smiled helplessly. "It makes sense inside my head," he said. "Or rather —it *doesn't* make sense, that's the entire point. I swear to you, I'm not as stupid as I appear."

"I see," John said, even though he didn't.

"But look at me," Henry said. "My father used to say I was

153

empty-headed, but I assure you, it's not true—quite the opposite, in fact. There's too *much* in my head, not too little. Pretend I never said anything. I meant to ask—what time shall I meet you, then?"

"Have you ever traveled thirty miles in a day?" John demanded. "Day after day, all in a row?"

"Of course." Latham looked almost indignant.

"On foot?"

"Ah…" A beat of hesitation. "Well… Not exactly? But I'm quite capable, really. Don't worry about me. Sunrise—will that do?"

"Sunrise is fine," John said in disbelief.

"Right. Then I shouldn't dawdle. I've a great deal to do in preparation. I'll see you then."

"Right," John echoed scornfully. He watched the other man leave with a shake of his head.

"What *was* that?" Marcelo asked.

"I don't know," John said, "but even odds, he'll not arrive in the morning. At any rate, prissy fellow like him—he'll beg off ten miles into the journey, complaining of blisters."

Marcelo nodded his head in agreement. "Lord above," he finally said. "I will never understand humanity. People are *strange*."

"Hmm." Latham's figure disappeared into the darkening night. John sighed. "Something tells me this one is particularly queer."

⚜

"Good day!"

John had taken his leave from camp. He'd carefully shaken the left hands of the men with whom he'd spent years cooking squirrels and stones into soup. Captain Olney had given him a nod and a final goodbye. Colonel Hamilton—with whom John had spent less than twelve hours on the battlefield—had clapped his good shoulder and made another idle promise—"If ever you're in need, let me know and I'll put my name to use to offer some assistance."

John had left the Continental Army encampment an hour after sunrise. By the time he walked out the gate, he'd managed to forget Latham—completely—again.

But here he was, standing next to the road, arms folded and smiling brightly. "It *is* a nice day, isn't it?"

John stared stupidly at him, it being too early in the morning for this level of explosive cheerfulness.

"How are you doing this fine morning, John?" He came over and clapped a hand against John's shoulder. Pain shot through him like lightning.

John didn't wince. He didn't even let himself shiver. Instead, he brought his good hand up, catching the other man's wrist, yanking it away from his shoulder.

Their eyes met.

Touching a white man like this, in reprimand… Not a good idea.

Latham didn't *look* likely to burst into violence, no matter what had been said about him on the battlefield, but then, you never could tell with some of these fancy types. Some of them could go from laughter to the most violent rage in the blink of an eye. It wouldn't matter that John had saved his life. It wouldn't matter if John had been his *brother*. John was black; Latham was white. And if Latham was one of *those*—one who would take offense at the slightest hint that he needed to treat John as human—then it was just as well John find out now.

"Not that shoulder," John said.

"Oh." Latham's eyes widened. "I am *such* an idiot. I had forgotten, and the sling is under your jacket…"

"Don't want everyone on the road thinking me an easy mark." John looked at him. "Not the other shoulder, either."

Latham frowned.

"It's not wounded," John explained. "I'm just not one for giving or receiving punches in various spots of my body to demonstrate my manhood."

"Oh. A handshake then?" Latham extended his arm.

It would be boorish to brush that off, and in all honesty, John was beginning to suspect that Latham was something of a puppy—earnest, exuberant, and utterly devoid of house-training. John sighed. Latham's shoes looked far too fashionable for a journey of five hundred miles. He'd quit in a day, two at the most.

Very well. John could handle anything for a day, even a puppy.

He held out his left hand. Gingerly, awkwardly, their hands met. Latham's gloves were some sort of soft leather against John's bare calluses.

"Well. No point dawdling."

"We're off," Latham said. "This is so exciting! I've never been on a walking trip, did you know?"

A *walking* trip, as if this were a jaunt through the woods for pleasure. He'd last three hours at best.

"Although, that's not true, come to think of it. I walked thirty-five miles to my gran's house when I was twelve and was scolded roundly. So, ha, perhaps I have a little experience. Although that took two days."

John glanced over. Latham kept going.

"*She* didn't scold me, mind—it was my father, and I suppose the dean, who seemed to think a trip to my grandmother's was superfluous when I had a Latin examination. As if avoiding the Latin examination were not the very point of the trip! Ah well. Sic transit gloria Henry."

John just shook his head at him.

"That's all the Latin I remember now, so maybe the dean had a point? But then, I've never needed to know Latin, so maybe I also had a point too. What did he suppose would happen?"

John did not hazard an answer. He wasn't sure who the *he* in that sentence was, and he didn't want to ask.

"If ruffians descend upon us and demand that I conjugate Latin verbs, I will be unable to save us by means of quick thinking," Henry said. "I apologize for my failures in advance. I also, however, will apologize to the ruffians, because I cannot imagine what sort of heartbreaking childhood would lead them to make such bizarre demands. Ah, maybe we'd have something in common! Come to think of it…"

Latham was going to give up. Any mile now, he'd beg off.

And even if he didn't, if John didn't say anything, Latham would have to stop talking. *Eventually.*

He would, wouldn't he?

LATHAM DID NOT STOP TALKING.

Not that morning. Not that night, as he asked about John's shoulder and if cold compresses helped, and if they didn't, if hot compresses did. He talked as he prepared some kind of a... thing...of cloth and herbs and warm heat over the fire for John. He talked as they ate and offered John bread and disgusting cheese.

John took the bread.

He talked the next morning—more cheese, more bread, more stories about goats and chickens and his father, whom he did not like, and his mother, whom he did. He did not stop talking.

Not that night. Not the next morning, nor the morning after, nor even the morning after that. John had imagined that Henry Latham would complain of hunger, weariness, thirst, and general malcontent.

Had John been given more than a few minutes to think the matter over, he might have realized that a man who greeted a nighttime assailant with "nice weather for a siege?" was unlikely to be a complainer.

He was just as unlikely to be silent.

He talked.

And he talked.

And he *talked.*

After the first few days, John had resorted to the desperate measure of not responding to even direct questions—not a nod of the head, not a grunt, not so much as a commiserating glance out of the corner of his eye—in order to satisfy his own curiosity about how long it would take Latham to run out of words.

Four days since they'd started their journey, and Latham was still going.

It had become a battle of wills: Latham wanted to engage John in conversation, and John refused to give in. Latham talked through the entirety of one day. Then the next. He talked until Virginia was gone, and Maryland, with its almost bare forests and its red, crunchy leaves underfoot, stretched before them.

Latham talked and talked, and one week into their journey, John realized he had made a grave error in his calculations: Latham talked, and John didn't hate it.

Chapter Three

HENRY LATHAM WAS ALL TOO aware that John Hunter seemed to be engaged in a heroic battle to avoid conversation. He'd managed to set up camp for two nights running without saying a word.

He hadn't complained when Henry had brought out the cheese.

"Here," Henry said, holding a slice of death-smelling cheese out to him. "Have some!"

A shift of Hunter's eyes out to the horizon was his only response.

"Day nine," Henry said. "I am eating the cheese. The cheese *will* be delicious. It will be amazingly delicious. It will positively melt in my mouth."

He put the slice on his tongue. It tasted like feet and frog shit. Henry choked, coughing, and reached for his tin flask of water.

Across from him, John tried very hard not to smile.

"Alas. The cheese prevails once again," Henry said. "The taste is not yet acquired. Ah, well. Tomorrow is a new day."

John just looked at him.

"You really should try the cheese," Henry said. "You seem like the sort of open-minded fellow who would find…something to love in this cheese."

John's mouth opened, then clapped shut. *Such* a valiant effort.

Futile, but valiant. From long experience, Henry knew that he was highly unlikely to shut up, not for any reason. He wasn't made for silence.

Nobody was, really. Henry had once been told—perhaps by one of the tutors whom his father had hired to try to make him a sober, learned fellow and who instead had been inexorably pulled into a lengthy discussion of some arcane, unimportant point of history—that resisting him was like trying to hold the ocean in place with one's fingers. It wouldn't work, and the ocean (if it felt anything about the matter, which it might, because who knew what oceans thought about? Not Henry, although he could speculate) regarded the effort with nothing so much as amusement.

They were three miles out of Philadelphia, one early morning, when Mr. Hunter finally gave in.

He stopped dead in his tracks.

He turned to Henry. He rubbed his head with his free hand. His hair was growing from short, tight curls into medium tight curls, not yet so long that they could be put into disarray. He glanced at Henry and finally spoke.

"Do you ever get tired of talking?" he demanded.

Henry gave him a delightful smile. "You lasted so long! Twelve entire days—really, I'm so impressed! That was excellent. Utterly excellent!"

Hunter narrowed his eyes at him. "What do you mean?"

"I wish we had those little medals you were talking about earlier," Henry said appreciatively.

"What? What medals?"

"The tin ones. The ones that said 'Well, at least you tried.' I would award you one right now. You definitely deserve it, don't you think?"

Hunter gave him an unblinking stare. For a moment, he tilted his head, as if trying to make sense of what Henry was saying. Henry could have told him there was no point in that either.

"You didn't answer my question," Hunter said. "Do you ever get *tired* of talking?"

Right. Henry had been so delighted at the fact of a question that he'd forgotten to answer.

"What an excellent question." He considered it now. "Tired of talking? What an odd idea. Let me check." The possibility had honestly never occurred to Henry. The back of his throat tickled—just a hint of incipient soreness, not enough to bother him—and if they hadn't passed a creek a mile or so back, his mouth would be dry. He tentatively tested his tongue, moving it in his mouth from side to side. His feet were a little sore. His tongue? No signs of fatigue at all.

"No." He cast a bright smile at his walking companion. "I don't believe I do. Is there a reason you ask?"

Mr. Hunter had been—over the past week or so—slowly losing his touch. The repressive look he gave Henry was scarcely forbidding. He looked as if he was on the verge of smiling.

Oh, he tried not to react to a thing Henry said. But he had failed. Henry had been counting Hunter's smiles. He was at four thus far this morning.

"Simple curiosity," Mr. Hunter said. He shook his head and started walking once more. "Thus far this morning, you've covered the finer points of piquet strategy, the musical oeuvre of Handel, and the various gaits of horses along with their utility in exacerbating lower back pain. It's not even midday. Aren't you afraid you'll run out of words? Or ideas?"

"Not in the least." Henry glanced over at Mr. Hunter. "I should warn you, I'm a talkative sort."

"I had surmised that to be the case sometime over the last hour or hundred."

"If it bothers you, I can keep quiet."

"Really? In that case…" The man seemed to be considering that as if it were a real possibility.

"I only meant for a minute, maybe two. I always forget that I'm supposed to be doing it," Henry added.

Hunter's lip twitched. "I knew the offer was too good to be true."

"Personally, I find that conversation works much better when two are involved. Haven't you anything to say?"

Hunter's eyebrows went down in contemplation, as if perhaps, he *did* have something—*one* thing—to say.

"Here," Henry said. "I'll give you some space to think."

"You will?"

"Of course!" Henry did his best to do something entirely unfamiliar: He tried to shut up.

Their strides lifted dust along the road, little plumes of light brown. Light brown. Now *that* was a nice color. Months ago, he'd marched through something red and claylike. It had caked his boots and stained his trousers—permanently, it turned out —thus ruining all hope he had of keeping his sharp appearance in the field. He wondered if that clay would make a good dye. Possibly. Probably. Definitely, if one could apply the stain evenly. He'd heard about dyes once. In fact—

"Did you know that beetroot—"

"That wasn't even a minute!" Hunter was laughing.

"Oh damn. I forgot! I was waiting for you to respond. You were going to do it this time, too!"

"What could I have said to any of your conversation earlier? I don't know much about piquet," Hunter finally said. "I've not had so many opportunities to play cards for money."

"In the infantry, you haven't? Well, good heavens. No wonder Britain was defeated. The Continental Army possesses far more discipline than I thought possible."

"I'm not precisely representative of the entire army." Hunter rolled his eyes. "As a personal matter, I choose not to risk what I have."

"Look at you, all reasonable and conservative with your funds." Henry drew back to punch the other man in the shoulder.

Hunter looked back at him repressively.

"Ah, right. You don't like that. I'd forgotten." He let his hand drop. "I'll try to remember. Definitely. If I can."

"Mmm. At least try to make it believable when you say it?"

Henry shrugged and made a mental note to definitely try to

remember. "Ah. Well. So let's not talk of piquet. What topic of conversation would you introduce?"

Mr. Hunter frowned.

"You can answer 'no conversation,' but then I shall just choose whatever flits into my head, and I have to tell you, that's a dreadfully mixed bag."

"I can't make you out," Hunter finally said. "When we first...ah...met...?"

"You mean when you tried to kill me?"

Hunter grimaced.

"Was it impolite to bring that up?" Henry tilted his head. "Oh dear. We can't let that come between us. You were doing your patriotic duty, and—as an observer who had more than a little reason to care about the outcome—I must say that up until the final moments, you did a commendable job of doing me in. Very good. You were very good at killing me."

"Not good enough. Are you capable of having a straightforward conversation? One that starts at the beginning and continues on in a straight line to the conclusion?"

Henry considered that. "Yes," he finally said, "but it has to be a very short line." He held up two fingers a raisin's width apart to demonstrate the precise duration of his focus. "I do tend to go off a bit. My father always used to shake me by the collar when I was young. 'Focus!' he'd shout in my ear. Then I'd forget everything altogether. But what were we talking about? Killing. Patriotism. Oh—right—you started by saying that you couldn't make me out. Good heavens. I was an utter cad in response. You introduced a perfectly acceptable topic of conversation, one about which I have particular knowledge, and I just went straight off onto some other ridiculous thing, as if I were a horse spooked by a spider."

"*Are* horses spooked by—no, never mind."

"Yes," Henry said consolingly. "You're getting the picture. It's best not to ask questions around me if you don't actually want them answered, I'm afraid."

"I have always been accounted a fast learner."

"So let us return to your original question. You wanted to ask about me. This is an excellent conversational theme. I know almost nothing about arachnids, not that I would ever let that stop me from expounding on them, but I know a great deal about me."

"I thought you were…" Hunter bit his lip, searching for a word. "That night, I thought you were despairing, perhaps. And yet here you are. I would almost call you…an idealist, maybe. You hardly seem the sort to *want* to die. Why didn't you want to go back to England?"

A cold shadow touched Henry's heart. He smiled brightly through that shadow and reached for the first semiplausible explanation that came to mind.

"You can't be that fast a learner," he scoffed instead. "I would have thought my reason to be obvious. That would be the treason."

"The what?"

"The treason," Henry repeated. "You know. Treachery? Aiding the enemy? The complete opposite, on my part, of the patriotic duty that you seem to have in such abundance? The treason is why I do not want to go back to England."

Hunter was staring at him. "I don't understand."

Henry didn't have the words to explain everything in his heart, and so he reached for easier words, ones he could utilize.

"It's not that difficult a concept. Think the consequences through for a moment. The treason would be such a bloody mess. Trials, beheadings. Blood everywhere. My mother would weep, my family would be launched into scandal, my sister's husband would become even more of a bore—which I would not have thought possible, but every time I think he's reached the utter zenith of monotony, he exceeds the physical limits of tedium once again. You know. Treason is just damned hard on everyone all around."

"I understand that," Hunter said. "But…treason?"

"What do you think I was doing at the redoubt? Following orders?"

"Well…"

"No. I thought to myself that it was an *excellent* night for a siege. Then Fusiliers Redoubt went up, and I thought it was an excellent night for a feint, too. I was afraid I was going to blurt it out in front of everyone, so I went to hide."

John looked at him. "Why?"

"You are not seriously asking *why* I thought I might say anything flitting through my head after this many days in my company, are you?"

"No—why didn't you *say* anything?"

"Oh, that. After I read the circular, I had to do *something*, even if the something I did was nothing. Up until that point, I'd managed to hide my treason in incompetence. 'Oh, you meant *that* left' works once, and 'didn't you say advance at *three* drum strokes?' I ran the most inept company in the entire British army, and my men loved me. We so rarely saw battle."

"You...didn't want to fight?"

"I told you it was treason."

"Well, but..."

"Technically, I'm not sure it *was* actually treason—possibly, my behavior at the moment was just a cause for court-martial—but purposefully evading orders and absconding from my position still brings us back around to willful disobedience and desertion. Which means weeping, scandal, boorish husbands, et cetera and so forth." Henry swept his arms wide. "I use the word 'treason' as a sort of shorthand for all of that. I prefer to live, all things considered, but if death is inevitable, I'd rather my family think me bravely, stupidly heroic."

If anything, Hunter looked more confused. His eyebrows drew together in a dark line. His mouth squished up.

"You are an incredibly odd individual."

"I know," Henry said. "It's my saving grace. People tell me all the time I'm a queer fellow, but if I'm going to talk as much as I do, I might as well give them something interesting to listen to, don't you think?"

"Mmm."

"My father hated it. He always wished I would keep my mouth shut. Stand in one place. Stop chattering about everything, or he'd knock me—" Henry stopped talking. Pasted a smile on his face. "Good thing I was a second son and he didn't have to actually succeed in reforming me! They tried me on all the second son things—law, church, you name it—and finally gave up and tossed me into the army. He'll be glad I'm dead." He considered this. "Honestly, I'm glad to be dead, too. The best solution to an awful mess; I had thought so for months, but hadn't quite figured out how to die without actually *dying*, a disfavored outcome, until you came along."

"That—it seems—perhaps excessive?"

"Ah, you'd agree if you knew him. He's a terrible father. The absolute *worst*. You couldn't imagine."

Hunter looked at him. "The man who fathered me owned me and my mother. He never beat me, but he did sell my mother when he gambled himself into a hard spot."

Henry felt his mouth go dry. He thought of his father yelling at him. Telling him to focus. Telling him to make something of himself, goddamn it, and...

"You win," he said. "You win. That is definitely worse."

"I had not realized we were playing a game. Do I get a medal saying 'You *didn't* try' now? Had I any choice in the matter, I assure you this is not a game I would strive to succeed at."

"Had you any choice in the matter, what would you have done, if not soldiering? If you were allowed to choose? Would you have gone to university?"

Hunter stared at him. "Are you completely ignorant of the world?" he finally asked. "I mean this honestly. Is something wrong with you? Did your father hit you too many times? University? In what world could I *choose* to go to university?"

Henry wasn't going to flush. He wasn't going to feel stupid—even though, apparently, he was an idiot of the most gargantuan proportions. "Ah. Um. This...hypothetical one, now? Where you could choose anything you wanted? Anything at all?"

Hunter rolled his eyes. "Good. Then I choose to be independently wealthy."

"An excellent choice, if I do say so myself."

"Nobody would sell my family." That was said on a growl. "I wouldn't ever have to worry about where they were, what they were doing, if they were alive."

"That seems like a...very good start. What would you do with all your wealth, though?"

Hunter looked at him.

"It's just a question! You could, I suppose, allow it to lie in a bank and make interest of some kind, or you could use it for... oh, I don't know, saving starving dogs? Educating orphans?"

"Is that what fancy British officers do with their wealth?" Hunter asked.

Latham felt himself flush. "I wouldn't know," he lied. "My father was...a...tailor."

Hunter raised one eyebrow at that rather obvious lie, and just shook his head. "Well." There was a pointedness to his words as he spoke. "If I were born a second son—and I suppose, in a sense, I was, although my father's first son would never have acknowledged such a thing—with all the attendant wealth that came with that, I would have gone into trade."

"Into trade." Henry felt dazed. "You'd have gone into trade."

"Of course." Hunter gave him a nod. "I grew up in a shipyard in South Carolina, you know. I used to listen to the traders talk in the shipyard—they never did notice me, even when I was right there—talking about their money and where it came from and where they'd get more of it. They'd find people in Africa, bring them to the Caribbean or the South, where they'd trade them for rum or sugar or cotton. Back to England, where they'd sell that for manufactured goods... It always made me think."

"You wanted to trade people?"

"No. They all seemed to have a want of imagination— trading the same things as everyone else. I wanted to show you didn't have to trade in human flesh, or the products of human flesh. I used to lie in bed at night and imagine a world where I stole one of the ships and made more money than the rest of them doing the things they'd failed to imagine."

"That sounds like a noble aim," Henry managed to say. Nobler than anything he'd ever thought of.

"Noble, ha." Hunter pressed the fingers of his left hand to his forehead, shutting his eyes momentarily. "I've learned long since to hope for smaller things, attainable things. I want my sister to be well. I want her husband not to be enslaved. I want to live with my family and not be separated from them except by my own choices."

The light in his eyes dimmed somewhat, but the fervor in his voice deepened. "I ask for what I can get. There's no room for childish dreams in my life."

"But those aren't childish dreams. I rather liked them."

Hunter wrinkled his nose as if annoyed that he'd spoken. "They're childish. Do you think that anyone would do business with someone who aimed to rewrite the way trading was done in its entirety?"

"Maybe," Henry said earnestly, "if you picked the right name. You could fool everyone. Pick something grandiose sounding, and they might not notice. Something like…"

"'Just the Usual Sort of Traders, Don't Mind Us' lacks a certain ring."

"No, something simple and ridiculous-sounding, like 'Lord Traders.' Who would think that *they* would be up to anything sneaky?"

Hunter sighed. "Forget I said anything."

For a moment, Henry tried. He looked over at Hunter, walking along at a regular clip. His injured arm was still bound to his chest in a sling; they'd checked it every night, and every night, Hunter hissed in pain when he attempted motion. Maybe his dreams were childish. Maybe they should be set aside. Still, it had sounded better than any idea that Henry had ever had thus far, and Henry had a great many ideas.

"Sorry. I can't. You see, we are…very, very different, of course. But I think we are of a similar bent."

"Oh?" Hunter was better at looking dubious than any man Henry had ever met. He could communicate disbelief in one syllable, with just a tiny hint of emphasis.

Henry was even better at ignoring those signs. "You ought to have asked me *why* I was committing treason. It wasn't on a whim. I *speak* on a whim; I commit treason with deadly seriousness."

Hunter just raised an eyebrow, and that absence of suspicion was more than enough invitation to expound.

"You see, around one year ago, I found this paper. It was

trash. Some revolutionary rubbish that someone had nailed to the walls of a barn to annoy us. I made the mistake of reading it."

"I can imagine what it was like. Bombastic. Full of derision for your sort."

"No, no. It wasn't, that's the thing. It's still in my pocket," Henry said softly. "I memorized the parts that mattered to me. *We hold these truths to be self-evident. That all men are created equal."* Those words had shattered him. He'd read them over and over, again and again, shaking them up and down inside his head. They had *hurt*, making his head ache as he tried to put them in their place. He'd tried to drown them out with chatter. With other ideas.

But that was the thing about Henry's mind. It never settled on any one idea for any length of time, but it always came swirling back to the thoughts that could seduce him day after day. Night after night.

All men are created equal, they'd whispered. *All men are created equal. Even you.*

Hunter flicked a look at him. "That sounds like the Declaration of Independence. It meant something to you? It shouldn't have. It's just a string of pretty words."

"It's *not,"* Henry said hotly. "Those are *ideals."*

A dismissive wave of the other man's hand. "Thomas Jefferson owns people. He no more thinks that *all* men are equal than the King of England does. It's all just words. That Declaration is nothing but ink on parchment, put there to make poorer men risk their lives so that Jefferson can pay less than his damned share of taxes."

"Well, they may be words, but they worked." Henry folded his arms. "An ideal set in motion is a dangerous thing. You can't control who believes it, or whether they take it to heart. 'All men are created equal.' Think of the power of that phrase."

"I have," Hunter said curtly. "'All men.' Ha. Tell me, when you were mulling over the equality of men up in your redoubt, did you ever imagine a man like me?"

Henry raised his head. He looked into Hunter's eyes—dark, in the warmer brown of his face. Fierce. Unrelenting.

He swallowed. He wanted to lie. To say that of course he had thought of *all* men. But… He was many, many things. Including a liar. He was definitely a liar. But lying now wouldn't just be pointless babble. It would be *wrong*.

He shut his eyes. "No. I didn't."

Hunter just shrugged. "Of course not." He said it quietly, with no bitterness.

He *should* have been bitter. He should have been angry. When people talked about all men, they should think about him.

And that made Henry think. And think. And think. And think some more.

Chapter Four

THE IMPOSSIBLE HAD HAPPENED: Henry Latham had shut up.

John hadn't thought such a thing would ever happen, but there he was—quiet for hours. He didn't speak when they stopped at a stream, dipping tin cups into cold water that tasted like stone and moss. He didn't speak throughout their late afternoon snack of dry bread and hard jerky.

Instead, he fiddled with an iron ring that he'd pulled from his pack, turning it around in his hands over and over.

Consider the equality of the black man, apparently, was a mental exercise that had left even Latham tongue-tied. No surprise; most people were easily befuddled when their cheerful principles overran their prejudice.

He didn't speak again until they came up on an inn just before twilight. Then, as John didn't spare a glance to the stone chimneys whose wisps of smoke promised heat, he stopped in the road.

"It's been a while," he said. "We've been sleeping on the ground for almost two weeks. Have you ever thought about halting somewhere for a night?"

Oh, Latham was so naïve. He was pretty, in the way of pretty men who knew they were pretty: high cheekbones, flushed from the day's exertion; smooth, bright hair pulled back in a fashionable club. His eyelashes flashed at John—not in so much as a bat but in the desperate entreaty of a tired man.

They'd made twenty-seven miles today, and he was no doubt tired.

"At an inn?" John made a face. "Hardly worth the coin."

"Uh. Coin isn't…" Latham flushed even brighter. "I have a bit on me, as it happens. I should think that a room at an inn…"

"Two rooms," John said. "That's what they'll be willing to give us. More like one room and a berth in the stables, if I'm lucky."

Latham understood his point immediately.

"Nonsense. You're sharing your journey; I'm sharing what I have. Any particularity on my part was lost during the last years at war."

John felt his nose wrinkle. "Who was your father again?"

"Um." Latham's eyes screwed shut. "A…man? A potter. Right. He made pots."

He'd been a tailor before. The truth was more like neither. With that talk of university? With the officer's braid John had seen on his shoulder that night? Unlikely. Even more unlikely with his mention of being a second son with the *usual* choice of law, church, or army.

Potter's son, John's good backside. What kind of potter's son developed any sort of particularity about sharing his room in the first place? Didn't matter, though. John had known the man was a liar from the first evening.

Instead, he jerked a thumb at the inn. "They will care in there. They'll let me stay in your room, but only if you pretend I'm your servant. And I'm not."

Latham's mouth scrunched together. He stared at the stone building, as if imagining the warm rooms inside. A cold breeze brought with it the scent of something savory—stew, perhaps, and John heard the other man's stomach gurgle. "We'll see about that." So saying, he marched in the direction of the inn.

He was going to get both their heads bashed in. John sighed, then followed.

Latham marched into the inn with the air of a man who owned the place.

The man who *actually* owned the place, a balding man wearing a stained apron, brightened when he caught sight of him.

"Sir," he said, completely ignoring John, "a thousand welcomes to you. You have the look of one who has been involved in the war. Officer?"

"Indeed," Latham said jovially. It was, John supposed, not entirely a lie. He *had* been in the war. He *had* been an officer. He just didn't mention that he'd fought for the other side.

The innkeeper bowed distinctly. "Thank you for your service, sir. How can I help you?"

"My good man. A room, if you please." Latham's manners had changed. They were like glistening icicles hanging from the eaves—cold and perfectly formed. Glancing at the tables nearby, he added, "Dinner as well. Your goodwife appears to set an excellent table."

The innkeeper nodded. "Of course, of course, sir. If you could come over here?" He gestured to John. "Your master's luggage—"

Latham tilted his head. "My pardon! I thought that was clear when we entered. Corporal Hunter here is no servant. We were comrades-in-arms."

"Former corporal," John muttered. "Now no longer in the infantry."

The innkeeper paused. He frowned at Latham. He glanced at his dining area.

"I've just a pack," Latham continued. "I'll take it up myself. But I'd like to wash and have dinner. If you could direct us—"

"I'll hold a table for you, sir, but your, ah..."

"Hunter is his name. And he is my traveling companion." John winced.

"Your companion may eat with the servants, if you please. And we have a place in the stables for him."

"It doesn't please. It doesn't please at all."

"It's not negotiable. I must think of the comfort of my other guests."

Latham frowned.

It wouldn't take him long to give up his principles. It never did. Rationality said that Latham could get his warm room and dinner, and if John couldn't... Well, it wasn't *Latham's* fault, was it? There was no principle so fine that it could stand up to a dish of warm stew at a comfortable table after a twenty-seven-mile walk.

Latham shook his head, let out a gusty sigh, and turned to John. "Well, Hunter." Their eyes met, and John did not look away. If Latham was going to abandon him for a warm bed, he'd not give the man the satisfaction of backing down. "You win."

"This game." John shook his head. "I really hate winning this game, and yet I find myself continually dragooned into playing."

Latham sighed. "Do we eat with the servants and bunk in the stables, or continue on?"

"We?"

Latham gave him a quirk of a smile. "I'm too overcome with exhaustion to make a decision. It's in your hands."

John met his eyes. Latham was a liar, and—by his own admission—a traitor. But he'd asked for his opinion.

And so instead, John shrugged. "I suppose tonight we can bunk in the stables. You'll toughen eventually, but for now, we'll compromise in deference to your softness."

"Excellent."

Latham turned to the innkeeper. "Dinner for two, then. With the servants."

<hr />

LATHAM GOT them a private corner to wash, and, after the innkeeper grimaced at the thought of an officer—a *white* officer—eating with the servants, a table in the back of the kitchen with stew for them both.

The innkeeper was even—almost—apologetic to Latham when he conducted them out to the stable. "Should be warm enough in the hayloft," he said, as they climbed the rickety ladder. "We've a full complement of horses tonight."

It was warm. The hay poked through the blankets they unrolled but it was—in a relative sense—the most comfortable that John had been on this journey.

Their bedrolls were inches apart, meaning that in the gloom, when John turned over, he saw Latham looking back at him.

Those damned eyelashes. Pretty was pretty. It didn't mean a damned thing at all, except that the random conformation of features that nature had endowed Latham with were, on balance, pleasing to the eye.

"How's your shoulder?"

John shrugged and unwound his sling. The doctor had said that he might recover full use of his arm, or that he might never have it. Slowly, he stretched his hand out to full extension, flaring his fingers. He could feel the answering pain in the ball of his shoulder, but it was dimming every day.

"I think," he said, "the doctor had no idea what he was talking about. It will be fine."

"Good." Henry's smile lit his face.

He was so damned pretty.

It had never bothered John that he liked looking at pretty men, no matter what churchgoers said. If he'd let the world around him decide what he ought to think of himself, he'd still be enslaved in South Carolina. Lizzie, the sister he'd raised, would be twenty-three and beautiful alongside him in slavery— if he were lucky—and sold somewhere else if he were not. If he'd listened to everyone else, there would be nothing he could do to protect her.

Instead... He thought of her last letter, of the months and months since she'd sent it, the panic that he refused to indulge lurking at the back of his mind. *I'm coming, Lizzie. I'm coming. Just be there when I arrive.*

In truth, John had found his natural inclinations to be incredibly convenient. When he'd been just out of childhood, he'd had no desire to start a family, even though his master had suggested he do so. Loving a woman, having a child—that would have made enslavement his home. It would have been the worst thing he could have done. They'd have tied him to his master even more than his sister had, and leaving her the first time had almost broken his heart. Lucky that he had never wanted women in that way.

It was luck that he liked looking at pretty men instead. Luck that his eyes traced Henry's forehead, and he wondered what he looked like underneath that shirt.

A prickle of awareness seemed to catch deep in his throat. It had always come naturally to him, with men. Looking at them and remembering to look away. Wondering *what if...*

He couldn't help but look at Latham and wonder *what if.* It was only natural. Latham was exceptionally beautiful, and unless the British signaled these things very differently than Americans, his inclinations ran parallel to John's. There were enough men like them; during the war, there had been times John had reached out and blindly sought comfort from a fellow soldier.

Latham, he suspected, had likely done the same.

There would be no seeking comfort between them, though, not unless he wanted things to change too much. John had a family, and who knew what trouble they were in? Every moment's delay meant precious hours when he could be with them instead. He had to make good time; he couldn't let himself become beguiled into lengthening this journey.

He felt it as instinctively as if he were still in battle, as if they were still locked in combat. It was Latham or John, Latham or John, and the stakes might no longer have been his life, but he'd promised Lizzie he would see her again, and if what he feared...

No, he couldn't think about his fears, not here, not in the darkness, not hundreds of miles away where he could do nothing about them.

"You were entirely right," Latham said softly in the dark. "I'm an inherently frivolous man, I'm afraid."

"You don't even shut up at night," John said unfairly. He *had* shut up that afternoon. Shockingly.

"I hadn't thought my principles through. If all men are created equal, it stands to reason that it includes all races. I hadn't thought about it at all until today, and I should have. You have every right to be annoyed. I had to go over the matter. It took me a bit."

"Well, then. It's good you set your mind at rest." There was a bit of a sarcastic edge to John's voice. He didn't even mean it that way; anything that distracted him from the things he'd heard about, of black families driven out in winter, no food, nowhere to go… Worrying wouldn't make it better. It just made his stomach clench. He sighed in the darkness. "I hope you sleep well."

"No, wait. I wanted to—that is, I needed to—" Latham reached out and set a hand on John's good shoulder.

John was too shocked to flinch away. Even through his undershirt, he felt that touch. A spot of warmth, a hint of nerves, sparked where the man's fingers lay.

Don't be an idiot, John.

"It's this," Latham said earnestly. "I hold these truths to be self-evident. That you were created equal. And that everyone who treated you as less debased themselves. I believe that you were endowed with unalienable rights: Life. Liberty. The pursuit of happiness. I believe that when you withdraw your consent to be governed, all men of conscience should stand by your side."

That spot blossomed into heat. They were face-to-face, inches apart, close enough that John could have leaned forward and touched Latham's lips with his own. And oh, for a moment, he wanted to do it. He wanted to forget his worries. He wanted to take everything this man offered—his principles, his person.

Ah, he thought at that unfurling emotion. *This. This. This is why I need to keep him at bay.*

He wasn't going to let go of his defenses for so small a gift as ordinary human kindness.

Life. Liberty. The pursuit of happiness. God, what he would have given for his family to have been born with the recognized right to just one of those. It hurt, having this pretty man—this treacherous liar—mouth sentiments that he'd yearned for before in the darkness of night. He wanted to reach out and lay hold of the man, to claim those lies for the truth he yearned for.

Instead, he made himself lie still. Told his overactive nerves to quiet down. He looked in the other man's eyes, made himself concentrate on the hay poking his side until the discomfort took over his desire.

"According to you," John said, "I was born with those rights. They're not yours to give. I won't thank you for them."

"It's just…" Latham sighed. "Never mind."

"Are you done?"

"Yes," Latham said. "I…think so."

"Good." John turned around, offering the man his shoulder. "Go to sleep. We've a long ways to go."

Chapter Five

JOHN COULD FEEL SLEEP TUGGING his eyes shut, fogging his brain. The hayloft was warm; the straw was comfortable. Beside him, Latham drifted off in no time at all, a solid presence that he could sense even in the darkness. It would be all too easy to fall into a deep sleep.

But even slumber seemed a lie. To sleep with his back to another man was to take that man for his comrade. It required a certain degree of trust, and to give it unearned seemed anathema. Comfort was a freedom-stealing lie.

Life. Liberty. The pursuit of happiness. Stretching for ideals like those, well... They just made him forget that at the end of the day, he didn't know where his sister was. If she was well. If she was *alive*. There was no room for ideals in his life. There was no room for anything except fighting. Surviving.

After Latham's breaths evened out, John slipped out of the blankets, made his way down the rickety ladder by feel, found his coat, and slipped out the barn door.

It was frigid outside the barn. The stables and the two wings of the inn made a little open-sided courtyard. The moon was a slim, silver crescent overhead, providing just enough light for him to make out a stone well in the center of that space.

There were stars overhead, twinkling with a faint, mocking light.

He should just leave. The open road called to him in the gloom, beckoning him on. Latham was too soft. Yes, he'd kept up thus far, but only because John's arm had restricted his movement. He was getting better—he stretched his arm out, feeling a twinge, but it was a good twinge. He could go faster, farther, longer.

He would do anything for his mother. For Lizzie. He would do anything in his power. He just didn't know what he needed to do, and the unknown ate away at him.

He should leave. John was doing his best to avoid despair; Henry preferred to stay in inns and eat freshly baked bread by the fire.

John's master had told him once that while he didn't hold with beating his slaves, others did—and that it wasn't cruelty because black men didn't feel pain the way white men did. That, he had said, was why he always had his slaves on the most dangerous jobs in his shipyard. If they fell from the heights, or if a beam pinched their shoulder... Well, it wouldn't hurt them as much, would it? It was simple humanitarianism, his master had said.

That sentiment was bullshit of the highest order.

John felt pain. The cold of the night made his skin into miniature cobblestones. It bit into his toes. John ought to have put his shoes on before leaving the stables. The cold did nothing to alleviate the ache in the pads of his feet, that persistent throb of flesh abused by the day's journey.

He sat on the edge of the well and felt his thighs protest.

He wasn't magic; he felt pain.

Lizzie, Lizzie. I'm coming.

He felt hope, too, no matter how much life had tried to rob him of that. He'd felt it in the afternoon. He'd felt it that night, looking into Latham's eyes. He felt it now, thinking of Lizzie's last letter. Life could not be so cruel as to take his loved ones away now, not when he'd survived an entire war to come...home.

Home, such as it was. Home was Newport, a city where his family was being threatened simply because they were free and black. Some home.

Life could be so cruel.

Latham was nothing but trouble, and really, John ought to leave.

That he didn't, that he sat out here in the cold looking at the stars, letting numbness seep into his fingers... That was idiotic.

The barn door creaked. He turned.

Latham didn't say anything as he crept out. He'd brought half the blankets with him, and he wore them draped over his shoulders like a multipointed cape.

"Couldn't sleep?" he asked once he stood close by.

John nodded.

"Looking at the stars?"

John nodded again. "My mother told me that the stars were different in Africa. When she first got off the ship in Charleston, it was night, and she thought she'd been taken to hell."

Latham didn't answer.

"I recognize," John said dryly, "that the earth is round and that the stars are fixed at a great distance. I labored for a ship-wright. I'm no fool."

"I had not said otherwise."

Somehow that just made John angrier. "It's really about your own feelings, you know."

"Your pardon?"

"All your talk of people being equal. It's not about me. It's about you. You want to believe all people are equal because it excuses your transgressions. You say 'all men are created equal' because back in Britain, you never questioned your tea or your sugar or your rum. You didn't ask who grew the cotton you wore. You never needed to. Your talk of equality is a sword, not an olive branch. If you say we are equals, you think I'll forget that you are complicit in the misery your kind inflicts on mine."

Latham still did not answer.

It was easier to talk this way than to think how helpless he was, how many miles still separated him from his desperation.

"All you idealists have a bit of Thomas Jefferson in you," John continued. "You fall short of your professed ideals and seek to make up the difference by condescending to those you see as beneath you. But your condescension does not make me feel equal."

Latham sat on the well next to John. He wrapped the blankets about himself, then set one elbow on his knee and his chin on his hand. Swathed in blankets as he was, it made him look like some sort of gnome.

"It's a fair criticism," he said quietly. "Very fair. In my defense, it's a new ideal for me. I'm still trying to make everything fit."

"That's a terrible defense," John replied. "Am I supposed to excuse you because it has only *recently* occurred to you that I could be on your level?"

"Also…a fair criticism." Latham frowned. "I've got these horribly awkward bits of elitist thought poking out everywhere, and I'm doing my damnedest to uncover them. It hurts my head, but clearly the situation has been, um, rather more personal to you than a little intellectual discomfort."

"Ha."

"You've been incredibly patient with me," Latham said. "I'm a horrible fumbler."

"Is that why you've agreed to accompany me? I'm nothing but a lesson to you. I suppose I'd be a valuable one at that. I'm black. I'm a former slave. If you wanted an object on whom to practice your equality, you could hardly do better."

Latham turned his head. "John."

The single syllable of his name echoed in the courtyard.

"I prefer to be addressed as Hunter."

Latham shifted toward him on the bench. "I am with you because you looked into my eyes on the battlefield and saw not an enemy but a man. You gave me your coat. I wasn't the only one who committed something like treason that night. You trusted me with your life when you could easily have taken mine."

"Idiocy," John muttered. "Utter idiocy."

"Empathy," Latham said. "I hold these truths to be self-evident, John. That all men are created equal. And yes, you're right. It *is* about my feelings. I desperately want to believe that I have the capacity, the right, to have everything that I've never dreamed possible. That even I—strange, odd, treasonous me, the Henry who can never focus on one thought long enough to finish a conversation—deserve happiness."

John didn't answer.

"Maybe that is selfishness," Latham said. "But then, maybe an ideal is nothing more than selfishness writ large. Caring for someone else with the hope that if you do, someone will in turn care for you. Maybe my ideals only feel so intense because my hope is so desperate."

"Ha," John said. "What do you know of desperation?"

"I don't. I don't know. But right now, I have blankets and you are freezing. If you are going to sit outside fretting, I can do something about that. Come here."

John looked over at the other man.

"I have no nicety of principle," Latham said. "I was in the infantry for years. I don't mind sharing body heat." His voice dropped. "In point of fact... I rather like it."

Strange. Odd. Treasonous. They were confusing words to come from a man who exhibited all the trappings of wealth. Not so confusing, perhaps, if that man had listened to church-goers talk about men who liked men, the way John had not.

"Come here." Latham gestured. "Stop freezing."

John let out a breath. So. Latham had wondered *what if*, too.

It didn't change anything. John refused to think of the other man that way. He wasn't going to let the contact, thigh on thigh, mean anything when Latham shifted six inches over. He was going to ignore everything when Henry—*Latham*, he meant—put his arm around him, arranging the blankets over the two of them like a little tent.

"Your fingers are ice." It sounded like Latham was scolding.

"Sorry, I'll keep them to myself."

"Nonsense." Latham's hands pressed around his, swallowing him in warmth. "What would be the point of that when I've warmth enough for two? You have to take care of yourself." The man *was* scolding. "You've several hundred some odd miles to travel still, and here you are, freezing yourself in the middle of the night and not sleeping. Sleep is necessary to recover from injury. How are you supposed to manage your distance tomorrow, and the day after, if you keep on like this?"

John didn't answer. Latham shifted again, pressing their thighs more firmly together.

What if John were to kiss him?

Latham, he was sure, would manage to talk through it, somehow.

His lips would be warm and his skin would be rough, but *God*, he'd know how to use his tongue.

Good thing there was never going to be a what-if between them.

"If you're going to fret," Latham said, "for God's sake, man, do it in a way that doesn't hurt yourself."

Latham's arm crept around his waist, a warm bar.

"You're a regular furnace," John heard himself say.

"Nonsense. We burn at the same temperature, didn't you know? I learned that from the camp doctor. It's not so surprising, after all. We have the same flesh, with the same ability to conduct heat and cold. I'm not naturally warm. I just wasn't outside as long as you, that's all."

"Mmm." It was hard to hate a man who shared his blankets. Harder still when his hand on John's waist—steady, not importuning at all—gave John ideas that he really ought not have, not about a man he was apparently going to be traveling with for quite a while.

Equality was well and good, but...

Strange, odd, treasonous me.

But the miles went by more pleasantly when Latham was around. His chatter was amusing, John had to admit. God knew John needed to be distracted from his thoughts of the future. He served a purpose.

And for all his chatter, Latham *listened* when John spoke. He never puffed up and demanded to know why John was questioning his character. He listened to John.

What if...

Slowly, John turned his head. Leaned in, so that his nose brushed the other man's shoulder. Deliberately, he set his hand —still cold, if not as frozen as it had been—against the other man's thigh. Even through the fabric of Latham's trousers, he felt his muscles tense.

He could feel the warm exhalation of Latham's breath against his cheek, a shuddering waft of air.

Yes, he thought. *I'm here. I'm like you.*

Latham did not move. Not for moments. Not until his free hand came up and gently—ever so gently—rested on top of John's hand on his thigh. He didn't move John's hand away. Instead, he acknowledged its presence. The inappropriateness of it. The implications—what it meant for both of them—and what his acceptance meant.

They sat in silence, on the well.

Just this much, John told himself. Just this much held no meaning. It was nothing more than an acknowledgement of something they both knew. John's own inclinations had to have been obvious as well, if Latham had come out here, sat like this with him.

It meant absolutely nothing.

"You're the one who needs sleep," John finally said. "We'd best go back to…" He paused. Not *bed;* that had its hidden implications, ones he didn't want to think through at the moment. "We'd best go back to the barn, Latham."

"It's Henry. I prefer that you call me Henry."

"Henry." John sighed and gave in. "But it's still Mr. Hunter to you."

IT WAS a lovely afternoon for walking, the second they had encountered in a row. The trees were mostly bare by now, which meant that despite the cold air, bright sun touched John's face, unfiltered by anything except a few branches reaching to the sky.

He'd left the sling behind several days ago. As he walked, he moved his arm, subtly, in its socket, testing the range—just enough to twinge, a good kind of pain, before backing off.

Henry was talking.

That, John realized, would be surprising to nobody in the universe who knew the man at all.

Henry was amusing, thoughtful, a complete chatterbox, and —incidentally—also an inveterate liar. Percentage-wise he probably didn't lie much more than the average man. But given the sheer volume of words that proceeded from his mouth, he uttered approximately a hundred times more lies than John. And he had a tendency to deliver them all at once.

"So at any rate," Henry was saying, "when I was taking articles—"

"One moment." John held up a hand. "When you were taking articles? Isn't that what one does when one wants to be a barrister?"

Henry wrinkled his nose. "Ah. Yes. Well, so it is."

"Didn't you tell me once you were a potter's son?" Or maybe it had been a tailor. There had been as many professions as there had been days.

"Ah, ha ha. Well. Yes, I did, and there are potters' sons who...still, possibly that might have been a bit of a...um, how do I say this? A bit of an exaggeration." Henry gave him a brilliant smile. "My father...did own a pottery works? It wasn't entirely a lie."

More than two weeks of walking. Two weeks of Henry talking; several days of thinking of him as Henry rather than Latham, a transition that had occurred all too swiftly. That much time, John had spent listening to the other man's exaggerations. He was used to it by now.

"So your father owned a pottery works. You were planning to be a barrister. How did you wind up in the infantry?"

"Did you know that people want barristers who are capable of talking about the same thing for more than two minutes at a time?" Henry shot back brightly. "I *did* know that, but my father had to be convinced that it was the case."

"Your father the potter?"

"Uh. Yes. Him." Henry simply waved a hand. "It does all make sense, and I'll explain as soon as I...um, take care of some business over by that copse of trees. If you know what I mean."

John did know what he meant, and he wasn't referring to

Henry's need to piss. Henry avoided all questions about his father, except to roundly decry him as terrible. The only thing John was sure of was that he *wasn't* a potter. He was likely not even a pottery works owner. Henry was hiding something.

It would be offensive, except he was so inept at hiding it hardly counted. It was like draping a blanket over a statue and pinning a sign to it that said *NO STATUE UNDER HERE, HA HA, WHY WOULD YOU THINK THAT?*

Henry's family was obviously wealthy—enough so that Henry, with his talk of equality and such, felt it an embarrassment.

But one could not hide the tracks left by wealth. John could hear it in his voice. He could hear it in his surprised exclamations.

"Who knew squirrel could be so delicious?" he'd remarked the first night they'd made stew of the hapless creatures who'd made the mistake of chattering excitedly at them from the road.

An officer in the infantry, and he'd never eaten squirrel? John knew that officers tended to use their own funds to purchase provisions, and that wealthy officers tended to eat well, but...

Never eaten *squirrel?*

He didn't complain about hard biscuit either. He acted as if it were a special treat.

"Goodness," Henry had said. "I'd always wondered what it was like, and now I know!"

He'd *wondered*. He had *wondered*, as if it were a line in a story and not the desperate reality for thousands of men.

Henry had just continued on the road, eating squirrels and hard biscuits with the absolutely terrible cheese that he tried every meal.

He may have been born wealthy, but his clumsy attempt to pretend otherwise was endearing. Or—at least—John corrected himself, it would have been, if John had been the sort to allow himself to be endeared. Henry hadn't even sighed wistfully five minutes ago when they'd passed a cottage. The wind had carried with it the scent of cooking food—savory meat and the yeasty smell of baking bread. Even John had glanced longingly in that direction before moving on.

It had been days since their last warm meal.

The wind shifted and John caught the scent of that bread again. He hoped Henry hurried his business up—story about his father or no, John hated wanting things he couldn't have, and bread was something of a personal weakness.

Crusty bread. Brown bread. Steaming bread, hot from the oven. Damn it.

John's stomach grumbled. At that moment, leaves crackled, presaging someone's arrival. He turned. Two men had come out of the trees. They were white, and they looked at John with narrowed eyes.

"Told you so," one said to the other.

"Walking about on the road, just like that."

God. The last thing John needed now was to be accosted by the locals. This, this was the sort of thing that might have happened to his mother in Newport. One day at the market, they might have—

He clamped down on that train of thought before it spread into panic.

"I'll be moving on," he assured them. "I've no desire to stay."

The two men exchanged glances. The one who spoke next had sandy-brown hair and a gap in his teeth. "But who knows what you've taken? That's what I say."

The other man—ruddy skin contrasting with dark, curly hair—nodded. "In fact," he said, "I think we should search your pack just to be sure you haven't stolen anything. We'll hold on to anything suspicious we find, just in case the real owners turn up."

So it was to be a kind of shakedown. He didn't have enough that he could afford to lose anything. John stepped in front of his pack. He was going to have to hold firm.

"Hand it over," said Gap Tooth.

John grimaced. "I would really rather not."

Curly Hair just shook his head. "It will be a real shame to have to report you to the constable. We live just down the road.

He knows us." He pointed in the direction of the cottage. "We're good, God-fearing folk. *Who* knows *you?*"

"Oh dear Lord." The words came from behind them as Henry materialized from between the trees. "You mean you *don't* know him?"

They turned as one. They caught sight of Henry. He paused, as if on instinct, to let them look him over. There was no sign that he'd been doing his business. There was no sign that he'd been on the road for weeks. Every morning, he wielded his razor like an expert. His cheeks were close-shaven; his clothing was almost new. His boots were dark, the leather not cracked by time.

Henry held his own pack over his shoulder as if it were a light jacket instead of a bag containing all his worldly belongings. He posed, arm cocked at his hip, eyes bright and wide. He looked like he belonged anywhere—his glossy not-quite-blond hair, his too-jaunty hat, his coat that spoke of riches. He wasn't trying to look like a potter's son now.

The men frowned, then exchanged glances with each other. Those glances said that they had no idea what Henry was talking about.

John had been feeling that way for the last fortnight.

"You've truly never heard of him?" Henry asked. "That's Corporal John Hunter. Corporal. Jonathan. Lewis. Hunter. Does that jog your memory?"

John didn't have a middle name, but Henry said it so sincerely that he almost doubted his own memory.

Gap Tooth shook his head. "Not...really?"

Henry continued on. "Corporal Hunter, Scourge of the Rhode Island Regiment?" He waited expectantly. Curly Hair shrugged.

"John Hunter, Bane of the British? Ruin of the redcoats? Enemy of the English?"

The two men just squinted at Henry.

"Surely you have heard of the Lacerator of the Loyalists? The Curse of the Crown? *That* John Hunter?"

"Um." Gap Tooth looked as befuddled as John felt. "No?"

"For God's sake. I knew the British had suppressed news of

our American heroes, but I didn't know they had been so successful. This is a travesty. An utter travesty."

Curly Hair's eyebrows scrunched down in confusion.

John had no idea what the other man was doing, but… Damn, this would not turn out well.

"Latham," John said through gritted teeth. "You're embarrassing me."

"Humble, too," Henry said, waving off the warning tone in John's voice. "Why, at the Battle of Germantown, he saved Washington himself from a detachment of British soldiers. They had snuck into the encampment before him. Had you not *heard* this story of attempted assassination?"

"No!" Despite themselves, the two men crept closer to Latham.

"Yes!" Latham was clearly warming to his story. "Major General the Lord Cornwallis, God rot his soul, had the most dastardly plan. He intended to kill Washington by subterfuge, thus depriving the Continental Army of its most powerful leader."

Curly Hair gasped. "Of course he did, that worm."

"Cornwallis had his men slay seven Continental soldiers— good men, including my comrade Duncan—but that's a story for another day." Henry paused, looking upward, as if to commemorate the passing of a lost soul.

Curly Hair tilted his head.

"The threat to Washington? How'd that turn out?"

John found himself mildly curious about what he was supposed to have done, too.

"Ah." Henry seemed to return to the present. "That evil man dressed his most trusted, most stealthy soldiers in Continental blue. He sent them into the encampment where Washington was quartered. Washington had sent scouts out to survey the land. His aide-de-camp, the, uh…" Henry faltered. "The esteemed, uh—"

"Hamilton," John put in. "His name is Alexander Hamilton."

Henry waved a hand in his direction. "Don't interrupt me, Hunter. As I was saying. The esteemed Hamilton had gone to oversee the front. Never believe that Washington was left unprotected, of course; he was no fool. But those cowardly, cravenly men in American uniform strode into camp as if they owned the place. They walked through the encampment, and before anyone knew what was happening, they slew Washington's inner guard. Washington cried for help—but only one man had the eagle ears to hear it."

"Who was that?" John asked.

Henry gave him an annoyed look, quickly masked by a sweet smile. "I am *so* glad you asked. It was Jonathan Lewis Hunter, *that* was who. Just as the spying, lying British soldiers surrounded Washington, Hunter here" —Henry clapped John on the back—"entered his tent."

John glared at Henry; Henry looked at his hand and yanked his arm away with a sheepish smile.

"Gah," said Gap Tooth. "One man, against so many?"

"Precisely. John was just one man. He hadn't any warning. He had naught on him but...a stick." Henry looked off into the distance. "A stick and a single carving knife that he had been using to whittle it into a ship."

John raised an eyebrow.

"How was he to defend his commander with such an item?" Henry posed this hypothetical.

"General," John interjected. "Washington is a general."

"General," Henry conceded. He didn't look at John, just smiled at the other two men. "I used the word 'commander' to describe what he did—commanded. In other words, I used it generally. To encompass generals. But back to the matter at hand. Corporal Jonathan Lewis Hunter had only those sparse weapons, to compare with the muskets and the wicked swords of his seven enemies. But he had one thing they did not."

"What?" Curly Hair asked.

A man willing to lie for him? John knew better than to provide that answer.

"Determination. He looked those devils in the eye and said one thing: 'I cannot allow you to kill my commander.'"

That sounded like a great deal more than *one* thing. Still...

"General," John interjected.

"General," Henry agreed. "That's what I said, isn't it? Stop interrupting. 'I cannot allow you to kill my general,' he said. 'You'll get to him when you go through me.'"

"So what happened next?" Gap Tooth asked.

"What, next? Oh." Latham paused. He looked up at the sun and sighed. "I'm sorry, gentlemen. We haven't had a hot meal in days, and we mean to make South Brunswick by nightfall. We must be on our way."

Gap Tooth glanced at Curly Hair. Curly Hair looked back. The two men gave each other a nod.

"I'm William," said Gap Tooth. "William Williamson. This is my friend David Poitier."

"Williamson. Poitier." Latham nodded at them. "We're pleased to make your acquaintance. I'm just Henry Latham, but I hardly need to introduce my traveling companion. Jonathan Lewis Hunter himself."

The men glanced at Hunter.

"He may shake your hand if you ask nicely," Latham said. "But he's very circumspect. Too humble, really. He hates admitting his role in things."

Poitier and Williamson had apparently forgotten that they'd started the encounter by attempting to rob John. They glanced at each other. Then Williamson turned to John.

"Mr. Hunter," he said, holding out his hand, "it's truly an honor."

"I…" John sighed. He took the other man's hand. "Right."

Poitier elbowed Williamson, who coughed and spoke. "Would either of you…want some soup?"

Chapter Six

THEY HAD SOUP—THICK soup, laden with beef, barley, and carrots. There was bread, cut in generous slices and spread with butter.

There was, of course, the continuation of Henry's tale, which he was determined to render with as much animation as possible. It had, after all, earned them a dinner. He invented details. He was the *best* at inventing details. John defeated one man with a map pulled off a table, another with his own musket. He confounded a third by slinging buttons pulled off a fallen comrade into his eyes—"very effective weapons, buttons are, if hurled hard enough," Henry explained, and the two men nodded, drinking in every word as if the tale were as good as the soup.

Poitier cut up apples, listening with starry eyes, as Henry made his way through the ending.

"As our good corporal faced the last man," Henry said, "bodies strewn about him, blood streaming down his face, his knife held before him in a low grip, well, what do you think he said?"

Williams was watching, wide-eyed. "I don't know. What did he say?"

"'You'll get to my general when you get through me.'" Henry gave a low growl. "He had no thought of his own wounds. He thought only of Washington, our great American Republic, and freedom. He raised his knife."

Henry gestured with his hands—one raised like the blade he'd described, the other gesturing an unknown assailant forward.

"What heroism!" Poitier clasped his hands together.

Beside him, Hunter rolled his eyes. "It was nothing," he said in a tone that conveyed that it had, in fact, been literally nothing.

Henry ignored that shameful failure to play along. "Faced with such courage, there was nothing the enemy could do. The man dropped his sword and ran, a coward to the end."

Poitier cheered. "Good riddance to the British bastard!"

Henry nodded solemnly. He was himself a British bastard; he ought to get some small satisfaction playing the role. "General Washington himself gave me the sacred command to accompany Hunter home. Loyalists still speak his name in hushed, envenomed whispers. Washington feared for his safety on the road. So here I am. And, gentlemen, we thank you for the meal—but we must be on our way."

Williamson sighed, as if he didn't wish to come to his senses. Poitier looked as if he'd been struck with a bouquet of daisies, a silly smile playing all over his face.

"Take some biscuits," Poitier said. "You'll be hungry come evening. It's the least we can do for such a hero."

"I'll wrap some roast chicken," Williamson offered.

"And the apples. We've an abundance of apples; we'll be sick of apples by midwinter."

They returned to the road fifteen minutes later, laden with fruit, nuts, and wax paper packets of chicken.

There was a feeling of exuberance that Henry got when he managed to make others happy. He felt it now. It put a lightness in his step, got him to whistling. Why, when he'd first encountered those men, they had been...

Um.

Too late, he realized that they'd been incredibly hostile to Hunter. So hostile. Good God, he'd forgotten about that, getting carried away with his story. He'd intervened, not

thinking of anything except lightening the mood. And then...
He had gotten a little carried away. They'd lost an hour's walking
time.

"So." He glanced over at Hunter. "Well. About that...story.
I'm sure...you're wondering where it came from."

Hunter looked over at him. His face was an unreadable
mask. "A stick. A knife. That's what I fought seven men
off with?"

"There were buttons," Henry protested. "Do not forget the
buttons."

"Did you know those two intended to rob me before you
appeared?"

"Indeed. I panicked, not remembering any Latin."

Hunter was probably angry. He had every reason to be. The
two of them had even been talking about Henry's lies when he'd
wandered off. Now the man must think him an even bigger liar.

And he wasn't *wrong*.

"I suppose..." Henry bit his lip. "Maybe... I shouldn't
have..."

John broke and snickered. He actually *snickered*. "No, please
don't apologize."

Henry stared at the other man a moment.

"You're not...angry?"

"That was the most ridiculous thing I've *ever* seen. You
just...you told them that I—and a *stick*—" Another round of
guffaws shook his shoulders.

"I got slightly carried away," Henry admitted. "I don't know
why I do this—these ideas just pop into my head and I say
them without thinking. I can't even blame my upbringing. My
father did his best to make me stop, but..."

"But people like listening to you talk," Hunter said, "and so
he never managed to make the lesson stick."

Henry blinked. He looked over at Hunter. "Did you
just say...?"

"Of *course* people like listening to you talk." Hunter
repeated that as if it were obvious. "You're funny, and even when
you're lying you say things that people want to believe. You're
not frivolous, no matter what you've been told. You mean well

and you like people, and you make them want to like you in return. Anyone who mistakes that for frivolity has no understanding of human nature."

Henry stopped walking. A brown bird flew overhead. The sky was clear and the air frigid. Reality seemed very close all of a sudden.

Hunter realized he'd stopped a few moments later. He turned, raised one eyebrow inquiringly. "What? If you're going to stop dead in your tracks every time I say something vaguely positive about you, this will be a very long journey. Hurry up now."

The implication that there would be *more*… Henry hastened to catch up, his head spinning.

"What?" Hunter asked. "Surely you've *noticed* that people like you by now?"

It had never been put to him in those terms. *People like you.* It was such a radical departure from the image he had in his own head—*talks too much, barely tolerated*—that for a second, he could not accommodate both thoughts. They warred in his head.

Nobody wants to listen to you.

Just thinking that it might not be true made Henry want to babble all the more.

"It's not that," Henry finally said, struggling to mask his feelings. "It's—it's amazing, I suppose, that instead of saying, 'Well, Henry, I think you're a decent fellow,' you have to hide behind general talk of *people* and such-like. Admit it. You like me."

"People like you." Hunter shrugged. "I generally count myself as a person. Where is the problem?"

"You admit it, then. You don't hate me!"

Hunter just smiled. "If I did, I'd have killed you outside Philadelphia. I've been known to take on an entire British regiment with a stick and a paring knife. You'd go down, no trouble at all."

Their eyes met. It was such a foolish thing, to be so happy that someone was issuing threats in his direction, but they weren't threats, and it was so lovely, so lovely. After a moment, they both laughed.

Oh, Henry thought, oh. This was nice. This was very nice. He could get used to this. He could get used to this, even though he knew he shouldn't.

"Hunter," he said, "I'll remind you that you said that later. No trouble at all. It sounds not very like me, doesn't it?"

Hunter just looked at him and shook his head. "Oh for God's sake."

"Mmm?"

"Call me John."

۞

"HERE." It was night. They'd made camp, and a small fire to warm their hands over. Henry leaned across the stone that sat between them, handing John something. "I'm not taking no for an answer again. Try it."

He dropped the slice of cheese into John's waiting palm. His fingertips touched John's hand briefly—a hint of warmth, quickly disappearing into the cold of night.

Henry cut off his own bit of cheese. The odor was rank this close, pungent and foul.

"Has it got any better?" John wrinkled his nose, inspecting the cheese.

"Not yet, but it should start improving any day now."

"You want me to voluntarily put this in my mouth and eat it?"

"Yes, and furthermore, while you do, say to yourself: 'The cheese is delicious.'"

John's eyes met Henry's. A spark from the fire popped, burning orange between them before going dark.

"'The cheese is delicious.'"

"Not in that monotone. Say it like you mean it. 'This *cheese* is *delicious*.' There. Like that."

John's voice lowered to something almost smoky. "This cheese is *delicious*."

Henry felt that last word inside him, like a caress.

"There." John brought his hand to his mouth.

Henry did likewise. It would have been almost romantic—looking into each other's eyes, raising their hands simultaneously to their lips.

It would have been romantic, except the taste of death hit his tongue, dissolving into a thousand liquid deaths.

The cheese was most decidedly *not* delicious.

Across from him, John coughed. He sputtered.

"Oh fuck me," John said, spitting the cheese out. "No warning! You gave me absolutely no warning."

Henry laughed through his mouthful. "I did! I told you it was terrible every night!"

"I knew it was bad—you said it was bad—this cheese is not *bad.*"

The main objective in the moment, Henry realized, was to not snort grains of foul-tasting cheese out of his nose. He clamped his hands over his mouth.

"*Bad* is for things that are ordinarily bad. *Armies* would unite to fight this cheese. This is the cheese of hell."

Henry swallowed his own cheese. "The cheese is delicious," he managed to choke out. "My...taste in cheese? May need some time to, um, become accustomed to that fact."

John pointed a finger at him over the fire. "That is not how reality works," he warned. "You cannot change reality just by insisting it's not so. That's called delusion, not reality."

"You're probably right. But—for the sake of argument—what if we were born deluded, and had to be, um, undeluded? I imagine it would take time."

"No amount of time would change the Cheese of Death into anything other than the Cheese of Death."

"Care to place a bet?"

"What stakes could possibly justify *that*? I'd have to eat the cheese. *Often.*"

Henry frowned. "Loser must provide the winner with a medal proclaiming 'Well, at least you tried.'"

Their eyes met across the fire. Henry waggled one eyebrow in what he hoped was a winning manner. And apparently, it worked.

"Well." John's lips twitched into a crooked smile. "Who wouldn't risk certain death for such a prize?"

⚜

"To you," John said, lifting his cheese like a libation of hard spirits about thirty miles from the Connecticut border. "The cheese is delicious."

Henry ate his own cheese. "A fine bouquet," he said, still choking on the taste. "There's...an underlying flavor, if you pay attention."

"Beneath the taste of death mold."

"Yes, beneath that."

"Once you ignore the feeling of impending doom that takes over your taste buds."

"Yes, definitely ignore that. There's an underlying subtleness that is almost...not completely terrible."

"Not completely terrible," John said. "You *are* making strides."

"Do you see what I mean? That...subtle...thing there, at the end? Surely you taste it."

"No," John replied. "It's all terrible."

⚜

"Speaking of not completely terrible," Henry said, two nights later after they'd performed their usual ritual of cheese eating and cheese complaining, "if you think Jefferson is so awful, how is it you were fighting with the Continental forces?"

John looked at him over the fire. Slowly, he sighed.

"You had to have *some* feeling for this...America...thing." He could not believe it had not occurred to him before.

John's eyes shut. "I wasn't fighting for the Revolution. I was fighting for Lizzie. And Noah."

Henry waited.

"When I was sixteen," John said, "my master hit hard times. Mostly self-inflicted—gambling was always his issue. He sold my mother."

John said that so matter-of-factly, yet at his side, his hand clenched.

"Up until that point, I had only dreamed of running away. I'd made elaborate plans. I knew when I'd leave. What I would say beforehand to allay suspicion. I even knew what to do to guarantee my freedom so long as I made it far enough. But…"

"You needed a push?"

"But there was my mother. And Lizzie, my little sister? I had told myself a pack of lies—that I could protect her, that I could make our master listen. She was his child. I thought that meant *something*, that one day, as long as I made myself useful…" John shrugged this away. "It was a delusion, and I lost my delusions. At the end of the day, he sold my mother, and my delusions were no comfort at all. So I left."

"As you should have."

John's hand clenched at his side. "I left Lizzie. She was too little to come, too little to even trust. I couldn't tell her I was going; if there was any chance she would spill my secrets, it would ruin everything. I left her there, in slavery, all alone, at eleven—no mother, no brother, no protection." His voice trembled. "Anything could have happened to her."

"Did it?"

John exhaled a long breath. His hands unclenched. "No. I made my way north. I found a job, I learned to read. I changed my last name to Hunter—it sounded strong, and the name he had given me did not seem like one I wanted to keep." A faint smile touched his lips. "I knew my master had been cheating his business partner, and that plan I had for freedom? When I left, I took his account books. Once I had a firm foothold in life, I found someone trustworthy to go to him and tell him that if he didn't release me and my sister and give us paperwork that declared us freed, I'd send his partner his account books."

"Did that work?"

"It did." John sighed. "My mother—finding her, raising the money to free her, that took another five years. But Lizzie came of age a free woman in Rhode Island, and…" John's smile was just a little sad.

"And?"

"She fell in love. His name was Noah Allan, and he was enslaved."

"In Rhode Island? I thought slavery was a Southern practice."

The fire flickered across John's face, illuminating those perfect cheekbones. He was looking away, at something.

"Mmm. Not so much. There are more than a handful of slaves in Rhode Island. As for Newport itself... It depends heavily on the slave trade. Or at least it did, before the British occupied it. I told Lizzie to love someone else, but... Well, apparently love doesn't work like that."

No, Henry thought stupidly, watching the fire play across John's skin. It didn't.

"We had plans for him, too. It was going to take time and saving. But then war broke out, and Mr. Allan's son enlisted, full of patriotic fervor. Some time later, Rhode Island announced that any slave who enlisted would be automatically freed. Noah was all set to enlist. Newport was occupied at the time, but it would have been no large matter for a slave to slip out in order to pass muster. But Mr. Allan cried that he needed the help, and Lizzie just cried, and..." John shrugged. "And I thought Lizzie had had enough of men she loved leaving her to obtain their freedom. So I made a contract with Mr. Allan. I'd enlist in Noah's stead, and in exchange he agreed to free him when the war ended, or upon my death, or after three years."

There was a way that John said Lizzie's name, something both soft and impenetrable, all at once. "You fought in a war you didn't believe in for *years* to free the man your sister loved?"

John shrugged, as if it were nothing. "People have fought wars for far stupider reasons. And this time I told her why I was going, and I promised to come back to her."

"And here you are. Coming back."

John looked away. "It was a lie," he said softly. "Every man who died on a battlefield had promised some sweetheart he would return. Some months ago, Allan freed Noah. He and Lizzie were married, and there began to be...incidents. Newport was much worsened by the British occupation, and people who have little often resent those they believe should have less. Rudenesses at first, then things left on my family's doorstep. My sister said she expected they'd be warned out at any moment."

"People are terrible."

"I promised to come back," John said softly, "and here I am, coming, as fast as I can. But I have not heard from Lizzie in six months, and I do not know if there is a back to return to any longer."

Henry swallowed. "I'm sure—"

John held up a hand. "You're not sure of anything. I'll say it all for you. The mail in the army has been wretched. It was wretched during the occupation, and it's not much better now. I try not to let the worry wear down my spirit, but…" Another shrug. "If I've been a bit harsh with you, that's why. I've been eaten up with worry these last weeks."

Henry sat up straight, started to reach out a hand, and then pulled it back. "Don't apologize."

Their eyes met again over the fire. A spark blossomed in his chest, painful and fierce and desperate, all at once. It was a wild feeling. A generous feeling. He wanted to take the world down, brick by brick, and put it back together again the way it was supposed to be. Nobody should have to worry, not like this. Least of all John.

Oh, Henry thought. *Oh. That's what this is.* It was… Friendship, but warmer. Care, but with a softness to it. It was a journey shared, coming closer to the end with every day.

"Very well," John said. "Then I won't apologize. You'll do it prettily enough for both of us if I just keep my mouth shut."

"*You* made a joke." Henry found himself smiling. "I like when you make jokes."

John didn't smile in response. That would have trivialized the light in his eyes, the amused purse of his lips. He didn't smile, but he shook his head. "I do that sometimes. That's what friends do."

Chapter Seven

JOHN EYED that night's cheese dubiously. It had become a ritual between them—cheese every night, just before dinner, so they could drown out the taste with whatever meal they had.

The fire was crackling; the brace of pigeons he'd fetched with his sling roasted merrily on a spit. When he stretched his arm, he could almost straighten it all the way out before his shoulder complained. He could mark the passing of this journey by these little things.

"The cheese is delicious," he said.

"Say it as if you mean it, John." Henry spoke from across the fire.

John looked up. Looked into his companion's eyes—wide, open, inviting.

"The cheese is *delicious*."

Speaking of things they were lying about…He didn't know why he did it—maybe for no better reason than it made him happy in a way that was deeply selfish—but he always tried to make eye contact with Henry when he said those words. He emphasized the word delicious, rolling the syllables off his tongue.

Delicious.

Henry flushed, right on cue. And if John's own cheeks

heated, well, that was no business of anyone's but his. Henry would never detect the blush.

John wasn't sure when Henry had transformed from *pretty British officer, not to be trusted* into *friend, definitely should be teased*. He wasn't sure if he was teasing himself or Henry. Both, he suspected.

That low sense of awareness built between them, coiling in John's gut, buzzing just beneath his skin. It simmered at night when they lay back-to-back.

But Henry hadn't said a word about it, for all his blushes, and if *Henry* didn't want to have a conversation about a topic, there was probably a reason. When Henry wanted to talk about his attraction to men in general, and John in particular, John trusted that he would do so. At length.

"Well?" That faint pinkening of Henry's cheeks—his entire face, nose, forehead—deepened under John's perusal. "If the cheese is delicious, eat it."

John put it in his mouth.

Maybe it was because he was still watching Henry. Maybe it was because he was thinking about Henry's attraction to him and avoiding the more salient, pressing matter of his own attraction to Henry. Maybe it was just the cheese.

Whatever the reason might have been, John's life changed forever in that moment for one undeniable reason.

He forgot to hate the cheese.

He forgot it so thoroughly, looking into Henry's eyes, that he didn't cough. He didn't spit out his mouthful. He chewed. He swallowed.

"My God," Henry murmured worshipfully. "It's happening. It's finally happening. I *told* you it was happening."

"What's happening?"

"I *told* you," Henry cackled. "I told you that it was starting to change. I told you that there was a richness to the flavor, but did you listen? No."

Oh. God. Damn. John straightened where he sat, tasting the lingering flavor on his tongue with something close to horror. It *had* been bad, hadn't it? Wretched? Disgusting?

"It wasn't *good*," he said defensively. "Don't get me wrong.

There was nothing *good* about it. Contempt for the Cheese of Death has wrought familiarity, that's all."

"Just wait. I've been doing this longer than you. This is how it starts."

This was how it started—watching the play of fire over Henry's skin, the shift of his smiles. This was how it started, treasuring the flash of his eyes, the ripple of the muscles in his behind when he stood and bent over the fire, poking the pigeons, sending a few drops of their juice to land sizzling in the coals.

It had started with teasing and friendship, and John had no idea where it would go.

John just shook his head. "This is how it *ends*."

৩⁺৩

"THE CHEESE IS DELICIOUS," Henry said a few nights later, biting into his sliver.

It wasn't delicious, not at the moment. But it had gone from utterly disgusting to almost palatable, and at this rate of progression, it would likely be ambrosia by the end of the year.

"The cheese is delicious," John echoed, sliding his own bite into his mouth. His tongue was shockingly pink, the cheese a white morsel against his skin. His skin drank up the firelight, reflecting orange and red and pink. Henry wanted to chase the sight of those colors with his fingers, tracing them, warm, along the path up John's neck. He shouldn't think of John's lips, but he did.

Also, he didn't think John *minded* him thinking of his lips, as he hadn't said anything like *why are you staring at my lips?* John would definitely have said that if he objected.

Possibly not.

"God rot it," John said in annoyance, frowning up at the starry firmament. "The cheese is improving. We can't have this."

"It's only natural."

"It is *not*. This should not work. You can't change the world around you just by claiming it's different."

"Of course you can," Henry said. "Once upon a time, somebody said 'Look, this piece of paper here equals a bit of gold,' and then everyone agreed that it was and here we are."

"Well, that's—"

"And once upon a time, someone stuck a bunch of sticks in the ground and said 'All the stuff inside these sticks is mine,' and everyone else said, 'Right-o' and went to fetch their own sticks. Most of the things we believe to be true are only true because we believe them, instead of the reverse."

"So if I believed you to be a rabbit..." John smiled at him.

"Ah, me!" Henry brightened. "My favorite topic of conversation. As it turns out, I am an *excellent* example of this phenomenon. You see, my father always believed me a frivolous man."

"Incapable of seeing beyond his nose, more like," John muttered.

"And so did everyone around him," Henry said. "Was he wrong? Or was his belief so powerful that he rendered me frivolous?"

"The fact that you can consider so ridiculous a question without bursting into laughter at the nonsensical nature of it rather agitates for the conclusion that you are not frivolous."

"My father told me, when he purchased my commission, that he hoped I died valiantly in battle, as it would be the only way I could do credit to the family."

John lifted the lid off the pot on the fire and poked at something inside it. "Your father is the anti-cheese. On inspection, he grows worse and worse."

"And then I arrived here," Henry said, "and I read that circular, and I had my thoughts. I engaged in the most frivolous treason anyone has ever engaged in. Even with him half an ocean distant, I couldn't undo his beliefs, though. I had made my peace with dying because he believed I should. It's hard to explain, but... I felt my choice was between living in England, frivolous and stupid, or dying here with a brain in my head. I couldn't imagine any other alternative."

"And now?"

"Now?" Henry sighed. "I'm living in a dream. In my dream,

I'm on a journey. It's a place removed from reality, and so I'm able to believe whatever I like."

"Yes," John said with a snort, "now *there* I very much disagree. I am not some figment of your dream. I exist. I am real. This is life, not some walking nightmare."

"For you it is," Henry said, eyes meeting his. "At the end of this journey, you'll have family and a home there to greet you."

John glanced sharply away.

"You told me to walk away from my life and not go back, but..." Henry sighed. "It's not practical. I have no skills except cheesemongering, and even that is suspect, as it takes any person weeks to find my cheese passable. Also, we are on the way to running out."

John did not point out that a potter's son ought to have had some skills. He didn't ask where the officers' commission had come from. With the exception of a few tiny comments, he let Henry's falsehoods lie when he could have made much of them. Henry was grateful for that. Still...

"I have sisters who are no doubt worrying about me, and a mother who is weeping, and even my terrible father may yet regret advising me to perish in a blaze of glory. I don't want to be a frivolous, irresponsible fellow, but walking away from the British Army in a fit of pique in the middle of battle may be the most frivolous thing I've ever done." Henry looked at John. "I don't want to die, but I don't know how to *live*, either."

John didn't say anything. He just stood, moved to sit next to Henry on the log. Having John close, having him sit down, his thigh warmed by the fire next to Henry—it was too much.

"And here you are," Henry said, "being kind to me when you have so many more non-frivolous things to worry about, and I'm spilling this *rubbish* on your shoulders."

John just took his hand. His fingers traced a pattern on Henry's palm. "Well, you know I can't outtalk you."

Henry's breath stopped. John was touching him. After weeks of distance, weeks of keeping a few careful inches between their backs at night... His mind ceased to function. He could feel his whole body shut down in appreciation. He looked blindly up at John, and even though his entire being was being consumed, he found he could still talk, because of course he could. "Nobody can outtalk me. It's a fact of nature."

"I don't know how to tell you to live. I rather think that's something you'll have to figure out for yourself."

His fingers traced a vein up Henry's arm, and oh, Henry wanted. He wanted to curl his fingers around John's wrist in return. He wanted to *live*.

"Yes, but—"

"But if I had made this trip alone, I'd have spent the entire time worrying myself into nothingness. I'd have had no conversation, nobody to make me laugh, nobody to feed me cheese, nobody to make me think."

"Nobody to save you from bandits with ridiculous stories," Henry said.

John reached out. The tips of his fingers brushed Henry's face, and Henry felt his heart stop.

Oh, God. If he believed his heart was stopping now, would he actually be dead? Was it possible to perish from a sharp influx of pleasure? Could one pass away from delight?

Henry took a breath, then another.

Apparently one couldn't, because John was touching him, and Henry had not died. That slow caress continued down his cheek.

"I don't know what to say to you except this," John murmured. "You have not been frivolous to me. You have been the foundation on which this journey is built. You have been necessary."

"Necessary?" Henry echoed.

John's thumb touched his lips.

"Necessary," John repeated.

Henry exhaled. He set his hand over John's. He should say something—anything. He didn't.

"When you figure out how to live again," John said, and he uttered *when* as if it were a foregone conclusion, not *if*, and Henry wanted, wanted, wanted, wanted to believe that *when* with his entire body. He wanted that *when* from the tips of his fingers, brushing against John's hand, to the thud of his heart. He wanted it from the aroused tingle that traveled down his spine all the way to his still-silent lips. "When you figure it out, then let me know."

Like smoke, John's hand slipped away.

৵৵৵

FOR SOME REASON—A haze of lust, perhaps, or inexplicable happiness, or some combination of the two—Henry found himself babbling throughout the next day.

No topic was too stupid for him not to remark upon. Chicken sexing (a noble career, although impossible to do, which Henry knew because he had tried when he was seven to no avail). Dogfighting (an ignoble career). Familial infighting (not a career, all too easy to do, but never as satisfying in reality as imagining a far superior outcome to the conversation in one's head).

He talked about everything except the one thing on his mind. Or perhaps it was not on his mind. Perhaps it was on his cock. In his cock? The particulars escaped him. How had they managed to *not* talk about this one thing over the course of their journey?

Henry had talked of literally everything else under the sun; why not this?

It wasn't that the topic was taboo.

Well. So. It was, technically, but that had never stopped Henry.

It wasn't as if he feared that John would fly into a rage or express disgust. They'd practically kissed last night.

Maybe it was simply that they had not talked about this one thing yet, despite its glaring obviousness, and it had now become awkward.

That awkwardness grew from morning to noon, from noon to late afternoon. By the time they were setting up camp that evening, the awkwardness—at least the awkwardness in Henry's mind—had grown to epic proportions.

So Henry did what he often did with awkward situations. He blurted out precisely what was on his mind, just as they were unrolling their blankets.

"So," he heard himself say, "I know I've never mentioned this before, but I'm certain you realize that I've fucked men?"

John's face went utterly blank for one heart-stopping second. Then he laughed. "Oh, God. Henry. Only *you*. Only you would announce it in that fashion."

Henry felt his face heat.

"No," John said, "I did *not* know that, not for certain."

"How could you not know? Was I insufficiently obvious?"

"Well." John considered that. "You were very obvious. But that only told me that you admired men the way I do."

Well. Good. They were both speaking about it.

"But I could hardly conclude anything about past behavior," John said.

Why *had* they not spoken of it when it was so easy? Apparently that was all that needed to be said to make it not awkward any longer. Henry laid his sleeping roll out, then fetched water while John skinned the rabbit he'd snared that morning.

They made the fire together. Henry clipped wizened bits of carrot and turnip into the stew pot while John broke down the rabbit carcass.

He peered into his pack, rummaged around, before sitting up with a frown. "We're out of bread."

"Ah well," John said. "We'll live."

They would. They'd done so before. But Henry liked bread, and he knew that John regarded him as just a little soft in comparison. He bit his lip. "There's a household not a mile back. I could pay for a loaf, I'd wager."

"We're both exhausted. Rest; we need to make our miles tomorrow."

"But John..." Henry tried to think of his very best argument. "*Bread.*"

"Oh, you think I'll give in if you bat your eyelashes prettily? Well, it's your coin and your feet. But you could stay here and tell me more about the fact you've fucked men."

"You're *teasing* me."

"Yes, and you don't dislike it. Did your father know? Did he do anything terrible to you?"

How John got to the heart of the matter so swiftly, Henry would never know.

"Here I am." Henry gestured expansively. "Sent into the army to atone for my terrible sins, preferably by dying valiantly."

John brought one hand up to his mouth as if to hide a smile.

"What? It's actually not funny. He was most insistent. He said awful things."

"I'm sure he did." John bit his lip, his eyes dancing. "I'm sure he was thinking, 'Oh, no, the *infantry*, that will definitely solve everything.'"

"He did!" Henry said. "How did you know? He said almost exactly those words!"

"I'm sure he said to your mother something like this: 'Dear, our Henry likes to fuck men, so let's surround him with men, preferably fit ones used to a march. Make sure they're dressed in tight trousers and sharp uniforms.'"

"There you veer off from reality. I am certain he did not say that."

"'Let's make him an officer. It will be his *duty* to watch them march. Let's surround him with *men all the time.*'"

"I see what you're getting at," Henry said, "and I believe he was thinking of military discipline."

"And did that stop you from fucking men?"

"Well—no."

"You and half the infantry, I'd wager. Henry, I hate to tell you this, but your father? I am going to guess he's something of a fool." John laughed. "He sent you into the infantry to teach you proper behavior?"

"Almost his exact words! In his defense," Henry said, "he'd never joined. How would he know?"

John laughed harder.

"And in his defense," Henry said, "I *have* become more circumspect. I'm much better at judging who is safe to talk to." He threw that out, holding his breath.

John looked over at him. "'Talk.' Is that how fancy British officers describe fucking?"

Henry's heart hammered in his chest. He looked John in the eyes. "What do you call it?"

John stirred the stew and shrugged.

"I've never had a commission bought for me. I've no choice but to be circumspect. I don't call it anything."

Henry exhaled slowly.

"I just do it," John said on a hoarse whisper.

Not a whisper. An invitation.

Their eyes met again. Henry felt a tug of energy go through him. In an ideal world, Henry would have intuited the perfect thing to say, something sweet and romantic, something that matched the growing lightness in his soul. He'd have said something that somehow captured the inchoate feelings that John aroused in him, and they'd have fallen—very slowly, very romantically—into a conveniently placed bower of petals.

Henry had never said the perfect thing in his life, and besides, it was almost winter and the closest they'd get to a bower of petals would be a pile of moldering leaves. With the wind whipping around them, even that was absent.

So what Henry said was this: "You must have done a great deal. You're so very pretty."

John's eyes widened. "Nobody has ever called me pretty before."

"No? Whyever not?"

"It's just not…done, I suppose."

"And now it has been done, and should be done a thousand times over. You're very pretty, you know. And intelligent. And —" He bit off a thousand other adjectives that came to mind. "If it were spring, I'd make you a daisy crown and prove it. But you have lovely, mobile, expressive eyes and a strong chin and a sharp jawline, and…"

And, oh, God, where was that bower of petals! He wanted to hide his face in it. His whole body, in fact. He'd just said, aloud, that John was pretty, in a tone that let all his more flowery sentiments show.

It was a pity there was no bower of petals. Henry could crawl inside and perish of shame. Hell, he'd settle for hiding in that pile of debris.

"Henry," John said easily, "you eat terrible cheese and think that Thomas Jefferson has good qualities. You'll excuse me if I find you lacking in good taste."

Ouch. John said it with a smile on his face, but it hurt. It hurt with an almost painful intensity. It hurt as if John were extending an invitation for just a fuck and no more, after all their weeks together. He'd had relations that meant no more, but this—

Henry stood. "You couldn't be more correct. I am an utter idiot. I should never have said any such thing."

John looked at him.

"I should have said," Henry said, "that you were devastatingly beautiful."

John still didn't say anything.

"But then, I have no taste," Henry said. "Me and my terrible taste, we're going to get bread."

"Henry."

"Good thing you're used to swill," Henry muttered. "Who knows what I'll come back with? After all, I have no good taste."

IT TOOK about ten minutes of disconsolately stirring soup for John's sour mood to fade, and for him to recognize the truth: He'd made a mistake. He knew how Henry longed for acceptance, and his words had been hurtful. However he might try to justify his sentiments, it was not right, nor was it fair, to treat Henry as he had.

Compliments... They made him uneasy. They always made him feel as if someone was trying to get something from him. And while Henry obviously wanted things from him, those things were mutual and pleasurable and not to be argued over.

John was in the process of constructing an apology when the dust from the road presaged Henry's return.

Henry, I was unfair.

Henry, I'm so deeply sorry that I hurt you.

Henry, I never want to see you with that hurt in your eyes again.

Henry turned off the road and came up to their camp under the trees. John *had* to get this right.

Oh, damn it. Henry had become important to him. He cared what Henry thought, felt a stab of pain in his own heart when he saw the hurt reflected in the other man's eyes.

"Oi, John!" Henry called as he approached, waving madly. "You'll never guess what happened!"

Oh, *no.* John was glad to see him. So glad that his heart lifted. They were less than a hundred miles from their destination. How dreadfully inconvenient.

"Let me guess," John said dryly. "Your traveling companion was an unconscionable ass, and you've obtained a cold shoulder to give to him."

Henry blinked at him. His lips compressed.

For a moment, he tilted his head in confusion. Then he laughed. "Oh, ha! I'd forgotten completely! I was annoyed at you for ten entire minutes, John!"

"Good God! Ten *entire* minutes."

"I know!" Henry set down the sack he'd slung over his shoulder and took out a loaf of bread, some radishes, and a bunch of carrots.

"Ten minutes on just one topic," he said, slicing bread. "How utterly single-minded of me. But then I got distracted! *Guess* what distracted me."

"Ah…"

"No, don't guess, it will take too long and I have no patience. I'm just going to tell you. It was cheese. That farmwife up there makes her own cheese."

"We have so much cheese. Why would you *buy* cheese?"

"First, we're running out. We do *not* have so much cheese. Second, I mean actual cheese. *Tasty* cheese. Cheese that one likes to eat. We don't have any of that. I was going to buy a small portion just for myself, so I could taunt you by saying you didn't want any of my cheese since I have no taste."

"Fitting punishment."

"But something happened. I tasted her cheese and…it didn't taste right."

"It wasn't good?"

"No. I'm afraid..." Henry swallowed. "I must confess. I'm very afraid that it *was* good. Objectively speaking."

"Oh," John breathed. "Oh, *no*."

"Oh, *yes*."

"John. It has *happened*. My tastes have become objectively *terrible*. You were completely right." He unwrapped the Cheese of Death and cut off a slice. He popped it in his mouth and chewed morosely. "I'm doomed. I like it. I actually like it."

"You should still be angry at me."

"Hush, I don't want to be. It's no fun."

"I shouldn't snap at you when you compliment me. That was terrible. I'm sorry."

"Well, then, boo." Henry wagged his fingers at him. "Consider yourself chastised. Want some cheese?"

"Henry. I'm trying to be serious."

"I am too. I realized it on my walk home. I ought to have been beaten to death for my mouth long before now. I'm scarcely tolerable as a white man, and people have been *trained* to tolerate me."

"Stop talking about yourself that way," John said. "Stop saying you don't deserve respect or care, because you do. It's not acceptable to me for anyone to dismiss you that way. Not at all. I'll fight anyone who says otherwise, especially when it's me."

Henry looked over at him. Their eyes caught, held. There was something—something bright and yet inexplicable in Henry's face.

"Oh," Henry said. "I wonder when that happened."

"When did what happen?"

"When did your good opinion become so utterly necessary to me?"

"I..." John trailed off. There was that word between them again. *Necessary*. It felt so much heavier than all the other words —lust, want, care, attention. It didn't fit, it couldn't fit, not with Newport so close. But Henry kept going.

"I feel pity for my former self, not knowing you at all. I can't garner a single ounce of regret for my childhood felonies any longer."

"What?" John pulled back. "*Felonies*? How did we get to felonies?"

"I was sixteen when I committed my first executable felony, you know. Buggery."

"Ah, that." John waved a hand as if batting a fly. "That's hardly even a felony. Henry, we were talking about—"

"Treason is my *second* felony. Being a hardened criminal dedicated to tearing down all the old institutions rather agrees with me, don't you think?"

There was nothing to do but give up and wait for the conversation to take them back to where they'd been. John tried to lead it there. He looked at Henry and said in his lowest, most sensual voice: "Felony looks good on you."

"Oh." Henry flushed. "I like it when you say it like that. Maybe I should add sedition to my list. My father will be so… What's the opposite of proud?"

"Annoyed? Dismayed? Outraged?"

"It will be glorious." Henry set his hand atop John's. The weight burned into him. "Let me lead you into a life of crime."

"Lead me? You can't lead me. I'm well ahead of you."

"Never! I cannot admit it. Name your crimes, sir. I *must* be the more dastardly."

"Aiding a runaway slave. Running away myself. Aiding another runaway slave. Fraud, blackmail in obtaining papers for my mother and sister." John shrugged. "The ever-present buggery."

Henry leaned in admiringly. "Damn you. You're right. You win. What excellent felonies. The *best* felonies. I have set my sights entirely too low! I need to break more laws."

"Ah." John smiled. "I've been an even worse influence than Thomas Jefferson, I see."

"What are friends for, if not to urge you on in the commission of crimes required by all men of moral character?"

Here was the tug he could give the conversation. John leaned in until he could see nothing but Henry's smile, the freckles on his nose. "Is it friends, then, that we are?" Their breath danced on each other's lips, warm and perfect.

Henry pulled away. "Here," Henry said in the way he had

that suggested he was speaking in perfect non sequiturs—or maybe not. "Have some dreadful cheese. It's still objectively terrible."

He cut a slice.

Oh, what the hell. John didn't take the cheese from Henry's hand. He leaned forward and took it in his mouth, letting his lips brush Henry's fingers.

He knew what to expect. He'd eaten the cheese often enough.

There was a burst of salt on his tongue, then a deep, rich flavor. Something that filled his mouth with an astonishing intensity.

And beneath that, there were layers—something sweet, something bitter, something sharp, coming together with a complexity that made absolutely no sense at all but formed an almost perfect balance...

"Oh no," John said. "It's happened."

"Has it?"

"How?" John pulled away. "How is this possible? How can this happen? How did the Cheese of Death turn into...this? What did you do? What were you thinking?"

"I was really thinking," Henry said, "that if you were going to kiss me, we had better both taste of cheese. But I can explain. It's simple. We hold these truths to be self-evident, that...all cheese is created equal."

"You are the most impossible man to try to kiss."

Henry just grinned at him.

"That when any form of cheesemongering becomes destructive of these ends, it is the right of the people to abolish it—"

"Do *not* continue, Henry. By no means are you to do this."

"*Make* me stop." Henry's eyes twinkled. "Where was I? Ah. It is the right of the people to abolish it and to institute new cheesemongers—"

In the end, there was only one way to shut him up.

Chapter Eight

HENRY COULDN'T REMEMBER the last time he'd laughed so hard. "It is the right of the people to abolish and institute new cheesemongers," he managed to sputter out between guffaws, and he was about to go on when John set a finger across his lips.

"Mmm?"

John leaned in. He set the back of his other hand against Henry's cheek. "Henry," he said on a low murmur. "Henry."

"I know. You don't need to tell me. I'm being an idiot."

The finger on his lips pushed in. "No," John said. "You're quick, and you're funny, and you're clever, and you don't stop thinking about a thing just because it hurts your head. You are further from idiocy than anyone I've ever met. Never let anyone say that you're stupid because you're not in the usual way."

"John," Henry breathed.

"I can't let you be this necessary," John said. "We'll be in Newport in three days."

"*John.*"

John leaned in, so close that Henry could feel the warmth of his skin. "And yet I can't stop needing you."

"Then don't," Henry said. "Don't stop."

Their lips brushed. It wasn't a kiss, any more than a touch of a hand was a caress. It was just the prelude to one—a meeting of lips so glancing that it was barely even an acquaintance. John pulled back.

Henry met John's eyes, rich brown and perfect, for one swimmingly sensual moment. Then they leaned in again, and this—*this* was a kiss.

John's arm wrapped around Henry as if he could keep the entire world at bay, as if he could protect him from the end of their journey.

Lips melded, then tongues, then mouths. Henry moved to straddle John, bodies pressing together.

John was kissing him, and it was magnificent.

Throughout his life, Henry had been kissed for too many reasons—because someone was angry, because they'd faced a battle and made it out the other end alive, because Henry was *there* and he was better than nobody.

He'd never been kissed by someone who thought him *necessary*. He'd always been the frivolous one. The flighty one. He'd always been That-Idiot-Henry, and never...this. Never someone to be cherished or valued or wanted.

John kissed him as if he were air itself, and oh, how Henry wanted. He wanted so much to be the man John was kissing. He wanted to stay on this road forever. He wanted to have no destination at all. He wanted this to be his life, dust and miles and jokes and a voyage with no end.

It could never happen. They'd run out of cheese. John had a family and so did Henry.

John pulled away first. "I spent all the war thinking of nothing but coming home." He shut his eyes. "I've worried so about my sister. Now, now that homecoming is upon me...I don't want this journey to end."

It doesn't have to, Henry didn't say. But it did. It *did* have to.

"What am I going to do, John?" he asked instead.

"You're going to go back," John said soothingly, stroking his hair. "You're going to tell lies about Yorktown, and you'll be good at it. You're going to claim you struck your head and have only now recovered your memories. Your wealthy family will welcome you with open arms."

"Oh." Henry shut his eyes. "You...know about that, then."

"Mmm."

"You're not angry? I…did rather tell a pack of lies about them."

"Yes," John said in a low voice. "You did, but the lies were so obvious they don't count, sweetheart."

Sweetheart. It hurt, that endearment, coming *now*, only when everything must end.

"I have to go back," Henry said.

"I know. You don't belong here with me."

"No," Henry said. "This is awful. I inherited eighteen thousand pounds from my aunt, and if I'm dead, my father gets it all. He's terrible, John. I cannot let him have it. But how do I go back?"

"Think of this as a dream," John said. "One in which you've acted differently, but—"

Henry sat upright. "You think I'm asking how to *stop* committing felonies? No, no. You have it all wrong. That is not the question that consumes me. How do I *keep* committing treason? It's easy when it's just principles spouted on an open road. But when my mother cries, when my father shouts, when my brother calls on me and tells me that I need to think of his son's reputation—how do I go on?"

"Ah." John smiled sadly. "That, I can't tell you. But every man's brand of treachery is his own. You've found so much of yourself. You can find this, too."

THEY OUGHT to have fucked that night.

Henry knew that. But somehow the act itself seemed so final. Intercourse of any kind would inevitably mean *goodbye* instead of *I love you*. And Henry didn't want to say goodbye until he had to. That night, they had made a single nest of blankets.

One kiss on the lips had turned into two. John's hands had found Henry's hips; their arms had wrapped around each other.

It had only been two kisses, but the second hadn't ended. It had gone on, breath heating, until condensation gathered on the sheet of canvas they'd stretched between two trees to shield them from stray drops. The kiss had endured until water dripped onto their skin and evaporated in the heat of their want. The entire world disappeared into that kiss until there was nothing but lust and humidity. John's muscled body hard on top of him, his mouth hot against his, the ground hard beneath his hips. That kiss went on and on, until it was no different than breathing, until weariness caught them both up and they fell asleep, curled in each other's arms.

They should have fucked.

Instead, they'd awoken that morning and packed their things as if it were a day like any other day.

"Kingston?" the man at the well said at noon. "It's twenty miles distant. Just beyond, you ought to be able to find transport across the Sound to Newport. You'll be there by tomorrow afternoon with any luck."

"Excellent news," John said.

It was. Henry was not so selfish that he would count it as anything except the best news, the most perfect news. John had worried, and here they were. It was good. It was great.

It was tearing him apart.

On that last night, with Newport a three-mile walk and a boat ride away from the camp they set, they ran out of cheese.

Their eyes met over the fire as they divided the last slivers.

"It's just as well," Henry said. "It is objectively horrible cheese." It was sublime when he put it in his mouth. "Stupid reality."

"I know," John said. "I'm thinking too much of reality now. Tomorrow I find out..." Henry could almost taste his fears in that pause, the way he looked over his shoulder. He could almost imagine unknown horrors in the way John swallowed and shook his head. "Worrying won't change reality, either. Distract me, Henry."

He said it the way he said the cheese was delicious, drawing out the syllables.

"I'm no use as a distraction." Henry sighed. "When I think of what will happen after tomorrow, I come up blank, too."

John just looked at him. "That's as good a distraction as any. What *will* you do?"

"Back home…" Back home, Henry was thought a frivolous, flabby fellow. One who thought a ten-mile walk sounded like an impossibility. "Back home, comfort is its own seduction. I wouldn't even have to try, and everything would work out for me. The footmen would bow to me. Men thrice my age will take my coat and consider me a jolly master for remembering their actual names and not just calling them all Jeeves."

John's fingers touched Henry's lips, and Henry let his deepest fears come out.

"I've been pretending this whole journey. I'm a frivolous fellow. I'm afraid my ideals won't hold up to reality. How can they? The advantages I have there are…" Henry was at a loss for words, and he was so rarely without them. "…A thing." He had no better word for it. "What am I supposed to do? I can't keep telling people, no, no, don't be nice to me."

"So don't do that," John said. "There must be a thousand ways to commit felonies. You're not the sort who is meant to be rude. Don't try to be any kind of felon but the one you are."

"Mmm." Henry let the conversation lapse—something he also rarely did. He only took it up again once they'd finished dinner, cleaned up, and retreated to their blankets.

"I don't know who I am there," he said. "I know who I am here, on this road, but there? Nobody there knows…"

Me, he almost said, but he had been so many people. A frivolous child. That unthinking idiot who had taken another man's coat without knowing the man who gave it to him.

"Someone who knows the me I want to be," he finally said. "The best me. The me I can be, the me I didn't know even existed a few months ago."

"Have someone in mind?" John's thumb stroked Henry's lips once more.

Henry couldn't help himself any longer. He leaned forward and kissed John with all his pent-up desire, with every ounce of his being. He wanted, he *wanted,* to be the man who could kiss John. He wanted to be the man who thought nothing of a five-hundred-mile journey.

He wanted to be the man who, ten years from now, saw John in the morning and thought, *here is someone I can trust with my life*. Hell, he wanted to give his own life over to him.

John's arm came around his shoulder, pulling him in. Their blankets rearranged, covering each other. Their bodies came together in the darkness, as the kiss went from lips to shoulders to hips, pressing firmly into one another. It was the best kiss. The loveliest kiss. It was hard and unforgiving like the road against their feet. It was warm and gentle, like winter sunshine in the morning melting the frost on dried grass.

John pulled off Henry's undershirt—cold air touched his skin, and it pebbled—but he scarcely had a chance to shiver. The other man bent his head and touched his tongue to Henry's nipple. It was joltingly, perfectly pleasurable—that little touch, his hands spreading across Henry's chest.

Henry let out a little gasp, then a larger one. His hands spread across the other man's chest. Down his ribs. John didn't object when he pulled away long enough to get the man's small-clothes off. He bent down and tasted John's erection, licking, sucking, hollowing his mouth around the man's penis.

"Oh God." John's hands slid through his hair. "You're incredibly good at that."

How many times had Henry thought of John at night? Of giving himself over to him?

More than the miles they'd traveled together. Every time they moved, the blankets shifted. Cold air hit them in short blasts, but Henry's body was a furnace of need now.

"I want you," he said. "I want you inside me. Do you —do we—"

He never got to finish his question. He never needed to.

John turned over, fumbling in his pack. Henry knew what he was looking for. Oil, its uses all too familiar... There. He turned back, sitting on his haunches, and hauled Henry to straddle him.

John's mouth was hot on his throat. Henry leaned down and inhaled the man's scent, wrapped his arms around the man's shoulders. Their naked hips pressed together.

"God, I want you," John said and tipped his head up.

They kissed again. It was dizzying, scarcely being able to see the man. Feeling the heat of his fingers running down Henry's back. His head bowed against Henry's chest.

John's fingers followed Henry's spine, down, down. They paused. Henry could hear the clink of the glass stopper, then the cool oil, slick against John's fingers, pressing against him, opening him up. His cock twitched against the other man's abdomen.

"You like that."

"God. I do."

"Let's try a little more, then."

John's hands steadied him. Guided him onto the head of his cock. Henry exhaled, sinking down. Down. Feeling his body open up so intimately... Feeling that pressure, so right, so perfect...

"God." He caught John's face in his hands. "You're perfect, John. You're so utterly perfect."

They kissed again. They didn't stop kissing.

John's hands came to Henry's hips. They moved, awkwardly at first, learning each other, learning the rhythm of each other's thrusts. Then less awkwardly—John wrapping one arm around Henry's waist, his other hand finding Henry's aching cock. His fingers felt like encouragement, and Henry gave himself over to the feel of them. Their shoulders grew hot, then slick with sweat. Every thrust was a perfect pleasure, stoking fires that could never be banked.

Had he thought the air cold? It was hot and humid, scented with their mixing musk, the silence broken by John's gasps of pleasure.

Henry was doing this to him. Squeezing him. Riding him. He could feel the other man's muscles tense. Feel John's arm squeeze him. He felt a spurt of heat, heard John let out a groan of surprise, then thrust hard, hard inside him.

He rode out the other man's pleasure, the groans, until John was a gasping, wrung-out mess.

"Henry."

"Yes?" He could not hide his own delighted pleasure.

"How close are you?"

"Very close. I should say—"

John cut him off with a kiss. He hadn't yet withdrawn from his body. His hand closed around Henry's cock with an almost possessive groan. He pumped once, twice, his kiss hard and demanding. Henry thought of the feel of John inside him, thrusting, groaning, being laid bare...

Very close. He was very close. He was—oh God. He spilled over the edge, his wet semen painting them both. For a second, his mind could not function. There was nothing but that achingly perfect pleasure. The absolute joy of touching someone he knew so well. Someone who trusted him. Who believed in him. Someone who thought that he could be so much. It couldn't be better.

Then John kissed him. "Let me find a cloth."

It was better. There was a little water still in the canteen, and even though it was half-freezing, having someone take care of him with such tenderness, being able to return the favor... It undid Henry. More even than the sex.

They curled up in the blankets afterward. Their arms, curled around one another, spoke all the words they had not yet said.

It hadn't been goodbye. It had been everything Henry wanted—desire, affection, a promise of what they could have.

It had been a promise of an illusion, like saying the cheese was delicious. No matter how their bodies had lied, the truth was simple. Henry looked into John's eyes afterward, trying to find the right words to say.

John found them first. "You're going back."

"I'm going back." Henry shut his eyes. "You're necessary, John. I need to know that I'm necessary, too. That I can be..." He trailed off.

He didn't have to finish the sentence.

John trailed his fingers along his shoulder. "We hold these truths to be self-evident," he whispered, "that all men are created equal, that they are endowed by their Creator with certain unalienable rights, that among these are life, liberty, and the pursuit of..."

John trailed off, shutting his eyes. For one heart-stopping moment, Henry wanted to be the thing John was pursuing. He wanted to be on that list of vital necessities. He wanted to dream that he could be so important.

"Home," John said instead. "The pursuit of home."

It wasn't home in the Declaration, but happiness. Happiness was *here*. It was evident in the flutter of John's fingers down his arm, the way their bodies fit together. Happiness was laughing with a man who let their conversation ebb and flow and never called him an idiot for the rapidly turning tide of his thoughts.

Happiness was this journey, and it was coming to an end.

Henry shut his eyes and tried to imagine going back to England. Back to his family. Nothing, still.

"Go," John whispered, brushing his hair back. "Pursue."

Chapter Nine

THEY WATCHED the sunrise together the next morning—a riot of pink and yellow and blue, tingeing gray clouds with hues that Henry could only remember seeing in a painter's palette. For a handful of minutes, the world was vermillion and gold, the unreal dream of a sleeping god.

Henry held John's hand throughout, clutching it as if it were the lowest rung on the ladder to heaven.

Then the sun rose. The clouds were gray. The dead leaves on the ground became just that—so much decaying plant matter. The dream, it appeared, was over. And because Henry was an adult and not a child, he just made himself smile. "Well. That's that. Let's be off, then?"

Their last hours together had begun.

They spoke as if it were any other day.

They had an argument on the merits of dogs and cats, and whether cats ought to have four or five toes on their feet, and if bulldogs were cute ("So ugly they're cute," Henry explained, while John insisted they were just cute without being ugly in the first place).

They spoke, and scattered farms gave rise to one village. The village tapered off but never quite seemed to end—there was always another house on the horizon, until finally the houses grew closer and closer, and the air smelled more and more of the sea.

The wind whipped around them as they approached the dock, bringing with it the scents of salt and seaweed and smoke.

"Does it smell like home?" Henry inquired.

John just shook his head. "It should, I suppose."

Henry negotiated passage and paid. John made an abortive gesture to his own deflated coin purse, but Henry ignored him, and John let him ignore him.

The waters of the Rhode Island Sound were gray and green, the waves just rough enough to keep the voyage on the pinnace interesting. Their path charted around one island, sailed between two others, desolate and craggy with shores of dark brown rock. They sailed close enough to occasionally make out yellow grasses broken by the occasional forest of tree stumps.

"What happened to the trees?" Henry asked.

The boat's captain spat. "Fucking British." It was his only comment.

"Fucking British," Henry agreed, and John shot him a smile.

It wasn't much. John's hands curled into fists on his knees. His jaw set, and no amount of Henry's cajoling conversation could soften his expression.

They landed in Newport later. The sun was shrouded by clouds, and Henry had no idea of the time. His legs felt strange on the solid wood of the quay; the world spun dizzily for a moment before his body remembered land again.

Newport had the look of a city that had seen better days. Many better days. Weathered stone buildings with slightly less-weathered squares on their walls suggested absent metal plates, undoubtedly ripped down and stolen for the British war effort. Henry had ordered it done himself, in the early days of his commission. But if the walls of the Newport buildings were stripped bare of all possible invitation, they seemed positively friendly in comparison with the inhabitants.

Perhaps the two of them did look somewhat shabby from the road. Perhaps they were watching John. Perhaps they were gawking at the two of them together.

"Companionable bunch, aren't they?" he whispered to John as they made their way up a muddy thoroughfare.

A small smile touched John's face. "Always. It looks...different. It's been years since I was here, you know, but I spent a good decade in Newport. It's odd not to recognize anyone."

"I can pretend to know someone, if you like."

"Mmm?"

"That man there? He's a chimney sweep."

John looked over at the fellow, then back at Henry. "He's six feet tall."

Henry shrugged. "I never said he was *good* at his job."

John's swallowed cackle of mirth was precisely what he'd been hoping for.

"That woman there? She's a knight. An actual medieval knight."

"But..."

"I don't know how it happened," Henry said. "One day, she didn't die, and that's not so unusual is it? She's just continued not dying ever since."

"I do recall *her,*" John said. "She sells fish." He gestured and they made their way onto an even muckier side street.

"Everyone needs a believable story to tell the masses," Henry said with a shrug. "Even undying medieval knights. After all that fighting, I imagine fish would be peaceful."

John just smiled again—a pretense of curved lips—and pressed his hands together.

"Now, that man—"

Before Henry had a chance to make up a story, John shook his head. "We're here." He turned, descended a few steps to a cellar door. He shut his eyes.

"John," Henry said. "It will be—" He cut off his reassurance at the flare of John's nostrils.

"Don't make up stories about my family. You don't actually know, and..." John's hands clenched. "You don't actually know."

No. He didn't. Henry bit his lip and hoped for the best. John inhaled, raised his arm, and knocked.

The silence that followed seemed interminable.

Nothing. Nothing. Then the scrape of iron on stone as a

bolt was drawn, followed by the irate protest of poorly oiled hinges.

A white man, gaunt and dark-haired, stared at them from the doorway. His gaze passed over John as inconsequential and landed suspiciously on Henry behind him.

"What the *devil* do you want?" It came out on a snarl. Even from here, Henry could smell the alcohol on the man's breath.

John's fist clenched harder. He let out a pained breath, his only sign of disappointment. Someone who didn't know him wouldn't know he was upset. They wouldn't understand the set of his jaw, the angle of his ears. John was reeling.

"I'm guessing," Henry heard himself whisper, "and—I'm not sure what makes me think this—that this isn't your sister."

John cast him a repressive glance. "Good guess." For a moment, he just stared at the doorway in shock. Then he shook his head, coming back into himself. "No. Sir, I beg your pardon. I'm looking for the previous occupants of this—"

"Don't know them," the man said. "Never heard of them. No use asking." With one last suspicious glance in Henry's direction, he slammed the door.

"Well." Henry frowned. "Um. Now what?"

John inhaled. His hands were still clenched, but he raised his chin defiantly. "Now," John said, "we go to Mr. Allan."

"Mr. Allan?"

"Noah's former master." John exhaled. "He thinks well enough of me, and if—when—they departed, they would have left word with him."

"Right."

"There's no need to panic," John said, almost certainly talking to himself. "There are so many possible explanations."

"For instance—"

"No," John said. "Please don't supply them. Talk of anything else."

They made their way to the other side of the city—up a bit of a hill, from which they could see the ocean spread before them, a wide expanse of gray glitter broken by islands and dotted by French ships—before turning into a shop. The bell rang; John waited.

A rustle sounded in the back room, and a minute later, a big, burly man made his way into the front. He paused in the doorway before smiling and taking another step forward.

"John. You've lost far too much weight. You've made it back, then."

"I have." John bit his lip.

"John, I'm sorry."

"*No.*" John's face crumpled in agony.

"I tried to convince them they could stay, that we could sort matters out with the constables, but things were getting bad, John. I did what I could, but…"

John's head had snapped up on the words *safe to stay*. "They're alive?"

"Why wouldn't they be? Noah left me something to give you with their direction, and I had a letter for you just two days ago. Let me find it…"

He turned to a cabinet, and John staggered, holding on to a table. "They're alive." His eyes glistened with a wet sheen. "They're alive, Henry. They're *alive.*"

"Good thing you weren't worried about it."

John smiled.

"Ah!" Mr. Allan said, turning around, papers in his hand. "Here they are!"

At that moment, the door swung open behind them, letting in a burst of cold air. Henry turned.

Five men stood there. One held a rake; one a rope. Two of the others wielded pitchforks. The fifth man—empty-handed— was Mr. Suspicious, the man who had answered the door for John earlier. He stood straight; the smell of alcohol on his breath mixed with something more pungent.

"There he is!" Mr. Suspicious proclaimed, pointing an accusing finger. "Get him!"

Henry didn't think. He stepped in front of John.

This, it turned out, was a brave but entirely futile gesture. They didn't care about John.

They cared about John so little that Henry stepping closer only egged them on. One man grabbed hold of Henry's right arm; another took his left. Mr. Suspicious stalked directly in front of Henry and glared at him, his gaze raking from Henry's eyes down his torso.

"I'd never forget a man," Mr. Suspicious pronounced. "It's him. It's definitely him." So saying, Mr. Suspicious punched him in the kidneys.

Henry felt pain flash through him along with an inexplicable sense of amusement. Ha. They'd been after him anyway. How foolish of him to volunteer himself! On the one hand, he hadn't known. On the other hand—

"How do you like the weather *now?*" Mr. Suspicious bellowed.

"It's very nice," Henry said, doubling over in pain and confusion.

"What is this all about?" Mr. Allan asked.

"I would know this man anywhere!" Mr. Suspicious gestured dramatically. "He's the one what popped my knee at Valley Forge and invalided me out. He was talking of the weather and all that in the middle of battle! I could never forget."

Henry's stomach felt like a mass of bruises. That had never stopped him from talking.

"In my defense," he said, "talking about the weather is hardly an identifying characteristic. Many people do it!"

"Shut up, you."

"In fact, you started the talk of the weather," Henry went on, "so how do we know *you're* not—what am I supposed to be again?"

He got a knee in the stomach for his troubles.

"He's a British officer," Suspicious went on, "and what, I ask you, is a British officer doing behind enemy lines while his superiors supposedly negotiate their surrender? Spying. That's what I say."

"Spying on a *carpenter?*" Henry said in disbelief. "How would that—"

"He admits it! He's an enemy spy! Kill the redcoat! Kill the redcoat now!"

"I didn't admit anything!" Henry said. Which was probably

good, because unfortunately just about everything Suspicious had said was true. "I'm not, I'm a—"

Medieval knight was the first thing that came to mind, and Henry just managed to catch those words before they came out of his mouth. *Cheesemonger* would have worked, except they'd eaten all the cheese. "I'm a—"

"Spy!" Someone bellowed. "He's a spy! Hang him!"

It was strange how the world worked. Henry had spent months wondering how to live. He hadn't wanted to die, but dying in a blaze of glory for his principles had always seemed better than any of the alternatives. So much so that every time he'd faced death on the battlefield, he'd not been afraid.

Now John was leaving and Henry had to go back and he had nothing, absolutely nothing. It was absurd that at this moment he realized that he wanted to live. He wanted it quite desperately. He wanted to figure out how to be who he was. He wanted to prove to himself, to *John,* that he was someone worthwhile. He wanted to live for years and years.

Amusing that he should learn that just as he was about to die. One man grabbed his elbow. The other took hold of the rope and gestured to the door. "The square out there," he said, "there's a—"

He never got to finish his sentence.

"He's not a spy," John interrupted in amused tones. "He's just outraged that you don't know who he is."

The men stopped. They turned to John.

"You don't know who he is? You *really* think he's a British officer?" John shook his head. "He was there when we stormed Redoubt Ten together and ended the war at Yorktown, but by all means, imagine him a spy."

"But—"

"I watched him almost die for another soldier so the redoubt could fall, but by all means, believe him a spy."

Mr. Suspicious frowned. "Who are *you?*"

"John Hunter, formerly a corporal of the Rhode Island Regiment under Captain Stephen Olney. I was at Yorktown," John said. "Mr. Allan here has known me a good decade—he can vouch for me. Or, if you don't believe me, write to Lieutenant

Colonel Alexander Hamilton and tell him you think that Henry Latham, of all people, is a British spy."

"Colonel Hamilton?" Mr. Suspicious paused, his suspicion flickering. "Washington's aide-de-camp? He *knows* him?"

"I'm not saying this man here saved his life, but…" John trailed off. "Sometimes men look like other men. It's nobody's fault. Believe what you will. I'm just saying that I've never heard of a British officer who could recite the Declaration of Independence as if it were a prayer."

One of the men with a pitchfork let the point drop six inches. "Well, then. That's as good a test as any. Let's hear it."

Henry took a breath. One of his ribs sent a stab of lightning through him, but he could have said these words through any amount of pain. He straightened, coughed, and started. "When in the course of human events, it becomes necessary for one people to dissolve the political bands which have connected them with another…" The words came easily, smoothly, cascading one after another.

Behind the men, John gave Henry a nod. He looked down at the papers in his hand, reading through them, shaking his head.

"We hold these truths to be self-evident." Henry was speaking to John, not anyone else. He'd said these words more than once on their journey; he'd always meant them. He felt that he'd mean them for John for the rest of his life. "That all men are created equal."

After the first sentence, Mr. Suspicious waved the others down.

John folded the papers. He hefted his bag.

John was leaving. They'd agreed that they would separate here. This was no surprise. Still. Henry was stuck here reciting words written by slave owners.

"…That they are endowed by their Creator with certain unalienable rights…"

John raised his fingers, not in a salute. He touched them to his lips and met Henry's eyes. It felt like a promise of everything they couldn't have.

"That among these are life, liberty…"

"Blimey," Mr. Suspicious said beside Henry. "You really *mean* it, don't you? You're crying. You're a true patriot, aren't you? I'm terribly sorry."

Not as sorry as Henry was. John slipped out the door on *the pursuit of happiness.*

Chapter Ten

"John!"

Henry caught up to John fifteen minutes later, just outside the docks.

John had not actually expected Henry to come after him, but now that he had done so, he found it impossible to believe he could have been put off so easily. He'd spent five hundred miles eating terrible cheese in the hope that it would change after all.

"Henry."

They looked at each other.

"I'm leaving," John finally said. "My arm's healed, and I know where to go. I've a letter that's a mere week old that says everything's well. And the longer you wait, Henry, the harder it will be for you to return."

"I know," Henry said. "I *know*. And, John...I need to go back to my family. I want to prove I can make something of myself."

"That's nonsense. You are something. You, as yourself."

"I want to make something more. I didn't hunt you down to *argue* with you, John."

"No?" A glimmer of amusement touched John's lips. "That's a first. Why *did* you hunt me down, then?"

"To tell you...thank you." Henry swallowed. "And to beg

you to write to me. I want to know…"

Everything, Henry didn't say. John didn't know how he heard it anyway.

"Thank you," Henry said. "For saving my life just now. For the entire journey. It's not that you changed my life. You made me see *I* was changing it."

John looked over at Henry. They were in broad daylight, on the docks. They couldn't embrace. They couldn't even touch. They were drawing eyes enough as it was.

"Thank you," John said, "for giving me something to believe in. Maybe a slave owner wrote those words, but they convinced people to fight for the proposition that all men were created equal." He looked around the docks, saw the suspicious looks cast in his direction. These people had tossed his family out; equals they were not. Not yet. Still… "Maybe," John said, "some day, some of them will even believe it. I cannot tell you how utterly necessary you have been to me."

"As necessary as you are to me," Henry whispered. "No matter where I go, or what I do, you and our time together will always be the foundation."

"Go." John's voice broke. He could not help it. "Henry, go now, before I do something foolish like grab hold of you and refuse to let go. *Go.*"

"Write to me," Henry said. "Write. You can reach me at my terrible father's home. It shouldn't be so hard to get a letter delivered. Just send it care of, um…the Duke of Scanshire?"

"Oh God." The roll of John's eyes was affectionate. "Of course he is a duke."

"He's definitely terrible. You'll write?"

John turned away, but not so quickly that Henry missed his reply.

"Every day," John said. "Every morning. Every night."

THE LETTERS from John's sister were comfort and companion on the remaining weeks of John's journey.

We were told to leave, the letter that she had left with Allan said. *Now that Noah's freed, there's talk of us becoming a burden on the charity of others. Never mind that we've done well enough for ourselves all these years. Still, we're leaving. We've met up with other freedmen, and we're heading north...*

Then, the latest letter: *We've found a space in Maine, where it can just be us, nobody else to bother us. Come join us as soon as you're able. May our love speed your feet.*

Some kind of love sped his feet—her letters, the thought of his mother in a safe space before a fire as winter came on. Imagining Henry's return to his terrible father. Henry was not here, but John imagined them having a conversation every day. It would flow over every possible topic.

He thought of Henry with every meal, with every bite of cheese that was insufficiently terrible, with every silent dinner where there was nobody about to exclaim *Squirrel! Who knew squirrel could be so delicious?*

৩৯৫৩

IT WAS early December when John found himself at the outskirts of the village, standing beside what was undoubtedly a farm. The directions had taken him this far, but no signs declared names. There was, however a black woman tending the winter frames in her garden. She looked up when she saw him and smiled.

"Ahoy."

"You. You seem familiar." She took three steps toward him, squinting. "Ah, that's it. You've the look of Lizzie Hunter."

John's heart leapt in his chest. "Lizzie Hunter? Not Lizzie Allan?"

"They've taken her name. You must be that fine older brother she's always boasting about."

They were here. John inhaled and felt almost weak. "She does...go on a bit."

The woman straightened and held out a hand. "Mrs. Wexford. My husband is about, and— *Alice!*" That last came out on a bellow.

A young woman materialized from the barn, skinny and gawky. "What, Ma? I milked the cow. I *told* you already."

"Alice, this is Corporal Hunter. He's home from the war. Take him to his family, and for God's sake, let everyone know he's back. There'll be a feast tonight."

Home. John had never been to this place, but he felt himself growing roots with every step.

What was home, then, but a place where people cared about your life, your liberty, the pursuit of your happiness? Mrs. Wexford had only just met him, but she smiled at him, misty-eyed, because he belonged here and he'd come back.

He'd never been here before, but that was precisely how it felt—as if he had just come back.

This village felt like *home* in a way Newport never had. He felt that sense of belonging more and more with every step. Black children rolled a hoop down the street, laughing at each other. Every two steps they were interrupted by another person demanding an introduction. Was this Lizzie's brother, finally? They'd heard so much about him. They felt like they knew him already.

He felt as if he knew them, too, brothers and sisters in a war for independence that they had not yet stopped fighting.

"Here." Alice Wexford stopped in front of a door. Instead of knocking, though, she called out. "Mrs. Hunter! Your brother's come! Hurry!"

The door opened a scant few seconds later.

Lizzie, Lizzie. His little sister—now round with child like a prize pumpkin—her hair back, a floury apron wrapped around her—

She burst into tears and threw her arms around him. "John. You're *back.*"

He hadn't let himself dream of this moment, not truly, not until now. She smelled of bread and Lizzie and *home.*

"There, there," John said. "I promised I'd come back, didn't I? You should believe me more often."

She sniffed. "You should promise less and stay home more."

He was home. Everything was perfect.

There was a feast that night, and introductions to people

he'd never met but who felt like old friends nonetheless. Home. He was home.

Still, that evening, he slipped away from the impromptu gathering and wrote his first letter, because sometimes home could be two places all at once.

❧

December, 1781

My dear Lord Henry,

My family is alive and well. They've joined a community of freedmen, and between the dozen of us, and with some help from a Quaker parish who feels the injustice done to us, we have every intent to purchase an island of our own. It is large and entirely inhospitable—hence our being able to afford it—but we have hope and determination, and so long as we make it through this first winter, all should be well...

July, 1782

My dear John,

I told you to desist. I must repeat myself. If you ever call me "Lord Henry" again, even in jest, I shall be forced to take drastic measures. It turns out that I am as good a liar as you believed. My superiors were, primed by my prior mishaps, all too willing to believe in my stupidity. After everything I'd done amiss before, my hitting my head and not remembering a thing and waking up naked in Yorktown? Apparently it was all too believable. The court-martial was nothing. They were delighted by my plan to sell my commission, as I am demonstrably less than useless as an officer.

I spent a week thereafter delighting everyone. It will never happen again.

My father was initially overjoyed by my plan to stand for election to Parliament at the next opportunity. He crowed to all and sundry that he had finally "made a man of me"—as if he were personally responsible for you Americans deciding to revolt and all that—and held a grand dinner so I could meet his friends.

In his mind, I am still not intelligent enough to develop thoughts of my own, so imagine his shock when I spoke in favor of abolition of the slave trade. Our discussion on matters of the East India Company were also helpful. I broached the concept, and someone asked, "But how will we have our cotton?"

I thought this a reasonable response: "Well, if we cannot have cotton except by means of threats, bribery, and corruption, perhaps we should not have cotton."

You would have thought I had shot a man. I published an opinion piece in the Times the next week, entitled "Perhaps we should kill fewer people" and it has caused a scandal. It is, perhaps, not the scandal my father expected me to cause in my youth, but he has expressed absolutely no gratitude for my circumspection. There is no reasoning with him on the matter; he stands firm. Killing a man for his coin is definitely wrong, but killing giant masses of men for tea, cotton, and sugar is our particular national business and must not be scrutinized.

Being a pariah has never been so much fun...

September, 1783

My dear Henry,
…Over winter, I intend to oversee our first major project—the creation of a handful of sloops meant for fishing. Fish can be salted and saved for the bitterest days; they can also be traded for warmer clothing, which is a necessity. But I'm hoping for something a little more frivolous. I dream of goats—there's cheese to be made, if you recall.

I have told tales of the cheese. The cheese is legendary here already, and nobody but me has ever eaten it.

The grand experiment will take longer, but my hope is that in a few years' time, we will have our first real trading vessel.

Along those lines, I finally told my mother and sister who I'd been writing to these last years. I had no choice in the matter. My *mother* looked *at me, and there's nothing to be done when she looks like that.*

Dozens of letters, she said. Is it a friend from the infantry? If so, how does he live in England?

I told them everything.

I never expected them to dislike me if I confessed the truth about my leanings—we've been through too much together not to love one another—but I did wonder if they might doubt my judgment or my character. My sister just held my hand and told me that there were enough people who thought us beneath them. She saw no point in adding to that score.

She then suggested that Patrick was single and didn't seem to have much interest in women. I had to explain that Patrick does not talk enough for my tastes...

May, 1784

My dear John,

I did not expect to win a seat in the House during the elections, but I must admit that my resounding defeat—which I have been told is an "emphatic rejection" of my "hasty and ill-conceived beliefs"—is a blow to even my inexhaustible optimism.

Even my allies tell me I must move slowly—that if we are to win hearts and minds on the abolition issue, we must hold firm on India.

Pah. I cannot stomach the thought of power won at someone else's expense. I also find that I am particularly unsuited to a career in politics. It turns out that one skill politicians must have is the ability to not say "you must be extraordinarily cruel" when someone says something that is extraordinarily cruel.

I am unsure what comes next.

I am only certain that without your correspondence, I do not know where I would be. Years may have passed since last we spoke in person, but you have always been—and will always be—the most fundamental necessity to me...

November, 1784

NUMBER 12, Rygrove Square in London was a small house—perfect for a political eccentric like Henry who had been disowned by his father but whose mother and sisters still came around for the occasional visit.

Over the last handful of years, Henry had gradually developed a knack for political essays. His tutors would never have approved of them—he still tended to ramble, and his style was shockingly familiar instead of tendentiously formal.

But his words were fun to read, and perhaps he would change a few minds here or there.

Sometimes he dreamed of more. Sometimes he dreamed that he'd answer the milkman's knock on the door and that it would not be milk.

That was an impossible dream, one he'd learned not to indulge in too often. Henry had always been a creature of high spirits; he preferred not to lower his mood with memories of a five-hundred-mile walk.

And so it was that on a fine November morning, a knock sounded on his door.

The milkman, of course.

Henry set aside the essay he'd been writing—somehow he'd dropped a four-page aside on cricket in the middle of the thing, and it would *not* edit itself down on its own—and went to get the milk.

This morning, it was not the milk.

John stood on his doorstep. He looked—no, not older. His head was shaved completely; he stood taller than Henry remembered. He caught sight of Henry and smiled.

His smile. God, his smile. It felt like a shaft of sunlight piercing straight through his soul. It lifted his heart.

Oh, Henry thought. *Oh, this. This feeling.* He hadn't let himself remember it except in his not-so-rare lapses in judgment. He only let himself feel like this on letter-days, when he perused the pages that had come across the ocean, committing them to memory.

"Good God," John said. "You wear spectacles."

Henry yanked them away. "Only when I write—which—good God, John." His heart hammered. All the wishes he so rarely let himself feel came racing to the fore. He wanted another journey. He wanted to walk around the world with this man and never stop. "John."

John held out a block of waxed paper. "I brought you some cheese."

"Is it...?"

"No, no. It's not *the* cheese. I think some days that *that* cheese may never really have existed. But it's...something we make on the island. Someday, it might come close."

Henry took the package. "See?" He turned, gesturing John to come in. "I knew it was milk at the door and behold. Just the milk I needed."

Henry did not manage to sort out his emotions on the short walk to the pantry. Slicing bits of crumbling cheese did not help him put his thoughts in order. His feelings filled his chest like shimmering tears. He wanted, he *wanted*, he wanted still, and he didn't dare ask if this was just a visit, or...?

Their journey felt like a dream now—one where he could forget the cold and discomfort and just...remember.

Ought he to embrace John? Kiss him? Beg him never to leave? All options seemed unfair, each in their own way.

The cheese was sharp and salty with a hint of musk, a deep, rich flavor that lingered on his taste buds.

It wasn't the same cheese. It would never be the same cheese.

"It's good," he finally said.

"A bit immature," John replied with a shrug. "We've only had it twelve months now. The flavors will deepen with age."

The pause that followed lingered in awkward curiosity, like a cat that had chosen to sit atop the newspaper when one had hoped to read it.

John smiled at him. "You never used to be quiet."

"I have too many thoughts, all stampeding their way to the forefront of my mind," Henry explained. "Eventually, all but one will be trampled to death in the crush, and I shall blurt it out in triumph."

Another long silence. Their eyes met. John squared his shoulders but didn't speak.

Henry gathered his courage. "John, I—"

John spoke at precisely the same time. "Henry, I—"

They both stopped. They looked at each other.

"Well," Henry said. "This will never do. We can't trample each other, or whomever will we speak to?"

"Ah." John rubbed his hands.

"You first," Henry said, because he was a cheater.

"I've seen the newspaper," John said. "Now that you're not running for political office, I imagine you're at loose ends."

"Well, there's always next election." Henry had thought as much to himself. Next time, next time, next time... Even Henry's naturally buoyant spirits quailed at the thought of applying himself to the Herculean task of altering the British national conscience, one person at a time.

"It seems a waste of unappreciated talent. I've heard there's a position open," John said. "You might take interest in it."

"A position?"

"There's a new trading company in the process of registering," John said, "one that is determined to do things differently. You may have heard of it."

"Ah?"

"They're registering as the Lord Traders," John said.

"Cheeky bastards." Henry's heart pounded in his chest. "I like their style."

"You would."

"I must confess—I know nothing of trade. Just what I've written in my silly little essays, you know."

"Yes, well, it's not a position as a *trader* I'm offering." John looked over at him. "You see, after considerable thought, we find ourselves in need of a personable white man with a fancy accent."

"Oh." Henry swallowed. "These are...qualifications I possess."

"Someone who can say, 'My dear sir, what's holding matters up? This permit ought to have issued six months ago.'"

Henry's heart fluttered in his chest. "I am exceedingly *good* at uttering words."

"I was thinking to hire someone who could wander into a customs office and talk and talk and not *leave* until everything was settled."

"This seems suited to my talents. How do I apply?"

"The pay is, for now, quite limited. And you'd have to travel with the captain. You'd be on ships for months at a time. It's a hell of a bad deal, Henry, and the only reason you should consider taking it is because if you stay here, you're likely to lose your temper eventually and say something that will get you arrested."

"Oh, I'd say that's almost inevitable." Henry stood. "My father threatened me with it just last week, and only desisted when my mother told him to be nice."

"I haven't even come around to the worst of it." John swallowed. "I should mention that I love you."

"Oh." Henry's head spun. His heart beat, far too many times. "Oh. That's—oh. I need a little time to think this over."

John straightened and looked away. "Of course. I'll be staying here for a week. If—"

"No!" Henry took hold of his arm, turning him back. "A week would be a great deal of time. I needed…oh, two seconds. I'm already done thinking."

The stiff look on John's face softened, and he laughed. "I should have guessed."

"I had to think about the salary, not anything else. I will require a larger salary."

"Henry…"

"I inherited some money from my aunt, as you may recall. I thought…perhaps…your organization might need a little capital?" Henry swallowed. "I figured that if I was paying my own salary, I could raise it a bit. That's all."

John's eyes had widened on this at first, and then narrowed. He shook his head. "I could not ask you to do that." But he didn't pull away from Henry's grip.

"You don't have to ask." Henry shrugged. "It's already done

in all but legalities. You already have my heart and my soul and my body. Why quibble about my fortune on top of those?"

John looked over at Henry. His eyes seemed dark and still, like an ocean at night. John reached out a hand, clasping Henry's fingers.

"If you need someone to say words for you," Henry said, "then I am your man."

"Henry." John's eyes shone.

"To be quite clear," Henry said, "I have never stopped being your man. Not since I started, sometime on the road from Virginia to Rhode Island."

"It's not bad, my life," John said. "My family is the best, my sister has little ones, and...I'm babbling, Henry. I miss you. In your last letter, you said I was necessary. Everything has been perfect except one thing. You're necessary—the most necessary person I've ever encountered—and you're *wasted* here."

"Oh."

"I ache, every time I get your letters." John tapped his heart. "We've tried being apart. Can we try being together?"

"How long?"

"I don't know how to measure the length of my wanting. Until the stars die and empires fall."

Henry smiled, his heart too full. "Until all men are treated as equal," he whispered. "Until everyone is allowed life, liberty, and the pursuit of..." He trailed off. *Happiness* was not enough to describe his emotion. He felt an incandescent joy, a sense that he'd finally clicked into place.

"The pursuit of home," John told him. "I told you that once, when we went our separate ways. Let me tell you it again, now."

The pursuit of *home*. That was precisely it, the thing he'd been searching for all these years on battlefields, in his father's parlor, in his political essays.

"Lizzie told me to tell you that you'd be welcome," John said. "That *we'd* be welcome. You'll like her, you know. And business will take us back here, and you can visit the members of your family who aren't terrible."

Home. Henry might have wept. Instead, he wound his hands in John's and let their fingers and their futures intertwine.

"I love you," he said again. "Please don't be disappointed when you help me pack. There's a great deal of ridiculous nothings that I'm terribly attached to and will have to bring along. I am something of a frivolous fellow."

John just smiled. "Tell me the story of everything on the voyage, then. We'll have all the time we need."

Epilogue

Harlem, New York, 1818

THERE WAS a clock ticking somewhere in the room, but John hadn't been able to find it yet, not without craning his neck. Which he was not about to do, not without appearing unspeakably rude. Instead it ticktocked somewhere to his right, mocking his inability to identify it.

Mrs. Eliza Hamilton sat in a comfortable chair before them. If she thought anything of the fact that the two men before her were men, or that one was black and the other white, she said not a word.

She just poured them tea.

"It's the least I can do, when you've traveled all the way from —Maine, is it?—just to deliver a story of my Hamilton."

"Ah, it's no problem." Henry picked up his teacup and took a sip. "We've traveled everywhere; we've an office in New York now, and we were due for a visit in any event."

John looked over at Henry. Decades at sea had aged them both, but on Henry, that age gave him a gravitas that almost managed to offset the impudent spark in his eye. He sat straight; his hair was a little lighter, strands of white mixing with gold and ginger. He had smile-lines at the corner of his eyes, and his swift, irrepressible grin had left creases on his cheeks—signs that he loved, and was well loved.

At the side of the room, a pretty black woman with her hair back in a bun sat stiffly in place. She had ink and a quill and she'd schooled her face to have no expression. "You don't mind if Mercy stays and takes notes?" Mrs. Hamilton asked.

"Of course not." John gave the woman a nod. *You there, you're one of us,* he tried to convey to her silently. *I see you, not a servant.* After a moment, she nodded back.

"Well," John said. "It is…not as if we could write our story down and send it along."

"We could have done," Henry interrupted, "but it would have been terribly imprudent, and John tries to keep me to three imprudent actions per week."

"I do no such thing," John protested. "You're going to make me look the scold already, and I haven't told you no since—"

"You *never* say no, but you look it. You look at me straight on and you say—"

John couldn't help himself. "'Henry, what are you doing?'" Their words spilled out atop each other; they both stopped before they could go any further. Henry laughed. John bit his lip.

"I see," Mrs. Hamilton said slowly. "You are…friends as well as business partners." In that pause, the one just before friends, John heard everything that it would be imprudent to say aloud. Lovers. Partners. Two souls twined about each other.

In the decades they'd spent together, they had plotted and planned, grown a business from a few small lines to a half-dozen ships and three offices. When they weren't out on business, they stayed at home. They gardened. They rested. They taught children what they'd learned. What they were to one another was obvious—but their small island of freedmen had had enough of hatred and tossing people out. They had a passel of nieces and nephews. Then there were the children who were not related to them in the slightest—who were also nieces and nephews now.

"Very dear friends," Henry said. "And in a way, I suppose we owe it all to your husband's leadership at Yorktown. It all started, you see, when… No, John, you tell it."

"It all started," John said, "when Elijah Sutton was preparing to bodily toss your husband into the redoubt at Yorktown."

"Mercy," Mrs. Hamilton said to the woman in the corner, "be a dear and remind me that I absolutely must speak to Mr. Sutton."

"Of course, missus. You've already noted it once before, you know."

They continued their story—Colonel Hamilton telling John to use his name to ease his way, the cheese, the journey, the stories about how they had borrowed his name to ease their way.

They did not talk of falling in love. There was no need to admit such a thing to near strangers, and in any event, John's words, transcribed, could never capture the look in his eyes.

"After that," Henry said, "after your husband had lent his name so willingly, it only made sense to pay him back. I had some property in England, and wanted to be assured that it would not pass to my dreary brother—"

John cleared his throat.

"Did I say dreary?" Henry smiled. "I meant my *dear* brother, who has quite enough property of his own. I should hate to put him to the task of managing my funds, particularly when I have proven such an embarrassment to him. I spoke to Colonel Hamilton in New York, and he worked a bit of legal magic on our behalf."

"How lovely."

"He enjoyed my essays. We argued about government some when we were in town."

"Did he correspond with you at all?"

"Yes, we corresponded a bit. We argued about what we were building here—a nation for all the misfits who never belonged elsewhere."

Mrs. Hamilton beamed. "That sounds so much like my Hamilton."

"I brought his letters, if you'd like a copy made."

This task, too, was shuffled off to the indispensable Mercy.

"And he was most sincere in his help," John said. "He introduced me to people who have been very helpful in making our venture the success it is."

"You seem very comfortable together," Mrs. Hamilton remarked at the end. "Mercy, you're getting all this down, aren't you?"

Mercy looked over at the two men. For some reason, she looked...well, sad, maybe. Perhaps angry. Or maybe that was pity John saw aimed in their direction, for some inexplicable reason. She bowed her head over the page, though, and whatever emotion she'd shown disappeared.

"Of course, Mrs. Hamilton," she said. "I would never miss a thing."

"Well." Mrs. Hamilton smiled graciously. "Thank you both so much for the tale, and the correspondence. I suppose you have business to do...?"

"A bit," Henry said. "More like, there are people whom I'd like to see, just to have a chance to talk with them. We're growing older. It's about time for us to hand off our duties to the next generation, you know. They tend to do a better job of it."

"Sometimes they do." She sighed.

"But then," John said, "that has always been the thought, hasn't it? We make the world we can, and tell those who come next how to make it better. I suppose we'll get all the way home eventually."

Author's Note

Thanks for reading *The Pursuit Of...* I hope you enjoyed it!

This story is a prequel (of sorts) to my next historical romance, *After the Wedding*—Adrian Hunter, a descendant of Lizzie and Noah Hunter, is the hero of that book.

If you want to know when that book (and the next ones I write) will be out, you can sign up for my new release e-mail list at www.courtneymilan.com, follow me on twitter at @court-neymilan, or like my Facebook page at http://facebook.com/courtneymilanauthor.

For a historical note on this novella, acknowledgments, and a list of other titles, please skip to the end.

To read *That Could Be Enough* by Alyssa Cole, just go to the next page.

THAT COULD BE
ENOUGH

BY ALYSSA COLE

Mercy Alston knows the best thing to do with pesky feelings like "love" and "hope": avoid them at all cost. Serving as a maid to Eliza Hamilton, and an assistant in the woman's stubborn desire to preserve her late husband's legacy, has driven that point home for Mercy—as have her own previous heartbreaks.

When Andromeda Stiel shows up at Hamilton Grange for an interview in her grandfather's stead, Mercy's resolution to live a quiet, pain-free life is tested by the beautiful, flirtatious, and entirely overwhelming dressmaker.

Andromeda has staid Mercy reconsidering her worldview, but neither is prepared for love—or for what happens when it's not enough.

For anyone with a heart of glass—shattered glass possesses its own kind of beauty.

Chapter One

Harlem, 1820

MERCY SHIVERED in the bracing morning air of her room and pulled her wrap more tightly about herself. She grumbled at the cold seeping up from the ground, then caught herself—it was better than the dank Gold Street cellar of her childhood. Perhaps her years at The Grange had made her soft at last, despite the hard work that kept her perpetually occupied.

She made her way across the small servants' quarters, walking confidently though there was no window and the sun's rays didn't illuminate her path. She could find anything in the darkness of her room after ten years at The Grange. That was the benefit of a simple, orderly life: no surprises to trip her up. Everything was as it should be.

She pulled out the chair at her desk, an old wooden thing that had made its circuit through the Hamilton children and now belonged to her. When she was young and foolish, she'd imagined she'd have her own writing desk in a home filled with laughter and warmth; lofty dreams for an orphaned Negro girl scraping by in New York City. She'd been promised those things many times over, but whispers in the darkness meant nothing once exposed to the harsh light of reality. She'd gotten her desk, at the very least.

It was a reliable and lovely old thing. She spread her hand over the surface in the darkness, traced her finger over the name *Philip* gouged deep into the wood. Mercy had always wondered if it was his handiwork, or a child's attempt at memorial to their brother. Perhaps it had been Angelica, who'd never recovered from the shock of his loss. These Hamiltons didn't let go of what they'd cherished. They tended to their love like keepers of the flame, nourishing it with ridiculous hope and hoarded memories. Mercy didn't understand them; she'd smothered her own flames, drowned them in tears and stirred the ashes until she was sure no embers remained.

She was fine now. She had a position in the home of a respected family. A room. A desk.

She'd received the desk after Mrs. Hamilton realized that Mercy could be of assistance with her interviews with, oh, just about anyone who'd ever crossed paths with Alexander Hamilton. Those damned, never-ending interviews that the widow threw so much energy into—both her own and that of everyone in her vicinity. That's what the desk was for: the work of preserving a legacy, and not even Mrs. Hamilton's own. Mercy sometimes wondered who Elizabeth Schuyler had been, and if she'd ever suspected that one day she would be sacrificed on the altar of her own devotion.

That was the thing no one told you: great love took more than it gave, and the greatest love could obliterate everything you'd been. It could eat up every bit of you—your past, your hopes and dreams—it was all-consuming, never satiated. Mercy's literacy and adeptness with words had been recruited to feed that awful hunger on behalf of Mrs. Eliza Hamilton, and thus Mercy's room had been outfitted with a desk. It was for efficiency's sake, nothing more.

Mrs. Hamilton didn't know about the words that had once pounded in Mercy's heart and in her skull and forced themselves through the nib of her quill like blood welling from a wound. Mrs. Hamilton didn't know the words had stopped, casualties of Mercy's own great love—they had been Mercy's sacrifice. It was all for the best, really. Those words had been dangerous.

Mercy had a brief flash of memory: paper curling into ash.

Her words—her world—being consumed by flames. A smile that she had once found lovely marred by contempt.

"Don't be foolish, Mercy. You seek beauty in everything, but sometimes there is no beauty in the truth."

Mercy still dutifully wrote every evening; the words were bland and dull now, but they were her own. She didn't know why she still indulged the urge; perhaps she retained a bit of the willfulness that had gotten her strappings for stealing books from the orphanage's library. Perhaps she was worried she'd simply disappear if she stopped putting pen to paper.

She reached for the striker and flint, lit the melted-down nub of her candle, and slid her journal in front of her. She tapped a finger on the page to ensure the ink had dried overnight, though if she smudged her banal musings it wouldn't be a tragic loss to the world of letters.

Awoke. Drank tea and ate a biscuit—must find new recipe for Sarah. Swept the parlor, study, and hall. Transcribed copy of E.H.'s interview with a Lieutenant Connor as requested by J.H. Sorted pack of correspondence between A.H. and C.M. ca. 1799, received from the lawyer of C.M. Walked Angelica about the grounds three times; she did not want to talk but was serene. Dusted Alexander in the foyer. Cleaned the front-facing windows and windowsills. Bathed. Yearned.

Mercy straightened in her seat, the abrupt scrape of the chair legs against the floor disturbing the morning quiet. That and the sudden skipping beat of her heart.

Yearned?

She had been exhausted the previous evening when she recorded her daily activities, but tired enough to slip and write *that*? It was rubbish, and she had no time for rubbish that wasn't being sorted or disposed of, especially not on an interview day.

She dipped her quill into the inkpot and carefully scratched out the word, starting with a line beneath it and then layering upward, walling it out.

Slept, she wrote in the space after the dark bruise of ink she'd created. That word was more fitting. Accurate, succinct, and something that was allowed to her in this life.

She stood up and dressed, slowly pulling on her stays,

chemise, and gown as she did every morning. She did up the buttons slowly and methodically; better to take her time than have to undo them and start again. She'd learned over the years that prudence in all things was the best course. It wasn't exciting, but she no longer had the constitution for excitement.

She lifted her elbow toward the ceiling and lowered her head to sniff; her dress would need a wash soon. Perhaps she'd try one of the suggestions she'd seen in the *Provincial Freeman*. She'd been meaning to try the brown soap and borax solution on her own clothing before washing anything in the household with it, but it was time-consuming with the overnight soak. Or maybe she'd get a new dress so she could go longer between washings. She had enough saved for one, for several really, but it seemed a bit futile. Who would notice?

She used a boar-bristle brush to scrape her thick hair down into a bun, squeezing a snood over the mass as big as her fist. With a tightening of her apron strings, she left her room and headed up toward the rectangle of morning light at the top of the stairs. When she'd first arrived, it had struck her that this particular moment was an ascension of sorts, and she had written just that in one of her letters to Jane.

Ascending the stairs into glorious light; like heaven's embrace after darkest night.

That letter was nothing but ash, as was the feeling that had pushed the words from her. Now she called it what it was: starting her workday. There was nothing poetic about it.

Mercy reached the top of the stairs and froze, caught up in the invisible grip of shock and pleasure and awe that had once been commonplace for her.

Beautiful. My heart...

There was an angel standing at the end of the hallway. Mercy was an irredeemable sinner, she'd been told, but she wasn't mistaken about the divine being before her.

Buttery rays of morning sun fought for the opportunity to dapple and highlight the woman at the end of the hall. Bright spots of lights formed a corona above her, the warm light silhouetting the shape of her against the wall of the foyer—and what a shape.

Her vivid green dress was expertly tailored, managing to be both sharp and soft as it hugged her curves, nipped in at the waist, then flared out to flow toward the floor. Mercy wasn't aware of the latest fashions, but she was sure the dress was on the outer limits of propriety. The bodice enhanced and drew the eye to the swell of her bosom. The split collar framed her neck, making one duly aware of the swanlike column.

The stranger's thick hair was pulled into a bun, too, and the mundane respectability of the hairstyle seemed at odds with everything else about the woman, but also somehow fitting. There was something in the way tufts of hair escaped at her temples and nape... Mercy could tell that those curls had been tamed into acquiescence with what was considered appropriate, and just barely. She wasn't so sure about their owner, judging from the jut of her hip and the way her chin tilted upward as she examined her surroundings.

No. Cease this train of thought.

Mercy knew better than to indulge in activities like observing a woman's shapeliness, but her gaze still clung to the stranger like damp cheesecloth, molding to her curves.

She had decided to turn back, to flee belowstairs where she belonged, when the woman looked in her direction. Their gazes caught, and even from that distance Mercy felt the tug of attraction.

No. No, no, no.

The angel began walking toward her. Marching, more like, if marching could be imbued with sensuality.

Large amber eyes set in a deep brown face; a smile that managed to be overfamiliar and curious at once. Those two features jumped out at Mercy, slammed into her with a nearly overwhelming force.

Not again.

Mercy raised a hand to the ache in her chest. There'd been a time when she'd felt beautiful things acutely. *Felt* them in her body and heart and soul. A flower pressed between the pages of a book had given her sustenance that even food could not. She'd shed tears at the sight of a bird with a ribbon streaming from its beak, flying toward its nest. She knew better than to expose herself like that now; years of experience and heartache had cured her of those naive tendencies. But the angel before her stirred that familiar sense of awe, of *want*, despite Mercy's hard-earned knowledge.

Mercy dropped her hand. Swallowed. Remembered who she was and what she was about.

"Are you being helped, miss?" she asked frostily. "It's rather early for uninvited guests; for those with manners, that is."

The smile didn't leave the angel's face. It shifted slowly, subtly, in a way that made Mercy reassess her first impression. This was no angel. The woman was most certainly a devil, come to tempt Mercy to wickedness. Lucifer had been the most beautiful angel of all, had he not? She'd read that in a poem, but Mercy couldn't imagine anything more beautiful than the woman approaching her.

The curve of the woman's lips was mocking, and the light, feminine sway of her hips took on a sudden, pendulous swagger. She approached, loose-limbed and fearless, making Mercy's rigidity more stark, more embarrassing.

Mercy had to look up a bit to meet the woman's gaze. Tension crept up her neck, spread over her scalp, as the woman stared down at her.

"Ahhhhh. You're one of those, are you?" the woman asked. Her voice was smooth and assured.

"One of what?" Mercy felt suddenly exposed. She tried so hard to keep her desires hidden, but it seemed this woman could see right through her. Her face grew hot and her breathing lost its rhythm so that she was suddenly aware that her body was doing it; for a moment, she forgot how to inhale.

The woman kept smiling, and assessing, and Mercy finally pulled in a breath.

"I am simply fulfilling my duty and trying to ascertain who you are." She tried to keep her tone firm and serious, as if she hadn't just gasped ridiculously like a trout at the seaport market.

The woman took a step forward, that teasing smile still on her lips, and Mercy saw that it hadn't been the effects of the morning sun casting the stranger in a good light; she was even lovelier up close.

"No," the woman said. "You were simply trying to put me in my place."

Mercy stared past the woman's shoulder, unable to look her full in the face. A wild sensation swelled in her chest; this beauty was painful. Mercy wanted to beat her fists against a wall, to scream. She'd thought herself done with such surges of emotion. She imagined this was the betrayal an old fisherman felt when a wall of water suddenly appeared on seas that had always been calm for him.

There was a brush against Mercy's face, and then the bare skin of the woman's thumb and forefinger pressed lightly into Mercy's jaw, guiding her face so that their gazes met. "Better than you have tried, friend. But if you'd like a go, I welcome the sport."

Mercy tried to think of a retort, but the press of those fingertips had the same effect on her thoughts as they would a candlewick, snuffing them out. Mercy couldn't tell if the woman's words were an invitation or a dare or both. Something Mercy had locked deep inside of her years before rattled the bars of its cage, eager to meet the woman's challenge. An image flashed in her mind of what sport could be had and a tremor went through her.

The woman's mocking smile returned.

"Miss Stiel?" Henry the butler's voice rang out in the hall, and both women turned toward it, though Mercy was the only one who jumped guiltily.

"Yes, I am Miss Andromeda Stiel, granddaughter of Elijah Sutton, he being a member of Lieutenant Colonel Alexander Hamilton's battalion, invited to Hamilton Grange for a meeting with one Mrs. Eliza Hamilton." The woman spoke at rapid-fire pace, though her demeanor was the picture of calm. "We went through this at the door when you attempted to leave me outside in the cold morning air like a beggar waiting for alms."

Andromeda. The name quite suited the woman.

"You were told to wait in the foyer," Henry said, not hiding his displeasure.

Mercy was impressed. This Andromeda wasn't making

Henry go all red-faced and befuddled; at least one of the staff had the situation in hand.

"Yes, I was, but the foyer is chilly and not at all where you leave a guest invited to your home," this Andromeda said. She tilted her head and looked at Henry for a moment, then sucked in a breath. "And, seeing how *I* am the one who's traveled all the way out to this far-flung corner of the earth, quite out of the way of the civilized regions of our fair city, to perform an act of kindness in granting Mrs. Hamilton's request for information from my grandfather Mr. Elijah Sutton, I thought perhaps I might see about getting a warm drink, as none was offered. Apologies if my desire to ward off the ague has put you out."

The words had been sharp and smooth, like Andromeda's dress, and delivered so quickly as to form a deluge of recrimination.

Mercy's eyes went wide as two red spots bloomed on Henry's cheeks. Henry? Blushing? None of the other servants would believe her if she told them.

"I beg your pardon," he said.

"And you shall receive it." She winked at Henry and his blush deepened. "Now about that warm drink?" She turned and caught Mercy's gaze, held it, then tilted her head meaningfully down the stairs before swaying toward the parlor.

Mercy understood two things quite well: one, *she'd* just been put in *her* place, and with an efficiency that was remarkable; and two, if she'd thought previous interviews she'd sat in on had been difficult, the one awaiting her would be the worst of them. Being in the same room as this Miss Stiel would be a test of will.

She raised a hand to her chin and notched her fingers where the skin still tingled from the woman's unexpected touch.

Andromeda.

This interview needed to be over with quickly; Mercy would only be able to breathe naturally again once the woman was out of her sight.

Chapter Two

MERCY OFTEN FOUND the parlor drafty, with all those large windows, but she was exceedingly warm that morning. The normally sedate room throbbed with the echo of Andromeda's words.

"After Lafayette wouldn't give in, my grandfather tried to calm Hamilton down. Hamilton wasn't having it, though, so he stormed off to Washington and the decision was made in his favor because *of course* he knew his ranking relative to every other man who might try to steal his chance at glory," Andromeda said with a shrug of her shoulders and roll of her eyes, as if she were speaking to an old friend and not the esteemed wife of one of the Founding Fathers of their nation.

Mrs. Hamilton had heard this story many times before, but she was rapt, nodding along with delight.

The interview had started off like any other, with Mrs. Hamilton going through the list of her husband's qualities that she wanted to highlight in her project: *elasticity of his mind; variety of his knowledge; playfulness of his wit; excellence of his heart; and his immense forbearance and virtues.*

Then Andromeda had made a joke bordering on lewd about Hamilton's other reportedly immense virtue. Mercy expected her to be escorted out, but Mrs. Hamilton had simply let out a peal of scandalized laughter before reminiscing about

Hamilton's bawdy humor. That had led to a detailed recounting of their courtship for Andromeda; she'd even removed her prized sonnet—the first he'd ever written her—from the pouch she wore about her neck and read it aloud. Mercy had stared into the fireplace and run through the chores she would have to do later, not needing to hear the poem again.

They'd only just started in on the actual interview.

Mercy glanced at Mrs. Hamilton, who leaned forward in her seat, captivated by Andromeda's storytelling. Mercy sat stiffly with the battered old portable desk on her lap, taking notes. She wrote salient points down, but in her mind, she was compiling her own dossier.

Andromeda was a seamstress with her own shop in the Montgomerie ward, though she had grown up on a farm in Suffolk County. Her grandfather, Elijah Sutton, had fought alongside Hamilton, and it was his story she was relaying because he had taken ill and was unable to make the journey. Her hands fluttered about when she grew excited, which was often. She gave each character in her story a different voice, as if she were telling a bedtime tale, and her French accent was endearingly bad. Sometimes she jumped out of her seat to act things out, and she had reached over and touched Mrs. Hamilton's arm multiple times as she talked. She was not one for social strictures.

Watching her is excruciating.

Mercy almost got up to open the window, just to soothe the restless itch this irksome woman induced in her. She usually sat silently in the background of these interviews, but she was too agitated this time, pouring tea, adjusting the drapes, tending to the fire. It didn't help that each time she did her job, Andromeda stopped her deluge of words and pointedly thanked her. Each time, what should have been a common nicety felt like a caress. Mercy took pride in her work, in doing her job well, but she didn't feel warmth unspool in her when Mrs. Hamilton commended her on the dusting.

Andromeda glanced at Mercy as she spoke, a wide smile on her face, as if she was waiting for Mercy to join in on the laughter and conversation.

Mercy looked down at her paper and jotted down a few more words. That's all she was there for. She knew what had passed at Yorktown, had heard the story from dozens of different perspectives. She had no real need of note-taking, other than as an escape from that honeyed gaze.

"Yes, of course my Hamilton did," Mrs. Hamilton said, beaming. "He wanted to fight more than anything. To create a legacy."

"My grandfather always admired that," Andromeda said, sipping her coffee. "He won his freedom from slavery by fighting in his master's stead, and he respected that Hamilton fought on the frontlines when he could have passed the war protected. He said that Hamilton took risks that were mad, foolish perhaps, but he was driven by a love for his country so strong that he couldn't do otherwise. Grandfather was the same, in a way. Escaped a British prison camp in Brooklyn with my mother and grandmother on horseback—across the East River! —just to get back to fighting."

"No!" Mrs. Hamilton exclaimed, delighted.

"Yes!" Andromeda said, excited as if it was the first time she'd heard the story too. "And after getting them settled, he headed straight for General Washington. As Grandfather tells it, he was initially refused an audience, until he encountered Colonel Hamilton. Grandfather explained that after Washington withdrew from Brooklyn, he had escaped a British prison camp, swam the river with a horse, and tracked Washington down. He said he believed in what America could be, and that he was going to fight for that bright possibility whether he was granted permission to do so or not."

Mrs. Hamilton laughed. "Oh, Alexander would have loved that. I can just picture his face." She stroked the sachet attached to her necklace.

Andromeda nodded. "I suppose he did, as Grandfather found himself in your Hamilton's battalion."

Mercy glanced up sharply. *Your Hamilton.* People didn't usually pick up on that so quickly or refer to him the same way Mrs. Hamilton did once they had. It made some guests uncomfortable, the bald possessiveness of the words. The covetousness. But Andromeda said it easily, as if it were a given.

Mrs. Hamilton looked through her folio. "I especially wanted to talk to your grandfather because several members of the battalion have related a story about him. They said Elijah Sutton was strong as a bull, and that at Yorktown he nearly launched Hamilton over the parapet and into the British lines like a cannonball!"

"Ah yes. Grandfather doesn't tell the story quite that way but he's exceedingly modest. He might have launched his commander to the moon but would have said he simply helped him get a bird's eye view of the battlefield."

Mercy watched as Mrs. Hamilton burst into giggles and Andromeda joined her. Was this her same mistress? Who worried over orphans and bills and her own children? Who was constantly in motion, only sitting still to remember *him*—often with tears standing in her eyes? Was she laughing with this forward visitor like a carefree girl? The only person who ever had this effect on her was her sister, Mrs. Church.

Perhaps Andromeda really was otherworldly.

Sarah, the brown-haired maid, scuttled into the room. "Mrs. Hamilton? Sorry to disturb you, but it's Miss Angelica…"

The laughter faded, and Mrs. Hamilton raised her brows. "Yes, Sarah, what is it?"

"She keeps asking after Philip, insisting that he was to take her out this morning. She's working herself up into a fit because he hasn't shown."

There was a rustle, and a shadow fell over the teapot and scones as Andromeda stood. "I must be going, so no need to worry about inconveniencing me," she said brightly.

"Oh, but you weren't finished!" Mrs. Hamilton's dark eyes sparked and her mouth pulled in tight. "Will you be able to come back?"

There was a hunger in her tone. It seemed she could never hear enough about her husband; she was doomed to be perpetually famished.

"Probably not anytime soon. I have my businesses to run. I made a detour while returning from visiting my family upstate, as I was supposed to escort Grandfather. But I will write."

"Yes, that will do, I suppose…" Mrs. Hamilton heaved a deep sigh, then her head slowly turned toward Mercy. "Aren't you due to go into town on your next day off?"

"Yes," Mercy said, her heart plummeting. She didn't go into town frequently, and since she didn't have much else to do, often worked on her day off. But that didn't mean she wanted to be *given* work. Especially when she had an idea of what that work would be.

"Well, you can meet Miss Stiel and transcribe her story, can't you? I'd give you an extra day's pay."

No.

But of course she couldn't say no. Even people who weren't servants couldn't say no to this woman. The fact that she was still in her comfortable home despite being widowed with seven children and crushing debt was a testament to that.

Mercy gave a sharp nod and looked over at Andromeda, who was regarding her with a curious expression.

"If she doesn't mind," Mercy said. She almost raised a hand to touch her chin where Andromeda had earlier, but stopped herself. "Perhaps she's too busy to meet and would prefer to write the letter."

"I can make the time," Andromeda replied. "If Mrs. Hamilton prefers I speak with you, I find that I prefer that arrangement as well."

Mercy tried not to let the warmth in Andromeda's tone wrap around her. She held on to her annoyance as stubbornly as King George had held on to the colonies; admitting that Andromeda affected her so deeply with so few words would certainly lead to madness.

"Excellent," Mrs. Hamilton said.

"I will be in town two days from now," Mercy said stiffly.

"My shop is in Montgomerie ward," Andromeda said. "Are you familiar with the area near Gold Street?"

Mercy nodded. She was all too familiar with the neighborhood. The memories of her past haunted those streets: her parents' laughter echoing over the cobblestones, Jane's lips brushing over Mercy's in the dark alley as they headed back from their work.

She gave a tight nod.

Andromeda's gaze ran over Mercy's body, lingering on her chest and hips. Mercy squirmed under the perusal. Was it… could Andromeda also feel… Mercy was confused, but then Andromeda spoke. "Perhaps I can take in your dress for you while you're in town, spruce it up a bit."

Heat rushed to Mercy's cheeks as she realized she'd misunderstood. She wasn't vain—she was quite aware she had no reason to be—but the insult stung.

"My dress is quite fine as it is," Mercy said, voice cool. "Not everyone desires to be so ostentatious."

"Pity, that," Andromeda said with a wink, then took her leave.

"She was delightful, wasn't she?" Mrs. Hamilton asked as she got up to attend to Angelica.

"She's quite forward," Mercy said, pursing her lips. "And talks far too much, and too quickly."

"Just delightful."

Chapter Three

ANDROMEDA COULD TELL from the stiffness of the knock at the shop door that it was Mercy and not a customer. She could just imagine her standing there in her dour coat and hat, knocking like the undertaker come to collect a corpse—mostly because she had already seen Mercy approach the shop, raise her hand to knock, then turn on her heels and flee, twice in the previous two hours.

Mrs. Hamilton's maid was pulled tight as the seams on a dress two sizes too small for its owner, and she didn't seem particularly amenable to being let out. Andromeda didn't know why, but from the moment she'd clapped eyes on Mercy, she'd wanted to take her shears to those taut seams, to snip them one by one until the woman could breathe again. She wouldn't mind seeing Mercy breathless, too, but under much more pleasant circumstances.

Andromeda had always been game for a challenge; she'd been the bane of her parents' and grandparents' existence on their family farm, her ceaseless curiosity and energy getting her into constant scrapes. But now she had too much on her plate between managing the shop and pursuing her other business ventures to deal with an uptight wench like Mercy.

Uptight but in no way unresponsive...

Andromeda thought of the way Mercy had gasped and gone

wide-eyed when she'd caught her by the chin. Andromeda shouldn't have done it—it was uncouth, grabbing at a servant like a lascivious houseguest—but it had been pure instinct. Mercy was like a lovely, classic dress pattern tucked into a drawer, or a fine set of shears gone to rust. Andromeda was impulsive, but not wasteful, and something in the way the woman had looked at her screamed loneliness, which was the ultimate waste.

And the way Mercy had responded to that brief touch...she hadn't pulled away, or been frightened or disgusted. Instead her eyes had blazed with a heat that her frosty tone could never ice over. Her lips had parted invitingly, and a shiver had gone through her. Mercy had liked Andromeda's touch; more worrying was the fact Andromeda had liked that Mercy had liked it.

You have neither time for nor interest in dreary housemaids... which is why you're wearing your best day dress and spent far too long oiling and plaiting your hair.

"Should you get that?" Tara asked. The girl was standing still as Andromeda poked pins into her dress, but leaned forward to peek at the front of the shop through the door of the fitting room. "Ouch!"

"Be still, now!" Andromeda said through lips pressed around several straight pins. She folded another bit of fabric down, pinned, then pulled the pins from where she clamped down on them and dropped them onto the floor.

There was another series of agitated knocks at the door.

"Change out of that and leave it on the chair there, and you can take Mrs. Kelley's dress for mending to put toward the cost of your own," Andromeda instructed, then walked into the storefront and pulled the curtain shut behind her. She ran her hand over her dress, giving a final tug at the sleeves and pull of the collar. She didn't need a reflective surface to know the dress fit like a glove and highlighted her assets; her shop was popular for a reason.

When she unlatched the door, Mercy stood there, brown eyes wide beneath her fine brows, lush mouth pulled into a frown. Her skin was a light brown with undertones of orange and yellow; she'd be stunning in something warm and eye-catching instead of the drab dress of a scullery maid. Andromeda imagined dressing her in the finest fabrics, draping swaths of it over that curvaceous body first to see how the colors suited her…

A blush rose to Mercy's cheeks and Andromeda realized she was staring, and not at all innocently.

"Hello. Pleasure to see you, Miss Mercy."

"Hello," Mercy said. Her voice trembled a bit, and she made a small hum of agitation that Andromeda found to be adorable. "My apologies for not coming earlier, but I was held up by some important matters."

Andromeda considered teasing Mercy about running away instead of knocking earlier, but the woman was already tensed and ready to bolt. Instead, Andromeda moved aside and allowed her to enter.

Mercy squeezed by, pressing herself against the doorframe while lifting her head high, as if that was a completely normal way to enter an establishment. She avoided even the slightest brush of her coat against Andromeda's dress, and exhaled once she was inside the shop, as though she'd bypassed a gauntlet.

A delicious, dangerous feeling swam up to Andromeda's head. It was the victory of having her suspicion affirmed mixed with the heady possibilities that lay before her.

Nothing lies before you but completing this interview and sending this woman on her way.

Mercy was attracted to her; Andromeda reminded herself that she needn't do anything with this knowledge. It wasn't a novelty, after all, nor was the fact that she was also attracted to Mercy. Still…Andromeda was intrigued.

"I'm just wrapping something up and then we can be off," she said, shutting the door and heading behind the shop's counter.

"Off?" Mercy's question was faint, and Andromeda noticed she was looking about the shop with a kind of wonder. That pleased Andromeda. She'd gone to great lengths to change her little shop from the hovel it had been when she'd received the deed: sanding, burnishing, and staining the floors and beams and counters; hanging eye-catching fabrics and building lovely display cases; making sure the space was inviting and well stocked. Mercy was staring at a little wooden bird hung from a rafter with red ribbon that swayed to and fro. There was actual pleasure on her face.

"Do you like what you see?" Andromeda asked, and Mercy glanced at her sharply. Her expression went guarded and closed off again.

"It could use a bit of tidying," she said. Her gaze went to the shelves of fabric, and now that Andromeda paid attention, they *were* stacked a bit haphazardly. Her receipts *were* scattered behind the register. Scraps of papers covered with sketches of dresses littered the shelves. While creation and presentation were her strong suits, tidiness was not. She'd grown up on a horse farm, and had learned that ideas of cleanliness were rather relative. The floor wasn't covered with horse muck and flies weren't swarming the shop, which was all many people could ask for.

"You would notice that, wouldn't you?" Andromeda asked, not hiding her amusement.

"It's my job," Mercy replied.

"It's your parry, more like," Andromeda said, casually nudging a pile of papers with her thumb. She was amused by Mercy, but she was prideful. She also enjoyed seeing Mercy's brows rise and the flush come to her cheeks as she watched the papers scatter and drift slowly to the floor. Mercy was quite lovely when she was piqued.

"Oh dear," Andromeda said, then stepped around the mess. "To answer your question, we're *off* to Lady Bess's, across the street. We can talk there."

Mercy's gaze shifted to Andromeda; her mouth was pursed in that disagreeable manner that made Andromeda want to kiss some softness into her. "I agreed to come to this establishment to conduct Mrs. Hamilton's business. I didn't agree to go to a tavern of ill repute."

Andromeda rubbed at her hands; her joints ached from doubling her workload the day before in order to leave time for the interview with Mercy. She wasn't fastidious when it came to cleaning, but she was a woman who cared about her business and didn't leave it to chance. "Well, I require sustenance," Andromeda said. "Feel free to stay here and hold down the shop until I return."

Tara came out from the back in her fraying muslin, carrying the dresses she'd take home to mend. She looked back and forth between the two women and handed Andromeda a few coins to pay toward her dress's completion, then headed out.

Andromeda handed the coins to Mercy, who still stood resolutely in the shop. "Put those in the till, will you? And perhaps you can give the place a sweep and get started hemming Tara's dress. I bet your basting stitch is *exacting*."

Andromeda pulled on her coat, giving Mercy directions on things that needed doing in a whirlwind of words all the while. She didn't let up for a moment, the words rushing out of her as they did when she was unsettled—which was quite something considering how quickly they already flowed when she was not. She had stepped through the door onto the square of clean ground in front of her shop when Mercy rushed out behind her.

"Feeling peckish after all?" Andromeda asked. "Really, perhaps you should eat more. Your dress is about a size too large and three years out of fashion. If you want, after we finish the interview, or after you sweep the shop, whichever you decide to do because really I don't understand why you would pass up a chance for delicious—"

"Enough! Miss Stiel. You are—"

Andromeda turned to see Mercy standing with her eyes shut tightly and her hands gripping her satchel, as if she were contemplating using it as a cudgel. Andromeda had wound the poor woman a bit too tightly, it seemed.

"Infuriating?" Andromeda asked, gentling her tone. "Over-confident? Irksome?"

She reached out and brushed her fingertips down Mercy's arm. It didn't matter that there were layers of fabric between her glove and Mercy's skin; she needed to touch her. Again.

A tremble went through the agitated woman, then she opened her eyes and fixed Andromeda with a frustrated glare. "Yes. Yes. And yes."

She really was lovely; Andromeda would have to find another way to bring the color to her cheeks and this brightness to her eyes.

"Anything else?" Andromeda asked.

Mercy's gaze swept over Andromeda's face and down her body and back up again, and Andromeda was shocked to feel her own face flush. There was something in that glance that she recognized: desire. Brief but blatant and not at all fitting with Mercy's prudish demeanor.

Heat and a heady sense of anticipation slipped over Andromeda's body like the finest silk. She wanted to see that look again, to fall into it and explore the delightful paths it might lead to.

Mercy opened her mouth, then shut it, shook her head. "Quite a character," she added to the list. She dropped the coins into Andromeda's hand and stood to the side as Andromeda locked the door to the shop.

"My words get away from me sometimes," Andromeda said. "My mother often said she could gentle the wildest horse but never stood a chance with me."

There was a spark of curiosity in Mercy's eyes, but the woman wouldn't be drawn into casual conversation so easily.

"I'm just not used to such a...*lively* personality," Mercy said, falling into step beside Andromeda.

Andromeda could tell she wasn't trying to insult her this time, so she didn't push back.

Lady Bess's Tavern was packed with the working class of the neighborhood: men, mostly, of all races, American-born and foreigner both. Carpenters, coopers, cordwainers, and more were all crammed around rough wooden tables, talking loudly as they broke bread and raised their glasses of ale.

Andromeda strode through the crowd, tipping her hat and clapping men on the back as her skirts brushed their tables. Most of the men were regulars, and she inquired about children, shops, horses, and whatever applicable bit of information she possessed about them. She responded effusively to good news and gave condolences on the bad.

She saw Mr. Porter having a pint and waved at him. He

grudgingly lifted his glass in her direction. She could have hoped for a better response from the man she was staking her future business plans on, but it was a start.

When she finally made it to her usual table, she'd worked up a thirst and an appetite.

She directed Mercy, who had gone round-eyed and stiff again, into a chair, then caught Bess's eye across the room and held up two fingers before sprawling into her own seat.

"This crowd is rather boisterous," Mercy said, drawing herself up straighter. "And rough-looking."

Andromeda laughed. "How long have you been tucked away uptown that you consider this rough-looking? We'll come back around midnight and I'll show you rough."

Mercy blushed and Andromeda grinned, because she hadn't even been trying that time.

"I'm no stranger to this area," Mercy said. "My family lived in one of the cellar apartments over on Gold." Her face had gone tight and proper again, all the softness of her flush gone.

Andromeda knew how terrible those cellars were: overcrowded, moldering from the damp, and often ravaged by outbreaks of disease. They were usually let out to Negroes while the houses above were rented by whites. Though she loved the city, she'd grown up in the open air of the country, surrounded by horses and trees and blue sky. She couldn't imagine how restrictive such a childhood had been. Perhaps that explained Mercy's demeanor.

"After my parents died of yellow fever, I was sent to an orphanage," Mercy continued. "So I know more than a bit about how rough things can get in this neighborhood, thank you."

Or perhaps *that* explained it.

Andromeda felt a sudden strong tenderness for Mercy as she thought of her own family and tried to imagine what her life would have been like without them. What did loss do to a person? She was lucky enough not to know. "I'm sorry," she said.

"Nothing to be sorry about," Mercy replied bluntly. "It was better for my parents to pass together; they would have been desperately unhappy without one another. And I did fine for myself."

Her feigned indifference said otherwise.

Andromeda felt that tenderness again. She wanted to take Mercy's hand, to give her comfort. She restrained herself. "That you did. I'm sure your parents would be proud of you."

"For being a housemaid? Perhaps."

"Is there something else you'd prefer to be?" Andromeda asked. She thought it a simple question, but Mercy closed up like a clam pulled from the mud along the Hudson.

"You didn't say how long you've been with the Hamiltons," Andromeda prodded, trying another tack. Mercy let out a breath of relief, seemingly pleased to no longer have to talk about her family or aspirations.

"I've been there, oh, ten years now."

"Ten years?" Andromeda raised her brows. "You hardly ever hear of someone sticking with a family for that long these days, and especially at a home so removed from everything. Most girls I know stay for a year or two and then move on. I get to hear customers complain as much, too. They simply can't imagine why these headstrong girls don't want to stay and empty their chamber pots."

Mercy lifted a shoulder. "It's quiet there. Being away from the city isn't such a bad thing."

Mercy's expression pinched at that last bit, pricking Andromeda's curiosity even more. Mercy was like an intricate puzzle with clockwork parts; Andromeda kept thinking she had her figured out, then a piece would shift and she'd be right back where she started.

"I thought it would be temporary when I took the job. It doesn't feel like ten years have gone by. I started around the time Mrs. Hamilton returned to The Grange after...certain personal matters had been resolved," Mercy said. She opened her bag and took out her pot of ink and quill and folio, placing each item down reluctantly, as if she hated to subject them to such a lowly resting place.

Andromeda rolled her eyes. "After Mrs. Hamilton cleared a path through that heap of debt she was left with after Hamilton's death, you mean?" A server placed two mugs of ale on the table and Andromeda took one up, taking two swift gulps of the bitter brew.

"A good servant doesn't discuss the private matters of their employer," Mercy said. She lifted her mug, sniffed, and placed it back down, and Andromeda felt another little chip at the flint of her annoyance and her intrigue.

So much for easier topics. Why was this woman so persnickety? And why did Andromeda so enjoy baiting her?

"Private?" Andromeda laughed. "Hamilton's business was all over Front Street, quite literally. In the form of a pamphlet. There's still a copy behind the bar, if you'd like to see it."

"Speaking of the dearly departed Hamilton, why don't we get this interview over with?" Mercy dipped her quill into the inkpot and then looked up, and Andromeda saw the same change in demeanor that she'd adopted that day in Eliza Hamilton's parlor.

"Parapet, cannonball, strong grandfather..." Mercy offered up when Andromeda didn't answer. "You know, the story I came here to collect."

Andromeda glanced at the way Mercy gripped her quill, the way she suddenly seemed a bit more in control of things. "Would I be wrong to venture that annotating Colonel Hamilton's life isn't the only thing you use that for?"

Mercy didn't answer, just stared across the table at Andromeda.

Andromeda had once found a tomcat in the family stable while mucking. She'd knelt down and held out her hand, waiting. The cat had hissed, glared at her, yowled in warning. Eventually, it had decided she was safe to approach, and its deep purr had vibrated through her hand as it rubbed itself against her, desperate for affection. Mercy seemed ready to hiss if Andromeda continued her line of questioning, but Mercy had also leaned into Andromeda's touch during that first meeting, before she'd remembered herself.

"It's just..." Andromeda tempered her words; Mercy was already prepared to bolt into the figurative underbrush. "When I take hold of a threaded needle, or work my shears through a fresh piece of fabric, it's not just work to me. There's something in me that, I guess you could say it sings, when I have a needle in my hand. I thought I saw a bit of that in you."

"You were mistaken," Mercy said in her clipped tone. "The majority of my writing is about Colonel Hamilton in preparation for his biography. As if he didn't churn out enough words about himself in his lifetime." She took a sip of her ale. "Mrs. Hamilton is continuing his grand tradition and I'm simply doing as she says, a pawn in a love story that should have been buried with the man instead of memorialized."

Andromeda had heard Mercy frosty and prim and judgmental, but there was *anger* in her words now. She thought of the way Mercy's brows had drawn behind Mrs. Hamilton's back every time the widow went on a tear about her departed husband, of Mercy's lips pressed tightly together in judgment. One wouldn't notice unless they had been paying attention to Mercy's every move, but then, Andromeda hadn't been able to do otherwise.

The serving woman appeared and placed two large plates of mutton and carrots before them, nearly nudging the small inkpot off of the table. Mercy scowled and grabbed it, corking it and placing it in her bag along with the paper and quill.

"I can't work like this," she said, gesturing toward the large plate.

Andromeda took up her utensils. "Then it seems you'll have to eat."

Mercy sighed dramatically, but didn't fight Andromeda for once. She began to eat, and wasn't able to hide her surprise at how good the food was. She seemed content to eat in silence, but the lack of conversation made Andromeda feel itchy.

"Does it really bother you?" Andromeda asked. "Your mistress's lingering affection for her husband? I think it's quite romantic."

Mercy had taken up a bit of mutton, but paused with the fork en route to her mouth. The telltale brows drew together. "Who says I'm bothered?"

"You, actually. You're not very good at hiding your opinions." This elicited a dainty snort from her companion. "During my interview, I caught sight of a lovely vein at your temple that showed itself every time she said 'my Hamilton.' Ah, there it is!'

Mercy lowered her fork.

"He wasn't *hers* though," Mercy said. The words had some force behind them, despite her supposed lack of botheredness. "Anyone who's read the pamphlet you spoke of is keenly aware of that. Anyone who's skimmed his letters with John Laurens could guess at that, too. He hurt and humiliated her while he lived, and she's still giving every bit of herself to him all these years after his death."

Andromeda wondered if Mercy realized she was cutting her mutton into smaller and smaller pieces as she spoke.

"Come now, Mercy. She loved him. And was loved by him."

"He had a fine way of showing it," Mercy said, finally getting a bit of the food onto her fork. "After all that, after she forgave him for humiliating her, for dashing their family's hopes, for Philip, he went and got himself killed! He left for his duel without even giving her the truth of his destination or a chance to stop his foolish plan. In the end, his pride was worth more to him than her undying affection. And yet she persists."

When Mercy looked up, her eyes were bright, and she chewed just a bit ferociously.

Mercy spoke of love as if it was muck she had to clean out of fine lace. Intriguing. Andromeda had loved before, and she didn't doubt its power. She had her grandparents and her parents as models of conjugal bliss and the work that went into it.

"Are you bothered by the fact that he hurt her or that she has forgiven him for it?" Andromeda asked. She shouldn't have cared either way, but it seemed her curiosity grew with each inadvertent revelation instead of diminishing.

"I'm *bothered* that people use love as an excuse to spend their lives pining away or devoted to some sainted memory. Love is impractical and unrealistic, and indulging it to such a degree is unsavory."

There was that lovely pique again. Mercy's nostrils flared and her fist was tight around her fork, but her eyes...her eyes flashed with challenge, like a lighthouse beckoning to a ship that must cross stormy seas to reach it.

An idea began to form in Andromeda's mind, like the outline of a pattern she just had to create. A scandalous, ill-advised pattern that should never see the light of day. Her favorite kind, if she were being honest.

"You're telling me that you don't believe in love?" Andromeda asked.

Mercy pursed her lips. "Look around this room. How many people do you think have found everlasting love?"

She jerked her chin toward a man pulling a bawdy woman into his lap.

"What's that got to do with anything?" Andromeda retorted. "I'm asking if you, Mercy, believe in love."

Just say yes.

"Of course not," Mercy said and stabbed a carrot on her plate. "It isn't worth the bother."

Oh hell.

The pattern in Andromeda's head took on a form that she couldn't resist—oddly enough, it was precisely Mercy's measure. Andromeda would have consigned it to the mental trash heap where she placed ideas that weren't meant to be, but she had the nagging feeling that it just might be her most beautiful creation ever.

She smiled at Mercy. Lord above, but Andromeda did love a challenge.

Chapter Four

MERCY TRIED NOT to show her relief as she gathered her belongings and placed them carefully into her bag. She thought she'd handled the situation well. She'd held herself at a distance, had batted off most of Andromeda's personal inquiries.

She'd kept her face impassive when Andromeda tried to charm her, and had mustered outright annoyance when Andromeda deployed her conspiratorial grin, as if asking Mercy to join in on the fun. Annoyance was safer than giving in to the desire to lean in closer to the intriguing woman across from her. To stop fighting against the curiosity—against the undeniable attraction.

No. There will be none of that. There couldn't be. What she'd had with Jane, and the girls before Jane, had broken her heart. It had broken her. She didn't remember ever feeling as drawn to them as she was to Andromeda, either. This new desire was too dangerous. Much too dangerous.

She placed the ink into her bag and closed it resolutely. She ignored the tension in her neck and shoulders, the slight twitch beneath her eye. There was nothing to worry over any longer. She would go back to The Grange. There was no cause to ever see the vexing Andromeda again. She should have been elated and yet…perhaps just one more question.

She'd read a few accounts of love from the members of the

battalion, and what they had done to gain it. Those interviews had intrigued and irritated her. Elijah Sutton's behavior was the most confounding of all.

"Your grandfather," Mercy pulled on her glove. Perhaps the ale had gone to her head. Yes, that was it. "He really stayed behind in a British prison camp after freeing his men? On the off chance he could convince your grandmother to leave with him?"

"Well, of course. He loved her," Andromeda said, as if that explained everything.

"He barely knew her," Mercy replied.

"I wasn't aware that there was a limit on how quickly a person might fall in love," Andromeda said. "Or on what they'd do to preserve it once they had."

Mercy felt that acutely. She'd once believed that the bonds of love were the strongest material in the known world. When she'd been young and foolish, of course.

"My parents loved each other like that." Mercy stared down at her glove and flexed her fingers. "'Love at first sight,' my father used to say. When my mother fell ill, he wouldn't leave her side. And when he caught the sickness too, they still sought each other out even in their deepest fever dreams."

Mercy remembered checking on them that last time, how the heavy silence had warned her but had not prepared her for their lifeless eyes and the way they held each other. For the realization that their love was so great that they had chosen to leave their only child alone rather than live without one another.

She'd hated her parents for leaving her, but had also wanted what they'd shared so badly. She'd gone from girl to girl, always devastated when things inevitably fell apart. She'd thought she'd found it with Jane—had finally, finally found it. She hadn't, but she'd learned why neither of her parents had wanted to be left behind. Love was a terrible thing, and powerful—and having tasted that power once, Mercy was certain she wouldn't survive its loss a second time.

Andromeda's hand came into Mercy's line of vision, then rested atop her own, stroking the back of it through the thin material of her glove. "Who took care of you, Mercy?"

God, that touch. Mercy could have cried from the loveliness of it. It was soothing and insinuating and sent both peacefulness and panic racing through her body. She pulled her hand away and looked about the pub, sure everyone would be staring at them after the intimate caress.

"What will people say?" Mercy's voice shook and her heart felt as if it would beat out of her chest. She should have just left without asking any questions. Without revealing anything of herself. Asking about Elijah Sutton had been impulsive, and she'd paid for it, as usual.

Andromeda shrugged, the picture of calm indifference. "Old Bill over there would say thankee for the wedding dress I made for his daughter for a quarter of my usual price. Hamish would tell me how his shop that I helped repair after the fire a few months back is coming along. Bess would tell me not to piddle about with a Miss with a branch up her arse, and to try a real woman like herself."

That drew a sharp gasp from Mercy; Andromeda smiled in satisfaction and raised a brow.

"No one judges you for…" Mercy moved her head and shoulders about, unable to say the words aloud. "You know."

"For being damn nigh irresistible?" Andromeda asked. She wasn't entirely jesting, but Mercy couldn't call her vain. She was justified in that confidence. "They might judge me. But they know I'm a good person and a good friend, and around here, that's what matters."

Mercy couldn't accept that. She felt a flash of anger at the casual confidence in Andromeda's tone.

"And I'm sure your family feels the same way." Mercy thought she'd delivered a line that would surely wipe that smug look from Andromeda's face, but the vexing woman didn't bat a lash.

"Oh, you know there were all kinds of people in the battalion."

Andromeda was right. There was Rachel…Jacobs? No, Mendelson. The woman had dressed in men's clothing to fight for her country. And a few years earlier, a soldier named John Hunter had arrived for an interview with his business partner. It had been quite clear to Mercy that they were partners in a great many more things, and oh how she had envied them. But still… she hadn't considered…

"Grandfather always told me that it didn't matter who a person loved, but how well they treated others and what they did to make this country and this world better. That has been the family philosophy pertaining to the general populace, and I'm pleased to report it also applies to me."

Mercy felt the words like a blow to the belly. That couldn't be true. No. Because Jane had said…well, if Andromeda's words were true, if she lived as she wished and was still accepted, then everything Jane told her all those years ago had been wrong. Lies. Mercy's tears, her pain—her words curling into ash and her world crumpling in on itself—had all been for naught.

She couldn't discuss it any further.

"You should return to the shop now," Mercy said as she fastened her cloak and drew herself up, preparing to leave. She couldn't stay a moment longer, with her thoughts scattered as they were.

She was met with silence.

Andromeda was examining her, head tilted to the side. It was the longest the woman had been quiet, and it made her nervous. Mercy knew her cloak was as unfashionable as her dress; her hair was done in two simple cornrows instead of a stylish bouffant; she was a plain woman. Andromeda was probably cataloguing her faults: priggish, frumpy, boring.

"Be sure to tidy behind the counter," Mercy reminded her curtly. Somewhat impolite, but better than *Stop reminding me of what I can't have.*

"An unprovoked parry," Andromeda murmured. The chastisement seemed to amuse her. "I do have work to finish, but…" Her head tilted even more, and Mercy realized the vexing woman was scheming. Yes. That tilt, that grin, the way crow's feet bracketed her eyes, highlighting the mischief in them. "What are you doing with the rest of your afternoon?"

"Returning to The Grange, of course," Mercy said. She began making her way through the tavern, which was quieter and less crowded given that much of the lunchtime crowd had come and gone.

Yes. That is it. That is all. You have achieved your task and should return home.

"Isn't today your day off?" Andromeda asked as they stepped into the street. She kept pace with Mercy's strides easily.

"It is my day of rest and I've yet to do that. I visited at the orphanage before I came here and I'm fatigued."

That soft, pitying look came over Andromeda's face again and Mercy wished she hadn't revealed that. She usually sent her donations in, but had stopped by on a whim. She had resisted returning to the orphanage for years, sure that it would be painful, but it hadn't been. Not *very*. She'd been happy to see that the facilities had improved, and to speak to some of the children. Her visit hadn't brought emotion crashing down about her ears.

She hadn't even flinched when the director of the orphanage mentioned how Jane had been in to visit with her husband and children a few months back. She was glad that her friend had gotten the life she wanted. In that moment, Mercy realized she'd never asked herself what she herself wanted in the years since Jane's decision had brought her dreams crashing down around her. Why was that?

Because you were too busy focusing on what you should not want.

"What did you do at the orphanage?" Andromeda asked, interrupting Mercy's introspection.

"I helped the children with their letters," Mercy said.

"So your entire day of rest has been spent in the service of others." Andromeda *tsk*ed, and the sound drew Mercy's attention back to the exasperating woman's mouth. It was a mouth that inspired queries: were her lips as soft as they looked? Would she kiss how she spoke, brash and unrelenting? It wouldn't be so terrible to find out, would it?

Questions that should remain unanswered, and further proof that Mercy should return home as quickly as possible.

"You can catch a later hackney," Andromeda said suddenly, as if she and Mercy had been in the middle of a discussion. She then nodded in agreement with her own assessment. "And if it gets too late, I can take you back myself. I'm quite the rider."

"Pardon?" Mercy wasn't quite sure what decision had been made on her behalf.

Andromeda took her by the elbow and flagged a passing coach, trundling her in, then climbing in after her. "Thomas Street, please," she called out. "The Grove."

This was unexpected. Mercy didn't like unexpected. She had planned to go home, to get away from Andromeda and the raucous feelings the woman and her self-assured charm aroused, and now everything was being thrown into confusion.

"Where are we going?" Mercy demanded as the cab began to move.

"Thomas Street," Andromeda repeated slowly. "The Grove."

"Are you in the habit of dragging women along on your adventures, without a care as to whether they wish to accompany you?" Mercy's face felt hot and her breath grew shaky. The muscles at the back of her neck felt uncomfortably taut. She had been so close to reprieve from the emotions Andromeda stirred in her, and now she was in even closer confines, stuck with the woman for who knew how long and going Lord knew where. "You can't just do with me as you desire!"

She gasped in a breath, balled her fists in her lap, and focused on the press of her nails into her palms instead of the tide of emotion trying to knock her legs from under her.

"Why must everything be such a drama with you, Mercy? And you wonder why I prefer Charles."

She squeezed her eyes shut and wished she could fling herself out from the carriage instead of further embarrassing herself. She tried to rein in her emotions, tried to avoid the awful breathless feeling that was closing in on her.

"Oh dammit, I've done it again," Andromeda said. "I can stop the coach. I will if you want. But I think you'll enjoy where I'm taking you, and I'll ensure that you get back to The Grange safely. Do you want to leave? Truly? Are you not the least bit curious?"

Mercy thought about what awaited her if she left that moment. A long ride back up to Harlem. More work. Mrs.

Hamilton. Angelica. Perhaps John come to visit, needing her assistance with the biographical work his mother had handed off to him.

Mercy scoffed at Mrs. Hamilton's obsession with her late husband, but if she looked back at the past few years, her own life had nothing to show for it besides that same work of preservation. And perhaps she'd had reason to immerse herself in someone else's life, their joy and grief. It had allowed her to ignore her own.

She opened her eyes. Andromeda was looking at her expectantly, hand raised to rap on the cab and make the driver pull the reins on his horse.

Mercy shook her head, and Andromeda lowered her hand. She still looked concerned, and—for once—uncertain.

"I don't like surprises," Mercy said, trying to brush away the panic that had almost overtaken her. There was nothing to fret about; she could leave when she wanted, and if she was honest with herself, she did not want to go back yet.

Are you not the least bit curious?

She was, despite knowing better. That stubborn, hopeful part of her stretched behind her rib cage like a cat awakening from a long nap, ready to scrounge about for scraps.

"Don't like surprises? Perhaps you haven't received a good one before," Andromeda said, venturing a smile. "But if you do not like them, this shall be the last."

Mercy wanted to remind her that they'd never see each other again, anyway, but she didn't. She let that thought calm her. It wasn't as if anything could come of a few hours more in this woman's presence. Her life would go back to normal as soon as she got back to The Grange.

And that is most definitively what you want.

Andromeda reached out and placed a hand on Mercy's knee. Her fingers stroked soothingly, but her touch sent a shivering thrill up Mercy's thigh, where it settled between her legs.

"I am impulsive, but I wish to give you pleasure, not cause you distress."

The thrill between Mercy's legs resolved into an ache, but then Andromeda pulled her hand away and smoothed out the creases in her own skirts. She began rattling something off about the pleats in her dress and Mercy received a shock when she realized that Andromeda was nervous, too. That calmed her a bit, to know that even someone brash and beautiful might feel anxious—and that perhaps she was the cause of it.

They pulled up in front of a squat brick building, and Mercy stared through the window in awe of what she saw. Other Negroes milled about, couples mostly, though there were groups of friends and families as well. They were all shades and from all walks of life, but all seemed to partake in a shared excitement about their destination as they all filed through a door at the ground floor level of the building. After paying their driver, Andromeda took Mercy's elbow again, and they followed suit.

They passed through a small, dark apartment, and for a moment Mercy was sure she had been dragged into some foolishness, but then they stepped out through a door leading to the backyard and Mercy gasped.

It wasn't quite beautiful—not yet. It was clearly a work in progress. The tables and chairs arranged around the large yard were worn and mismatched, and the ground was packed dirt. The sparse trees had only the beginnings of blooms on them and loomed somewhat menacingly in their skeletal state. But most tables were occupied by Negroes of every station, and they all faced a stage. And on the nearly bare stage were players, also Negroes. They were dressed in common clothes, and one or two held manuscripts. When they opened their mouths, out came the words of the Bard.

That sharp, sweet joy that Mercy had denied herself for so long spread through her as she watched the players strut about. She didn't take her eyes away from the stage, even as they were led to a table and seated, even as Andromeda ordered them refreshment.

"A fellow from the Caribbean just opened this pleasure garden and theater. They're going to have musical performances, dance, and put on plays."

Mercy nodded, leaning in toward Andromeda a bit even

though she still watched the stage. She had been wrong—the Grove was already beautiful.

"I'm making the costumes for the players—today is just a rehearsal, as the show doesn't start in truth for another month or so," Andromeda said in a low voice. As low as she could manage, that is. "I'm sorry if you don't like it. The boy says they're already in the second act, and I'm sure you can't stay to the end. But I thought..."

"Shh!"

Andromeda looked hurt, and Mercy shook her head. "You misunderstand. You have many things to apologize for, but not this, so hush. I am..." She swallowed against the emotion that buffeted her about although she was still in her seat. Andromeda had known just the right place in the teeming heart of New York to bring Mercy. No one had ever known before. No one had ever *endeavored* to know. It had always been Mercy fumbling about trying to please others, all for naught. "I am delighted. Thank you for bringing me with you."

She expected Andromeda to grin or make a sly remark, but instead the woman gave a small nod and sat back, her gaze turning toward the stage. Mercy followed suit, then caught sight of something in her peripheral vision.

Andromeda had reached her hand out, gaze still on the players. Mercy trained her gaze back on the stage, too, but she felt the first contact of Andromeda's fingers with the metal chair back, the vibration as they curled through the ornate iron bars. The slow brush against the fabric of Mercy's cloak and then a final vibration as Andromeda gripped the metal tightly.

Mercy exhaled and then leaned back, telling herself it was perfectly all right that Andromeda's knuckles pushed gently into her back. Four of them in a line. Four points of pressure connecting her to the woman beside her.

She did not move away.

"We that are true lovers run into strange capers," one of the players recited, and Mercy let the beauty of the words overtake her.

They watched in silence, and at act four Andromeda walked out with her to hail another hackney, one that would take her back to The Grange. Mercy couldn't think of past betrayals or pretend that she hadn't enjoyed herself. Her heart and her head were full of words that had nourished her—she hadn't realized she'd been starving until she heard them, and she held them close as she parted ways with the woman who could be the ruin of her if Mercy wasn't careful.

It wasn't until the coach was approaching The Grange that she realized she hadn't said goodbye.

Chapter Five

SPRING light streamed into the parlor through the wall of windows, ridding the room of the oppressive air that sometimes lingered like sprits trapped between worlds.

Angelica sat at the pianoforte in the parlor, running through the same songs that she played any time she was near the instrument. Mercy knew she'd been an accomplished player in her youth, but now she tapped at random keys, the notes occasionally coalescing into some semblance of rhythm before falling apart.

Mrs. Hamilton was on the chaise, a soft smile on her face as she read over the final version of Andromeda's account of her grandfather's story.

Mercy shifted uncomfortably and fussed with the sewing in her lap. She generally never worried that her work might be lacking, but she had never really cared about what she was writing before. Or rather, she hadn't cared about the source of the words.

After returning from her visit into town, Mercy had lain in the darkness of her chambers and reexamined the day's events without self-censure. She'd allowed herself to feel every bit of Andromeda's beauty instead of blocking it out, to laugh at the jokes she'd frowned disapprovingly over. She'd allowed herself to relive every touch: a caress along the back of her hand; a stroke of the knee; the press of four knuckles against her back.

Mercy had felt Andromeda's touch all through her body, like the first time she'd tasted spiced rum. Warmth, burning and sweet at once, had suffused her. Mercy wished to practice temperance in matters of the heart, but Andromeda's brief caresses, and her curious wit, had set her down the path to temptation.

No. It is finished. Do not think of her.

"Mercy."

She realized Mrs. Hamilton was calling her name. The pages rested in the woman's lap, and she wore an amused expression.

"Sorry, missus. My mind must have drifted." She stifled a yawn; she hadn't been sleeping well.

Every time she closed her eyes, she saw Andromeda's lovely, expressive face. The way she twitched her nose when she knew she'd said something risqué, or how she leaned forward and locked eyes at the end of a particularly long sentence instead of pausing to take a breath. Andromeda spoke as if she wasn't quite sure she'd get the words out before keeling over but was determined to try.

"I said that this is wonderful." Mrs. Hamilton looked at her as if she expected an explanation for that.

"Thank you. I simply relayed Miss Stiel's words."

Mrs. Hamilton shook her head. "No. That is what you usually do. While she is quite the storyteller, I'm talking about *you*."

Mercy felt like a bird who had flown through an open window that slammed shut behind it. She'd been so careful, before this. Not too much deviation from the original recounting. Simple words instead of ones that would make the story soar.

"Your descriptions of the storyteller herself are quite vivid," Mrs. Hamilton continued. She opened a huge ledger that contained the stories of the other battalion members she had been able to contact, and tucked the pages concerning Elijah Sutton in between other packets. "You described her laughter as 'carrying like the burble of a spring through the vale.'" Mrs. Hamilton closed her eyes as if savoring those words.

"I'm sorry," Mercy said.

Mrs. Hamilton's eyes opened and her brows lifted. "You must know after all these years of hearing about my Hamilton that I appreciate a finely turned phrase. Excellent work."

Guilt and pleasure pulled and pushed at Mercy: guilt at the unkind thoughts of her mistress she'd shared with Andromeda, and pleasure at someone complimenting her writing after all these years. It wasn't the same heady rush that had sent heat up her neck when Andromeda complimented her, but it was pleasant all the same.

She stood and bowed her acknowledgement. "I am glad to have pleased you. Shall I take Miss Angelica for a walk around the grounds, if she so desires?"

She glanced over at Angelica, who was still tapping away, and that's when Mercy realized something. Angelica wasn't picking keys at random—she was playing one half of a duet.

Her chest went tight for a moment, and though Mercy didn't believe in bad presentiments, she would take that one-sided declaration of love as a warning.

Not again. Never again.

"I would like that, yes," Angelica said, a smile breaking through the somber mask of concentration she'd worn while playing. "Father once told me that walking sharpened a mind made dull by repose or conversation with John Adams."

"Yes. Walking is good for the constitution," Mrs. Hamilton said. She smiled as if remembering something pleasant, and Mercy could see the resemblance in the two women, then—a resemblance that was more than the shared pain between them. "I have some matters concerning the orphanage to deal with that came in with the post. There also something for you, Mercy."

She handed over a slip of thick, rough-edged paper that had been folded and sealed with a dollop of wax. Mercy didn't recognize the hand behind the scrawl of her name, but there was something about the way the letters sloped to the right, as if running full-tilt toward the future, that made her heart beat a bit faster. She wanted to rip the seal off immediately, but no. She would wait.

Patience. Temperance. She'd worked hard on developing those habits in her daily life. She couldn't throw them away after one trip to the theater.

She tucked the letter into her apron pocket, then walked over and helped Angelica with her shawl.

They walked slowly through the gardens, arms linked. Mercy ignored the weighted flap of her apron pocket in the wind.

"Do you think that birds have music in their souls?" Angelica asked suddenly, and Mercy leaned her head to the side as she pondered the question.

"I would say so. They sing beautifully, do they not?"

"I'm of the same mind," Angelica said, pleased with Mercy's answer. "Do you think birds can love?"

Mercy was struck with the memory of a bird flying by with ribbon trailing from its beak. "They mate, and build nests, and raise children. I suppose they can love, in their own birdish way. Why do you ask?"

"Don't you see?" Angelica looked at her as if the point was obvious, then continued when Mercy simply stared. "Music can make you feel anything: happiness or sadness, longing or excitement. If the birds can create their birdsong, then they must be able to feel. And if they can feel, they can love. Imagine what that's like, being able to fly and to sing and to love! It's not fair, really. I wish I was a bird."

She flapped her arms playfully and gazed up at the spring sky, and Mercy inhaled deeply. She should have warned the woman, reminded her that flying too high was dangerous, but Angelica was enraptured by the sparrows wheeling overhead. Mercy followed her gaze. When was the last time she'd looked up instead of at the ground? Appreciated birdsong as something other than an indicator of the time of day?

"It must be quite something," Mercy said. The letter in her apron slapped at her thigh again, as if seeking her attention. Quite as distracting as Andromeda herself.

"Do you think I should read the letter I received, Miss Hamilton?" she asked.

"Of course," Angelica responded, gaze still on the birds. "I love receiving letters, don't you? I expect one from Philip soon. He always writes from school. Whom is yours from?"

"Mine is from…" Mercy pulled the paper out and unsealed it, and a wave of something too close to happiness went through her. Too close to a bird wheeling and chirping, carried on invisible currents.

"An admirer?" Angelica guessed.

Yes. No. She shouldn't be. Oh, but I want her to be, though.

"A…friend, I suppose."

"Friends can be admirers," Angelica pointed out helpfully.

Mercy read, keeping in step with Angelica's amble.

Dear Mercy,

I hope your voyage back to the wilds of Harlem was not too taxing. I admit, I was saddened to see you go, and not just because your dress was in the same sorry state as when you arrived. While it's no secret that you find me a bit vexing, I am having some difficulty finding a matching flaw in your person. I suppose you are somewhat priggish, but I don't find this trait a flaw as it pertains to you. I do hope to have the pleasure of your company again, if only to see if I'm mistaken about that.

I imagine The Grange to be a lonely place, and thus I offer myself to you. In friendship, I suppose. That's a start.

Curiously yours,

Andromeda

The letter was bold, and possibly dangerous if anyone else had opened it, but Mercy would wrinkle her brow about that later. For a moment, just a moment, she allowed herself the throb of possibility in her blood. The remembrance of Andromeda's fingertips on her jaw, so close to brushing her bottom lip. Four knuckles pressing into her back. Then she folded the paper and tucked it back into her pocket.

Mercy had been quite sure that she was above such foolish emotion, but even her mental reprimands could not stop certain *notions* from stirring. She wanted to press her hands to her chest, to push and push until she crushed that fledgling feeling beneath her palms like an insect.

Never again.

"You look sad now," Angelica remarked.

"Just a bit fatigued," she said. "Shall we head back?"

Angelica looked at her with sympathy and nodded. "Let's."

❦

My dear Mercy,

I dined at Lady Bess's today and found that I missed your company. There was no one to give me peevish looks when I spoke too loudly, or to write my every word down as if I was a person of consequence. Was it really only a few hours that we passed there?

I remember that the tips of your index finger and thumb grew dark with ink, but that seemed to be the one bit of mess in the world that didn't aggravate you. I also remember that before your coach carried you away from the Grove, you spared me a rare smile, one that I should like to look upon again.

My recollections may be wishful thinking, though—you did say I had a way of making even the mundane seem grand. I thought you were quite grand from the moment I saw you, so you might be able to imagine what I think of you now.

Fondly yours,
Andromeda

❦

My dearest Mercy,

I have been hoping that you would muster a bit of your namesake and find a moment to respond, but no matter. My aforementioned overconfidence will carry us through in the meantime. How go things at The Grange? I hope you find your work agreeable.

Here in Montgomerie, I've been wildly busy. The costumes for the show are coming along, but other plans are not running as smoothly. The building next door to my shop is for sale. I wish to purchase it, and to open a boarding house for people in the neighborhood. The proprietor wishes to sell it to someone else. I won't speculate as to why he believes this fellow a more attractive prospect than me. We're all well aware of how attractive I am, after all.

Don't fret (I will be presumptuous enough to presume that you might fret over me); I don't believe in failure. With that said, you should expect another letter soon.

Persistently yours,
Andromeda

THE GROWING FAMILIARITY of the letters should have put Mercy off. It did not. She received and read, received and read, and after the sixth letter she finally did what she'd said she would not.

It's common courtesy, she told herself. *It would reflect badly on the household if I didn't.*

She picked up her quill and wrote a response.

She wasted eight sheets of good paper due to a shaky hand, muddled words, and stilted sentences. Eight sheets in the waste bin only to produce this stunning bit of verse on the ninth:

DEAR ANDROMEDA,

I have very much appreciated your correspondence. I hope all is well with the shop and that you are able to successfully purchase the building. All is the same here at The Grange.

Your obedient servant,
Mercy Alston

SHE HEMMED and hawed about the letter for a full day. She wanted to say more, so much more. She wanted to tell Andromeda how the letters had awoken feelings that left her tingling, like blood rushing into a limb gone numb. She wanted to tell her that she thought her incredibly brave for her attempts to purchase a building. She wanted to tell her that she did fret over her, and in more ways than Andromeda could imagine. But that was too much to contemplate.

She posted the insipid little letter.

She wrote in her journal before bed: *Copied interview with a Mr. Porter on the subject of Hamilton's creation of the treasury. Did the laundry—new detergent was a success. Wondered if there wasn't some way to retrieve that blasted letter from the post. Honestly, what was I thinking? Three lines of banality buffered by rote cordiality. She will laugh when she reads it. She will know me for the fool I am.*

She waited for a response.

Chapter Six

ANDROMEDA DIDN'T QUITE KNOW what she was doing with these letters. She had thought to send one or two. Charming missives to put a smile on Mercy's face. The nervy woman had obviously been hurt in the past. Andromeda had wanted to soothe that hurt, and then...what exactly?

When she was inventive and impulsive with her dress designs, she often succeeded, but that was because she was working from a basic template. She already knew the approximate shape of the finished product, and when she'd have to cut the final thread. What she had started with Mercy had no such set ending point. She was weaving instead of sewing now, and that was a task she'd never before attempted.

When Mercy had finally responded, the reply had been surprisingly short, given her obvious affinity for writing. But it hadn't been a rejection. Mercy had proven herself more than capable of serving up cutting remarks, so Andromeda had taken heart in the lack of them.

There had been a shyness to the letter that Andromeda had found endearing. And the next time Mercy had written there had been less formality, more words, and more...Mercy.

Dear Andromeda,

I hope this letter finds you well. I am glad to hear that you are kept so busy with your business pursuits. I'm sure the costumes for the players will be more than adequate. I have seen only two of your designs, but they were both pleasing to the eye. Although I rebuffed your previous offer, I am indeed in need of a new dress.

Any news about the building you seek to purchase? It seems such a brave venture, buying your own building and starting not one but two businesses. I always thought of ownership as something for other people, so much so that I forget it's something afforded to us, too. It seems I've been mistaken in my assumptions about many things.

Your obedient servant,
Mercy

৩৵৶

Dear Andromeda,

Last night I went into the garden with Miss Angelica to watch the meteor shower. Did you see it? I imagine perhaps you were up to something more enjoyable; if you were, you missed quite the sight.

For a while, clouds obscured our view, but then a fortuitous wind pushed them onward in their journey, revealing the brilliant star-studded night sky. Most of the stars appeared to be stationary, except for a few that seemed to tremble with excitement for the descent of their brethren, making their final journey. We waited, and waited, and we were rewarded. One, two, three—too many to count. Brilliant, beautiful streaks of light! My heart leapt in my chest that such magnificence might exist and that I might look upon it. It was the second time I have encountered that particular sensation in recent memory.

Yours cordially,
Mercy

MERCY'S LETTERS, read sequentially, were like a flower unfolding, petal by petal. Andromeda wanted more; she wanted the full bloom.

She had more pressing matters to attend to, though, like speaking with Mr. Porter about the purchase of the building. She reminded herself of that as she waited outside the office of the man who held that goal in his hands.

The door to the office pulled open and he stuck his lined face through the door. "Miss Stiel?"

"Mr. Porter. How good to see you." She smiled.

He didn't return the sentiment, simply turned and went into the office, waving over his shoulder for her to follow him.

"I was hoping we'd be able to discuss the finalities of the purchase," she said. "I have plans that I'd like to jump into right away, you see. There's work to be done to get the place fit for letting and—"

"I do believe you're getting ahead of yourself, Miss Stiel," Mr. Porter interrupted. He leaned back in his chair. "I have other offers for the building. Offers from people with a bit more standing than you."

Anger rose up in Andromeda, trying to escape from her lips, but she was impulsive, not self-destructive. Getting something from him that he didn't want to give her would be worth more than allowing him to write her off so easily.

She turned doe eyes on him.

"I don't understand, Mr. Porter. You know as well as I do that my current business is one of the anchors of the neighborhood. I provide work for young women, give back to the community, and I'm seen as a knowledgeable businessperson. I know everyone in a mile radius, and what's more, they know me and they like me—or at the very least they respect me. I doubt anyone else wanting to buy can say the same."

"No one else wanting to buy is an unmarried Negress," he said, his tone suggesting he'd listed not one but two faults in her character.

"Oh, how sad for them," she said, tilting her head to the side. She was bothered, but she couldn't even get angry at this because people underestimating her usually worked out for her, when all was said and done. She got what she wanted and they learned not to let their prejudices blind them to the obvious—that Andromeda Stiel was a force to be reckoned with.

"I currently own and operate one successful business as an unmarried Negress. Is there something about owning a boarding house that requires either acquiring a husband or transforming into a…what is the word you'd use for the white counterpart of a Negress?" She looked at him expectantly. Waited.

He shifted in his seat and made a sound that was somewhere between a snort and a sneeze. "Selling to an unattached woman of any persuasion is not something to be taken lightly."

Andromeda tried to look thoughtful, though the only thing she was thinking was how fine it would be to stick this man with a straight pin in a sensitive area. "Once the building is sold, it has nothing to do with you. I absolutely won't let it go to ruin, but what business would it be of yours after the exchange of money?"

She had enough money. More than enough. She had been working years now, and in addition to her shop, she'd invested in other businesses—those of washerwomen, cobblers, domestics, and many more—always getting her money back with interest. She was not rich, but she was certainly well positioned to buy the building and turn it into a boardinghouse that would be affordable, safe, and clean for the people of the Montgomerie.

"Miss Stiel, I'll be frank. I don't give two figs whether you are married, or going to be married. I'm unmarried myself." Andromeda resisted the urge to look about his messy office and kept her gaze trained on him. "But it's not just me. There are partners, bankers, people who simply won't take the risk. If the property were to devalue afterwards, or if you were to get with child and lose the ability to bring in income—"

"Mr. Porter, there's little chance of that happening and you know it." She smiled, but she could feel the tension around her eyes from trying not to glare at him.

He sighed. "In making business decisions, it pays to go with the lowest risk. That is not you, Miss Stiel. Unless you have plans you haven't told me about. Plans that I could pass on to anyone who might share my reservations, perhaps?"

He gave her a curious look, and Andromeda realized that she hadn't just found an opening—the codger had given it to her. She galloped straight into it.

"I do actually. I've been talking to a childhood sweetheart from home about our future, and it seems our affections have not waned. There's to be a marriage soon, you see, so there's actually nothing to keep me from buying."

"Excellent. And you'll be able to provide evidence of this?" He raised bushy white brows.

Andromeda gave him a tight smile. "Of course."

Her childhood sweetheart had herself just been engaged, but Andromeda would make it work. Failure wasn't an option.

She left Mr. Porter's office and headed back to her shop, turning over plans in her head.

"There's a letter come for you, miss," Tara said when she walked in.

Andromeda snatched it from the girl, then gave her an apologetic look. Tara simply shook her head and walked away.

Mercy.

No. She felt a brief disappointment when she realized it was from someone else—her letter should have arrived days ago. Her spirits lifted when she recognized her grandfather's handwriting. She perused the short note, trying to make sense of the words. It seemed Grandma Kate had taken ill. She was recovering, but it still left Andromeda unsettled.

"I'll have to head up to Suffolk to visit my family again, Tara," she said. "Will you be able to handle things here?"

"Yes, miss. And my sister can come in, too, if you want."

"That would be perfect," Andromeda said. "I should only be gone a few days."

She thought of her childhood sweetheart up in Suffolk, and her fiancé and his new profession, and a devious smile worked its way across Andromeda's face.

If luck was on her side, she might have found the solution to her problem.

Chapter Seven

❧

THE WIND outside The Grange howled, and the sound of snow and hail battering the side of the house nearly drowned out Angelica at the pianoforte. The late spring storm had come upon them sudden and unexpected, as if mirroring Mercy's tempestuous mood.

Never had a week felt longer or more wretched. Perhaps she exaggerated; she had certainly experienced worse, but time and distance had dulled past pains, even the ones that had made her lose her words and lock her heart away. This new paroxysm of torturous infatuation was a fresh and inescapable torment.

Why did I send it? Why?

She groaned in mortification as she ran the feather duster over the bust of Hamilton in the hallway, and his stone smirk seemed to mock her inner turmoil.

Not feeling quite so superior to my Eliza now, are you?

She swiped at the bust with a vicious barrage—as vicious an attack as could be meted out by feathers—but the smirk remained. So did the ache in her chest.

She'd thought herself so careful over the past several weeks. She'd had a system in place for when each letter arrived. She wouldn't be foolish enough to allow herself to tear at the seal like a lovesick girl waiting for word from her lover. It was simply correspondence between two friends, she reasoned. She wouldn't want anyone to be confused about that, least of all herself.

She waited forty-five minutes exactly before opening each letter. Forty-five minutes of telling herself that she wasn't excited, that each slide of the minute hand across the clock face didn't make her pulse race faster until her whole being was fairly throbbing. That finally sitting at her desk, removing the seal, and revealing Andromeda's barely restrained script didn't give her a delicious gratification that swept down from the nape of her neck to her toes.

She had developed a strict pattern for reading the letters too. Once quickly, once slowly, then once again the following morning, before she wrote out her response. She wouldn't overindulge like a child let loose in a sweet shop, and she wouldn't tempt herself by reading before bed. Because though Andromeda spoke of her shop, her plan to open a boarding house, and all manner of banal observations, there was a definite undercurrent to the words that might lead Mercy astray in her dreams, and she was already dangerously off course.

Andromeda had talked about Mercy coming in for a new dress, and then she'd described how she would take Mercy's measurement—down to the very last detail. Mercy wasn't certain how anyone could survive a fitting by Andromeda Stiel; she'd hardly survived just reading about it.

Holding herself away from everything had grown easy for Mercy, until Andromeda had come along and mucked it up. Mercy had been foolish, had read too much into Andromeda's friendliness. She'd driven her away. Just the thought of it made her body go tight with anxiety.

Two weeks before, she'd taken a deep breath and, instead of her usual reply, she'd copied out a poem she'd written in her journal. The first poem she'd written in years.

Delicate hands flutter like two brown birds
Winging free over the verdant vale
Riding the currents of the warm spring gale
Stopping to sip at rushing creeks
Moving ever faster as they sing a song of
Unimaginable beauty

And, oh, how I wish
These untamable creatures
Would impart their wild wisdom
Upon me

She'd folded the letter, sealed it, taken the extra precaution of putting it into an envelope, and then mailed it out.

She hadn't received anything from Andromeda since then.

Mercy had created a thousand excuses as to why a letter should take so long to arrive when they had been coming so regularly—her imagination really was back in top form. But she had eventually resigned herself to the fact *she* was the reason. She'd ruined everything. Why had she sent the poem? Had she thought to impress Andromeda?

The rebuke to the last poem she'd shown to the object of her admiration echoed in her head.

"Enough of these foolish words! I will marry, and that is final. What did you think would happen?"

Mercy skulked about The Grange, pinched with embarrassment every time she remembered that she'd exposed herself so shamefully. Again. She imagined Andromeda opening the letter, imagined her frowning at the flowery words on the page. Turning it over and holding it up to the light with that exaggerated manner of hers to see if she was perhaps missing something of note that would explain why Mercy would send her such a thing. What had Mercy thought could come of such audacity?

Nothing could come of it.

Nothing. What Andromeda should be to you.

Yes, she should be nothing. But somehow, nothing had become what lifted her out of bed every morning. Nothing was what made her feel like she was ascending again when she marched up the stairs, the possibility of a waiting letter pulling her into the light. Nothing had quite possibly become the something she had been hiding from all of these years.

And she had ruined it.

She had finished her dusting and was heading down to the kitchen when she heard the sound of hooves approaching during a lull in the storm.

"Henry, are we expecting anyone?" She poked her head into

the kitchen in time to see the butler's brows crease in annoyance. He placed the teakettle on the tray along with the cup.

"No, and even if we were, no one of sound mind would show up in this weather."

"Perhaps I was mistaken," she said, shaking her head. She handed him an extra cube of sugar to place beside Angelica's cup; he knew she liked her tea sweet but discouraged her from the habit.

He sighed and accepted it, then both of their gazes darted abovestairs as the sound of the heavy knocker echoed in the hallway.

"Go get it before Angelica does," Mercy said. Sometimes the woman would jump up in excitement and rush to the door, expecting Philip. "I'll bring her tea."

Henry dashed up the steps and Mercy hurried behind him as quickly as she could without spilling the hot liquid. She got to the door of the parlor just in time to intercept Angelica.

"Come, it's time for your tea."

"Whoever is at the door?" Angelica asked, eyes glossy with unshed tears.

"Likely someone lost in the storm," Mercy said.

"Perhaps it's—"

"No, it's not him," Mercy said gently. *It will never be him.*

"You don't know that," Angelica said mildly. "I miss him. Why hasn't he come to visit us? Doesn't he miss us?"

Her heart ached for the woman, trapped by the eternal torment of love. It wasn't fair. It wasn't fair to be punished for your capacity to care. Andromeda looked into Angelica's tearstained eyes and wished the world weren't so cruel to those who found the most beauty in it.

"He does miss you, very much. But he wouldn't want you to worry so," Mercy said. "He would want you to be happy."

"It's hard to be happy when the people you love leave you," Angelica said. Mercy closed her eyes and heat pressed at her lids. She thought of her parents, cold and still. She thought of Jane's lovely face, lovely even as she burned Mercy's letters.

"You think me selfish, but this will protect you, too. One day you'll understand."

She opened them and tried to smile at Angelica. "It is hard, and we cannot always achieve this goal. But we can try, yes?"

Angelica nodded.

"Come, sit before the fire. Your hands must be chilled from playing."

"Mine are about frozen through from holding the reins, so I do hope that's an open invitation," a familiar voice said, and Mercy nearly did drop the tray then. She turned and found Andromeda shivering in the doorway, arms wrapped about herself. Henry had taken her coat, but the skirt of her blue dress was dark with moisture and her hair was still festooned with snow and ice.

Mercy put the tray down carefully. "What are you doing here?"

"Lovely to see you, too," Andromeda said through chattering teeth.

"Why were you out riding in this weather?"

To see me? The hope lodged in her fast and sharp.

"My grandmother was ill, so I went up to Suffolk for a few days. I was coming back when this storm blew in." An involuntary shudder shook her from head to toe. "I didn't think I could make it back to town and got a bit desperate."

"Oh. Of course," Mercy said. It had been silly to think that anyone would come explicitly for her. That didn't stop the lump from forming in her throat at even the thought of the sickness that could beset Andromeda. Of the possibility Andromeda's boundless energy wouldn't pull her through it. She blinked away sudden ridiculous tears, the sight of Andromeda and the state she was in conspiring to overwhelm Mercy's emotional parapets.

This is why. This was why she hadn't wanted to feel. This was why she couldn't. It was too much, and for what? Certain heartache.

Henry cleared his throat. "Given the…unusual circumstances of Miss Stiel's arrival, I believe that Mrs. Hamilton would wish that she warm herself here. I'll have Sarah arrange the fire belowstairs, too."

Mercy wasn't quite sure where Andromeda should go either. During her previous visit, she had arrived as a guest of Mrs.

Hamilton's, but now she was a Negro woman who had called unannounced.

Henry left and Mercy turned her attention back to their guest.

Andromeda's eyes were overbright and she shivered uncontrollably. It reminded Mercy of her final days in the cellar on Gold Street, of her parents shaking with fever and her powerless to help them.

She wasn't thinking when she marched over to Andromeda and grabbed the woman's hands. Mercy pressed them together as if in prayer, then rubbed her own hands over them.

"You're chilled to the bone!" She knew her voice was shrill but she couldn't help it. She wanted to cry; shrillness was the preferable alternative.

"Well, I am now, but I'll soon burst into flames if you keep at that," Andromeda said.

Mercy wasn't sure if Andromeda meant the innuendo in her words.

"I do need my fingers for my work, Mercy. And for other more pleasurable pursuits." Andromeda's voice went low at that last bit—she'd meant the innuendo, and then gone for more. It seemed even a devil of a chill couldn't keep her from playing at seduction.

Mercy shook her head and began pulling Andromeda toward the hearth. "Of course you'd be foolish enough to ride out into a storm and catch your death of cold. Irresponsible, impulsive—"

Mercy was stopped by Andromeda tugging back, pulling her up short. Andromeda's icy fingers slipped through Mercy's, drawing their palms together. When Mercy turned back, the irksome woman was grinning at her.

"Careful," she said, her voice still shiver-shaken. "I might think you'd care if I did."

They looked at each other for a long moment, and it was Mercy who tore her gaze away first.

"Would you like some tea?" Angelica asked. Mercy had nearly forgotten her mistress was there.

"Actually, if you have any of that coffee…" Andromeda

turned toward Mercy and batted her damp lashes. The glow of the flames illuminated her face, her stark beauty, and Mercy reminded herself of the hell this woman could drag her into if she let her.

She always had preferred the heat, unfortunately. She could only hope that she wouldn't be burned too badly this time around.

Chapter Eight

"WELL, this isn't quite the reception I expected," Andromeda muttered as she finished plaiting her hair into a single braid. She received no response, as she was quite alone in Mercy's chamber.

She sat on the edge of Mercy's bed and looked about the space. An old wooden desk with Mercy's writing implements lined up neatly across the top of it. A wooden chair. A bureau for her clothing. There was no color, no decoration—nothing to reflect the vivid personality that had eventually come through in Mercy's letters. That personality was nowhere to be found in Mercy herself, either, truth be told.

She told you she didn't like surprises; you should have taken her at her word.

After the outburst in the parlor upon Andromeda's arrival, Mercy had kept her distance, claiming a surplus of work. There had been no more worried looks or tender caresses. Andromeda had soaked in a hot bath to warm herself, eaten the meal she'd been given, and now lay in Mercy's bed with a few warm bricks that had been brought by Sarah, another servant. The wind still blustered outside.

She had left against the advice of her family, but she'd had the solution to her problems in her bag and had thought she could beat the storm. She had been restless worrying that the building would be sold out from under her, that if she let even a moment pass, her opening would be blocked off forever. When the storm grew too dangerous to navigate, another opening had emerged.

Mercy.

Their exchanges had become warm, personal. Andromeda had assumed that Mercy would be pleased to see her. Instead she had been vexed, agitated, and on the brink of tears. Andromeda hadn't given up, but she was starting to reconsider her choice to seek shelter at The Grange.

It grew late, and she was wondering if Mercy would sleep in the hallway rather than join her when the door pushed open with a quiet scrape against the jamb.

Andromeda kept her eyes closed, listening to the sway of Mercy's skirts and the near-silent creak of the floorboards. Was she tiptoeing? In her own room? There was silence, and Andromeda opened her eyes.

Mercy stood beside the desk, holding a mug in her hands, and the scent of floral tea filled the air. She was staring at Andromeda. There was no tightness or prudery in that expression, no. It was open and unguarded and filled with such longing that Andromeda felt pinned by the weight of it. She had been worried she alone felt the intense desire, but to be looked at like that dispelled all doubt.

Mercy closed the door, then stepped forward and held out the cup. "I thought you were asleep," she said.

"Sorry to disappoint," Andromeda said, pushing herself up to a sitting position. "I can pretend to be if you like, but I'm fairly awful at pretending to be something I'm not. You may have picked up on that."

Mercy's mouth formed something resembling a smile, but also not far from the face a person made before they were violently ill. Andromeda should have been put off by the fact that she couldn't tell the difference, but she was ever optimistic.

"Here. You should take this. Something warm to keep away the chill." Mercy handed over the cup, and then wrung her hands, the very picture of a fretful woman.

Andromeda thought of what her mother had told her during her visit when she'd finally admitted that her above-average levels of absentmindedness had been driven by infatuation.

"You've got no patience. Remember when you tried your hand at horse training? Scared the mares half to death and had the stallions ready to break down the fences. Go slow, my child. Rushing headlong into love means you might run right past the person you're after."

Her father had listened to this advice with a peculiar smile on his face that Mercy didn't want to know the cause of.

Patience. Feh. Andromeda made a sound of annoyance and Mercy flinched. Perhaps her mother was right.

"Thank you." Andromeda bought the warm glass to her lips and took a sip. "I'm about ready to burst from all of these warm drinks, but I appreciate them."

Mercy's gaze was still anxious, but annoyance crept in. "Well, I hope they prevent you from getting ill. Riding about in the wind and ice is dangerous. You must be careful, Andromeda."

"Why?" She took another sip of tea and kept her gaze on Mercy. "Death comes for the prudent and the impetuous alike, you know."

"Perhaps," Mercy said. "But rushing into danger that might be avoided is foolish. There are worse things than death, Andromeda."

"I know," Andromeda said carefully. "That's why we must make sure that we take our pleasure where we can. Life is hard, and then you die. Prudence is well and good, but there'll be time for that in the afterlife, don't you think?"

She kept her gaze locked on Mercy, who looked completely flustered.

Be patient.

"And thank you for allowing me to stay with you."

"Yes." Mercy's reply was short. "You came here by chance and you didn't want to put Mrs. Hamilton in a bind. I... It is fine."

She turned her back, ending the conversation by dropping into the wooden chair before her desk.

ALYSSA COLE

Andromeda didn't think it wise to reveal that it hadn't been entirely chance, so she simply sipped her tea.

Mercy had taken up her quill and was studiously ignoring Andromeda.

"I'm more concerned that I put *you* in a bind," Andromeda finally said. "I know that responding to my letters is one thing and having me show up on your doorstep is another."

"It isn't my doorstep on which you arrived," Mercy said. The only sound was that of quill on parchment. She finished whatever it was she was writing and turned in her seat. She had that stiff, priggish look about her again.

"I wondered if my last letter displeased you. I know it was an odd thing to send." She didn't meet Andromeda's gaze, and her expression was disconsolate.

"The letter about the toad that hopped into the soup pot when the Washingtons came for dinner? Why would that displease me?"

"I sent one after that," Mercy said. She lifted her head and met Andromeda's gaze.

"I've been away from the shop for a week now. The trip to my parents' is long and it makes sense to visit for a few days. And I needed time to work out the details of something regarding the purchase of the boarding house."

She wouldn't bore Mercy with the details of the intricacies of a printing press. On second thought, Mercy would likely love to hear such boring intricacies. But there'd be time for that later.

"You didn't receive it!" The smile that news caused to grace her face was different from the smiles Andromeda had seen at the Grove; she hadn't even borne witness to half of Mercy's beauty, it seemed. The woman's shoulders dropped and her head tipped back a bit in relief, and the slight give in her made Andromeda want to toss the tea aside and kiss her.

Patience. She sipped again, knowing the warmth couldn't match that of Mercy's mouth. She hoped she'd be able to prove herself right, and soon.

"Thank heavens," Mercy said. "I would have been rather embarrassed had you read it. I shouldn't have sent it." Her shoulders drew up again.

Andromeda pulled back the reins on the swell of anticipation that had begun to gallop in her blood. "Oh. Was it a letter telling me to desist?"

Andromeda was already debating whether to press her case or just let Mercy be.

"No! No." Mercy shook her head. "It was just…something silly."

Andromeda gave a sigh of relief. "I'm a seamstress, Mercy. While I will critique your clothing, your words are safe from me. I'd be happy to get ten pages of silliness from you. A hundred."

Mercy stared at Andromeda, her brown eyes luminous in the candlelight. "I know. It's just…I didn't want to disappoint you. And I was convinced I had."

There it was again: that inclination of the head that made Andromeda itch to reach out and stroke her. Mercy had grown up in cellars and orphanages; how did she come through all that with this kind of fragility? Andromeda thought of Mercy's rigid uprightness.

Ah. That's how.

"I won't say that you could never disappoint me, but it would take much more effort than posting a silly letter."

Mercy glanced up and Andromeda smiled. It was like getting a thread through the eye of a needle, finding the right smile for that moment: not too eager, not too aggressive.

Gentle.

Mercy leaned forward a bit and Andromeda knew she had succeeded. "As luck would have it, I'm here now. Whatever it was you wanted to say can be said to my face."

Mercy stood abruptly; the thread had slipped past the eye of the needle, it seemed.

"I should prepare for bed," she said.

Andromeda finished her tea and passed over the cup, then flopped back on the bed and rolled onto her side. She heard Mercy groping around for what seemed like much too long. "Need help with your buttons?" she asked.

"Not at all."

"I have two perfectly good hands that c—"

"Andromeda." The word had the same near-hysterical tone as when she'd stormed out of the shop, and later in the coach. Andromeda quieted.

There was the sound of Mercy blowing a puff of air between her lips, and then darkness descended upon the room. Then there was a creak in the floorboard and the shift of the mattress as Mercy climbed onto it. She lay down stiffly and Andromeda imagined her lying in repose with her arms crossed over her chest, like one of the antiquities she'd seen a sketch of. It hadn't struck her as the most comfortable position.

There was no talking for a long moment, and Andromeda supposed Mercy had fallen asleep, tired from the work of her day.

"How go things with the purchase of the building?" Mercy asked. Her words were benign, but she was only a few inches away and Andromeda could feel the heat of her. It seeped through the ticking of the mattress, spread through the rough sheets. Perhaps Mercy was always this warm, but Andromeda had touched her several times. Even when Mercy had taken her hands in that odd, moving attempt to warm them, she had not produced this kind of heat. What had she been thinking of in that long silence, before asking her question?

Andromeda turned onto her side facing Mercy, closing a bit of the space between them in the process. She could see nothing in the darkness, but she could feel the shape of Mercy before her.

God, if she burns like this from a distance...

"I am still having trouble with the sale. It seems the proprietor doesn't approve of selling to an unmarried woman, never mind that I earn more than many men."

"Have you no intention of being married?" Mercy asked. It was asked in a polite tone, as if she didn't particularly care to hear the answer.

"No, though I suppose many women have no such intention and become wives all the same." Andromeda hated the silence that followed her words, mostly because of the thing she hadn't said. She felt uncertain and it made her uncomfortable, so she did exactly what she'd been chastised for her entire life: she rushed headlong toward what frightened her.

"Actually, I've had my mind set on one person in particular, of late, but I'm still unsure of how I'll be received. I'm reaching rather far above my station, you see."

"Oh." There was a shift, and despite the total darkness, Andromeda knew Mercy had turned her back to her. Rejection barreled into her. She knew not every woman was open to being wooed by another of their sex, particularly one who had invited herself into her bed, but she had thought Mercy felt *something*...

A kind of panic filled her. How was it that she had planned on doing the wooing but was now the one bereft at being set aside?

"I hope he is not foolish enough to reject you," Mercy finally said in a rough voice. "I think any man would be lucky to have you."

Andromeda's ability to be gentle had reached its end. Her hand shot forward in the dark, landing on the bare skin of Mercy's arm. That soft skin beneath her palm sent a charge through her, but she ignored it.

"He?" she asked.

"The man you desire. The one above your station."

Andromeda couldn't see her, and couldn't imagine what expression she was making because she hadn't heard this wavering, weak tone before. She hadn't had time to learn it yet; she barely knew Mercy, which made what she did next all the madder.

"You really are a fool," Andromeda said. And when she heard a soft gasp of surprise, she angled her mouth toward it and didn't stop until Mercy's warm lips were pressed against hers.

Chapter Nine

MERCY COULDN'T BREATHE. She couldn't.

There had been the shame of her incorrect presumption, then the shock of Andromeda's hand on her arm, and after that there was only the earthy scent of tea-warmed breath and the slide of a luscious mouth over hers.

Her death wouldn't be an honorable one; her tombstone would read *Here lies Mercy Alston, asphyxiated in the throes of lust.* Not honorable, but she'd imagined many ways to die and this seemed like the best way to do it—and one she hadn't ever thought possible.

She'd been trying to remain calm, to hold off panicking because the woman who had undone her resolve after so many years was in her bed. Her body hadn't complied, really—she'd burned with both embarrassment and need as she stared up into the darkness trying to gather her wits. She'd felt a bit of relief mixed in with her regret when she learned that Andromeda seemed to have her sights on some man. That was how love worked for women like her, or perhaps just for her in particular.

The painful words of her last, and most resounding, heartbreak still rang in her ears.

"And how did you suppose we would spend a life together? You think some pretty words will provide for me? You think no one will gossip?"

She wanted to press her hands to her ears, to bite her cheek at the awful memory; she could still hear the ripping of the packet of letters, smell the flames that had engulfed her years of words.

This was why she didn't want to feel. This was why she'd been relieved, in a way, to be mistaken about Andromeda's attentions. She'd thought that she'd made an early escape from that inevitability. But then Andromeda's hands…her mouth…

Andromeda's lips moved over hers gently, so featherlight that the brush of them shouldn't have made Mercy's thighs press together and her nipples grow taut. But each little brush dredged up hidden feeling in her, like the lobstermen hauling up their cages from the briny deep. In the darkness, there was just the solid presence of Andromeda above her and the warm sweetness of her mouth.

Mercy took a deep breath through her nose, then pushed up into the kiss. It was the wrong decision, she knew it even as her elbows pressed down into the scratchy ticking of the mattress and her tongue tangled with Andromeda's.

There was a moan in the darkness, and then Andromeda's other hand was at Mercy's shoulder, pressing her down into the pillow. Her mouth clung to Mercy's as she gave in to the pressure and sank down into the bed. Andromeda made low, hungry groans as she kissed her, noises that sent unspeakable pleasure thrumming through Mercy's veins.

"I want to see you, but I don't trust you not to change your mind while I search about for the flint," she said against Mercy's mouth.

Arousal flared anew, higher and hotter than Mercy had thought imaginable.

"You'll just have to use those hands you're always boasting of," Mercy replied, and was pleased to hear Andromeda's scandalized laughter.

"So you're one of those," Andromeda said, sitting back so she straddled Mercy's thighs. Mercy froze for a moment, remembering their first encounter.

"One of what?" she asked in a worried voice, and heard Andromeda huff in annoyance.

"A missish little thing who was just waiting to be caught in the dark with an ardent admirer to show her naughty side," Andromeda said. Her weight shifted, and she nudged her knee between Mercy's thighs. Her hands were moving, cupping Mercy's face, then sliding down her neck. Andromeda's fingertips traced Mercy's collarbones, then tugged at the neck of the loose chemise she'd worn to bed. She pulled slowly, slowly, and Mercy could feel every fiber of the rough material graze the taut tips of her breasts before the cool air of the room hit them. The textured material was replaced by the warm pads of Andromeda's thumbs, brushing back and forth over the sensitive skin. Her thumbs were rough, surely resistant to pinpricks, but so gentle.

Mercy trembled and tried to hold her hips still as sensation spread through her, both from Andromeda's touch and the echo of her words.

Ardent admirer.

Andromeda's thumbs slowed but didn't still, a torturous tempo that inexplicably seemed to increase the pleasure she was receiving.

"Wait," Andromeda said. *Stroke. Pause. Stroke. Pause.* "Did you really think I would insult you? In the midst of this?"

Mercy knew it was foolish, but she also couldn't lie, not with Andromeda making her feel so much that she could barely think straight.

"It wouldn't be the first time," she said. Her hands went up to finally smooth over those curves she had fantasized about since she'd first come upon Andromeda bathed in sunlight. An angel, she'd thought then. An angel who was at that very moment driving her mad with lust. That was all well and good, for Mercy was already fallen.

Mercy cupped Andromeda's waist, slid her hands up so that the weight of Andromeda's perfect breasts rested against the backs of her hands. "It's all right."

Andromeda stopped moving for a moment, then one of her hands slid back up to Mercy's neck, tugging her up toward her. Mercy knew the kiss was coming, but was surprised by the ferocity of it, and the tenderness.

"I will never hurt you, Mercy," Andromeda whispered fiercely. Then her knee notched up between Mercy's thighs, until it was pressing into that throbbing flesh. After that, it all happened so quickly. The sweet friction between her legs, Andromeda's mouth at her neck, then lower, as she drew Mercy's nipple between her teeth and teased at it with her tongue.

"Oh Lord," Mercy whispered, then pleasure arced through her, piercing her like the rays of morning sun bursting through the clouds to spread over the Hudson. It went on and on, spreading joy through her body, joy so intense she was certain that she must be illuminating the dark room with her pleasure. She collapsed back onto the bed, but Andromeda's caresses didn't stop.

"Andromeda," she panted, backing up and away from what had become too much pressure—too much pleasure.

Andromeda moved beside her, pulled her close, and they lay in sated silence for a moment.

"So, what was it you wanted to tell me in this letter?" Andromeda whispered.

In the darkness, Mercy felt like anything was possible, but she was too raw to discuss the poem just then. "I—I've started writing again," she said.

"'Again' implies you stopped. What's that about?"

She sounded so curious. So interested. Mercy wouldn't tell her everything, but something was a start.

"Many years ago, I thought I was in love. No, I was most definitely in love. I thought I was loved back. That was the part I was misinformed about."

"And what happened?" Andromeda asked. "Is there someone I should take my sewing shears to?"

Mercy was surprised to find herself laughing. Laughing while talking about the things that had wounded her so dearly.

"She didn't love me, or if she did, she stopped. And then it happened again. And again. And the last time was so terrible I decided I was done."

She didn't describe the burnt letters or Jane passing her in the street with her husband, pretending she didn't know her.

"With…her?"

"No, with *it*. With love."

It seemed silly when stated like that, the pain that had been her driving motivation for years.

Andromeda took a deep breath and Mercy steeled herself. "Hm, a bit of a hasty conclusion I'd say, but I've made some hasty decisions myself." Andromeda's words were slow, measured. She was taking her time in responding and Mercy knew that was something that didn't come naturally to her. It was that consideration that did Mercy in. She loved Andromeda. Simple as that.

Can you really be so brainless as to fall for this again?

Mercy felt two arms wrap around her, and then a hand smoothing over her hair, and the anxious thoughts fell away. "Tell me about this writing."

Mercy didn't know what she had expected, but she found herself relaxing in Andromeda's embrace. "A poem. That's what the letter was. A poem, for you."

She turned her head in toward Andromeda's neck, hiding although it was too dark for her face to be seen.

"Brilliant," Andromeda breathed, stroking a hand over Mercy's shoulder. "I knew you were brilliant."

"You haven't read it yet," Mercy said. Her lips brushed against Andromeda's collarbone and she was surprised and pleased to feel Andromeda tremble against her.

"I've read your letters, and you weren't even trying in those." Andromeda's mouth was near Mercy's ear. She nipped at the lobe and it was Mercy who trembled then. "So yes, a poem, which is trying by its very nature, is going to be brilliant."

Mercy couldn't argue with that—her mouth was suddenly occupied with a much more pressing matter.

Chapter Ten

MERCY AWOKE in the darkness and stretched. She could tell she was awake earlier than usual, and was certain she wouldn't fall back asleep. The night had been spent learning Andromeda's body by touch in the darkness and, when she could stand it no longer, by candlelight. Beautiful dips and curves of smooth brown skin. Scars on her knees and elbows from a life of rushing into things fearlessly.

Each dark brown mark had filled Mercy with an unexplained joy. She hadn't kissed them, but she'd run her fingertips over them—as she had over every part of Andromeda—and felt a brief rush of bravery. The feeling that it was okay to be hurt, again and again, by your own recklessness. Perhaps that's what life was, and hiding from it as Mercy had been doing was living a half life.

She'd tried to temper her emotions, but she couldn't. One couldn't remove foundation stones from a dam and expect it to hold. She'd built up her entire world around denying herself happiness, and now she felt so strongly for Andromeda that it scared her.

It can't last. It won't.

She shook her head and rolled away from Andromeda's warmth into the cold stillness of the room. For the briefest of moments she felt utterly alone in the darkness, but she took a deep breath and reminded herself that Andromeda was still there. So were the questions she had asked, lingering like the scent of their arousal.

"What do you want?" Andromeda had asked once, then again, and a third time between their bouts of lovemaking.

"You," Mercy had answered each time, reaching for her.

Finally, as the candle guttered, Andromeda had shaken her head and asked one last time. "What do you want from life? I am quite the catch, but what else do you want for you?"

Mercy froze. She didn't know. She'd only just allowed herself the possibility of love; could she ask for anything more? Was that allowed to her?

As she pulled on her robe and slipped through the door toward the kitchens, she started to think maybe it could be. But she had spent so long *not* thinking of it that she wasn't sure where to begin.

To write again. Fear pulsed in her at the thought, but she'd mentioned her poetry and Andromeda hadn't laughed. She'd thought it brilliant.

To be a part of the world again. No, that wasn't right. She was already a part of the world; that had never changed, try though she had. She could expand her world to include Andromeda. She needn't travel far for that, after all. She just needed to be where Andromeda was. She had enjoyed the security of a life at The Grange, far from her painful memories. She didn't regret her choices, but ten years was a long time.

She felt her way through the dark hallway, certain she wouldn't fall because she knew every possible obstacle. And that had been part of the appeal of life at The Grange, hadn't it? That and the reminder in the everyday devotion of the Hamiltons. She'd scorned Mrs. Hamilton and Angelica for living their lives for those who had loved them and passed on, but she'd been living her life for someone who hadn't even truly loved her in return.

She was done with that.

In the kitchen, the embers of the cooking fire glowed in the hearth, and Mercy set to work breathing it to life. She needed warm water for the coffee she'd bring to Andromeda.

Andromeda was always so sure of herself; she could help Mercy figure out what she wanted from life. Surely she could.

Mercy puttered about in the kitchen for a bit. It was when the water had finally begun to boil that she noticed crinkled sheets of paper clipped above the fireplace. They looked like they'd been wet through and hung to dry. She grabbed the edge of one between her fingers and scanned it. A local Negro paper, judging from the announcements. A baptism. A barn raising. An engagement announcement.

No. NO.

"Miss Andromeda Stiel to wed Mr. Martin Shear, her childhood sweetheart, in an early summer wedding…"

Mercy pulled her fingers away from the broadsheet as if burned. She hadn't misunderstood after all. Andromeda had said she'd been planning something. That she'd found a solution to her problem with the sale. But then Andromeda had said she wanted Mercy, hadn't she?

Why would she choose you over her livelihood? It's been well established no one would. You assumed. You were wrong.

Andromeda hadn't said she wasn't to be married—she'd said she didn't want to. Was that what this had been? A lark before taking her vows?

She thought of Jane again and a thousand horrid memories assailed her at once. She stumbled out of the kitchen and back to the room. When she opened the door, Andromeda's gravelly morning voice called out to her. "Mercy?"

"Yes?" She was surprised at how calm she sounded. She wanted to rage, to scream at the unfairness of it all, but all of her energy was focused on rebuilding the dam and stopping up the emotions that had flown freely for one night. She'd known Andromeda would ruin her, and that knowledge had been confirmed. Why should she humiliate herself further? Andromeda would leave, taking the illusions of more with her.

"Come back to bed," Andromeda said and the heat in her voice made Mercy tremble. A tear slipped down her cheek, and she was glad for the darkness.

"I can't," she said, managing to hide the pain fairly well, she thought.

"But I was thinking about the boarding house. And how I'll need someone to run it." There was the sound of a hand slapping the mattress. "Come back to bed."

"I said I can't." That was sharper than she intended, but she thought of how beautiful Andromeda had been in the candlelight and it hurt. Damn it all, it *hurt*. "And you should probably get on your way. I'm sure you have to attend to the business of the sale. I know you'll want to get everything squared away now that you've figured out your solution."

Miss Andromeda Stiel to wed Mr. Martin Shear, her childhood sweetheart...

"What are you on about?" Andromeda had the nerve to ask.

"I have to work. You have to go. That is all," Mercy replied. She hated the frigidness in her tone, but it was either that or let the weight of what she'd read crush her. Ice was cold, but it was strong if it froze hard enough.

...in an early summer wedding.

"Don't do this, Mercy," Andromeda said.

"I'm simply going to work," she said. She was pulling on her dress with trembling fingers.

"No. You're putting me in my place," Andromeda said. "You're so scared I might hurt you that you'd rather run away than talk about whatever tick has crawled up your arse."

Mercy cringed at the honest anger in her tone. Perhaps Andromeda should look into taking up with the players at the Grove. But Mercy knew what she'd read. And, more than that, she knew what she deserved—it wasn't someone like Andromeda. If there wasn't a husband, there would have been something else eventually. Perhaps she should look on this as a blessing. She was ruined, but she might still be able to preserve some sense of self. To have what she'd had the night before last a few months more and *then* be snatched away would have killed her for certain.

"I'll have Sarah gather your papers from the kitchen and the rest of your things. Goodbye."

She turned toward the door. She'd walk out and it would be over. Just like that.

"You know, you despise people who hold on to love for a

reason," Andromeda said from behind her. There was a sniffle. Was she crying? Surely not. "It's because you're jealous. You're too cowardly to ever show your love and then you wonder why no one gives it to you in return."

Oh, that would leave a bruise.

Mercy closed the door behind her and walked up the stairs to do her job.

Chapter Eleven

"ARE YOU WELL, MERCY?"

Mrs. Hamilton clutched the packet of letters and the notes Mercy had taken, but hadn't turned an eye to them yet. Instead, she looked up at Mercy, the soft wrinkles around her eyes deepening with concern.

"Just feeling poorly," Mercy said. It wasn't a lie. "I'll go open the windows and let some air in."

"Yes, some spring air will do us all good," Mrs. Hamilton said.

"I can walk with you in the garden later, if it lifts your spirits," Angelica offered from the sofa.

"Thank you, miss."

Mercy went about her work, keeping her mind first on putting one foot in front of the other, then on pulling back the curtains and undoing the latches.

She'd been in a fog since that morning a week ago when she'd hidden in Colonel Hamilton's office, skulking by the window and not coming down until she'd seen Andromeda trot off on her horse. She'd convinced herself that Andromeda's stiff posture and the fact that she hadn't looked back meant that she hadn't really cared.

But...

That was when the fog had set in; it was as if some part of

her knew that if she tried to see too far ahead, there would only be the lonely road she'd consigned herself to. If she let her thoughts become too clear, she'd revisit those last moments she'd spent with Andromeda, the horrible words battering her over and over again. Thinking led to feeling, so she'd simply...stopped.

And that worked out well the first time, didn't it?

Mercy tugged hard at the cord to the curtain and there was a tearing sound.

"Everything all right?" Mrs. Hamilton asked.

"Yes. Sorry, missus."

Perhaps not quite all right. Mercy had dropped a vase, burnt one of Angelica's favorite dresses with the iron, and spilled ink on the carpet due to her inattention, but that was better than *feeling*. Because with feeling came the unvarnished truth: she had erred, and badly so.

She *had* been a coward. If Andromeda had lied, that would make her a liar, but Mercy hadn't even done her the courtesy of asking if that was the case. She'd already decided that things would not work out, and she'd jumped at the first proof she had to support it. She'd treated Andromeda like a stranger after sharing a night of passion—more than passion. Simple lust wouldn't have frightened her as much.

But if she had asked Andromeda about the engagement and been proven right, what then? She couldn't very well have stopped her from marrying, could she?

You could have tried.

But that would have been ridiculous. To think that she could have fought for love and come out the victor.

"I wasn't aware that there was a limit on how quickly a person might fall in love. Or on what they'd do to preserve it once they had."

Mercy pushed at the window, the swollen wood catching on the sill. It was silly, but tears sprang to her eyes at the resistance.

Why does nothing ever go easily for me?

She banged her fist against the wooden frame, but still it didn't budge.

How could I have hoped for someone like her?

Mercy pushed again, angrily, and the window finally gave. She was suddenly leaning out into the garden, and everything hit her all at once: the singing of the birds, the sunlight on the river, the scent of flower blossoms on cool spring air just verging on warm. The beauty filled her, fast and sharp, and oh, she thought she would burst from it. Had it always been like this?

Yes.

The beauty had been there before Andromeda walked into Mercy's life, and would be there if she never returned. It was in that moment that Mercy realized she hadn't stopped herself from feeling for all those long years—she'd stopped herself from living.

Go.

The command was in the flow of the river and rush of the wind through the trees.

GO.

Mercy remembered the way Andromeda had looked at her. Her words. Her touch. She allowed herself, for a moment, to believe that happiness could be hers. Why should she give it up so easily? Engagements were broken every day in America, and for lesser reasons than Mercy Alston loving a woman with her whole heart.

She thought of how she'd felt as she padded to the kitchen that morning she'd last seen Andromeda. She'd accepted that she was in love, and she hadn't felt lesser for it. She hadn't given anything up; she hadn't begun to lose herself. With Andromeda, Mercy had started to *find* herself. She'd started to become more than the doubts and the anger and the fear.

Mercy had been wrong once again—great love gave more than it demanded. Great love was what gave Eliza Hamilton a strength of will that was marveled over by men who'd shaped a nation. Great love gave Angelica the hope that each day might bring her grandest wish to fruition. The only thing a great love demanded was trust, and Mercy was ready to pay that cost once again.

She thought she might jump through the window and march downtown, not stopping until she was at Andromeda's door. But no. She could wait a day, until she was off from work.

Can I?

"You've been poorly since Miss Stiel's visit," Mrs. Hamilton said in that thoughtful way she had. "Did you catch a grippe from her? I hope it isn't the fever going about in the wards."

Mercy's head whipped back as she looked over her shoulder. "What fever?"

"There's a sickness about. Some are saying it's another plague of yellow fever. Oh, just thinking of what my Hamilton and I went through when we were ill with it." Mrs. Hamilton shook her head. "I wouldn't wish that on anyone."

Mercy had spent years hiding from her emotions, but she couldn't force away the worry that gripped her now, thinking of Andromeda shivering and alone. She thought of her parents gone cold and still in that dank basement of her childhood.

"Do you think Androm—Miss Stiel might be ill?" she asked.

Mrs. Hamilton raised her shoulders. "I should hope not. But she would have been rather susceptible after being caught in that storm."

Mercy threaded her fingers together and tugged with worry. She was a coward, perhaps, but even cowards sometimes found something worth fighting for.

"Mrs. Hamilton, I must ask something of you. I understand if the answer is no, but—"

"Yes, you have my leave to go into town today in addition to your day off tomorrow," Mrs. Hamilton said. She was going through the notes now, but a smug smile graced her lips. "If there is one thing I know well, it is heartbreak. If you have a chance to mend your heart, or someone else's, do not wait. If you have a chance to forgive, or be forgiven, do not wait."

Mrs. Hamilton sighed, and her gaze skipped toward the entry to the hallway, where Hamilton's bust resided. "No one, not even the best of men, is guaranteed the time to fix all their mistakes. All we can do is attempt to do right by others with the time the good Lord provides us."

Tears sprang to Mercy's eyes. Could Mrs. Hamilton know? Could she really be encouraging…? She thought of how kind Eliza had been with John Hunter and his partner. How she

ALYSSA COLE

listened attentively not only to stories of what had happened on the battlefield with her Hamilton, but of the lives and loves of the people she interviewed. It had been in front of her all this time: not forgiveness, for what was there to forgive about herself, but acceptance. What she'd thought could never be hers.

"Thank you, Mrs. Hamilton. Miss Angelica, I'll see you soon."

She turned to go.

"Mercy?" Angelica called out.

Mercy stopped and looked back. The woman had a bright smile on her face. She flapped her arms playfully as she had in the garden. "Good luck."

Mercy thanked her, and was off. She hadn't allowed herself to fly on hope's wings for years. She needed all the luck she could get.

<hr>

MERCY DIDN'T COME and go three times before knocking this time. She marched straight up to the door and rapped like a redcoat in search of patriots.

She had thought she'd be able to figure out what to say on the way down from Harlem, but she'd been scared out of her wits that the dress shop would be closed for the evening, or that Andromeda would be ill, or that she would have moved up the wedding date. Now Mercy was in front the shop and still had no idea what to say. Well, she had one thing to say, but it would have to wait, for the sake of fairness and propriety.

She knocked again and there was the thump of heels on floorboards before the door was pulled open. Mercy had already suspected it wasn't Andromeda from the graceless cadence of the footsteps, but her stomach sank and panic rose in her when the door opened to reveal a young woman with frizzy hair and an annoyed expression on her face. It was the same who had rushed out from the back and handed Andromeda coins the last time Mercy had been at the shop.

"Sorry, miss, but we're closed now," she said, already

pushing the door shut again. Mercy threw an arm out, stopping the door before the latch could be pulled down.

"I'm here to see Miss Stiel," she said.

"She ain't here," the girl said. "I have a lot of work to do, miss. I been holding down the shop for three days now and it seems everyone in the world needs a new spring dress."

"Three days? Where is she?" Mercy asked. What could keep her away for so long? Illness? Her hand went to the wall beside the door.

Andromeda couldn't really be sick. She had to be all right. She had to—

"Is there a reason you're haranguing my apprentice?"

Relief flowed through Mercy so fast that she didn't remember to panic as she spun and grabbed Andromeda by the shoulders.

"You're all right!" she exclaimed.

One side of Andromeda's mouth lifted in what could barely be called a grin. "I suppose you could say that." She pointedly took a step back, pulling herself away from Mercy's grip.

Mercy didn't know what to do with her hands, so she tugged at the sleeves of her dress.

Right. I must say something.

"What do you want, Mercy?" Andromeda asked. Her tone was as hard as her eyes. The vibrancy and cocksureness that had both irked and enthralled Mercy were nowhere to be seen. Perhaps Andromeda *was* ill. Perhaps—

A sudden realization hit Mercy: she'd been so busy comparing Andromeda to Jane, searching for the method by which Andromeda would finally fail her, that she'd failed to see that she, Mercy, was the Jane in this situation. The cold words she'd spoken to Andromeda had been a most artless parry; she'd meant to do more than deflect. She'd meant to hurt Andromeda, to sever the link between them. She hadn't thought that she *could* hurt Andromeda, which may have been worse than actually succeeding.

"I want—" She swallowed, the panic finally rising in her. She said the first thing that came to mind. "I want a dress."

Andromeda's eyes narrowed to slits. "You can visit the Widow Murphy down the street if you need a dress."

"But I want a dress from you," Mercy said. "You know very well that no other dress can compare to the loveliness of yours. The sleek lines, the sharp contours." Heat rose to Mercy's neck, and she choked out the words. "No other dress will do."

"We're closed, miss," the girl repeated from the doorway of the shop.

"Oh, that doesn't matter, Tara," Andromeda said, and Mercy felt a sliver of hope, like the sun cresting the horizon. Then a storm cloud passed before it, obliterating it from view. "Some customers want everything on their terms. They can only see that which conveniences them, and everyone else must accommodate their capricious nature."

The certainty that had driven Mercy to the shop was eroding quickly, but though the words were harsh, they were not unfair.

"Your mistress is quite right, Tara." She looked at Andromeda and took a deep breath. "Hang the dress. I would like to talk. I once trusted you enough not to jump out of a moving coach when you spirited me off, and while I can't guarantee that what I say will bring you pleasure, I do not wish to cause you distress."

Andromeda stared at her, and Mercy really looked at her. The dark circles under her eyes. The way her shoulders were hunched, her dress was wilted, and her hair was flat. She was no less beautiful, but she was sad. Mercy had seen that same sadness reflected back in her looking glass, but now she was the cause of it.

"Please," she said.

Andromeda whirled and entered the dress shop, waving a hand over her shoulder to indicate that Mercy should follow. "Tara, take your work home with you. I'll see you in the morning."

The girl gathered up a basket of dresses and scurried out, throwing a curious glance back over her shoulder.

Mercy walked into the shop and looked around. "I see your apprentice has cleaned up a bit."

"She wouldn't know how to clean if her life depended on it. She can barely manage a needle, let alone a broom."

"Oh." So it had been Andromeda, then? Mercy regretted having said anything that first day. The spotless shop lacked the character it had when she'd walked in and looked upon everything Andromeda had created for herself.

"Come on, then." Andromeda's voice was still rough, and she was motioning Mercy to the back, where measurements were taken. Mercy swallowed.

"I don't really need a dress."

Andromeda let out a hearty laugh at that. "Oh, but you do. If anything good comes of this mess, I hope it will be the improvement of your wardrobe."

Mercy was taken aback at the sharp words. Perhaps she had been wrong; there might be no way to make things right.

"I beg your pardon. That was rude," Andromeda said, rubbing her hands over her skirt.

"I deserve no better," Mercy replied in a low voice, and was met with Andromeda's exasperated sigh.

"Truly, Mercy, have you learned nothing?" she asked.

"What—"

"Come." Andromeda went into the back room, the heels of her boots hitting the floorboards with enough pressure to declare her annoyance, and Mercy followed after her.

Chapter Twelve

ANDROMEDA HAD LONG FANTASIZED about having Mercy on her pedestal, but not like this. Not after days of working her hands raw alongside hired workers making repairs to her newly purchased building to get it fit for boarders. Days spent trying to avoid thoughts of Mercy, followed by sleepless nights where thinking was the only thing she could do.

Night after night of lying in the darkness, remembering the shock of Mercy's cold words, like a pan of icy water thrown into the bed that they'd shared. Andromeda had been confused, taken aback by the cruelty of Mercy's withdrawal, and had lashed out instead of being patient. She'd had every right to, of course, but her anger hadn't solved anything. She'd ridden her horse hard away from The Grange, the tears freezing on her cheeks in the bizarre cold of the spring morning. She'd given up. Perhaps it had been for the best, but perhaps not.

"So I'm guessing you'll want something high-necked," she said, as if she didn't have pages of sketches she'd designed just for Mercy. She held her measuring tape against the slim column, wrapped it around to get the measurement. She could feel Mercy's pulse throb beneath her thumb. She'd placed her mouth against that pulse and suckled the last time they had been together.

She pulled the tape away, saw the tremor go through Mercy

as it caressed her skin. She should have pushed her out of the shop and slammed the door in the wench's face. Instead she moved behind her, pressed one end of the tape to where arm met shoulder, and slowly pulled the remaining length across the span of Mercy's back. She kept the pressure of her fingertips light, just enough to graze Mercy through the fabric of her dress.

"I—I want…"

Andromeda noted the measurement, then moved to Mercy's side and repeated the torturous motion, this time spanning from shoulder to wrist.

"Oh, I know what you want," Andromeda said. "Something in the style of a burlap sack. You want a dress that makes everyone forget that you exist."

She noted the measurement, then wrapped the tape around Mercy's wrist, right where she imagined the sleeve of a beautiful, stylish-but-sensible dress should fall. There was that pulse again, thrumming away as a reminder of how fragile Mercy was beneath her rigid exterior. Andromeda had grown up surrounded by nature, but life in the city had allowed her to forget that fragile things often tried to appear more frightening than they were to repel predators.

That didn't excuse Mercy's behavior, but it also didn't excuse Andromeda's. She hadn't known love could hurt like that, that time and distance could be a physical pain. She'd told the story of her grandparents so often; of Grandma Kate spurning Grandpa Elijah. She'd always thought the spectacular part of their story was the escape by horseback across the river, but no. It was how he'd waited for her on a river bank in enemy territory, unsure that his love would be returned but willing to risk everything on the hope that it would be. It was Grandma Kate, building a life for them during the hardships of war, unsure if the man she'd given her heart to would return from his time with Hamilton's battalion. Love wasn't always about bluster and heroics. It was also having patience during the lulls in excitement, when victory wasn't assured.

"Did you read my letter?" Mercy asked as Andromeda crouched down.

Andromeda pushed her hand beneath Mercy's skirt, tried not to remember how the skin beneath her fingertips had felt against her mouth. Her hand slid up, up and Mercy gasped.

"No, I didn't read it," she said, looking up into Mercy's eyes. "I couldn't. I couldn't bear to read your words. I knew they would—" She paused, and had to look away from Mercy's gaze. She focused on pulling the tape taut against her leg. She didn't need the measure really—she'd memorized the dimensions of Mercy's body with her hands and her mouth. She knew exactly her measure; or she'd thought so before Mercy had come back into her room and pushed Andromeda away. "I knew that it would be too painful, to read your words, to hear them in your sweet voice, and to know that I had meant nothing to you."

She pulled her hands away and stood, catching Mercy's hapless gaze.

"You think that you mean nothing to me?" Mercy asked, with a kind of awe in her tone. Mercy was like a startled deer, caught unawares, frightened out of her wits but oblivious of how dangerous her hooves were when she reared and kicked out. Andromeda could not withstand another kick.

"High neck, slim-fitting sleeves, ruching along the collar, high waist. Is that something you'd want?" Andromeda asked. She reached out to get the measurement of Mercy's waist.

"What I want is to apologize," Mercy said. Her voice quavered. "I should not have been so hasty."

"Haste? That is what you apologize for?" Enough. Andromeda could take no more. Perhaps Mercy really was so cold; perhaps the woman she'd met in her letters and shared a bed with had been the bait, Mercy the predator, and Andromeda had been the prey all along.

She turned to move away and Mercy grabbed her by the collar. It wasn't a rough tug—strong enough to force her to look upward but not enough that she couldn't easily pull away—but it surprised Andromeda. She looked up into eyes that had just been filled with uncertainty, but the gaze that met hers now was sharp as the tip of a pin.

"No. I apologize for giving you up so easily," Mercy said. Her voice was angry, but Andromeda could see that her anger was turned inward. "Do you love him? I can accept it if you love him, but if this is simply for the purpose of business, then I believe I will have to voice my strenuous objection to your union."

Andromeda didn't know what Mercy was talking about, but discovered that she was even lovelier in her determination than she was in her pique.

"Love whom?" Andromeda asked. She could think of nothing but the stubborn set of Mercy's mouth and the slight pull at her collar.

"Martin blasted Shear," Mercy said in a tone bordering on a growl. She looked down at her hand on Andromeda's collar and seemed to remember her manners, for she released her. Andromeda felt a stab of disappointment.

"Martin…" Andromeda's stomach dropped and then flipped and then flew up to her throat as confusion, then understanding, then hope made their appearances in quick succession. "You read the paper," she said.

"Yes. I found it drying in the kitchen and I was furious. I was hurt. But I should have spoken with you. Because you…" The hand that hovered near Andromeda's certainly rumpled collar lifted and cupped Andromeda's jaw. Her thumb brushed over Andromeda's bottom lip and the sensation went through Andromeda like lightning. "…you are irksome and overconfident, but it appears I find that to my liking. And if you do not love this Martin blasted Shear, and you perhaps feel for me a bit of what I feel for you…"

Mercy's eyes had gone glossy and Andromeda's own throat was rough.

"I don't love him," Andromeda said. "Because he doesn't exist."

"Pardon?"

"While at home, I paid a visit to an old friend," she said. "She'd recently been engaged to the owner of the local Negro newspaper. I asked if she could do me a kindness by printing something special up for me that I could use as the proof I needed.

"I had to wait until the next printing day, but I left home

with an engagement, on paper, that would put Mr. Porter at ease, and a fiancé who would meet a sad end after the ink on the deed was dried. Martin blasted Shear fell down a well, I've heard. A pity. He was a good man and helped me immensely."

"You mean…" Mercy's hands went to her mouth and she took a step back, wobbling on the pedestal. Andromeda caught her at the waist and held her steady for a moment before releasing her and taking a step back.

"There is no fiancé. I told you that I would never hurt you, which in retrospect is a rather lofty promise. I imagine marrying someone else while I'm madly in love with you might qualify as hurting you, though. And myself."

"Madly in love?" Mercy looked about and Andromeda allowed herself a chuckle, a bit of her fear starting to ebb. Perhaps one day they'd even laugh about this. The fact that there might be a "one day" suffused her with hope. The sadness that had weighed Andromeda down fell away. She grinned and took a step closer to Mercy.

"Yes. With you. I was going to ask…I'll need help with the boarding house and as you seem not entirely happy at The Grange, perhaps we might form a partnership? There's keeping the rooms clean, maintaining the property, and keeping the boarders in line. You know, all of those things you seem to get some strange pleasure from. And there would be time for you to write, if that's what you want to do. I'd make sure you had time."

Andromeda looked up at Mercy, imagining what their life could be like together. There would be spats and disagreements over trivial things, to be certain, but there would be days at the Grove and Lady Bess's. Conversations with friends. Quiet nights in front of a shared fire as Andromeda sewed and Mercy wrote. Not-so-quiet nights when they retired to their bed early. They might have all that ahead of them, and Andromeda was champing at the bit, to be sure, but she would be patient. For *this*, she could be patient.

"So…this is an offer of employment?" Mercy asked quietly.

"Oh, no. This is an offer of me. Us. Together. The employment is just a means to an end."

Mercy's eyes briefly closed, and when they opened, they shimmered with tears. "Moving back to the city would mean giving up the quiet of The Grange."

"I can be quiet," Andromeda said quickly. "Truly. Sewing is quiet by its very nature, and I can walk about in stocking feet, and try not to ask too many questions. I'll be busy much of the day, you know. You won't even know I'm about, that's how quiet—"

"Andromeda?"

"Yes?"

"Perhaps you should finish these measurements. I'll need a new wardrobe if I'm going to be among the fashionable town-folk now."

Andromeda nodded, joy surging through her, and roped her measuring tape around Mercy's waist. Instead of cinching it tight, she used it to pull Mercy forward so that they were pressed against one another.

"I don't believe this is part of the measurement-taking process," Mercy said. That determined look was still lighting up her eyes, and her expression was open and inviting.

Warmth flowed through Andromeda; she thought she might float from the happiness that rushed to her head. "It's an exclusive service, reserved for my most important client."

"Ah. Starting my return from the far-flung countryside in grand style. If that's the case, carry on."

"As you wish." Andromeda continued where she'd left off, pulling Mercy close and standing on tiptoe to meet that sweet, soft mouth. The kiss was gentle at first, but then Mercy's hands cupped Andromeda's face and held her in place. Mercy kissed her deeply, possessively, and without an iota of prudish restraint.

Lord above, Andromeda did love a challenge. Luckily for her, so did Mercy.

Epilogue

Mrs. Hamilton,

Enclosed you will find a recollection from Mr. Calvin Porter, whom I encountered at Lady Bess's Tavern, a local establishment which I frequent with Andromeda. I overheard Mr. Porter recounting his participation in the theft of several cannons from the British at the request of Alexander Hamilton. Learning that he had not yet shared it with you, I asked if I might send you a summation. Please forgive the length of the piece, but I wanted to ensure that I conveyed the humor in Mr. Porter's vivid storytelling. It seems I, too, am invested in your Hamilton's legacy. I hope you find the tale useful.

In your previous letter, you asked how things are coming along. Both the boarding house and Andromeda's dress shop are flourishing, and she is already looking for her next investment. I volunteer my services at the orphanage twice a week, teaching the children to read and write, and a few of my poems have been published in local papers. I have also started working on a play to be put on at the Grove.

I do miss the quiet of The Grange, but although things are not always easy, I am quite content. That is more than I'd ever imagined for myself; that is more than enough.

Your obedient servant,

Mercy Alston

Author's Note

Dear Reader,

I hope you enjoyed Mercy and Andromeda's story!

If you're curious about Andromeda's grandparents, Kate and Elijah Sutton, the story of their battle for love and freedom can be found in my novella *Be Not Afraid*. It's already available.

If you'd like to be notified about upcoming releases, feel free to sign up for my newsletter at www.alyssacole.com! You can also follow me on Twitter at @AlyssaColeLit, or on Facebook at https://www.facebook.com/AlyssaColeLit/.

For historical notes on all three novellas, please continue reading.

END NOTES: ROSE LERNER

Acknowledgments

There are always so many people to thank, but this book has more than most. Thank you, of course, to Tiffany Ruzicki, beta reader extraordinaire. I rely on you. Thank you to my uncle David for looking over the military stuff. Thank you to the friends who shared *Hamilton* fandom with me: Susanna Fraser, Olivia Waite, and especially Tiffany Gerstmar, my partner in Aaron Burr ambivalence.

Thank you to Courtney and Alyssa, for including me in this amazing project. This wasn't an easy book to write, especially now, and I don't think I could have done it with anyone else. Hopefully you will never know how much I admire you both because it would be a little embarrassing.

Thank you to our copyeditor, Kim Runciman, for your expertise and for thinking Nathan was adorable.

Thank you, as always, to Sonia, my partner in creativity and in life. There's no one I would rather have waited outside the *Hamilton* stage door with. I would always rather do everything with you.

Thank you to Elizabeth for sharing your knowledge of halacha and Jewish history and practice with me. Remaining errors of fact or judgment are, of course, all my own.

Younger readers familiar with Hebrew might notice that Rachel and Nathan's pronunciation is different from what they're used to. Like many things in modern life, the language has been standardized in recent decades; most synagogues today use the modified Sephardi pronunciation that is spoken in Israel. Rachel and Nathan know Ashkenazi Hebrew. I don't, although I remember my mother said certain words differently than my rabbi does. Heartfelt thanks to Miranda Dubner and her family for your help, as well as to Elizabeth. I apologize for any lingering mistakes!

I would like to thank Revolutionary War reenactors for your exhaustive expertise, and for your commitment to making it available on the internet. I would have had no idea what to do about tents without you. Thank you to Thomas Fleming for your insightful, detailed books on Yorktown and the Revolutionary War, and to Michael E. Newton for writing *Alexander Hamilton: The Formative Years* and loving footnotes even more than I do.

Thank you to Jewish historians for safeguarding our memories; I am grateful every day for your work and your strength.

Last but not least, I would like to thank Lin-Manuel Miranda, for creating *Hamilton* and for making me want to write about America.

Historical note

I hope you enjoyed Rachel and Nathan's story! This is my first Revolutionary War story—my first story, actually, that isn't set in Regency England—and I had a wonderful time researching and writing it.

The burning of the HMS Charon really happened. John Laurens, cinnamon bun that he was, wrote in his diary, "It was allowable to enjoy this magnificent nocturnal spectacle, as the vessels had previously been abandoned by their crews." In my story I had him share that thought with his men.

Women in uniform were a reality in every eighteenth-century army and navy. The difference between men and women isn't as wide or as fixed as we sometimes imagine, and people don't pay that much attention to each other anyway. Plus, while soldiers and sailors lived in close quarters, they usually didn't bathe much or have more than one set of clothes. Rachel's role model, memoirist Hannah Snell, served successfully in the British marines for three years from 1747 to 1750.

Deborah Sampson served in the Continental light infantry for seventeen months. After the war she petitioned for and received a military pension, authorized a biography, and went on a successful lecture tour in 1802, as part of which she performed military drills in uniform. I highly recommend Alfred F. Young's recent biography, *Masquerade*.

Many Jewish soldiers served in the Continental Army, both as officers and enlisted men. Fritz Hirschfeld's *George Washington and the Jews* is a good starting place to learn more (not to mention a great name for a band). Haym Salomon, Nathan's spy mentor, was real. He often gets referred to as "the financier of the Revolution," and it's true that his help as a broker was invaluable to finance superintendent Robert Morris, desperately wheeling and dealing in Philadelphia to keep the army afloat.

But what gets forgotten (maybe because most historians don't see Jews as action heroes) is that before he fled New York for Philadelphia, Salomon was a spy who used his knowledge of German to turn disaffected Hessian officers. He was twice suspected of setting major fires in the city to sabotage the British occupation. He spent all his own money on the Revolution (he even paid James Madison's personal bills) and died broke in 1785. If he had lived just a few more years, Alexander Hamilton's insistence on full repayment to holders of Continental debt would have restored his fortunes.

Was Hamilton Jewish, as Rachel and Nathan wonder? The evidence is entirely circumstantial, but personally, I think there's a case to be made. The story about him attending Hebrew school as a boy is true. It's too complicated to get into here, but if you're interested in learning more, visit the *Hamilton's Battalion*'s DVD extras page on my website: I've written a long blog post about it.

Believe it or not, I didn't make up the Great Yom Kippur Window Controversy of 1755 either! Solomon Hays (who sounds like a real jerk) was eventually readmitted to the synagogue after he apologized and agreed to stop writing a tell-all book. But I doubt people forgot. And Rachel was right that the grudges and loyalties formed during the Revolutionary War would never be forgotten either. When I read Thomas Fleming's *Washington's Secret War*, about the general's struggle to improve conditions at Valley Forge while Charles Lee and Thomas Conway worked to undercut him, I was surprised at how many of the players were already familiar to me as Hamilton's friends and enemies from his later political career—and how little the battle lines changed.

Antisemitism—to state the obvious—did not go away after the Revolution. It remains a frightening force today. However, the United States was the first Western country to grant Jews full national citizenship and legal equality.

Article Six of the Constitution clearly states that "no religious Test shall ever be required as a Qualification to any Office or public Trust under the United States." This meant that unlike in England, no one could be required to affirm their belief in specific religious principles (for example, disavowing the Pope or taking an oath "on my faith as a Christian") before serving in the military, civil service, or government. In the 1788 parade in Philadelphia to celebrate the Constitution's ratification, a rabbi marched with other city clergy, and the banquet afterwards provided a kosher table—unprecedented in Europe at the time!

(The "no religious test" clause only applied at the federal level; several states did exclude Jews, atheists, and/or Catholics from state office in their new constitutions.)

So, part of what Rachel and Nathan hoped and fought for was realized.

One day, may it all be. May no one be left in the wilderness. May justice and integrity and kindness be first in Americans' hearts. May we fight to make it happen, and win.

As we say every Passover: Next year, may we all be free.

Also by Rose Lerner

Lively St. Lemeston series

Sweet Disorder

True Pretenses

Listen to the Moon

A Taste of Honey (an erotic novella)

Not in any series

In for a Penny

A Lily Among Thorns

All or Nothing (a novella)

END NOTES: COURTNEY MILAN

Acknowledgments

My gratitude must first go to my Raptors—Bree Bridges, Alisha Rai, Alyssa Cole, and Rebekah Weatherspoon—who were in the (WhatsAppChat)room where it happened when we had the initial idea for this anthology. (I won't tell you how it happened. It started out of spite. The best things usually do.) Their encouragement and help and gut-checks, from the first moment to the last, made this a better story.

Second, my thanks to Rose Lerner and Alyssa Cole, who immediately were carried away by this idea, came up with the premise for it, and delivered utter magic. You are the best partners in crime that I could possibly wish for, and in the event that I ever find myself in need of committing felonies, I will consult you first.

As always, my thanks to Lindsey Faber, Kim Runciman, and Anne Victory, for helping me deliver this story as well as I can, to my dog for his patience, my husband for...well, for nothing, which tells you that he never reads the acknowledgments, and to my vast and wonderful array of friends who are so numerous that I can't possibly list them all.

My eternal gratitude to Lin-Manuel Miranda for envisioning an America that calmly accepted me as a part of this country, while simultaneously earworming me forever.

Finally, I want to acknowledge my gratitude to you, my

readers, who have been so incredibly patient with me and my slow writing. I am never as fast as other authors in the best of years, and to characterize this last year as "proceeding at a snail's pace" would be to belittle snails.

Thank you for your patience, your words of encouragement, and your kindness.

Historical Note

This story touches—briefly—on the history of racism and slavery in the North, a history that is sometimes surprising to Americans who learned of slavery as a thing that existed south of the Mason-Dixon line. For those who are wondering, yes, there were enslaved people in Rhode Island at the start of the Revolutionary War, and yes, Rhode Island, after not having enough soldiers enlist, decided to open their rolls to black men —and on February 14, 1778, the Rhode Island Assembly voted that "every slave so enlisting shall, upon his passing muster before Colonel Christopher Greene, be immediately discharged from the service of his master or mistress, and be absolutely free."

This law stood in place for four months before slave owners insisted on its removal, but by that time, many enslaved men had already took steps to secure their freedom. The Rhode Island First Regiment—which was later collapsed with the Second into just the Rhode Island Regiment—came to be known as the Black Regiment because of the large number of African American soldiers who fought in it.

As for what happened afterward to John's family in Newport, this was also an incredibly common practice. In theory, "warning out" was a practice in the New England states which was used to coerce outsiders into leaving before they could become a drain on the town's resources—usually because the town deemed them unable to care for themselves. In practice, communities warned out those whom they deemed undesirable for many reasons. African-Americans were disproportionately warned out as compared to their peers.

For those interested in learning more, I highly recommend Christy Mikel Clark-Pujara's dissertation, "Slavery, emancipation and Black freedom in Rhode Island, 1652-1842," which you can find at: http://ir.uiowa.edu/cgi/viewcontent.cgi?article=4956&context=etd

And for those wondering how likely it was for a community of African Americans to find an island in Maine and settle there...the answer is, very likely! So likely that it's already happened. At one point, Malaga Island in Maine was settled by a mixed-race community. The inhabitants were incredibly poor, and as often happened to poor, mixed-race communities, they were eventually forced to leave. But the inevitable consequence of kicking out everyone that doesn't look like you is that those people go and find their own place.

And if you want to know what happens next to our intrepid band, well… there's always next book.

⚜

I had the idea for this novella early in 2016—what we might call a younger, more hopeful, more innocent time. At that point, my thought for what would happen in this book was something along the lines of:

1. Meet at Battle of Yorktown! Fight! Abscond!
2. …?
3. …?!
4. …!!
5. HAPPY ENDING

I had some ideas, but had other projects that needed my attention first, and so I set this to the side.

I turned back to it in December of 2016. Now, it turns out that December of 2016 was a very different time than March of 2016, mostly because sometime between March of 2016 and

December of 2016, November 8th happened. And…then, November 8th kept happening.

Those of you who know a little bit about my personal history know that from 2006 to 2008, I served as a law clerk—first to Alex Kozinski on the Ninth Circuit and then to Justices Sandra Day O'Connor and Anthony Kennedy on the Supreme Court. I care about this country—its legal history, its founding documents. I care about the evolution of this country in small and dorky details, like the incorporation of the Bill of Rights against the states, or the modern Commerce Clause jurisprudence, or footnote four in Carolene Products. Most importantly, I care about the Thirteenth and Fourteenth Amendments to the Constitution, amendments that came many decades after the founding of this nation, and which finally began to deliver on the most fundamental promises that were made in the Declaration of Independence—that all ~~men~~ people were created equal, and should be treated equally under the law.

It has been hard to watch the ideals (if not history) of this country come under attack—birthright citizenship, equality under the law without regard to race or religion.

This history is very personal to me. When my great-great-grandfather first came to this country, he did not bring his wife for a variety of reasons. One of them was that it was difficult for Chinese women to immigrate under the law. For two generations, my forebears lived in this country, returning to China only for brief visits to marry, visit spouses who would not come with them, and say hello to children whom they might never see again. My mother's mother is my first maternal ancestor to bear her children on US soil.

When my parents married, their marriage—between a Chinese woman and a white man—was illegal in seven states.

If I had happened to fall in love with a woman instead of a man, up until two years ago, *I* would not have been able to marry.

Progress has been good to me and mine. Regression, knowing where we have come from, is a little frightening. I found it hard on a very personal level to write a story about the

Also by Courtney Milan

The Worth Saga

Once Upon a Marquess

Her Every Wish

The Pursuit Of…

After the Wedding

The Devil Comes Courting

The Return of the Scoundrel

The Kissing Hour

A Tale of Two Viscounts

The Once and Future Earl

The Cyclone Series

Trade Me

Hold Me

Find Me

What Lies Between Me and You

Keep Me

Show Me

The Brothers Sinister Series

The Governess Affair

The Duchess War

A Kiss for Midwinter

The Heiress Effect

The Countess Conspiracy

The Suffragette Scandal

Talk Sweetly to Me

The Turner Series

Unveiled

Unlocked

Unclaimed

Unraveled

Not in any series

A Right Honorable Gentleman

What Happened at Midnight

The Lady Always Wins

The Carhart Series

This Wicked Gift

Proof by Seduction

Trial by Desire

END NOTES: ALYSSA COLE

Historical Note

The initial draft of *That Could Be Enough* was the first thing I wrote after the Election of 2016 (this is how I imagine it will appear in future history textbooks). I was demoralized. I was sad and angry, but also numb. I felt like I had been hopeful, and that hope had been crushed underfoot.

I realized I couldn't write explicitly about America. My novella *Be Not Afraid,* which features Andromeda's grandparents Elijah and Kate Sutton, is about choosing to believe in the future of America. My two most recent releases had been about heroes and heroines who cared so much for this country, even when it didn't love them back, and worked hard to make it a better place. To be quite honest, I felt almost as if I had betrayed those characters. So I started writing this: a story about ordinary people living their lives against the backdrop of a country that was still finding its way. A story with a heroine who felt so much, and so deeply, that she thought the only solution was to not allow herself to feel at all—to not allow herself to care.

In writing this story I remembered that, above all, the story of America is one of a great multitude of individuals with so many things stacked against them who...lived. And loved. And thrived. No matter the time period, and no matter the obstacles placed before them. People from marginalized groups have always made their way by finding their place within their communities and holding tightly to the things most dear to them. They fight, in small ways and in large. They hope, though common sense may tell them not to, and sometimes America is worthy of that hope.

Mercy and Andromeda are queer, and they live together and are accepted by their community. Yes, I *know* you likely just read the story, so you're aware of this, but I wanted to make it clear that this is not anachronism in the name of happily ever after: queer people have always existed, and though society has generally excelled at making their lives difficult and dangerous, there were people who lived as openly as they could and were accepted within their communities.

Andromeda is a Black woman who owns her own business, makes loans to other Black women for which she receives interest, and has a strong entrepreneurial spirit. Again: this is not anachronism for the sake of happily ever after. Free Black women then, as now, started their own businesses out of both necessity and ingenuity. In a society in which they couldn't count on many mechanisms of support, they created their own and uplifted each other while doing so.

Some of the resources that were most helpful to this story, and touch on the aforementioned subjects, are as follows:

Hodges, Graham Russell Gao. 1999. *Root and Branch: African Americans in New York and East Jersey, 1613-1863*. University of North Carolina Press.

Clever, Rachel Hope. 2014. *Charity & Sylvia: A Same-Sex Marriage in Early America*. Oxford University Press.

Harris, Leslie M. 2003. *In the Shadow of Slavery: African Americans in New York City, 1626-1863*. The University of Chicago Press.

Also by Alyssa Cole

Loyal League
An Extraordinary Union
A Hope Divided

Reluctant Royals
A Princess in Theory

Off the Grid
Radio Silence
Signal Boost
Mixed Signals

Let us Dream
Let it Shine

Be Not Afraid
Agnes Moor's Wild Knight
Eagle's Heart

CPSIA information can be obtained
at www.ICGtesting.com
Printed in the USA
LVOW07s1109071117
555310LV00006B/112/P